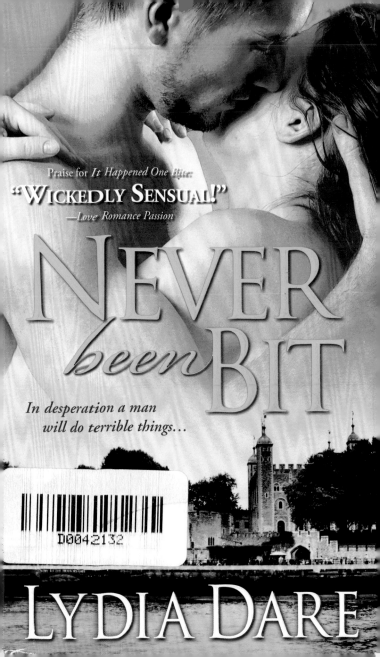

NEVER been BIT

In desperation a man
will do terrible things…

D0042132

LYDIA DARE

ALSO AVAILABLE FROM SOURCEBOOKS CASABLANCA AND LYDIA DARE

978-1-4022-4507-7

978-1-4022-4510-7

ISBN-13: 978-1-4022-4513-8

"Sexy, witty, and wildly passionate... Just as riveting, sexy, and hot as the first two in the series."

—*Star-Crossed Romance*

"Ms. Dare has proven herself with her writing, characters, story lines, and imagination. I'm a fan for life."

—*The Good, the Bad and the Unread*

"Heart warming... Filled with high jinxes, laughter, and love."

—*Bookaholics Romance*

"Fiendishly enticing... four stars for its originality and fast-paced fun!"

—*Books by the Willow Tree*

"The authors flawlessly blend the historical and paranormal genres."

—*Romance Novel News*

"Hot romance, sizzling and palpable chemistry."

—*Steph the Bookworm*

"Lydia Dare's intrigue, sexual tension, and humor will keep you reading well into the night."

—*Love Romance Passion*

"Delightful... funny and romantic and a joy to read... each book sucks you in from the first page to the last."

—*Anna's Book Blog*

NEVER
been BIT

LYDIA DARE

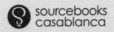

sourcebooks
casablanca

Published by Sourcebooks Casablanca, an imprint of Sourcebooks, Inc.
P.O. Box 4410, Naperville, Illinois 60567-4410
(630) 961-3900
FAX: (630) 961-2168
www.sourcebooks.com

Printed and bound in the United States of America
QW 10 9 8 7 6 5 4 3 2 1

Kimberly K.—You once told me over a glass of soda that I was in the wrong profession. Thanks for the nudge.

Tori—Thank you for always being in my corner, for your strength and advice over the years. I am so grateful for our friendship. As Alec and Sorcha have been your favorites since the very beginning, this is for you.

One

EVER SINCE SORCHA FERGUSON HAD MET HER FIRST Lycan, she'd been determined to have one for her very own. And her coven sister had *promised* there would be Lycans at the Duchess of Hythe's house party. Since the day that glorious news had reached Sorcha's ears, she'd planned her entire visit south around the idea of falling in love with a beast just like two of her very best friends had done. Yet she hadn't seen *even one* Lycan since she'd been in Kent, and she'd already been at Castle Hythe for a sennight.

There was only one thing left to do. If they wouldn't come to her, she would go to them. But first, she had to fix the shambles that was the Duchess of Hythe's orangery. Sorcha had been nearly overcome with sadness when she'd seen all the plants in such a sad state of neglect.

She scoffed. She was feeling very much like the plants these days. Every one of her friends had married within the last year or so, and she was the only witch in her coven left to find a husband. She snorted. She hadn't even come close to finding one, and all because those promised Lycans had yet to make an appearance.

Sorcha walked from row to row in the orangery, laying her hands on the forsaken plants. The lilies could use a kind word to boost their spirits. Their stems sagged, and there was not a single bloom to be found. She blew a lock of hair from her eyes in distraction.

A piece of Irish ivy reached out to touch her ankle. The poor thing was yellowed and aching for attention. She smiled and touched her hands to the vine, watching it strengthen and fortify itself right before her eyes. "Ye're welcome," she murmured when the vine stroked across the toe of her shoe. She wiped her hands together. The duchess would be appalled if she saw the dirt beneath Sorcha's fingernails.

"There you are," Lady Madeline Hayburn called from the other side of the orangery. "I've been looking everywhere for you!"

Sorcha bit her lip. She shouldn't have stopped to tend the plants. But she couldn't just allow them to suffer, could she? "I was just thinkin' of goin' out for a bit," she said evasively, avoiding the other girl's gaze as she lifted herself up to sit on a low table.

Maddie's face fell. "Oh," she said with an understanding nod. But Sorcha could tell her friend was disappointed. And she'd be the worst sort of friend if she abandoned the young lady to go in search of a man. Or men. Or Lycans. *Or her destiny*.

Maddie wouldn't have any idea how to go along without her. Sorcha patted a place beside herself. "I just thought I'd pay a visit ta Eynsford Park. The ride isna too far, from what yer grandmother said."

Maddie smiled as she settled beside Sorcha, her blond curls bouncing about her shoulders. "I can't believe how wonderful Grandmamma's plants look. Just a fortnight ago, this place looked as though it had died a less than peaceful death. You are a miracle worker."

Sorcha remembered. It had hurt her very heart to see the plants in such shape. "Oh, I just have a bit of a green thumb."

"Something I clearly lack." Maddie smoothed her skirts out in front of her. "What is so important at Eynsford Park?"

Only Sorcha's future. "I just want ta visit my old friend."

Maddie leaned in conspiratorially. "For years," she whispered, "the villagers swore a monster resided at Eynsford Park. Did you know?"

Sorcha knew all about that particular monster. And she could hardly wait to lay eyes on his half brothers, especially as the monster, or Lycan, in question was married to her coven sister and dear friend.

"Monster?" she giggled, determined never to give the secret away. "Cait, I mean, Lady Eynsford, would no' put up with a monster on her grounds."

Maddie giggled then too. "I can't imagine the marchioness scaring a monster away. She seems of the sweetest disposition."

"Ye've never seen Cait in a temper." Sorcha nudged her new friend's shoulder with her own. "Ye can take my word for it, Maddie. A monster would no' wish ta make her angry." Cait in a temper was a force to be reckoned with. Any self-respecting monster would steer clear of her wrath. That was what her husband did, after all.

"She sounds like Grandmamma."

The two were a bit alike with their commanding presence, now that Sorcha thought about it. "And would a monster *dare* enter Castle Hythe?"

Maddie laughed again. "Not if he had any idea of the dressing down he'd receive. 'How dare you trod upon my roses!'" She mocked her grandmother's imperious tone. "'Did you just eat my footman? Out with you, and don't come back until you learn some manners.'"

Sorcha could well imagine her coven sister barking in just that same manner at her wolfish husband. "Well, there ye have it. If a monster couldna dwell here at the castle, it couldna dwell at Eynsford Park either, if it ever did. Would ye like ta ride over there with me?"

She wouldn't be able to speak freely with Maddie about, but she hated to leave her behind. The English girl was terribly timid when left alone.

Her friend sighed. "I would love to, but Grandmamma would have a fit of apoplexy if I did. She's expecting more of *those* gentlemen to arrive, and she'll expect me to be there to greet them."

Ah, *those* gentlemen. Men of privilege the Duchess of Hythe had handpicked as acceptable matches for Maddie, men she might want to choose for a husband during her first season. This house party was an opportunity for her friend to see which men she might fancy ahead of time. It also would allow the duchess to investigate their character more closely and determine if a match might be made.

Sorcha had a reasonably sized dowry, one that would be considered large at home in Edinburgh, but it didn't compare to the fortune attached to Lady Madeline Hayburn. Hopefully, the gentlemen present would see more than pound signs when they looked at Maddie. She was the sweetest girl and deserved a gentleman who appreciated all her good qualities.

If more of *those* gentlemen were arriving today, Sorcha's excursion to Eynsford Park would have to be put off. She wouldn't throw Maddie to the wolves. That made her giggle. *She* was the one looking for a Lycan, after all.

"We doona have ta go as far as The Park. We could just ride around the castle grounds. I'll send Lady Eynsford a note askin' her ta come visit me instead."

If only there was a way to beg Cait to bring some of Eynsford's Lycan relations with her, but her coven sister was adamant that a beast was *not* in Sorcha's future, so the odds of that happening were slim, to say the least.

Maddie's green eyes twinkled almost as brightly as her smile. "Let me go get my habit, and I'll meet you in the east drawing room."

After changing into her riding habit, Sorcha penned a note to Caitrin Eynsford. That took a little longer than she had expected as she tried to find the right words to entice her coven sister to bring along her pack. Finally, note in hand, Sorcha left her chambers and made her way through the twisting and turning corridors that made up Castle Hythe. Once on the main level, she handed her note to the Hythes' stoic butler with directions that it be delivered to The Park at once.

She smoothed her sapphire riding habit into place and frowned. It was a bit long. She'd have to fix that later when no one was watching. Magic spells tended to make most people a little squeamish. Looking at her feet to make sure the hem didn't touch the ground, Sorcha started toward the east drawing room without even glancing up and promptly ran headfirst into an immovable object that blocked her path.

"Ouch!" Her head shot up. As she reached for the injury, she looked right into the black-as-night eyes of an old friend. Tall and handsome as ever, he was a friendly face in this English world, and she'd never been so happy to see him.

"Alec!" she gushed. "I had no idea ye would be here."

❧

Alec MacQuarrie's mouth fell open when his eyes landed on Sorcha, of all people. What the devil was she doing here? He hadn't imagined he'd cross paths with the witch again, not since his life had been irrevocably changed. Alec took a step back, and if he'd needed to breathe, he'd have taken a steadying breath. As it was, he could hear the blood pounding in her veins. She smelled, like she always did, of Scottish apple blossoms in the springtime. Damn his mouth for watering! This was *Sorcha*, for God's sake. "I—uh—How are you, lass?"

She grinned at him, her pretty face upturned and filled with joy as it always was. "Wonderful. Well, I would be if this riding habit was just a bit shorter."

Even in her unflattering dress, she wasn't the child he remembered. Damnation, when did Sorcha become a *woman*?

"I was supposed ta meet Maddie in the drawin' room. Come with me?" She linked her arm with his and led him down the corridor before he had time to respond.

"Maddie?" he asked, once his mind caught up to him.

She stopped walking, and he nearly tripped over the little wood sprite. "Lady Madeline, I should have said." She beamed up at him. "I wonder, are ye one of *those* gentlemen?"

Had she ever made sense? Not that he could remember, now that he thought about it. "What gentlemen?"

"Oh, I bet ye are." She again began towing him down the corridor. "Maddie—Lady Madeline—would do well ta choose ye, Alec. Ye'd see her for the sweet lady she is. I ken ye would."

"What are you talking about, Sorcha?" He planted his feet in the corridor, drawing her to a stop and forcing her to look up at him. "Tell me or I won't take another step."

Her soft brown eyes sparkled with exuberance. "What do ye want ta ken?"

Alec tipped her chin up so he could see her more clearly. "I have no idea what you're talking about. Why are you at Castle Hythe?" He didn't remember an association between the Fergusons and the Duke or Duchess of Hythe. He hadn't even realized Sorcha was acquainted with the family.

"Well, Her Grace invited me at Rhi's weddin'. And

I've made fast friends with Lady Madeline, her grand-daughter. But that's no' why I've come. No' really."

Alec had been so hurt, so angry during that wedding. Knowing that his maker, his *mentor*, had abandoned him to a dark world with which he was unfamiliar. No wonder he didn't remember anything that had transpired that day. Alec shook his head as the rest of her words sank in. "Why *have* you come?"

A mischievous grin spread across her face. "Because," she whispered, "I am searchin' for a Lycan of my very own, and Eynsford Park is within ridin' distance."

If she'd coshed him over the head with a broadsword he wouldn't have been more stunned. Cait was nearby? He hadn't realized. Good God. How had he *not* realized it? Damn fool that he was. He'd spent months avoiding polite society, making a place for himself in his new life. After *one* summons from the Duchess of Hythe, he was right back where he'd started—thinking about Cait.

Sorcha gasped and covered her mouth, her eyes silently begging to be forgiven.

"It's all right," he lied. "She married Eynsford. I've accepted that."

Certainly, even Sorcha could see through him. He had to get away. Alec turned around and headed back for the entrance. He could be back in London in the blink of an eye and forget he'd ever come to Kent, or at least try to.

He halted, unable to move an inch. What else had Sorcha said? She was searching for a Lycan of her own? And the only Lycans that would be present at Eynsford Park aside from that blasted marquess were

Eynsford's *relations*, whom Alec was fairly certain were the man's brothers, or half brothers, as the case might be. Viscount Radbourne and the wild Hadley twins. Three of the most depraved men in all of Britain. They were walking scandals. They were trouble. They were *dead* if even one of them felt the urge to claim Sorcha.

He glanced back over his shoulder at the little witch. A horrified expression still lingered on her face. Well, he was feeling just as horrified. Alec was back in front of her in a flash.

"Do you mean to say," he whispered so softly that no one but she could possibly hear him, "you were hoping to catch yourself one of those drooling beasts?"

Her horror quickly grew into indignation. "They doona drool."

Blast it, she did hope to catch one! "Oh, I happen to know they do," Alec grumbled.

Sorcha heaved a sigh as though he was the most troublesome man in existence. Then without a word, she spun on her heel and stalked off toward some unknown destination.

Alec was only a step behind her. "Have you lost your mind? Those creatures aren't for you. I can't believe your father would approve."

She paid him no attention as she burst into a drawing room. Inside on a small divan, a young blonde in a green habit smiled at their entrance.

"There you are," the chit gushed, rising from her seat. "I'm having our mounts readied, and—" She blushed crimson when she spotted Alec. "H-hello," she stammered.

Sorcha thrust her arm backward as though to deny his existence. "Pay him no mind, Maddie."

Stubborn little witch! Where had she gotten it in her mind that she should saddle herself with a bloody Lycan? What the devil was so enticing about the beasts? "Sorcha, I'm not done speaking with you."

"Pity," she bit out. "I'm done speakin' with ye."

"Ah!" a crackly voice came from the corridor. "Mr. MacQuarrie, I am so glad you accepted my invitation." The Duchess of Hythe, a dragon of the first order, stepped into the drawing room. Her icy blue eyes raked over Alec as though she was admiring his form.

He gulped. "Thank you, Your Grace."

The duchess gestured to the blond chit. "Have you met my granddaughter?"

Not unless one considered Sorcha's "Pay him no mind, Maddie," an introduction. "I'm afraid I haven't."

Her Grace rose to her full height and beckoned her granddaughter forward. "Mr. Alec MacQuarrie, this is Lady Madeline Hayburn and her delightful friend, Miss Ferguson."

"We've met," Alec growled. At the duchess' imperious expression, he softened his voice and amended, "That is, Miss Ferguson and I are old acquaintances."

"Neighbors in Edinburgh," Sorcha clarified as though to distance herself from him even further.

The duchess shifted her gaze to the lass who still had her back to Alec. "You are so well connected, Sorcha," she replied in a very congenial tone, not one usually associated with the Duchess of Hythe. Had Sorcha managed to charm the old dragon too?

Apparently. The woman had called her by her Christian name.

Of course, Sorcha had that effect on everyone. Anyone who came near her adored her. And… his eyes lowered to her perfectly rounded bottom, which he'd never noticed before. He could easily move his hand to caress her if he was of a mind to do so.

Damn it all to hell! Those bloody Lycans would be all over her in an instant. She'd get her wish in that regard, but she wouldn't be happy with the outcome. In the last few months, his path had unfortunately crossed that of the Hadley brothers on more than one occasion. A more degenerate group of men didn't exist.

Poor Sorcha wouldn't realize that until it was too late, however. She was sweet and innocent and… out of her bloody mind if she thought he would stand by and let her literally throw herself to the wolves. Especially *those* damned wolves. Eynsford's pack. His stomach roiled at the very thought.

"Sorcha, if I might have a word alone with you," Alec said to the wood sprite.

She glanced back over her shoulder at him, and Alec forgot what he was going to say. When had her eyes become that bedeviling? She blinked, her long lashes sweeping across her cheeks. Freckles. Why had he never realized she had freckles? It made him wonder if she had those little spots of color all over. Dear God. Now all he'd be able to think about was what marks the little witch wore on her most sensitive places.

The Duchess of Hythe raised her eyebrows. Well, she raised one of them. The other one scrunched up in a most offended fashion. "Is this a word that cannot be shared with the rest of us, Mr. MacQuarrie?" she asked.

He opened his mouth, however nothing but a croaking sound came out. He closed it. He must resemble a fish. A very uncomfortable fish. He'd hoped to save Sorcha from Lycans, and instead he'd somehow turned into a blasted salmon.

"If he shared the word, Yer Grace," Sorcha piped up, "then it wouldna be a surprise." She looked up at Alec, and her eyes danced at him in warning. He would kill her. Or kiss her. He wasn't certain which.

"A surprise?" the duchess gasped as she laid a hand on her chest. Her flesh jiggled at the edge of her bodice. "For me?"

He swung his gaze to Sorcha's bodice. Definitely a better view. In fact, it was one he couldn't take his eyes off.

"Mr. MacQuarrie?" the duchess prompted.

"Yes, Your Grace," Alec said with a small bow, ripping his gaze from Sorcha's person. "If I told you, the surprise would be ruined."

The shrewd old woman's eyes narrowed. Then she giggled. That old matriarch giggled like a girl still in the schoolroom. "I do so love a surprise." She clapped her hands together with glee. "May I have just a hint?" She held her fingers up with about an inch of space between them and looked at him as though he'd hung the moon and stars.

"Grandmamma," the little blonde said. She had a name. But Alec would be damned if he could remember it. Not with Sorcha standing directly beside her. "Let the man have his fun. It appears as though he and Miss Ferguson have been in one another's pockets for quite some time."

"Young man, if I find you anywhere near Miss Ferguson's pockets, I will—" the duchess began.

"Yer Grace!" Sorcha protested. "He has never been anywhere *near* my pockets. I can assure you it's the furthest thing from his mind."

But it wasn't, though he felt more comfortable keeping that to himself.

The duchess held up one hand to stop Sorcha's diatribe. "If I find you anywhere near Miss Ferguson's pockets…" she said as she threaded her arm through his and started down the corridor, leading him along. The duchess dropped her voice down to a conciliatory whisper. "…I will be most delighted."

Good God. Now he had Sorcha to watch after *and* a surprise for the duchess to create out of thin air. If that wasn't bad enough, Her Grace had him thinking lascivious thoughts. And she clearly wasn't at all ashamed for having placed them in his mind.

The duchess reached for his lapel. "Where did you get that flower, Mr. MacQuarrie?" she asked. "It's quite remarkable."

He wasn't wearing a flower. Well, he hadn't been a few minutes earlier. He glanced down at his jacket to find the happiest white orchid peeking out of his buttonhole. Alec looked back over his shoulder to find Sorcha grinning at him. That little witch was trouble. Beautiful, beguiling trouble.

Two

"WHY WERE YOU QUARRELING WITH MR. MacQuarrie?" Maddie asked as a groom helped her onto her sidesaddle.

Sorcha, already atop her spirited chestnut, tossed her head back to look at the clouds as though she hadn't heard her friend's question and let the sun warm her skin. After all, what was she to say? *Well, the irritable vampyre doesn't care for werewolves since one stole the love of his life last year.* Hardly. She might as well ride for London and admit herself to Bedlam. She lowered her head, smoothed her hand over her horse's neck, and cooed to the animal.

"There you are, milady." The groom took a step backward and smiled at Maddie. "Don't go too far. You know how Her Grace worries."

"Thank you, Johnny." Maddie urged her bay closer to Sorcha. "But there's no need for concern. Miss Ferguson and I will be careful."

The lad nodded and then started back for the stables.

Maddie's green eyes twinkled when they landed on Sorcha. "I *know* you heard me. Am I to take from your silence that you don't wish to discuss your handsome neighbor?"

Sorcha looked down at her reins and shook her head. "It was nothin' important, Maddie. Mr. MacQuarrie and I simply doona see eye ta eye about the Marquess of Eynsford." That, at least, was the truth.

Despite Alec's assertion that she had lost her mind, Sorcha felt a tug of guilt in her heart. She hadn't meant to blurt out Eynsford's name, and she couldn't quite forget the look of pure torture that had flashed across Alec's face when the name left her lips. If she could have snatched the words back, she would have done so. Poor Alec had been devastated when Cait chose Eynsford over him.

They started toward the west side of the property at a slow trot, and Maddie sent Sorcha a sidelong glance. "Your neighbor is in good company then. Grandmamma is a bit wary of the marquess as well. He was quite estranged from his father before the old man's passing. Did you know?"

Yes, Sorcha was quite aware of Eynsford's rift with his father, or at least the man all of society believed to be his father; but that was neither here nor there. She shrugged her response. "Many men choose paths their fathers do not agree with."

Maddie agreed with a nod. "True. Papa has been quite put out with Nathaniel and Robert most of their lives. What about your Mr. MacQuarrie?"

"*My* Mr. MacQuarrie?" Sorcha somehow managed to keep from tumbling from her seat. She'd never thought of Alec in those terms before.

Maddie giggled. "Does he follow his father's path? Or is he more the rebellious sort like my brothers?"

She'd heard quite the scandalous tales about the Earl of Bexley and Lord Robert Hayburn ever since she'd befriended Maddie, always in very hushed tones, however, to keep anyone else from hearing. Their exploits certainly didn't sound like Alec, at least not the man she'd once known. "He always pleased his father who, alas, has since passed on," Sorcha replied.

"Hmm," Maddie mused. "I simply cannot understand his arrival at Castle Hythe."

What was there to understand? Hadn't the duchess invited more than a dozen eligible gentlemen for Maddie to meet? "For ye ta become acquainted with, I'm certain."

"No." Maddie shook her head. "He's not one of *those* gentlemen."

Her friend had Sorcha's complete attention. "Why do ye say that?"

Maddie shrugged as though the answer was clear. "Because, you goose, he's not titled."

Not titled? That was hardly a deterrent as far as Alec was concerned. Sorcha gaped at her friend. "I assure ye, his fortune is one of the grandest in all of Scotland." Not to mention he was one of the most handsome men of Sorcha's acquaintance. And kind and generous.

Maddie certainly shouldn't discount him so easily simply because of his lack of a title. No, the better reason to discount Alec would be that he was incapable of loving anyone other than Cait. But most marriages weren't love matches, and he was admirable in every other way, even for a vampyre.

Maddie grinned. "I'm sure it is, Sorcha. That's not what I meant. It's only that Grandmamma has beén adamant that I'll marry a peer. All the others either already possess their titles or are their fathers' heirs apparent."

Sorcha hadn't realized that. How had that fact escaped her? She frowned. "Well, I doona ken then, Maddie. Perhaps Mr. MacQuarrie has other business with yer grandmother."

"Perhaps," her friend agreed, and then she cocked her head to one side as if she was contemplating something. "He doesn't sound Scottish."

Sorcha shrugged. "Doona let him hear ye say that." At Maddie's confused expression, Sorcha took pity on her. "Alec is English educated," she explained. "He left Edinburgh at twelve, but he returned home often enough."

"Oh." Maddie nodded. "I suppose that explains it." Then she pointed at a large tree off in the distance. "Race you to that oak over there."

Sorcha agreed with a nod, but her mind was still on their conversation and her heart simply wasn't in the race. She followed in her friend's wake, reaching the specified tree well after Maddie had already arrived. Why *had* Alec been invited to Castle Hythe? The mystery would remain, as she couldn't very well ask the duchess, but she'd keep her eyes open and see if she couldn't learn the truth for herself.

❧

"She's a delightful chit, isn't she?" Nathaniel Hayburn, the Earl of Bexley, broke into Alec's thoughts as he watched from the library window while Sorcha and her friend rode across the meadow.

"Aye," Alec replied, though he wasn't certain which *she* they were discussing. He stepped away from his position near the window and sauntered toward the middle of the room where the Englishman had dropped into an overstuffed leather chair.

Bexley grinned roguishly. "But Grandmother has threatened to sever both my hands if I even consider touching her."

So the earl wasn't discussing his sister then. Alec managed not to frown at the dissolute nobleman. He knew Bexley more by reputation than from sight, but what he did know was more than enough to make Alec certain the earl was not the man for innocent, enchanting Sorcha. Damn if she didn't need a keeper. If it wasn't because of her inane fascination with Lycans, then it was due to debauched Englishmen's fascination with her, not that he could blame the man. She *was* delightful.

"Your grandmother is a formidable woman. I certainly wouldn't want to cross her." Thank God the old woman had taken Sorcha under her wing, if for no other reason than to keep Bexley at bay.

The earl laughed. "You have the right of it, MacQuarrie. And she does hold the purse strings. Even Father is terrified of angering her." Bexley rested his head against the back of the chair. "So I shall endeavor to find other pursuits to occupy my time in godforsaken Kent."

"You could always return to Town," Alec suggested. The miles between London and Castle Hythe would keep Sorcha safe from at least one depraved Englishman, just in case the fear of his grandmother wore off or the lure of the little witch proved too tempting.

Bexley shook his head. "I've been ordered here for the duration of this party. To make certain no one makes improper advances toward Madeline."

At least the man cared about his sister's virtue. That was something, Alec supposed. He dropped into a seat across from the earl. "So what pursuits do you have in mind, Bexley?"

"Well," the man sighed, "tomorrow evening there's a ball. But tonight I shall have to make my own fun. I plan to head into the village with Radbourne. He always manages to find the most willing chits. Care to join us?"

Bexley *and* Radbourne? The combination was nauseating. Still, Alec did need to feed and barmaids were generally easy marks. After a little enchantment, the women wouldn't even remember their encounter. Then the rest of Bexley's words hit him. "Did you say 'ball'?"

The earl grimaced. "Unfortunately. All the guests and local gentry. Did Grandmother not tell you?"

No, Her Grace had failed to mention the event. *All the guests and local gentry.* Alec's stomach twisted. The odds that Cait, Eynsford, and his blasted pack would be present were not in Alec's favor. "Radbourne is attending, I assume?"

"Everyone at The Park."

Bloody perfect. Alec groaned. He'd have to see Cait. Well, he didn't *have* to see her. He could skip the blasted ball, but in doing so, he'd be throwing Sorcha to the Lycans—or rather she'd throw herself at them

and he wouldn't be around to prevent her foolishness.
If only he could talk her into packing her trunk and
heading home, he wouldn't have to stay in Kent himself.
Though the likelihood of that seemed nonexistent.

"You all right, MacQuarrie?" Bexley asked, sliding
forward in his chair.

"Why wouldn't I be?" Alec hedged. Who wouldn't
want to see the girl of his dreams happily married to a
slobbering beast?

The earl shrugged, looking less concerned, and
settled back against his seat. "So, up for it?"

"Up for what?"

The man scoffed as though speaking to Alec was a
chore. "For our jaunt into the village this evening."

As long as Bexley, Radbourne, and his brothers
were headed away from the castle, Alec wouldn't
have to watch over Sorcha. And by the end of the
evening he would be in need of sustenance. Though
the company was not of his choosing, he didn't have
many choices here at Castle Hythe. He could always
entice a maid at the castle, but he hated doing so. It
was always a bit precarious to partake where he slept.
Someone could overhear or see something.

Alec raked a hand through his hair. "Oh, of course.
Into the village. Sounds amusing." About as amusing
as catching the plague.

❧

Sorcha flopped onto her bed and stared up at the
ceiling. She'd waited the entire day for some sort
of entertainment. Not that Her Grace wasn't entertaining in her own right. But Sorcha had hoped

for more. Alec had slunk away as soon as he had disentangled himself from the duchess' grasp. And Maddie had had to suffer more dress fittings for the upcoming social events. Even Cait had cried off, stating she was too tired for a visit in the note she sent back to Sorcha. And not a single Lycan had made an appearance. How on earth was she to catch a beast of her very own if she couldn't even be in the same room with one?

Sorcha was nearly certain the duchess had cards or charades planned for the night's activities. Mindless pursuits were better than no pursuits, she thought with a heavy sigh. But then the jingle of tack outside caught her attention. She moved quickly to her window and pushed aside the heavy drapes. Three men sat astride prancing horses that danced in their places, appearing to be nearly as anxious to get moving as the gentlemen were. Sorcha shoved the window open, and the crisp country air filtered into her chambers.

One of the men reached into his pocket, pulled out his watch fob, and then glanced up at the rising moon. Sorcha's breath caught in her throat. After waiting more than a sennight, the objects of her desire had finally arrived. "Bexley had better hurry up, or we'll head into Folkestone without him," Archer Hadley, Viscount Radbourne, complained.

Sorcha nearly sighed. All three of the Lycans were directly beneath her window. How wonderfully fortuitous. Radbourne was just as handsome as he'd been the previous spring at Rhiannon's wedding.

"You could be a gentleman, Archer. You know,

go to the door and request his presence like any other man of good breeding would do," one of his twin brothers teased. If they'd just look up, she could tell them apart. Weston had a very dashing scar across his cheek, while Grayson was unmarred.

"And ruin my good reputation?" the viscount asked. "It took too many years to cultivate the image I have."

"He's right." The other twin laughed. "No one would expect the dissolute Lord Radbourne to do anything gentlemanly."

"Did someone take your name in vain, Radbourne?" A tall man sauntered from the castle.

Hmm. Sorcha had had no idea that Maddie's oldest brother was acquainted with the Hadley men. That was most useful information.

Lord Bexley strode toward the wolfish trio who still sat atop their horses. The earl's groom tossed him the reins to his own horse. "Heaven forbid anyone should make such an egregious error as to call Archer Hadley a gentleman," Bexley joked merrily as he mounted.

"Who's the extra horse for?" Lord Radbourne asked. "Is Robert in residence?"

Bexley shook his head. "My brother is still hiding somewhere in Yorkshire. No, I've asked Mr. MacQuarrie to join us. Hope you don't mind," he said glancing toward the door. "He should be here in a moment." Bexley turned his gaze back at the Hadley men. "You are acquainted with MacQuarrie, aren't you?"

"Indeed," Lord Radbourne grumbled, appearing less than pleased by the addition to their party.

"Had anyone told me this night had gone to the

dogs, I'd have probably cried off," Sorcha heard
Alec reply as his long legs ate up the distance from
the main door to where his horse stood saddled and
ready for him. She fought the grin that pulled at the
corners of her lips. *Gone to the dogs.* She snorted a little
as she covered a giggle with her hand. Alec took the
reins and hoisted himself atop the beautiful beast as
smoothly as a cavalry officer. "Shall we?" he asked.

Just then, Lord Radbourne must have noticed her
as she hung so indecorously out the window, trying
to capture their every word, because he doffed his hat
and bowed his head toward her. "Miss Ferguson,"
he called, which had everyone's head turning in her
direction. It was much too late to duck behind the
curtain at this point. So, instead, she simply waved at
the collection of men beneath her window.

"Such a vision of loveliness, Miss Ferguson. Should
I stay and be your companion for the evening?" Lord
Radbourne asked. Not even a hint of a smile crossed
his lips. He simply regarded her stoically, waiting for
her response.

She opened her mouth to reply, but Alec spoke
first. "Miss Ferguson can do much better than the
company of mutts like you."

"Beg your pardon, MacQuarrie," Weston Hadley
replied, fingering the scar on his cheek. "Unless you'd
like to discuss your own bloody habits, I'd suggest you
leave ours in good company where they belong."

Sorcha noticed the use of the word "bloody," and
Alec must have as well, because he simply swung his
mount around and headed down the lane.

"Until next time, Miss Ferguson." Lord Radbourne

touched the brim of his beaver hat in farewell and followed Alec down the drive.

Sorcha could hardly believe her luck. Finally, she'd spotted her coveted Lycans... But they were moving as far and as fast away from her as they could. She wouldn't have it. Her destiny lay with one of those Lycans; she just knew it. After all, Cait and Elspeth had both married beasts of that variety and they were gloriously happy. The Hadley men were as close to perfection as Sorcha was going to get.

She jumped to her feet, searching everywhere for her dark cloak. She finally located it in one of her many trunks and tossed it over her arm. She smoothed her dress in front of the looking glass and found her appearance to be quite normal.

They were headed to Folkestone, according to Lord Radbourne. She and Maddie had gone into the village the previous afternoon. It was fairly close, all things considered. If only she had some clue as to their ultimate destination once they reached the village, she'd know how to dress. Well, there was nothing for it. She'd have to go as she was.

Sorcha crept from her room before realizing she was drawing attention to herself. Foolish. She'd do much better to act as though she wasn't up to something nefarious. She rose to her full height and smoothly made her way to the main level.

Luckily, the household was teeming with people. When she streaked out the door and toward the stables, no one even took notice. The groom, Johnny, sat outside the stables on the edge of a wooden fence, his feet wedged between the boards to keep himself in place. When he saw Sorcha approach, he dropped to the ground to stand before her.

"Miss Ferguson," he started, obviously unsettled by her appearance out of nowhere. "What brings you to the stables so late?"

It would have been so much easier if she could have borrowed a mount without anyone realizing. Sorcha bit the inside of her cheek and racked her brain for a reason to be in such an awkward position. And to put the poor groom in such an awkward position. She really should go back to the house. But to do so would be to abandon her pursuit of a Lycan for her own, wouldn't it?

"Johnny," she began quietly, batting her eyelashes in what she hoped was a coquettish move. Instead, she probably looked like she had dirt in her eye. "Do ye remember yesterday when Lady Madeline and I went ta the village?"

"Of course, miss." The man nodded. "I accompanied you myself," he said.

"I lost something there." She looked at him. And waited. His eyes scrunched together. She'd lost her mind. He would never fall for it.

"Was it something of value, miss?" he asked. He cared. Oh, dear. He had a conscience. It was too bad Sorcha had abandoned hers back in her chambers.

"Oh, *very* much value," she said, praying it was dark enough to hide the nervous tic above her eyebrow.

"Do you remember where you lost it?" he asked. "I can go and look for it. I'll do it right now." Such a dear young man. Guilt bit at Sorcha's lust for a beast of her own, but she pushed past it.

"I don't remember, but I think if I went back there,

I might be able ta retrace my steps and find it. Do ye think ye could take me?"

"Certainly. I think the duchess would grant me leave."

"Oh, I just talked ta the duchess and she did grant ye leave." She would be forgiven for her lie, wouldn't she? Certainly she would.

"Then first thing tomorrow," he replied with a nod.

She shook her head frantically and blinked as though she blinked back tears. "Ye doona understand how important it is." She grasped his hands in hers and squeezed. She knew the very moment she had won him over. It was when he sighed heavily. "The duchess said ye can take me tonight. Right *now*." She waited for his response.

"If ye say so, miss," was his only reply. "I'll just ready a carriage."

Sorcha paced from one side of the barn to the next as he prepared their conveyance. Nothing good could come of this, could it? Well, perhaps something could. Perhaps a Lycan would fall in love with her and claim her under the light of the moon. Well, not tonight's moon, since it wasn't full. But some day. Sooner rather than later, hopefully.

"Do you have a companion, miss?" Johnny asked as he handed her inside the carriage.

Blast it. No companion. "I do, but the poor dear has taken ill. And I do so want ta go ta the village tonight, ye see."

He looked doubtful for the first time all night.

"It was my mother's. The item I lost." She really should have decided what that item was. "It belonged to my mother." When he still looked undecided, she continued. "She's dead." Certainly her late mother would forgive her subterfuge.

"I'm sorry to hear that, miss," Johnny said, his eyes softening.

"Now do ye ken why this is so important ta me?" *Because my entire world is hinged upon the impropriety of this event.*

The young groom nodded and said, "We'll find it, miss. I won't stop looking until I do."

Oh, he would break her heart into a million pieces if he didn't stop being so wonderful. He'd be terribly disappointed in her when she slipped away from him in search of her Lycans once they reached Folkestone. But a lass had to take matters of the heart into her own two hands if that lass wanted to be successfully married to a beast of her own.

Three

ALEC'S HUNTER ATE UP THE GROUND AS HE RACED EAST, farther and farther from Castle Hythe. If only he could lead those flea-ridden wolves so far from Sorcha that they would forget the way back to her. Wishful thinking, he knew, but it was the only thought that calmed his nerves.

What the devil was wrong with the lass? She had actually leaned out her bedchamber window trying to catch the attention of Radbourne and his sycophantic pups. The littlest witch had to be the most difficult in her whole coven. Elspeth was reasonable. Blaire was pragmatic. Rhiannon knew her own mind, but she made wise decisions. And Cait… Well, it was best not to think about Cait. Even so, Cait had never been as difficult to deal with as Sorcha.

"I say!" Bexley called from somewhere behind him. "We're not racing in the Ascot, MacQuarrie. A nice leisurely jaunt will do."

Alec pulled back on his reins, slowing his mount to a more relaxed gait. "Sorry," he replied over his shoulder.

"That thirsty, are you?" Radbourne's mocking voice made Alec grind his teeth together.

If he tore the Lycan's head from his shoulders, he could make Bexley forget the entire event, but then he'd still have to deal with the twin pups. He truly shouldn't even consider the option. His old mentor had been very adamant that Alec not start some war. ...But Matthew wasn't around any longer, was he?

Getting rid of the blasted wolfling would at least keep Sorcha safe. Alec hadn't missed the way Radbourne had leered at the little witch. It had been enough to make his vision turn red at the edges. The damn viscount was lucky he hadn't been within reach when it happened or he'd be missing an arm or a leg or something even more vital.

"Or just in a hurry to enchant a little piece of baggage?" Weston Hadley asked as he rode up on Alec's right.

The irksome twin most assuredly deserved the scar he wore on his face like a badge of honor. Alec hadn't been present when a powerful vampyress had marked the pup for his impertinence, but he could certainly sympathize with the lady who had been driven to reprimand the young Lycan. He glared at the wolf at his side. "Callista sends her regards, Hadley."

A satisfying look of fear flashed in the Lycan's eyes, and Alec bit back a smile. It truly was a shame he'd missed that whole event the previous spring. And it truly was a shame that both of the wolf's brothers hadn't been punished in a similar fashion. Perhaps Sorcha wouldn't find them so enthralling if they were all scarred.

"Callista?" Bexley asked as he rode up on Alec's left. "Who is this little baggage?"

Callista would *not* appreciate being referred to in such a fashion. Thank God she wasn't in Kent. Alec aimed for what he hoped was an expression of ennui. "An acquaintance of Mr. Hadley's. No one you'd be interested in."

"Pretty name," the earl added with a shrug. "Someone you'd care to tell me more about, Wes?"

"You wouldn't want to meet her." Alec chuckled more to himself than at Bexley. "She's positively ancient." In all honesty, he wasn't certain how old the vampyre was, but he wouldn't be surprised if she'd been with Caesar when his forces first entered Britain.

The earl frowned. "What a shame. I've cut my swath through Folkestone more times than I care to count. A new, pretty face would be most welcome."

"Miss Ferguson has a pretty face," Radbourne remarked from behind them.

Alec clutched his reins even tighter. Had blood flowed through his veins, it would have been pounding in his ears. How dare the man even say her name?

"Indeed," Bexley agreed. "I would love to taste a bit of Scotland myself." Then he groaned a bit as though he imagined doing that very thing.

Alec cast the man an admonishing glare. "Your grandmother has warned you off of her," he reminded the earl.

Bexley agreed with a nod of his head. "True. It really is too bad. Such a tempting little lass with the prettiest lips."

Not bad at all, but good fortune for Sorcha even if she didn't realize it.

"And so charmingly untried," the earl continued. "There's nothing quite as nice as an eager pupil."

Alec pressed his hunter forward a bit more. If he had to listen to this all the way to Folkestone, every bit of patience he possessed would vanish. "How much farther to the village?"

"Not far," Bexley replied, completely oblivious to the perilous rope on which he walked. One really shouldn't go about provoking vampyres, certainly not to the extent the Englishman did. Not if one wanted to keep his head attached to his body at the end of the day.

Just in the distance, Alec could see the lights of what appeared to be a tavern. Thank God. He glanced over his shoulder at his companions. "I'll meet you all there."

The four men chuckled as Alec rode on ahead. "My, he certainly is eager," one of the twins muttered, but Alec didn't look back to see which one.

❧

Night had fallen very quickly. Sorcha peeked out through the curtain of her pilfered coach. Certainly, they must be closing in on Folkestone by now. Sure enough, a warm glow emanated from a grey stone building up ahead. The Knight's Arms. The hinged sign rocked back and forth, swayed by the ocean breeze. She'd noticed the tavern the previous day. Raucous male laughter filtered from the establishment and Sorcha shivered. What had possessed her to embark on such a foolish journey?

The Hadleys, Alec, and Lord Bexley must be in the tavern. It was the only place she could see or hear signs of life in Folkestone. But the Hythe carriage pushed farther into the village and finally stopped right outside the small bookshop she and Maddie had explored at length the day before. A moment later, Johnny opened the coach door and offered his hand to assist Sorcha from the conveyance.

"Nothing is open, Miss," he said regretfully. "But you can still retrace your steps. We can come back in the morning, if you think your trinket is in one of the shops."

Her *item* had turned into a trinket now. She really should have spent the drive into Folkestone deciding what exactly she had lost. "Thank ye, Johnny." Her eyes glanced over his shoulder, back down High Street toward The Knight's Arms. It really wasn't so far away. She could be there within moments, if she could just get away from the helpful groom.

Then inspiration struck. Johnny would be left with a headache and she'd have to drive the coach back to Castle Hythe herself, but she was proficient with the ribbons. There were some advantages to having a much older brother who was easily persuaded to teach her things she had no business learning.

Sorcha opened her reticule and willed a valerian seed to find its way to the top. She smiled at the seed and clasped it into her palm. Within seconds, life began to sprout within her fist. She opened her hand and watched a white flower burst open. Its sweet scent tickled at her nose, which was the very last thing she wanted. "No' me," she whispered to the plant. Then she closed her fist again and the new flower disintegrated in her hold, leaving her the perfect amount of dried herb.

"Did you say something, miss?" Johnny stepped closer to her.

Only a tiny bit of guilt ate at Sorcha's insides when she opened her hand and blew the herb right into Johnny's face. He collapsed in a heap at her feet. Sorcha gasped, even though she knew that had been bound to happen. She glanced down the street, making certain no one had seen the magical display, and dropped her reticule to the ground.

She stepped back, bent over, and tried to heft the young groom by his armpits to let him sleep off the effects in the coach. *Havers!* Who would have thought Johnny was so heavy? Did he collect stones in his pockets? What she wouldn't give to have Blaire's strength in that moment. Her battle-born coven sister would have easily dispensed with the groom and been halfway to The Knight's Arms by now.

Sorcha tugged again at Johnny's jacket and was relieved when she moved him half an inch. Still, at this rate it would be all night before she could get the groom inside the coach. "Next time, give him the valerian when he's *inside* the door," she berated herself.

"Did you say something, lass?" a deep voice asked, directly behind her.

With a gasp, Sorcha spun around to stare in the dark amber eyes of Viscount Radbourne. He was so devilishly handsome with his light brown hair illuminated in the moonlight that she struggled to find her voice.

"Now, Miss Ferguson," the Lycan began as he took another step toward her and gestured to the groom lying at her feet. "Tell me, may I be of assistance?"

Sorcha bit her lip and racked her brain, trying to find a story that might be worthy of the Lycan. A story? That would be pushing it. A lie. That was much more appropriate. "It appears as though the Hythe's groom is a bit under the weather?" she tried.

"Did you cosh the fool over the head, Miss Ferguson?" He raised his eyebrows at her as he leaned casually against the side of the coach.

"What makes ye think he's a fool?" she countered, trying to avoid his question.

"He's on the ground at your feet," Lord Radbourne said pointedly as he gestured toward Johnny. The Lycan bent and smacked the side of the man's face. Johnny didn't even flinch. He didn't groan or make any sound at all.

"He won't wake up for while," Sorcha admitted. "At least I don't think he will." She fidgeted under Lord Radbourne's heady stare. "I hear that's the way of it when one has imbibed too much."

Radbourne snorted. "He doesn't smell like drink."

Sorcha wanted to slap her own forehead. Of course a man with a heightened sense of smell would know whether or not Johnny had been imbibing. Foolish. Foolish. Foolish.

"Then perhaps it was something he ate?" she tried.

"Or some scheme conjured up in your mind?" he chuckled. "What shall we do with him?"

She searched around the darkness. "We can't just leave him here in the street." She looked up at Lord Radbourne

with what she hoped was her most bewitching smile.
"Will ye help me get him inta the coach?"

The Lycan groaned loudly as he hoisted the unconscious groom into the coach. Her mother hadn't lived
long enough to teach Sorcha the right way or wrong
way to catch a Lycan, but something told her this was
the wrong way.

"That was a bit like moving a dead body," Lord
Radbourne mumbled as he dusted his hands and
stepped out of the coach.

"Ye've moved a dead body before?" Sorcha gasped.

He chuckled. "That's a discussion for when I know
you better, Miss Ferguson." His gaze drifted slowly
down her body. "Much better."

Sorcha was certain that she would be ten shades
of red if not for the darkness that hid them both. She
took a deep breath. Then she blurted, "And how long
will that take, Lord Radbourne?"

His eyebrows rose in question as the corners of
his lips twitched. There was a very long pause during
which Sorcha questioned the brashness of her words.
He'd probably think her an untried youth out to snag
a handsome peer. "It would take just long enough for
Eynsford to realize my intentions. Then he'd trounce
me. And Cait would feel obliged to come to my rescue.
And then all hope would be lost for you and me."

Sorcha giggled at his words.

"So, Miss Ferguson, what shall we do now?" he
asked, appearing to be most intrigued by her plight. "I
can escort you back to Castle Hythe."

So close. She'd been so close to catching a Lycan.
But by her own foolish actions, she'd forced the man

to *move a body*, which in turn had probably made him lose any interest he might have had in her.

She motioned toward the closed carriage. "I suppose I'll just wait for Johnny ta wake." She kicked at a clump of dirt with her toe. "Ye should go back ta yer pursuits, whatever they may be." Then beneath her breath she added, "Or whomever they may involve."

"You make it sound as though I slay pretty lasses with my witty repartee on a daily basis, Miss Ferguson."

Sorcha couldn't hold back a groan. When would she remember that Lycans could hear every mutter she made? Every comment she tossed out under her breath went straight to their ears. "Why do I always forget about their impeccable hearing?" she asked herself. Since she was already talking to herself like a ninny, she would probably be safe to continue. "He's listening right now, in fact, though how he can hear me over that atrociously sized foot in my mouth, I've no idea. I had no idea Lycans were *that* astute."

"Pardon me, Miss Ferguson," Lord Radbourne said, standing taller as he appeared to sober before her very eyes. "I'd appreciate it if you wouldn't bandy that little fact about in such a cavalier manner. It's a well-kept secret. One I was unaware you knew about."

"Oh, doona worry. I have secrets of my own that I'd no' like ta be bandied about. The fact that ye are what ye are is no' somethin' I would discuss with anyone else. Ye have my word on it."

For some reason, she felt the need to reassure him. Probably because he looked so discomfited by the fact that she knew. She reached a hand up to smooth his lapel. And let it linger there as her eyes sought his.

She needed him to understand that she would never, ever tell.

Four

Alec MacQuarrie stepped out of the tavern and looked up at the night sky. He'd needed only moments of surveying the taproom to realize that an adequate dinner would not be possible tonight. At least not at The Knight's Arms. Being a vampyre was a damned nuisance, especially when one was a gentleman beneath all the darkness.

Life would be so much easier if he had fewer scruples, or perhaps if he had the ability to block out the feelings of the whore who was to be his meal. But to his dismay, when he took from a woman and allowed a bond to be created between them, when he sealed his mouth over her skin and drank her in, he took in too many harmful emotions along with her life-giving blood. Despair coursed through Alec in those moments, so he avoided unfamiliar chits at all costs.

At least at his club in London, the Cyprians were accustomed to his idiosyncrasies. The women at *Brysi* would let him drink his fill in exchange for pleasure and coin. They no longer expected more than he was able to give, and they didn't need to be enchanted. He hated usurping a woman's free will, which is what he would be doing if he spent any more time inside The Knight's Arms with his traveling companions.

He'd lost track of the Hadley twins almost as soon as they'd entered the establishment. They'd set their sights on two pretty little wenches who seemed determined to fight over which one of them would get to tup the one with the scar. What was alluring about having been branded by a vampyre, Alec had no idea. Yet something apparently was.

Bexley had settled at a table with local fellows involved in what appeared to be faro. Radbourne had somehow disappeared. And Alec was bored out of his mind.

As his foot hit the top step, a gentle wind came up to brush the hair from his forehead, and along with it came the scent of apple blossoms. Apple blossoms? Why did that scent seem so familiar? He racked his brain, trying to remember where he'd last smelled that delightful aroma. Just thinking about it made his mouth water.

Then he heard her giggle.

Alec spun around quickly and looked into the darkness. His excellent vision didn't let him down. He saw the back of a nearby coach that was stopped outside a tiny bookstore. And standing in its shadows was a lass. He closed his eyes and inhaled deeply, though he didn't need to do so. He wouldn't mistake Sorcha for anything. That was her scent. That was her lovely hair piled atop her head. That was her... *touching Radbourne*? By God, she was!

Alec was across the street in the blink of an eye. He stood behind the coach and listened, hoping to hear their conversation for a moment before ripping the mutt's limbs from his body, simply because he had let Sorcha touch him. Alec froze in place.

"It is a sad day when gentlemen must resort to eavesdropping, is it not, Miss Ferguson?" he heard Radbourne ask Sorcha.

"Eavesdroppin'? That's a terrible practice. One I never indulge in unless I absolutely have ta ken somethin' that no one will tell me about." Alec heard her giggle and felt a grin tip the corners of his own mouth.

"There are things that people refuse to discuss with you?" Radbourne asked. "Such as?"

"Such as what it's like ta kiss a Lycan," Sorcha said quietly, her voice barely more than a whisper.

"What a travesty." Radbourne's voice deepened. "Shall I show you?"

That was it. That was all Alec could possibly take. He couldn't stand on the opposite side of the coach and let Radbourne introduce Sorcha to passion. And he had no doubt this would be her introduction. He strode quickly around the coach and stopped in his tracks. The pair of them stood there laughing at him.

"It's ill-mannered to eavesdrop, MacQuarrie," Radbourne said. A good six feet of space separated the Lycan and Sorcha. Thank God.

"What's even more ill-mannered is to have her out in the dead of night without a chaperone," Alec clarified. He took Sorcha's elbow and turned her to face him. "What the devil do you think you're doing, Sorch?" he asked. "Your reputation will be in shreds if one word of this gets out." He opened the door of the coach and made a motion to usher her inside. But a foot fell out of the door instead. A man's foot. Which was solidly attached to a leg. What the hell?

Radbourne shrugged. "He's a big man. I'm afraid it was nearly impossible to fit his body in such a small space without folding him."

Sorcha giggled. "Looks as though he's come unfolded."

"That much is obvious," Radbourne said, a chuckle behind his words.

"Who is that?" Alec ground out.

"He's no' dead," Sorcha said, almost as though she was put out by his questions.

"I'm well aware of that," Alec ground out. "I can hear his heart beating."

"She knows what you are?" Radbourne asked, his voice incredulous.

"I ken everythin'," Sorcha said. Then she immediately bit her lip at the scathing glance Alec sent her. "Well, I ken a lot." Then she clarified again. "I ken enough. Just barely enough."

"She knows what I am too," Radbourne said casually as he leaned against the coach.

"She knows enough to get herself in heaps of trouble," Alec countered. Would his entire holiday be spent removing Sorcha from sticky situations? Evidently it would. He inhaled deeply and faced Radbourne. "Your services are no longer needed. You may go." He raised an eyebrow at the Lycan. "And I trust that you value your skin enough that you will not tell anyone of this impromptu encounter."

Radbourne pushed away from the coach with a groan. "What encounter?"

"Exactly," Alec returned.

He could almost hear the words in Sorcha's mouth before she spit them out. "What if *I* tell someone? What then?"

Infuriating little witch. Alec had no idea what to do with her. "Then one of us could be forced to marry you. Or see you ruined."

"And since I was with you first…" Radbourne said.

Sorcha's eyes grew wide. "It's that simple? Truly? Ta catch a beast of my very own, I simply have ta let him compromise me?" She put her hands on her hips and tossed Radbourne a saucy grin. "Then consider yerself compromised, Lord Radbourne. Shall we race for Gretna?"

Alec's mouth fell open. Damn if she wouldn't kill him, which wasn't an easy task as he was already dead. But then amusement broke across her features and she laughed until she had to wipe tears from her eyes. Thank God, she'd been teasing. Still it left him ill-humored.

"I'd like to know why this is so amusing to you," Alec said, sounding like an old spinster aunt to his own ears. He would have a soft spot for old spinster aunts from this day forward. The poor dears must be the most put-upon souls in the land.

When Sorcha had caught her breath, she said, "Because I have an unconscious groom in the carriage. And I have a Lycan scoundrel who couldn't be considered a scoundrel at all, or at least not with me, because I had him carry a body and ruined any chance he'd find me enchanting. And I have a vampyre who's playin' nursemaid." She wiped at her eyes again. "Ta me, that's quite amusin'."

"Who's to say you ruined any chance with me, Miss Ferguson?"

"Oh, ye may call me Sorcha, Lord Radbourne," she said with a breezy wave of her hand.

"He may do no such thing!" Alec growled.

"In that case, Sorcha," Radbourne drawled, "do call me Archer."

No, Alec had no choice. He would have to murder the Lycan right here, right now. "Absolutely not! There are some lines that should not be crossed."

Sorcha narrowed her eyes at him. "Why no'? Ye seem ta be crossin' one or more of them at this very moment, Alec."

"Who else would protect the Lycans of the world from you, Sorcha?"

An infuriating smile lit her lips. "Does he look like he needs protectin' from me?" She turned to Radbourne. "Do ye fear me at all, Archer?"

Alec bristled at the use of the man's Christian name.

"Not a bit," Radbourne replied smoothly.

"Oh, you should fear her," Alec said. He shook his head in dismay. God, *he* already feared her. "You may go, Radbourne. I'll see her back to the castle."

"Is that what you want, Sorcha?" the Lycan asked, and Alec was certain that was just to needle him.

"Well, I assume my plans for the night have been thwarted by my nursemaid," she said, flicking her wrist in a most annoyed manner at Alec.

"We will discuss your plans," Alec bit out, "as soon as we're alone."

She put her hands on those hips again, and he had an absurd wish that his hands were holding her hips instead. "Oh, ye can feel certain we will discuss it, Alec."

Blast and damn. He was trying to save her virtue. Why on earth did she have to look so annoyed with him? She'd called him her nursemaid, for God's sake. Well, he might as well play the part.

Alec scowled in Radbourne's direction until the blasted Lycan tipped his head in farewell. "Until tomorrow, sweetheart," the wolfling said and then he started off toward The Knight's Arms.

Tomorrow was several hours off, and Alec would have to make sure Sorcha had regained some sense before her eyes landed again on the Lycan or his younger brothers.

"Well, I hope ye're satisfied." Sorcha folded her arms across her chest. "It wasna easy gettin' all the way ta Folkestone alone."

Most likely not, especially for a lass who didn't have the power of enchantment the way he did. "Well, what does that tell you, Sorch? That perhaps you should have stayed at Castle Hythe like you were supposed to?"

Her dark locks bounced as she shook her head. "If somethin' is worth havin', it's worth workin' for."

She sounded just like her father. Always a man of business, even though a gentleman. Alec sighed. How could one reason with Sorcha? How could one get her to see the danger she'd put herself in? He'd probably have a better idea if he had a sister of his own. As it was, he had no clue. "Well, you'll have to *work* on it some other time. I'm taking you back."

Sorcha sighed and reached for the carriage door. "I'm pretty sure Johnny is out for the night."

Alec pushed on the door to keep her from opening it. "Sit up in the box with me, and we can continue our conversation." Perhaps inspiration would strike him before they reached Castle Hythe.

Five

SORCHA SETTLED INTO THE COACHMAN'S BOX AND waited for Alec to assume the place beside her. Why was he being so difficult? She wasn't anything to him, not really. Friends, neighbors. Nothing more. Was it simply that he didn't wish anyone else to find the happiness that had eluded him? Well, that wasn't terribly charitable of him.

Or was this just the way of vampyres? Did they enjoy ruining everyone else's plans? She hadn't known Lord Kettering when he was a vampyre. And she'd only briefly met Lord Blodswell when he was still a vampyre, though the man had seemed most agreeable even in that state. Of course, since then, both gentlemen had found their true loves, the women for whom their hearts beat once more, and been restored to the men they had once been, albeit in a time period much later than when they were born.

Alec slid into the spot beside her, and she couldn't help glancing at his profile. She could tell that he was unhappy with this new life of his. He frowned more than he used to, and the warmness that had once exuded from him had been replaced by cold, vacant emptiness. Sorcha folded her hands in her lap. They drove past The Knight's Arms and the merriment within, headed straight for the darkness past Folkestone.

She wished that Alec could find the same peace Kettering and Blodswell had discovered, that he could be transformed back to the man she'd once known. But that was never to be. His true love, Cait, loved another. Poor Alec was doomed to spend an eternity without the one woman he'd always assumed he'd love, marry, and have children with.

Thinking of him that way made it much more difficult to be annoyed with him. Could she do something, anything, to make him smile the way he once had? Something that might return the old twinkle in his eye?

"You are completely out of control." His irritated voice bit into her thoughts.

Sorcha's head snapped up to meet his gaze, but he wasn't looking at her. His eyes were trained on the road before them. She wasn't out of control. She knew exactly what she was doing. So her plan hadn't gone as... well, planned. *She* wasn't out of control, and it wasn't very nice of him to say so. "Ye have become quite opinionated since ye've become a vampyre, Alec."

"I thought I was a nursemaid," he grumbled.

"Aye, that too," she agreed. "I think I liked ye better before."

He scoffed. "Aye, me too."

Well then why was he behaving this way? He was in control of himself, after all. "I doona ken why ye have appointed yerself my protector."

"Perhaps because you need one and I'm around."

Sorcha rolled her eyes.

"I can't believe, Sorch," he continued, "that Seamus Ferguson would be happy with you chasing after men of their ilk."

Men of their ilk? Sorcha somehow managed not to snort. "Ye mean Lycans, do ye no'? They are noble beasts. No' 'men of their ilk.'"

Finally, he shifted his midnight gaze to her and she almost shivered from the intensity of it. "I'm barely keeping my temper at bay. Don't provoke me."

"Or what?" she muttered to herself. But she knew he had heard her because he clenched his jaw even tighter and a muscle twitched right beside his eye. "Doona pretend that this is about me, Alec. We both ken better."

"I beg your pardon," he growled.

Sorcha sighed and shifted away from him on the bench. "We both ken this is about Cait, no' me. But she doesna need or want protection, and neither do I."

Alec's frown deepened as he returned his eyes to the road before them. He was quiet for the longest time before he finally made a sound. "Cait's lost," he said quietly. "I know that. But you don't have to be."

But Cait wasn't lost. She was happier than she'd ever been. Though Sorcha couldn't bring herself to say those words to Alec. No matter how infuriating she found his sudden overprotectiveness, she could never purposely hurt him worse than he already had been. Doing so would be cruel, and she'd always adored him. He was kind and honorable. Intelligent and admirable. Not to mention, the most handsome man in all of Edinburgh.

She'd been just as surprised as Alec when Cait had married Eynsford. Of course, all of Edinburgh had been surprised by their sudden wedding. Sorcha, along with the rest of the city, had been convinced Cait would eventually accept Alec's proposal, and they'd be the prettiest couple in all of Scotland. Wealthy and powerful too.

Even so, if she'd been listening carefully to Cait, Sorcha wouldn't have been surprised. Cait *was* clairvoyant, and she had declared most fervently on more than one occasion that Mr. MacQuarrie wasn't in her future. But Sorcha had always suspected that Cait would eventually give in to the handsome Scot. After all, who would say no to Alec? And who could keep saying it?

"Is it so hard ta believe I might ken what's best for me?" No one else thought she did, but she thought it wise not to admit that.

"Those… *men*," he bit out, "aren't for you, Sorch." She sighed.

"Is it so hard to believe I might want what's best for you? That I might know what that is. And that it might *not* be what you want?" He flicked the ribbons harder, pushing the team of bays along the road at a faster clip. "Though why you would want one of those beasts I have no idea."

Because they were loyal, spirited, and lived life to the fullest, at least if they were anything like the other Lycans of her acquaintance. And Alec's acquaintance. "Are ye still angry Lord Benjamin dinna tell ye the truth of his circumstances?"

❧

The truth of his circumstances? That his oldest and dearest friend was a drooling beast of a man who sought the moon like it was part of him? That he was not the man he'd portrayed himself to be and had kept that fact a secret from Alec since they were twelve years old? He had every reason to be angry about that.

He hadn't realized the truth until after that terrible night when he'd been transformed into the monster he was now. Once his sense of smell had been enhanced beyond measure, Alec had known upon his first scent of his old friend that Ben was a Lycan. The betrayal was still difficult to accept after all they'd been through together. "This has nothing to do with Ben."

And it didn't. Not at all. Ben wasn't at Castle Hythe or Eynsford Park, trying to lure Sorcha down a dark path not meant for a lady of her sweet innocence. She was as delicate as the flowers she controlled with her thoughts and emotions, not a chit to be toyed with the way Radbourne and his brothers were wont to do.

"Little Rose was born, ye ken?" she said, completely knocking his thoughts off-balance.

What had she said? Little Rose Westfield had been born? Yes, he knew that. It would have been impossible to miss. Ben had sent more than one letter announcing the blessed event. More than one *unanswered* letter.

"She has the prettiest mop of red hair, just like Elspeth," Sorcha continued merrily.

He could hear the smile in her voice, and strangely enough, it made him smile too. It had been so long since he'd done so that the smile didn't quite feel right on his face. "Does the tiny little witch have her mother's green eyes too?"

"No, silly," she laughed. "Bairns have *blue* eyes. Though Benjamin swears they'll change ta look just like his."

"They haven't yet?"

"They're blue as cornflowers. And gettin' bluer every day."

Alec could just imagine the infant witch in his mind's eye. His oldest friend's daughter who must look amazingly similar to her mother. He smiled despite himself.

"Benjamin wanted ye ta be Rose's godfather. He said he sent ye letters askin' ye ta do so."

The smile vanished from Alec's face and he was glad to see Castle Hythe on the horizon.

"He has brothers who can fill that role."

"But they're his brothers. *Ye're* his friend. Ye're the one he wants ta look after Rose's future."

"I can't step foot in church, Sorcha," he growled, even though he didn't want to. It wasn't her fault that he'd been attacked by an enraged vampyre. It wasn't her fault that his only choice had been to die or become the same sort of monster who had stolen his life. It wasn't her fault that he couldn't be little Rose Westfield's godfather. "Ben should have known better than to ask."

She leaned against him and slid her hand around his arm. Her warmth and apple blossom scent enveloped him. "I am sorry, Alec."

He nodded because there was nothing left to say. She was sorry. Ben was sorry. Damn it, even Alec was sorry. But sorry couldn't fix all that had gone wrong in Alec's life. It wouldn't make Cait love him. It wouldn't make him human again. It was just a sorry excuse for a word.

Alec focused on the castle, growing larger and larger each moment as they neared it, and he tried to clear his mind. "The fellow in the carriage. He'll be all right in the morning?"

"The valerian dust will leave him with a headache, but he'll be all right."

"Will he remember you coercing him into taking you to the village?"

Sorcha shrugged. "Probably. But I think Johnny has a soft spot for me. I doona think he'll say anythin'."

A soft spot. Any man with eyes would have a soft spot for Sorcha and a very hard something else. "It's better not to take the chance. I'll have a *talk* with him in the morning to ensure his silence."

She sucked in a breath beside him. "Are ye goin' ta enchant him? Can I watch?"

If he hadn't been holding onto the reins, he'd have fallen right off the bench. He *had* planned to enchant the groom, to wipe his memory of the previous night. But how the devil did she know about that power?

"No, you can't watch!" he barked. "How do you even know of such things?"

Completely immune to his ill humor, she smiled up at him. The stars reflected in her dark eyes, and she reminded him once more of the most innocent of creatures.

"Blaire," she answered cheerily. "She told Rhi and I that we were never ta look a vampyre in the eyes. That ye can control a human by enchantin' them."

"Apparently Rhiannon didn't pay any attention to

that lesson," he grumbled. And Blaire Kettering should know better than to go around talking about vampyre powers. Others of his kind weren't particularly happy about their secrets getting out.

Sorcha giggled. "Well, Rhi *had* ta look Lord Blodswell in the eyes. How was she ta get him ta fall in love with her otherwise?"

How indeed? Alec shook his head. "No looking vampyres in the eyes, Sorch. Blaire was right. And no following Lycans around the countryside unless you want to get yourself mauled."

She laughed again. The sweet, melodic sound made him think of Scotland and of a less complicated time. "But I can look in yer eyes, Alec. I ken ye'd never hurt me."

No. He'd never hurt her and he'd make damn sure no other man, be he Lycan or human, did either.

"Can I ask ye a question, Alec?"

As though he could stop her. He sighed heavily. "What is it, lass?"

"When was the last time ye had a bit of blood? Ye look a little pale."

"It's the moonlight," he hedged. "You look pale too."

"Do I?" she mused aloud. "Hmm. But ye dinna answer my question."

Of course she'd notice that. "About when I last had sustenance? Yesterday before I left London."

"Oh. I thought maybe ye'd found a maid or someone at the tavern in Folkestone."

She would never cease to amaze him. How the devil did she know such things? She must have read his expression because she shrugged once more.

"Blaire says they're the easiest targets for a vampyre."

"Blaire should learn to keep her mouth closed."

Sorcha grinned up at him. "I'll let ye tell her that yerself. I doona need any bruises." She snuggled closer to him on the bench. "She also says ye can go days without feedin'."

True. The more one moved around, the more one needed to feed. And he needed blood soon.

"Well, if ye doona want ta enchant a barmaid, ye can always take what ye need from me."

Alec choked on a cough. Good God! He couldn't believe she'd said that. Now all he'd think about the rest of the night was sipping her blood and sharing his passion. Bloody perfect!

"Are ye all right?" She hit his back, as though that would stop his sputtering.

"Sorcha!" he hissed. "You can't go around saying things like that. Some less principled vampyre might take you up on that offer."

She blinked at him and lifted her wrist up to him as though it was an offering. "Well, I have plenty. I think it would be all right ta share. Especially if ye doona want ta go back ta Folkestone."

"Sorcha!" he growled louder.

She sighed as though he were the most troublesome man of her acquaintance. "Or ye can visit the butcher shop in the village. I noticed it yesterday when Maddie and I were shoppin'. But I'd think I must taste better than whatever ye could find there."

He was one hundred percent certain she was right. Sorcha would taste of sweetness, innocence, and light, and he would be the worst sort of cad if he took her up on her offer. Now if he could only forget the images she'd planted in his mind.

Butcher shop in the village. Damn it all to hell.

He stopped the carriage, closed his eyes, and drew in a deep breath, even though he no longer needed one. She'd already planted the seeds in his mind, so he had the taste of her on the tip of his tongue; it was easy to make his teeth descend. They were teeth that could pierce her flesh, taking the source of her life into his own body as sustenance. He turned to her and smiled, fully aware that his rakish grin of years past, the one she was used to seeing, no longer existed.

"Oh, my," she gasped as one hand fluttered to land on her chest in surprise.

"Oh, my, indeed." He nodded as he moved to pick the reins back up.

"Wait," she said as she pressed her hand to his arm.

He tried to keep the bite out of his voice, but he was fairly certain he was failing miserably when he said, "*What*, Sorcha?"

"Well, ye canna let me have a peek and then turn away. At least let me look at ye. Doin' otherwise is a bit like givin' a child a birthday gift and then takin' it back." She huffed in indignation.

"You are too curious for your own good," he grunted. "Or mine," he mumbled under his breath. But against his best judgment, he turned back toward her. The vision that met him was enough to floor him.

Sorcha sat beside him, her delicate little hand pressed against his arm. Only the Sorcha he remembered was gone. With her head tilted in curiosity, the moonlight caught her face, transforming the girl he'd once known to the woman who sat beside him. When *had* she grown up?

"I think they're quite handsome," she said with a nod of approval.

She reached out as though to touch his mouth. "Don't," he said as he captured her hand in his.

❧

He needed to let someone touch him. He needed it more than anything. Alec had once been so loving and so casually free with his emotions. Now he was this big ball of tormented vampyre with the weight of the world on his shoulders. Sorcha tried to turn her hand and extract it from his heavy grasp, but he just covered it with his other so that her hand was sandwiched between his.

"You're so warm," he said absently, his voice tortured, as though his words were wrenched from his very soul.

"And ye're so cold," she replied, but she raised her other hand to cover his and squeezed. He closed his eyes. Such a tormented man. "Ye need someone ta warm ye up."

His eyes flew open. "There is no one who can do that for me. Not anymore."

"So, ye think ye're doomed ta live this life? This life ye canna tolerate? This life is no' meant for ye, Alec. I'm certain of it."

"Don't assume my life will be returned to me like Blodswell's and Kettering's were. I'm not like them." She could almost hear the words she knew to be in his head. *My heart is not mine to recover because I gave it away.* He'd not say the words aloud. Not now.

"Ye have a ring," Sorcha said as she searched for the relic with her fingertips and lifted it toward the moon. "That is all ye need. That and ta fall in love."

He snorted.

"Do ye think yerself unlovable? Is that it? I can promise ye that is far from the truth."

In a sudden move that nearly scared her, he took her shoulders in his hands and brought her face close to his. "Do you think you know me?" he snapped. "Do you think you know all that I've become? You have no idea, Sorcha. You have no idea what I have to do to survive now."

"Then tell me," she urged softly as she reached up to touch the side of his face. He leaned into her hand, almost like a cat that wanted to be petted. He didn't even seem to realize it. But she did. So, she threaded her fingers into the hair at his temple and tried to soothe him with a gentle stroke.

He immediately realized her intention and jerked his head away, just when she got too close for comfort. For his, not hers. She could be much closer and still be comfortable. "That may work for Lycans, a scratch behind the ears, but it will not work for vampyres. We're a completely different breed," he ground out.

"Fine," she quipped. She'd had just about enough of his brooding. "I'll find a Lycan who might like my strokin' more than ye do." Then she put her hand back down in her own lap.

"Over *my dead body*," he growled.

"That should be easy ta do seein' as how yer body is as dead as yer heart. It is, is it no'?" she goaded him.

She knew she was crossing a line, but she couldn't help it. The brooding vampyre act was growing tiresome.

"My heart *is* dead," he affirmed. "The rest of me, apparently, is fully alive, as long as I act the part of the parasite I am and take the life source of others." He said the last drolly with a casual flick of his wrist.

"The rest of ye is alive?" she cried. "How *dare* ye tell me a lie like that, Alec MacQuarrie?" She turned and scrambled down from the carriage, landing solidly on her feet. He was only seconds behind her.

"Where do you think you're going?" he asked as he stalked her.

"As far from ye as I possibly can," she tossed over her shoulder. She wasn't going to sit there and let him lie to her. She'd walk all the way back to Castle Hythe on her own.

However, Sorcha had only taken a few steps before Alec overtook her. "Why are you running from me?" he asked as he spun her around.

She blew a wisp of hair from in front of her eyes. It landed back across her brow, and he very casually reached out to push it back, as though it was something he wanted to do. "I absolutely despise a liar," she bit out. "And I have had just about enough of ye ta last me a lifetime. So, go on, Alec. Go on and wallow in yer own self pity. But stay away from me. I plan ta find a nice beast of my own ta settle down with. And ye are standin' solidly in my path."

He looked at her as though she'd grown two heads. "Just *why* are you mad at me?" he croaked. "You dashed from the carriage as though the hounds of hell were barking at your heels."

"No," she clarified. "Just ye." Her toe began to tap in frustration as she crossed her arms beneath her breasts and glared at him.

"When did you become such a shrew?" he taunted.

"I'm too young ta be a shrew," she tossed back. "Ye really should apologize for callin' me names. I've done nothin' but try ta help ye tonight."

"Help me?" Alec scoffed. "I don't recall that. Though I certainly remember you infuriating me at every possible opportunity." He began to tick items off on his fingers. "One, you sneak out in the dead of night to chase after some Lycans who don't even know you're alive because you have some misguided notion that one of them is in your future." He bumped another finger. "Two, you drugged the Hythe's poor groom with something even I'm not familiar with and then convinced a Lycan to fold the groom's body up in the carriage." He ticked off a third finger. "Three, you forced me to leave my search for a good meal in order to escort you home."

"Do ye always get so surly when ye're hungry?" she shot at him.

He groaned aloud. "Probably. Do you always have a quip for everything?"

"Probably," she replied. "Are ye finished with yer list? If so, I'd like ta go back ta Castle Hythe."

He appeared to mull it over in his mind. "No, I'm not finished." He ticked off another finger. "Four, you vex me to no end."

"Now are ye done?" she asked.

"For the moment," he replied.

"Then listen ta me and listen ta me well, Alec

MacQuarrie. From this moment forth, ye will stop tryin' ta be my protector. Ye can stop tryin' ta be my friend, if that's what ye desire. Because I canna stand the broodin' and the anger any longer. Yer circumstances have changed, yes, but yer choice of how ta behave is yer own. I'll no' have any part of ye from this day forth unless ye can approach me with civility. And an occasional smile would be nice too."

"Sorcha—" he complained.

"Ye had yer turn. I'm no' finished," she snapped.

"Oh, well then, please continue," he said with a sarcastic sweep of his hand.

"Ye may no' have any hope for love or anyone to share yer life with, but I do. I want more than anythin' ta be a wife ta a husband who loves me. Ta wake up beside him every day and know that no matter what happens, he's mine. And I'll do whatever it takes ta find one. So, help me God, if ye stand in my way, ye will see the full force of my powers."

"You control plants, Sorcha," he scoffed. Then his eyes narrowed. "What else can you do?"

"My *husband* will be the one who shares those secrets with me," she said, knowing her tone was as brittle as old parchment.

"Bloody hell," Alec said under his breath as he ran a frustrated hand through his hair. "How did such a perfectly normal night become such a mess?"

"I believe that was when I told ye that ye're worth more than ye think ye are," she said.

"You don't know—" he began, his voice tight and controlled.

"I ken that I want ta be alive. And ye want ta die. Or at least make yerself miserable for the rest of yer days."

"That's not true," he interjected.

She continued as though he hadn't spoken. "I haven't even been kissed." She looked up at his face, searching for an expression of bemusement. But what she saw there surprised her.

"Never?" he asked.

"Never," she repeated.

"Then I think we should remedy that right now," he said. Before she could even gasp, one arm slid around her waist and he tipped her chin up with his crooked index finger. "You deserve one good kiss."

She could barely croak out her next words. "And ye think ye're the one to give it ta me?"

Before she could even move, his head dipped toward hers.

Six

ALEC HAD WANTED TO KISS HER SINCE HE HAD FIRST seen her face in the moonlight, her pale skin glowing with something he wasn't willing to look further into. She was absolutely radiant. She'd given him a well-deserved setdown, as only she could do. Sorcha, with her innocence and wise counsel. She wasn't willing to let her dreams of romance and love be pushed to the side, and particularly not by a jaded man like him.

He brushed with gentle fingers at the little lock of hair that kept falling across her forehead as he bent and kissed her cheek, lingering there longer than he should. But he was enjoying the thump of her heartbeat. It was beating like mad, like his grandmother's knitting needles used to clash together when he was a lad, slightly erratic and rhythmic at the same time.

"Tell me why I should waste my first kiss on ye, Alec. It's no' as though ye care for me." Her voice was quiet but strong.

"I care for you, Sorcha. Otherwise, I wouldn't be taking such great pains to keep you safe." She began to sputter out a retort, but he pressed a finger to her lips. "I don't want you to be hurt."

"Ye think ye ken somethin' about hurt?" she asked quietly, her body melting a little against his.

Alec pretended to think it over. "Maybe a little," he finally acquiesced. "I'm afraid you have these grand notions of how love should be. And that no one is going to live up to your expectations. Then you'll be disappointed and disillusioned."

Before he could say one more word, Sorcha reached up and pulled his head down to hers. Her lips very shyly and very softly touched his. He kept his eyes open and stared at her, and she stared back. She had a "What do I do now?" look in her eye.

Very gently, he sipped at her lower lip, drawing her body flush against his with the arms that were still around her waist. Her eyes closed, and her breath kicked up as he tilted his head and fit his mouth to hers. Her apple blossom scent reached his nose twofold, nearly overwhelming him. He'd hoped to teach her a lesson. That she should be careful of dangerous men. That kissing some monster in the dark wasn't what she really wanted. That it wasn't any part of the love she sought. But *he* was the one who was flabbergasted.

Her hands slid from around his neck and then down his lapels, where they slid beneath his jacket. Then they were everywhere, and Alec didn't know when his intentions changed. But he suddenly went from being her instructor to the one being taught. She learned as he kissed her, every tilt of the head that he tried on her, she tried out in return. She sucked at his lower lip as her hands roved across his waist and around to his back.

Alec's hands went on a journey of their own, emboldened by her raw sensuality. He slid around her waist and down her back to roll over her pert little bottom, which he squeezed gently, drawing her against his stiffness. She gasped and pulled back, her mouth open as she tried to catch her breath. She looked from his eyes to his lips and back again, as though deciding her next move.

His teeth ached almost as much as his manhood. The essence of her called to him. He wanted to partake of every part of her, from her drugging kisses to her sweet little derriere, and he wanted to kiss all the places in between. But then he heard the beat of hooves on the road behind them. "Sorch," he groaned.

"What?" she breathed back.

"We can't do this," he said as he pulled her arms from his waist where they still roamed, driving him crazy.

"All right," she acquiesced breathlessly as she let him set her from him. She swayed only slightly before she reached up to touch her lips with her fingertips. Then her eyes met his. And he wanted to drag her back into his arms.

Radbourne and his motley twin brothers pulled up short beside the coach and took in the scene before them. The twins instantly put their heads together and began to talk. Radbourne walked his mount toward Sorcha. If he put one finger on her, Alec would rip his head from his wolfish shoulders. "Did you have trouble with the coach?" the viscount asked.

"No." Sorcha dragged her eyes from Alec to

focus on the three wolves. "I had trouble with Mr. MacQuarrie," she sighed. "I was just about ta walk home. He's a beastly man when he's in a temper."

"Then allow me to be your knight in shining armor," Radbourne said.

Knight in shining armor? Alec somehow managed not to snort. His maker had been a benevolent knight in the service of Richard the Lionheart and had followed his King into battle. Viscount Radbourne was a poor imitation of the Earl of Blodswell or any other man of his stature.

The viscount kicked his foot out of the stirrup, where Sorcha replaced it with her own, and pulled her up in front of himself with very little distress. Alec was plenty distressed, though, by the fact that her skirts only hung to her midcalf as she straddled Radbourne's mare. Damn lucky horse. Alec shook the highly inappropriate thought away.

"Sorcha," he began. He'd yank both of them from the saddle if Radbourne didn't unhand her.

"You look like you could use a moment to collect yourself, MacQuarrie." The viscount flashed his pearly white teeth at him. Alec realized that not only did he have a raging manhood that was most obviously drawing attention, but he also had descended incisors. "You'll want to take care of that before you return to Castle Hythe. Bring the groom with you?" Radbourne tossed over his shoulder as he kicked his horse into movement.

Bloody hell, he'd made a mess of things. Alec seethed as he watched the blasted pack ride off with Sorcha. How could she kiss him, run her hands across him, drive him to the brink of madness, and then ride off so willingly with those mutts? But he already knew the answer. She was right where she wanted to be. In the company of drooling, flea-ridden wolves.

❧

Sorcha was finally right where she'd always wanted to be. For nearly a year, she'd plotted and planned, looking for opportunities to locate the Lycan she was destined to spend her life with. She sagged against Lord Radbourne's very hard, very warm chest and closed her eyes, blocking out the dark countryside they passed. Now that she *was* right where she'd wanted to be for so long—specifically, in the arms of a Lycan—all she could think was that it wasn't where she belonged at all.

Havers! She'd kissed Alec! Caitrin's Alec, not that he belonged to her friend, but still she'd always thought of him in those terms. *Mo chreach!* She'd actually pulled his head down to hers and she'd kissed him. She'd kissed him! What was worse was that she didn't feel bad about it at all. At least she didn't think she did.

On the contrary, it had been heavenly. Her first kiss, and it had been perfect.

Even through the fine lawn of his shirt, she'd felt the muscles of his chest and back with her fingertips, and she'd held on for dear life, clutching him to her, wishing she never had to let him go. But then she had. His voice had seeped into her consciousness, telling her they shouldn't. And her heart had nearly broken. What a foolish thing to have done! What madness had driven her to kiss Alec MacQuarrie? Of all the men of her acquaintance, she had kissed the one man—no, vampyre—whose heart was irrevocably lost to her or anyone else. It was utter insanity.

"You do seem prone to finding trouble, lass." Radbourne's husky voice broke her from her reverie. His breath warmed her cheek, and Sorcha's eyes flew open to find the viscount staring down at her with a most concerned expression.

She forced a smile to her lips, hoping he wouldn't see through her feigned cheerfulness. After all, *this* was the man she was supposed to be trying to charm, not a brooding vampyre who was incapable of loving her. "I doona ken what ye mean, my lord."

He refocused on the road before them, fanning his hand across her middle and securing her against him. "Oh, I think you know exactly what I mean, sweetheart. First, you beguiled a groom who is quite possibly half in love with you and willing to face the wrath of the dragon who is the Duchess of Hythe to win your favor. And then there's MacQuarrie. Between you, Cait, and Rhiannon, I can't help but wonder if all you Scottish lasses have the ability to enchant poor men with only the bat of those absurdly long eyelashes."

Sorcha's heart leapt to her throat. Alec? Could she enchant him? Had Radbourne possibly seen some sign of affection, some sign that Alec had felt a *bit* of what she'd experienced in his arms? Was that too much to hope for? "MacQuarrie?" she echoed, hoping her voice hadn't cracked on Alec's name.

A grin quirked on Radbourne's face and he glanced down, only briefly, to catch her gaze. He was a striking man with those dark amber eyes and that strong chin.

Why wasn't she swooning just from being in his company? From being held so closely to him and inhaling his woodsy scent? From feeling his warmth penetrate through her pelisse and the gown that was hiked up to her knees to sit astride his horse? Lord Radbourne was the embodiment of what she'd dreamt about since she met her first Lycan. With only the bat of her eyes, she could try to enchant him as he'd suggested, yet she didn't feel the urge to do so. Not now, at any rate.

"Don't pretend you don't know what you just did to him."

Pretend? She didn't have a clue. What *had* she done? What had Radbourne seen? "I assure ye, sir, I doona ken what ye're talkin' about. Perhaps ye've imbibed too much this evenin'. My brother has a habit of doin' that himself."

Radbourne chuckled. "I assure you, Sorcha, I never get foxed. High tolerance for spirits," he explained. "My, you are a little minx, aren't you?"

"I doona think I am." And she didn't. No one had ever said so before. Weren't minxes akin to sirens or such things? She was just... Sorcha.

"Well, I am certain of it." The viscount frowned as they passed through the gates of Castle Hythe and the pebbled path crunched beneath the horse's hooves. "I know you think you know that creature back there, but I assure you he isn't the man you once knew. It would be best if you kept your distance from MacQuarrie—and all other vampyres, for that matter. A little thing like you would merely be a between-meal snack for his kind."

A snack for Alec? A giggle escaped her throat. "He would never hurt me." At least she didn't think he would. Of course, an hour ago she wouldn't have thought he would have kissed her, either. However, she *had* started those dealings hadn't she? Yet, he had kissed her in return.

"I'm serious, sweetheart. I'd rather not have to explain the evening's events to Eynsford. You know how hearing MacQuarrie's name can set him off like nothing else. So, please promise me you'll stay away from the bloodsucker. I'd rather keep my head on my shoulders where it belongs."

Havers! Eynsford. Sorcha somehow managed not to groan. Caitrin, the seer, would already know everything. There was never a way to hide anything from her. But would she have confided all to her husband? If Cait thought getting her wolfish husband involved was in Sorcha's best interest, she would have. "It's probably too late for that."

"For keeping my head on my shoulders?" Radbourne's voice raised an octave. "I do hope not. I rather like it where it is."

She certainly couldn't explain what she'd meant by that. None of Eynsford's half brothers knew about Cait's powers of second sight or about the coven. "Of course ye do. It's a very handsome head. I'd hate for ye ta lose it as well."

The viscount dipped his very handsome head closer to hers and whispered, "Did you notice my brother's face? Weston, I mean. The scar across his cheek?"

How could she miss it? The line stretched from his ear to his mouth. It was a most notable disfigurement, though it made him appear dangerous and dashing at the same time. She nodded.

"One of MacQuarrie's kind did that to him. With only her fingernail. And *we* can heal from anything. Imagine what could happen to a sweet thing like yourself, Sorcha. Vampyres are not to be trifled with."

"But Lord Blodswell and Lord Kettering," she began as they reached the stables. "They became human once more."

"Anomalies, sweetheart. Blodswell was just as surprised by his transformation as anyone else. No one, not even a vampyre, has ever heard of such things before. It wouldn't do for you to pin your hopes on such a probability."

No, it wouldn't. But if it *was* possible, if Alec *could* be transformed back... she knew what to look for, didn't she? Both Kettering and Blodswell had suffered chest pains before becoming human again. Elspeth believed their hearts had been flexing, preparing to beat once more after each had met his true love. And Blodswell had suffered from headaches and the inability to drink from anyone other than Rhiannon. If Alec began to show such signs, Sorcha would certainly recognize them.

Radbourne swung from his saddle and offered his hand to her. "You look a million miles away."

Sorcha accepted his assistance and landed safely on her feet. "Just woolgatherin'."

One dark brow rose in mild amusement. "Somehow that statement terrifies me."

"Well, then ye frighten too easily, Archer." She grinned up at him, so handsome and wolfish, and wished she felt something for him. A fluttering in her belly. A dryness in her mouth. Something other than a simple appreciation of his sense of humor and wolfish nature.

Sticking to her original course would be so much simpler. Find a Lycan and help make him fall in love with her. This Lycan would probably make a fine husband, in fact. But all she could think about was the brooding vampyre somewhere behind them in the darkness of Kent and the soul-searing way his kiss had stolen her breath.

Radbourne tipped his hat in farewell as he remounted. "Do remember what I said."

"Of course," she agreed with a nod. "I'm certain I will find it very difficult ta think of anythin' else."

At that moment, both Hadley twins rode up behind them. "Pray say you'll save me a dance tomorrow evening, Miss Ferguson?" unscarred Grayson Hadley asked.

Weston Hadley's face dropped. "I was going to ask her, Gray."

His twin shrugged. "I usually beat you out, Wes."

How strange life was turning out to be. She had not one Lycan's attention, but three. Sorcha shook her head with a laugh. "Thank ye both for the flattery. I would be honored ta dance with each of ye tomorrow." A few hours ago she would have been floating up to the clouds with this, heady from her spectacular success. But something else now weighed her down. She turned her attention once again to the viscount. "Will ye tell Cait that I would like very much ta speak with her?"

"It'll be my honor, sweetheart."

"And tell her I willna appreciate it if she puts me off again."

She could tell Radbourne bit back a grin because his amber eyes twinkled with mirth. "I shall toss her over my shoulder and personally deliver her to you in the morning, Sorcha. Will that do?"

She couldn't help but giggle at that particular image. Blast, why didn't Lord Radbourne make her heart leap? "That will do very nicely, sir."

Seven

ALEC MANAGED TO UNFOLD THE HYTHE'S GROOM FROM the ducal carriage and left him to sleep off the remnants of whatever Sorcha had used to drug the poor lad. For a moment he watched the young man's chest rise and fall with each breath he took in his deep slumber.

Finally, filled with the most bizarre sense of jealousy, Alec stalked back toward the castle. He snorted at his own foolishness. Jealous of a poor, uneducated English groom. But the man *would* sleep peacefully, and Alec was certain that particular luxury was not in his immediate future. Not after he'd kissed Sorcha. Not when all he could think about was tasting her on his tongue. Not when he needed every bit of strength he had to keep from marching up to her room and finishing what they started that evening.

But that would be the most foolish thing he could do. She was *Sorcha*, for God's sake. He'd known her since her birth. And, despite her wholly intoxicating and innocent kisses, she wanted someone else, *something* else. And he'd gone down that road before. He knew how that particular story ended, and it wasn't in his favor.

He stalked toward the garden path and glared up at the night sky. The damned moon was nearly full. A few more nights and those drooling beasts she seemed so enamored with would transform into actual snarling wolves. After this evening's debacle, he could well imagine her finding a way to place herself directly in their path. And then… well, then she'd be forever lost. No longer the sweet, innocent he adored, the lass he cared so much for.

Alec couldn't allow that to happen. But he also couldn't allow himself to care for her anymore than he already did. Ruin lay down that road. He needed to think. He needed to feed. *Butcher shop in the village.* Sorcha's melodic voice echoed in his ears. Damn it all to hell. He'd already determined that there was no one in the tavern he could take from. So he didn't really have a choice, did he? Besides, he really should retrieve the horse he'd ridden into Folkestone and keep Bexley from wondering what had happened to him.

Alec looked over his shoulder to make certain no one was about in the garden. Certain no one would see his rapid disappearance, he bolted off in the direction of the village and that damned butcher shop.

He grumbled to himself as he picked the lock of the darkened building, searching for his evening meal. He could have been at home where he could partake of all the wenches he wanted at *Brysi*, the club for those of his kind. It was a veritable fountain, with Cyprians lining up to share the pleasure that came with coupling with a vampyre. There was no desperation in those women's eyes. There was no fear. No enchantment was needed to get one of them to accept him. In fact, he'd become something of a legend at *Brysi*, known for his stamina and the amount of pleasure he could give a wench in exchange for her life force. But here he was, stuck in Godforsaken nowhere and forced to scour a butcher shop to find sustenance.

He shivered lightly. Lamb had been one of his favorite meals when he was alive. But not anymore. Thankfully, everything he needed was right there before him. Except for a warm body to drink from. Perhaps that was better, because the very thought of a warm body made him think of Sorcha.

Sorcha... What would she think if she could see him now? Standing in a butcher shop, partaking of his evening meal. Hell, the chit had come up with the idea. And it was bloody brilliant. He wouldn't have to face the conscience of a single whore. Nor that of a single widow. He wouldn't deflower a single innocent.

But the very thought of Sorcha made his body react. He'd known as soon as he'd volunteered to give her first kiss that he was dicked in the nob. She should have shrunk shyly away from him. But no. Not Sorcha. She had to throw her whole self into it. Every delectable inch of herself.

He glanced down at the glass of life-giving fluid he sipped from a cup there in the dark. It would be so easy to blame the whole encounter on the wood sprite. But, truth be told, he'd wanted to kiss her as badly as she'd wanted to be kissed. How the devil had that happened? If someone had asked him only hours earlier how he felt about Sorcha Ferguson, he'd have said she was a very nice lass. Now all he could think was that she was a sorceress in the disguise of a young maiden, one who was bent on his destruction.

He could still taste her on his tongue, even after his second glass of animal blood. She had tasted as good as she smelled. Why hadn't he ever noticed her smell before? Three things he'd discovered about Sorcha— she smelled like apple blossoms, had freckles that he'd bet covered more than that pert little nose, and she was bent on self-destruction.

Alec muttered as he let himself out of the butcher shop and stepped into the darkened street. He startled when a voice spoke from the darkness. "What on earth were you doing in there?" Bexley asked. Of course, someone would catch him. And, with his good fortune, it would be the Duchess of Hythe's grandson, a known reprobate and defiler of women.

Alex could already imagine the conversation they might have. *Well, Bexley, you remember that chit you saw with your sister, Miss Ferguson? Well, I want to drink her blood. But I settled for the stores the butcher had set aside. Aren't you glad you asked?*

He snorted out loud instead. Not very gentlemanly of him. Not at all.

"Are you foxed?" Bexley asked when he got nothing from Alec.

God, he wished he was foxed. It would be so easy if he could wash his troubles away with a bottle of whisky. But he was doomed to live this life where he couldn't imbibe spirits, couldn't eat real food, and couldn't partake of Sorcha Ferguson. "No, I'm not foxed," he finally said.

"What were you doing in the butcher shop?"

Bexley wasn't going to let this die, was he?

"I just got a little turned around," Alec mumbled.

"You mistook the butcher shop for the tavern?" Bexley asked and then laughed so hard he bent at the middle, clutching his stomach.

"So glad you find it humorous."

Bexley had obviously enjoyed himself more than Alec had this night.

"I'm going back to Castle Hythe. Are you coming?" Alec crossed the street toward the stables, with the earl quick on his heels.

"First Radbourne and his brothers left, and now you?" Bexley complained. "I hope the lot of you learns patience sometime soon." He clucked his tongue.

Reaching the stables, Alec gestured to the young lad in the yard to retrieve his horse. "Patience?" He glanced back over his shoulder to glare at Bexley. It wasn't patience Alec lacked. In fact, he had it in abundance. He'd shown it tonight when he'd set Sorcha away from himself.

"If at first you don't succeed, you have to try again," the earl coaxed. "In fact, I have two lovely wenches waiting inside for us. Come and join me for a bit of fun first?" When Alec didn't respond, a corner of Bexley's lips lifted in a sideways grin. "Don't tell me you're afraid of the chits." He faked a look of a shock and gasped. "Don't tell me you're an innocent?" He could probably hear Alec's teeth grinding, because he suddenly sobered. "Fine," he huffed. "If you insist, I'll abandon my pursuit of the two barmaids and escort you back to Castle Hythe. Then I'll get you some

warm milk and read you a story to help you sleep."
He muttered something even Alec couldn't hear, but
it sounded like *damn them all*.

"You needn't give up your pursuit of the wenches,
Bexley," Alec said. Then he took a jab at the man.
"Some of us don't need to chase skirts the way you do.
Women simply drop at my feet, ready for a tumble.
Must be my dark eyes."

"So, that's how it is?" Bexley countered. "You've
had enough for one night?"

He'd had enough of Bexley. But not nearly enough
of Sorcha Ferguson. He'd most definitely had enough
of this conversation.

The stable boy brought Alec's horse into the yard
and handed him the reins. Alec pressed a coin into the
lad's hand. "Many thanks."

"Best get mine too," Bexley grumbled, sending the
boy back into the stables once more.

Alec sighed as he swung up into his saddle. He
would have been happy to ride back to Castle Hythe
alone, but he wouldn't have that luxury now. He
couldn't abandon Bexley, much as he'd like to.
Instead, he waited for the earl to mount his own
steed, and then the pair of them started back for Castle
Hythe in relative silence.

Apparently, the earl was annoyed about leaving the
village earlier than he'd wanted, because he barely
made a sound most of the way, uttering only an occasional grunt or grumble.

After finally reaching Hythe grounds, Alec glanced
over at Bexley. The fellow hadn't needed to leave
on his account. And if he truly had a lovely pair of

wenches waiting for him in Folkestone, that would explain his surliness. "There's a pretty little maid who works in the kitchens. I could put in a good word for you," he offered. Just because Alec was miserable in Kent didn't mean Bexley had to be.

But the earl just laughed. "I had *her* yesterday."

"Why doesn't that surprise me?" Alec returned as they both came to a stop in front of the stables.

After they had handed their horses off to a couple of grooms, they entered the castle and started toward the duke's study. Behind them, the Hythes' butler coughed gently to get their attention.

"Did you need something?" Bexley asked the man.

"A letter came for Mr. MacQuarrie," the butler said as he held out a silver salver with the note on top.

Alec took the note and gazed down at the elegant scrawl he knew by heart. *Cait.* It was from Cait. The room began to spin a bit, or perhaps it was just his world turning upside down. What could she possibly want from him?

"Good night, all," Alec grunted as he dashed up the stairs to his own quarters, determined to answer that question. He ripped into the letter, tearing apart the sealing wax with haste, so anxious to see what she had to say that he couldn't move quickly enough.

> *My dear friend Alec,*
> *I am certain you have no wish to hear from me, and that saddens me more than you know. Please be aware that I have always valued your friendship and hold you in the highest esteem. I have been worried about you these past months and was relieved when*

I learned you would be staying at Castle Hythe for a time. You belong among the living.

I know you are the last person I should ever ask a favor of, but I find I have no choice. By now, you must have seen Sorcha at the castle. The duchess has taken a special interest in our friend, and truly, such an interest can only be beneficial for Sorcha. She has a brilliant future ahead of her, but she is stubborn. It must amuse you to hear me, of all people, say such a thing about anyone else. Perhaps that will impress upon you how truly stubborn she has become.

I know I can trust you, Alec, with what I am about to impart. Sorcha's future has always been very clear to me. I have always known what path she should follow and which man was destined to be her one great love. Unfortunately, she pays little heed to my advice on this matter. She has convinced herself a Lycan is her destiny, but she is mistaken. Such an alliance would be disastrous for her.

You do not owe me anything, Alec, but I know you care for Sorcha. While you are in residence at Castle Hythe, I beg you to watch after her. You are the only one I trust to do so. I will call on Sorcha tomorrow. I will understand if you do not wish to see me.

> *Always your friend,*
> *Caitrin*

A friend. She'd only seen him as a bloody friend. Alec tossed the letter on his bedside table. Really, what had he expected? That she had seen the error of her ways in marrying Eynsford? That she would beg Alec to rescue her from the worst decision she'd ever made?

Alec snorted. He was still a damn fool. But he'd loved Caitrin so deeply for so long that he supposed old habits were difficult to break. If only he could remove her memory from his mind, it would be so much easier to get on with his life.

He leaned back against his pillows and closed his eyes. He heard Cait's voice in his mind, repeating poignant parts of her letter. Sorcha was mistaken in her estimation that a Lycan was her destiny. Thank God. He hated to think about one of those mangy beasts drooling on her soft, white skin. But Sorcha was deucedly stubborn. Cait was right about that. Look what Sorcha had done this very evening. And an alliance with a Lycan would be disastrous for the little wood sprite. He didn't even want to know what Cait meant by that.

He didn't have a choice now, did he? There was no one else around to keep Sorcha out of trouble. But how was he supposed to keep her out of trouble when he couldn't even trust himself around her?

Eight

SORCHA SNUCK INTO THE HYTHES' ORANGERY, HOPING the flowers and plants would bring a little peace to her soul. She could use a little peace. She'd slept very little the previous evening because memories of Alec's kiss had kept her awake more than half the night. Then like a fool, she'd rushed to the breakfast room and remained there all morning, hoping he would make an appearance, before she realized vampyres didn't need to eat breakfast. Well, they might have breakfast, but it wouldn't include capers or baked eggs.

Still it had been disappointing. She hoped he wasn't avoiding her after what had happened the night before. Or perhaps he'd stayed abed with a headache like the ones Lord Blodswell had suffered from before he became human.

It was a foolish thought, she well knew. Alec was still entirely devoted to Cait. He wasn't going to become human after sharing one kiss with Sorcha. Or was he? After all, she'd been completely set on a Lycan of her own until she had shared one kiss with him. That kiss could have affected him as much as it had her, couldn't it? But if so, wouldn't he have sought her out this morning?

She shook her head. The kiss probably meant nothing to him at all. In fact, she'd wager that he had kissed lots of lasses the same way. After all, he was very good at it. A most delectable shiver crawled up her spine as she remembered how his lips had taken hers and how he'd masterfully made her want to surrender more than just her mouth to him. That had to come from practice, didn't it? The very thought of Alec kissing someone else brought her even lower.

Sorcha noticed a sad little daffodil on a worktable. Poor thing. Her ill mood had probably made the flower droop. Sorcha took a few steps toward the flower, which was wilting before her eyes. A happy thought would help. She caressed the yellow petals and closed her eyes; Alec's face appeared in her mind. His black-as-night eyes were filled with desire, as they had been the previous evening.

A very male voice came from behind her. "Maddie said you have a green thumb."

Sorcha's eyes flew open, and she leapt backward right into something very hard. She gasped and spun around, surprised to find Lord Bexley's green eyes twinkling down at her. "Oh!" He'd almost caught her using magic. That would have been disastrous.

"I didn't mean to frighten you, Miss Ferguson." The earl grinned roguishly.

Sorcha stepped away from him and touched a hand to her heart. "I was only startled a bit." She affectionately stroked a leaf on the drooping little plant. She'd come back to it later.

"My apologies, my dear." He gestured to a small set of chairs by a wall of windows overlooking the garden. "Since I've already interrupted your solitude, care to join me?"

"I havena seen ye in the orangery before, my lord," she said as she took his outstretched arm.

"I confess I don't come to the orangery often. But I'd heard of the miracles you were working here. When I didn't see you above stairs, I was hoping you had paid Grandmother's plants a visit this morning."

Had he come here to search her out? "Ye wanted ta speak with me?"

Lord Bexley held out one of the wooden chairs for Sorcha. "I do enjoy your delightful company, Miss Ferguson."

"Ye're very kind."

"What a horrible thing to say." He chuckled as he took the spot across from her.

Horrible? What had she said? "Are ye sayin' ye're no' kind?" Sorcha frowned at him.

"I've never been accused of it before." Then he shook his head. "No, Miss Ferguson. I am opportunistic, if anything."

"Opportunistic?" She must sound like a mockingbird, repeating everything he said the way she was. But she didn't have a clue what he was talking about.

"I have been hoping to find you alone for quite some time."

He had? He'd barely looked in her direction until a few days ago.

He shrugged. "Amusements are few and far between here in Kent. How are you keeping yourself occupied?"

Sorcha wasn't quite sure what to say. Kent seemed perfectly fine to her. Castle Hythe was more secluded than what she was accustomed to in Edinburgh, but she'd been quite happy with her visit. "I've enjoyed Maddie's company immensely, my lord."

A mischievous glint lit his green eyes. "I am certain, my dear, that you would find me much more entertaining than my sister, were you to give me half a chance."

Half a chance at what? "I'm no' quite sure——" she began, but she was interrupted by the clearing of someone's throat from the threshold.

"Miss Ferguson." The Hythes' stoic butler caught her eye.

Sorcha leapt to her feet. "Yes, Palmer?"

Lord Bexley rose from his spot as well and smoothly dropped his arm across her shoulders. "Can this wait, Palmer? Miss Ferguson and I are in the middle of a conversation."

The butler kept his old eyes leveled on Sorcha. Was that censure for Lord Bexley she saw in the depths of them? "Lady Eynsford has just arrived, Miss Ferguson. She said you were expecting her. I've placed the marchioness in the golden salon."

Thank heavens Cait was here, if for no other reason than to end her bizarre conversation with Lord Bexley. "Thank ye."

"Allow me to escort you." The earl once again offered Sorcha his arm. "I find I am not quite ready to give you up, my dear."

The butler sighed. "And His Grace is asking for *you*, Lord Bexley."

Bexley's arm fell to his side, and his brow furrowed with disbelief. "Grandfather is asking for *me*?"

Sorcha was just as surprised as his lordship. She hadn't laid eyes on the duke during her stay at Castle Hythe. Maddie had explained that her grandfather was quite sickly and never left his chambers. She glanced at Bexley, still beside her. "Doona let me keep ye, my lord. I can find my own way ta the golden salon."

"Thank you, Miss Ferguson," he said quietly. "I hope we can continue our conversation soon."

Sorcha wasn't quite certain she wanted to continue their conversation, but she smiled politely before rushing off toward the main section of the castle. She could hardly wait to see Caitrin and she bustled, most unladylike, down the corridors to reach the golden salon. Thank heavens the duchess wasn't around to see the spectacle she was certainly making of herself.

Finally · reaching her destination, Sorcha burst through the doors. Standing beside one large, arched window, Cait was as radiant as ever in a sky-blue gown that perfectly matched her eyes. Her flaxen curls were piled high on her head, and an all-knowing smile graced her face.

"Cait!" Sorcha gushed, throwing her arms around her friend's shoulders. "Ye came."

Caitrin giggled. "Ye dinna give me much of a choice, did ye?" Still she returned Sorcha's embrace and kissed her cheek. "Archer said if I dinna make the jaunt of my own accord, he'd toss me over his shoulder and drop me at yer feet." She took a step backward, and her eyes raked Sorcha up and down. "Aye, ye have all of Eynsford Park in an uproar."

Sorcha frowned a bit. She knew the look in Cait's eyes. She'd seen it all of her life, always right before her friend began telling her that what she wanted wasn't in her future. "Doona start, Cait. That's no' why I wanted ye ta visit me."

"Doona start what?" Her friend feigned innocence better than most.

"Ye ken exactly what I mean. I'm no' in the mood for ye ta tell me once again that a Lycan is no' in my future." It didn't matter that Sorcha wasn't the least bit concerned about Lycans at the moment. She still didn't want to hear Cait's irritating, all-knowing advice on the subject. People should be allowed to make their own decisions about some matters.

"Make yer own choices, will ye?"

"Well, why no'? I should be able ta have whatever in life I want, no matter what or who ye see for me."

At that, a broad grin spread across her friend's face. "Now ye sound like Alec."

Alec. He was exactly the creature Sorcha needed advice about, but asking Cait for such in theory was much easier than asking for it in person. Sorcha knew she needed to be very careful how she went about all of this. Cait might have married Eynsford, but a part of her would always care for Alec. "I'm certain I doona sound a thing like that self-pityin' vampyre."

Cait smoothly rounded a white brocade settee and then gracefully sat on the very edge. "Oh, ye sound exactly like him. One of the last conversations, or arguments rather, that we had before I married Dash was on predetermined fate and whether or no' a man should have a say in his own future."

Because Alec had been so in love with Cait and hadn't understood why she refused to give him a fair chance. In his place, Sorcha would have felt exactly the same way. She dropped onto the settee beside her friend and tried to keep her face from dropping just as quickly. "He's still in love with ye."

Cait disagreed with a shake of her head. "He thinks he is. Once a man gets an idea in his mind, it is hard to get him to shake it. Just like ye and yer fascination with Lycans. See, the two of ye are very much alike after all—stubborn, independent-minded Scots."

That hardly sounded flattering, the way Cait said it. But she was wrong. Lycans were no longer at the forefront of Sorcha's mind. "Cait, have ye seen a future for Alec? Is it possible he could be transformed the way Lord Kettering and Lord Blodswell were?"

Cait's blue eyes narrowed, and she folded her arms across her chest. "Ye ken I canna answer a question like that, Sorch."

Well, she *could*; she just chose not to. Blasted principled witch. A simple nod or shake of her head would do. "But I'm worried about him. Please tell me somethin'."

Cait leaned back against the settee and sighed. "I'm worried about him too. I canna tell ye specifics, Sorcha. Ye ken that. However, I can tell ye that Alec's happiness is no' lost forever. It just will be different than he ever imagined. He canna be allowed ta return ta the darkness in which he's been livin'. Doin' so could jeopardize whatever future he has."

"Darkness?"

"A place so void of life and so debauched that I will never speak of it. Seein' him there tears at my heart." Cait leaned toward Sorcha and touched her hand. "But ye're so full of life, Sorch. And he's always adored ye. And ye're here with him at Castle Hythe. Do ye think ye could help remind him that life is worth livin'?"

Remind him? How was she to go about doing something like that? Well, he'd certainly felt alive when she'd kissed him, not that she would ever divulge that to Cait. She would like to kiss him again. Especially if it was for his own good. If his future depended on being reminded what it was like to live. But how could she even try to kiss him again if he was avoiding her? "Cait, do ye remember the promise ye made me?"

Cait laughed. "I am sure I have made ye many promises over the years, Sorcha. What are ye talkin' about?"

"Ye promised ta tell me all about the marriage bed."

Cait's face immediately flushed as she began to fan herself. "I promised no such thing," she whispered vehemently. "And keep yer voice down." Her eyes scanned the room, the windows, and the doorway.

Sorcha couldn't stop her giggle from erupting. "Ye're an old married woman and still embarrassed about what happens in the marriage bed?"

"I'm no' embarrassed by it, Sorch. I just doona want ta discuss it where other people could be listenin'. It's no' proper." Cait sat back with a huff.

"So ye *would* discuss it with me if we were alone?" Sorcha narrowed her eyes at Cait. "For some reason, I feel like ye're stallin'."

Cait's eyes gave her away when she refused to raise them to meet Sorcha's. The witch *was* stalling. She'd promised. She'd promised on the day of her marriage.

"Fibber," Sorcha accused.

"It's no' that I doona want ta tell ye. It's just that some things are sacred between Lycans and their mates." She finally met Sorcha's eyes. "And ye already ken about reproduction. From the flowers and the plants. The fertilization with pollen and all that…" She whispered the last.

"Ye're comparin' what goes on the marriage bed with *flower reproduction*?" Sorcha snorted. A very unlady-like sound, she well knew. But she did it anyway. That was the most absurd thing she'd ever heard.

"Yer husband will teach ye all that ye need ta learn," Cait said as she covered Sorcha's hand with her own and gave it a quick squeeze. "I promise."

"Some help ye are," Sorcha grumbled.

Cait pressed a hand to her chest. "I married Dash," she said quietly. "There's a bit more ta a Lycan relationship than a normal one."

"And I'd like ta catch one myself, so it would be nice ta be prepared," Sorcha huffed.

Cait opened her mouth to speak, probably to deny that Sorcha would marry a Lycan, but a clatter from the hallway brought both ladies to their feet.

"See, I told ye someone could be listenin'," Cait said with a self-satisfied grin.

Through the doorway, the Duchess of Hythe bustled in, tugging an unwilling gentleman behind her. "Your Grace," the man sputtered. "I have an appointment I must keep."

The duchess gave one last jerk of the man's arm, and Alec tumbled into the room, protesting all the while.

"There," the duchess said with a self-satisfied smirk as she dusted her hands together. She turned to address Cait and Sorcha. "Lady Eynsford and Miss Ferguson, I am so happy to see the two of you together."

"That makes one of us," Alec muttered as he righted his clothing. He looked as though he'd been brawling in the street.

The duchess continued as though he hadn't said a thing. "I met Mr. MacQuarrie in the corridor and impressed upon him how much I'd like to learn the details of my surprise. You do remember the one you mentioned the other day?"

Sorcha pressed the back of her hand to her lips to stop the giggle that wanted to erupt. Poor Alec. He clearly didn't have a clue what to do about the duchess' surprise.

"I told Her Grace that patience is a virtue," Alec tried.

"A virtue I apparently lack," the duchess chimed in. "So, I'll have my surprise now."

Nine

A<small>LEC HAD DONE ALL HE COULD TO AVOID THIS LITTLE</small> gathering. He'd smelled Cait's scent as soon as she'd entered the castle. He'd heard the blood rush through her veins. For months, he'd avoided running into her at all costs. Yet there she was, standing a few feet from him, close enough that he could touch her. But, for once, he didn't want to reach out and touch her. And the little piece of his heart that always ached when he saw her didn't so much as give a little twinge. Of course, his heart was dead. But up until this very moment, he'd felt *something* every time he'd come into contact with Cait. Yet now, he felt nothing aside from a lingering fondness.

Instead, his eyes were drawn to Sorcha, who stood before the Duchess of Hythe with a hand pressed to her lips to stifle a laugh. The very sight of it made him want to laugh with her. How odd was that?

"We havena quite finished yer surprise yet, Yer Grace," Sorcha said. "But I do promise." She paused long enough to draw the tip of her finger across her breast. "Cross my heart that we'll have it for ye by tonight."

The duchess narrowed her eyes at them both. "Might I have a hint at what it is?"

"Uh." Alec grunted. He had no idea what the blasted surprise was supposed to be. This had been Sorcha's idea. Not his.

"I'm sure it would ruin the surprise if they told ye," Cait said quickly. "Sorcha was just tellin' me that they have some finishin' touches ta put on it."

"I was?" Sorcha sputtered from beside Cait. But Cait nudged her with her elbow until she spoke up and said, "I was. Aye. I was just tellin' Cait about the surprise and how we had a little more ta do with it before we could present it ta ye."

The duchess put her hands on her hips. "Then why are you standing here? You, MacQuarrie, were stalking the corridors like a lion in search of your next meal." He was. Quite perceptive of her. "And, you, Sorcha, were here *socializing* with Lady Eynsford?" She looked affronted. "And all of this is while my surprise goes unfinished?"

Her gaze landed on Cait. Was that a twinkle in her old eyes as she scolded Caitrin? He was almost certain it was. The duchess pulled Cait to her side. "I suppose I'll be forced to entertain your guest, Miss Ferguson, until my surprise is complete." She looked over at Cait. There was most definitely a twinkle that time. "You two should get on with it and don't dawdle. I'll expect my surprise by tonight." And with that, she tugged Cait over the threshold.

Cait waved and grinned at them both as she was dragged through the open doorway. "I'll see ye both later at the ball."

"Not if I see you first," Alec muttered as their footsteps receded.

Sorcha punched him in the arm. "That wasna very nice. I wasna ready for Cait ta go yet. We'd just started a very interestin' discussion."

Alec folded his arms across his chest and looked down at her little pixie nose, which was still covered in freckles. God, he loved those freckles. "Do you think there's something going on there?" He gestured to the open doorway.

"Do I think there's somethin' goin' on in the corridor?"

Alec frowned at her. "Do you do that just to needle me?"

"I doona have any idea what ye're goin' on about, Alec."

He wasn't sure he did, either. "Did you notice the glances between Cait and the duchess?"

Sorcha looked at him as though he had sprouted a third eyeball.

"If I didn't know better, I'd think the two of them were plotting something."

"Plottin' somethin'?" Her warm brown eyes sparkled with mirth. "Like a way ta wrestle the English crown from the Hanoverians? Do ye think they have a Stuart waitin' in the wings ta take over the throne? Bonnie Prince Charlie died without issue. So I doona think—"

"Sorcha!" Damn, he wanted to kiss her. Or throttle her. Maybe both. "That's not what I meant at all. Do you think they're plotting something about... us?" Perhaps that was just wishful thinking on his part.

"Us?" Sorcha laughed. "That's the most ludicrous thing I've heard all day."

Was it? The images that had been plaguing him all night said differently. "More ludicrous than Cait and the Duchess of Hythe wrestling control away from Prinny?" Alec couldn't help the grin that spread across his face. The very idea of those two women plotting to overthrow the government was too ridiculous for words.

"Indeed."

Did she just say *indeed*? Alec wanted to ask why that was. Why the most ridiculous scheme he'd ever heard was less ludicrous than the two of them being together. But he already knew the answer to that. Sorcha couldn't think of them as an *us* because her mind was set on one of those drooling beasts. That, according to Cait, would be disastrous for the little wood sprite. He couldn't let it happen.

"What are we to do about this surprise?" Alec changed the subject. "Heaven help us if we don't have something for Her Grace this evening."

Sorcha winked at him. "I've got just the thing." Then she motioned for him to follow her from the salon.

Alec groaned and set off behind her. The sway of her little round bottom had his complete attention as they twisted and turned down corridors. He could barely draw his eyes from her backside long enough to look at where they were going. But within moments, he found himself in the orangery. The scents of many different flowers teased his nose. Of course, she would bring him to the orangery. It was her favorite place.

"Ye're the second gentleman ta visit me in the orangery today," she remarked absently.

That caught his attention and he dragged his eyes from her derriere. "Who was the first?"

"Lord Bexley was here earlier. He's a curious fellow, is he no'?" She reached for a large, empty pot and set it on a nearby table.

Damn it to hell. The hair on Alec's arms stood up. "What did *Bexley* want with you?"

"Ye make it sound as though no one would want ta spend time with me, Alec," she said, laughing.

At least he hadn't offended her. Yet. But Bexley was someone she shouldn't be alone with. "Oh, I have no doubt men want to spend time with you, Sorch. But you should take care with Bexley. He has a sordid reputation."

"As do ye," she reminded him with a glare. "Will ye pass me that pot over there?" she asked as she filled her container with soil.

He reached for it absently. "But I would never ruin you. Bexley, on the other hand..." He didn't even want to envision Sorcha alone with that reprobate. "What exactly did he do?"

Sorcha shrugged. "He was just bein' a bit odd, actually. I'm no' certain what ta make of it. He invited me ta sit and talk for a bit. And he put his arm around me."

"He did what?" As soon as Alec got his hands on the blackguard—

"Doona act like ye canna hear me, Alec," she scolded.

"He touched you?" Alec asked, reining in his temper.

"No' like that," she clarified. "No' like ye did,"

she said more quietly as a pretty little blush crept up her cheeks.

"About that," Alec said as he shuffled his feet. "That was a poor choice on my part." He hadn't been thinking clearly, and now he couldn't stop thinking about her. A poor choice indeed. He wasn't certain he'd ever forget the feel of her soft lips against his.

Sorcha nodded. "I thought ye might think so." Suddenly, she seemed very interested in the plant she held. Where only a moment before she'd been looking up at him as she talked, she no longer did. She focused all her attention on the plant. "I mean, a man like yerself, ye've kissed scores of lasses. I am but a drop in the big, old bucket that's yer love life."

She wasn't a drop in a bucket at all. She was all he could think about, all of a sudden. "My bucket's empty," he said. Then he waited for her reaction.

She snorted. "Somehow I doubt that." She was up to her elbows in dirt, and she'd never looked prettier. She swiped a hand across her brow to brush back a stray lock of hair, but it fell right back over her eyes. "Can ye help me?" she asked as she blew at the tuft of hair.

She'd swiped a large streak of dirt across her forehead, so Alec took out his handkerchief and reached for her chin to steady her with one hand while he tucked the lock of hair back into her coiffure and wiped at the streak with the other.

The sweet scent of apple blossoms washed over him as she blew heavily. "There," he said as he bent and kissed that shiny clean forehead quickly. "That better?" Why on earth had he done that? He never did anything like that. Not anymore.

"Much," she breathed. Her heart was suddenly beating rapidly within her breast. He could hear the wash of blood in her veins and see the pulse that beat at the base of her throat. His teeth began to ache. Alec took a step back from her, hoping to regain a bit of his control.

"So this surprise," he started. "What exactly is it?"

She pointed to the half-potted plant on the table. "I found this the other day when I was out here workin'. Sad little thing, is it no'?" She turned back to her work. "The gardener told me it's a precious orchid the duke bought for the duchess years ago. They did all they could for it and finally gave up hope that it would survive and tucked the poor thing inta the back of the orangery. There it has sat. All alone with its leaves droopin'."

"Sorcha, that thing is dead," he informed her.

"No, it's no'."

He lifted one of the dry, brittle leaves and it broke apart in his hand. "Aye, it is," he said more firmly.

"*No, it's no'*," she argued. "It's just waitin' for someone ta love it."

"Sorcha," he argued.

"Watch." She tucked the plant into its new soil and pressed the mound gently but firmly. Then she poured the smallest amount of water into it. She stroked her hand across one of the dry, brittle leaves, and the little thing perked up. It still looked dry and brittle, but it actually looked... happy?

"Did you do that?" He couldn't help but ask. He knew she could control plants, but he'd never seen it with his own eyes.

She shrugged. "All I did was love it. It brought itself back to life when it realized its own potential. That's what it's all about. The plant has ta believe."

"Plants can think?"

"Of course, they can. They're no' doomed ta live in one little pot. With care and love, they can become so much more." She stroked across the stem of the plant, and even more of it perked up. One of the leaves even reached out to tickle the back of her hand.

Alec felt a grin tugging at the corners of his own mouth as he listened to her giggle. "I can't believe you did that."

"I just provided the medium. The plant did the work." She shrugged again. Then she turned to him, a look on her face so radiant that he had to take a step back. She was innocence personified, with a streak of allure that he'd love to look further into. But with him being what he was, it wasn't meant to be.

"Now we have the surprise for the duchess," she said quietly. "She'll be very happy with it."

"And my contribution to this surprise?"

Sorcha shrugged. "It was so nice of ye ta bring me my special soil all the way from Edinburgh. I doona think the orchid would have recovered without ye."

Clever, adorable little witch. "So, what were you arguing with Cait about?" He thought it best to steer her toward safer waters before his interest in her grew to astronomical proportions.

"It's nothin'," Sorcha murmured as a blush crept up her cheeks.

Clearly it was something. He nudged her with his shoulder. "Tell me."

"It's no' somethin' I can discuss with ye, Alec," she said, her face becoming even more rosy.

Bexley. Had Bexley taken advantage of her? "Tell me what it was about, Sorcha," he said quickly. "Did Bexley try anything with you earlier?"

She turned back around and buried her hands in a new pot, ignoring him completely. "If ye must be so curious, I had questions only a *lady* can answer. Now, go away. The surprise is done. Ye can come back later and get it."

The devil he would. If something was wrong, he might be able to help. "I'm not leaving until I find out what you were arguing about," Alec said as he crossed his arms and glared at her back.

"Then ye will be waitin' for a very long time," she informed him.

Blast the stubborn little witch. He approached her until he was merely an inch from her, his front lined up with her back, so close he could look over her shoulder. Her hair tickled his nose, and he brushed it gently to the side.

"If ye think ye'll intimidate me by breathin' down my neck, Alec MacQuarrie, ye are sorely mistaken," she said quietly. But that little pulse at the base of her throat was beating like mad. "And ye'll no' enchant me inta tellin' ye a blasted thing."

Those little freckles sparkled against the skin of her shoulder. She must have them everywhere. He was an idiot when he asked her, "Do you have freckles like this all over?" before he pressed his mouth to her shoulder.

Sorcha gasped. "I thought ye were interested in findin' out what I was discussin' with Cait. Now ye're wonderin' what path my freckles travel? Have ye lost yer mind?" She spun quickly to face him.

He'd nearly forgotten about the discussion with Cait. Who knew freckles could be so distracting? "What *were* you talking about with Caitrin?" he asked.

She inhaled as though fortifying herself. "If ye must ken, I asked about personal relationships."

"Personal relationships? As in?"

"As in the kind between a man and a woman." Even her freckles blushed that time. She avoided his gaze.

"Did she answer you?" More importantly, what did she say?

"She refused, with little regard to the fact that she had promised me forever ago that she would tell me all. She said my husband would teach me what I need ta ken." She inhaled deeply. "But I'm curious." She watched his face closely. And must have seen his eyes darken with that comment, because her mouth fell open.

He took full advantage. He dipped his head quickly and took her mouth with his. She raised her hands to hold his face close as his tongue stroked against hers. She may have only just received her first kiss, but she was a damn fine student. He sipped at her lips until the ache of his teeth nearly overwhelmed him. He knew they were fully distended. He pulled back from her and looked away.

Damn. He was just as dangerous as those Lycans of which she was so enamored. "Your husband will teach you what you want to know. Cait's right. And you shouldn't go around being so curious. It could get you in trouble."

"Ye mean like the kind where ye kiss me senseless."

She did look a bit witless as she rested her face against his chest, her arms sliding around his waist as she breathed. She made him want to breathe with her.

"Exactly," he confirmed as he set her away from him. He needed to feed so he wouldn't be quite so hungry. For some reason, he doubted it would help with this type of hunger. But he had to step away from her regardless. "I'll see you a bit later," he said as he slunk away from her.

"No' if I see ye first," she teased. But there was something in her gaze. Something different. She looked… mischievous.

He walked out of the orangery and straight into a cluster of English lords as they strode down the corridor. "I say, MacQuarrie," the Earl of Chilcombe boomed. "The next time you tup a fair lady in the orangery, you should clean yourself up a bit before you leave." The man pointed to Alec's face and shirt.

Alec rubbed at his cheeks and groaned aloud as he realized that mud coated his jaw. And two very obvious, very muddy, very feminine handprints stained his waist-coat. Sorcha. She knew. And she'd let him leave looking like he'd just been rolling in the mud with her.

"I say we should journey into the orangery and meet the object of MacQuarrie's affections," Lord Loughton said.

"Do it and die," Alec warned.

Ten

NOTHING WAS AS WONDERFUL AS A WARM BATH. SORCHA closed her eyes and rested her head against the edge of the copper tub, inhaling the sweet blossom fragrance she had added to the water. It made her think of the apple orchard at her father's estate in Southwick. She smiled to herself as she remembered her last visit there.

More species of wildflowers grew there than anywhere else she'd ever been. It was heaven. Anyone who visited in spring would be in awe of the meadows filled with butterflies and skylarks. Perhaps she could get Papa to send Alec an invitation. Southwick was the furthest place from darkness she could think of. His spirit would be lighter by at least tenfold.

And wouldn't it be lovely to kiss him in that magical setting?

A knock at the door interrupted her musings. Sorcha gasped, sat up in the tub, and sloshed water over the edge. "Who is it?"

She heard the door creak open. "It's me," came Maddie's disembodied voice from behind the changing screen. Then the door closed with a click.

Sorcha breathed a sigh of relief and leaned back against the edge of the tub. "I'm in the middle of bathin', Maddie."

"And I'm in the middle of hiding. Do you mind if I stay here for a while?"

Sorcha sat up again, sloshing water over the brim. "Who are ye hidin' from?"

"Everyone." Maddie sighed. The four-poster creaked as though her friend had thrown herself onto the bed.

Hiding from the Duchess of Hythe, Sorcha could well imagine. But, "Everyone?" she echoed. This sounded much more important than finishing her bath. She reached for a towel and stepped out of the tub.

"Hmm. The strangest thing really. Do you think there's some sort ailment that affects only men?"

Sorcha slid her arms through her yellow silk wrapper and emerged from behind the changing screen. "I think anythin' is possible."

From the middle of the bed, Maddie rose up on her elbows to look at Sorcha. "Do you remember Lord Chilcombe?"

An earl of some sort, if Sorcha remembered correctly. "Tall fellow with reddish hair?"

Her friend agreed with a nod. "He sought me out in the music room and he looked me over in the most bizarre fashion and then he asked me if I enjoyed spending my time in the orangery. As I was in the music room, I thought it most peculiar."

"That is a little odd."

"You haven't seen him in the orangery, have you?"

"No." Sorcha shook her head. She'd seen Lord

Bexley in the orangery, and she'd thoroughly kissed Alec in the orangery. However, Lord Chilcombe had never darkened that particular doorway, at least not while Sorcha was there. "What did ye say?"

"I told him I thought orangeries were very nice. And then he got the most curious look in his eye. Like a hound right before it pounces on a cornered fox. Luckily, your Mr. MacQuarrie rounded the corner. He sent Chilcombe a scathing glare that made the earl scurry off."

"That sounds like Alec," Sorcha agreed with a smile, not correcting Maddie at all when she referred to Alec as hers this time. "He is forever savin' one lady or another. Chivalrous ta a fault." She sat at the edge of the bed, closer to her friend.

"I wish I'd had his assistance with Lord Loughton a little while ago."

"The baron from Shropshire?"

"The very one. The man asked if I'd remove my glove so he could see my hands. Said there was nothing so lovely as a lady's fingers."

Sorcha couldn't help the sputtery laugh that escaped her. "That's the most ridiculous thing I've ever heard."

"I thought so too. And I told him that he'd have to find some other lady's fingers. But he was most persistent. He even tugged at my gloves. Nathaniel frightened him off, but even he's been odd today."

"I thought ye told me Lord Bexley was odd every day." Sorcha grinned, hoping to bring a smile to her friend's face.

Maddie agreed with a nod. "All brothers are odd."

"Mine certainly is."

"Nathaniel was more odd than normal, though. He spent the day with Grandpapa, and it has darkened his mood." She sat forward, folding her arms across her middle. "Honestly, Sorcha, every gentleman I've come in contact with is behaving strangely today. This hardly bodes well for the ball this evening, and I was so looking forward to it."

"Are ye acquainted with Lord Radbourne and his brothers?"

Maddie's green eyes grew round with surprise. "I know the viscount is an acquaintance of Nathaniel's but I haven't met him. Grandmamma says the Hadleys are bad *ton* and I'm to keep my distance."

"Bad *ton*?" Sorcha shook her head. "I find them delightful."

Maddie's mouth dropped open as though she was scandalized by the very thought of Sorcha being acquainted with the Hadley brothers. "Do you *know* them?"

Sorcha shrugged. She knew more about them than she probably should, but she couldn't divulge any of those secrets to Maddie. "I wouldna say I ken them very well. I've enjoyed a few conversations with them. They're scandalous and charming rolled into one."

"Well, they'll be here this evening. As they're guests of Lord and Lady Eynsford, Grandmamma couldn't get away with not inviting them. But she said that she will not, under any circumstance, allow the degenerate Hadley men an introduction."

Hearing something like that would only make Sorcha more determined to meet the gentlemen if she were Maddie. "Do ye want me ta introduce ye? Secretly, of course."

Maddie shook her head as though Sorcha had lost her mind. "Why ever would I want to meet those gentlemen? Not one of them is a potential husband and I need to remain focused on my ultimate goal."

Sorcha shrugged. "Suit yerself. Ye doona ken what ye're missin'."

Maddie fell back against Sorcha's pillows. "And now my dear friend is behaving just as oddly as everyone else. I think I should go back to my chambers, climb into bed, and start the day over. See if it makes more sense the second time around."

Sorcha laughed. "I promise ta be myself at the ball. We'll have a grand time."

"Promise?" Maddie lifted her head to make eye contact.

Sorcha nodded and traced an X above her chest. "Cross my heart."

❧

With a beautiful potted orchid in his hands, Alec made his way to the Duchess of Hythe's private sitting room in the family wing of the castle. Sorcha had fashioned a pretty blue ribbon around the pot, something he would never have thought of himself. Somehow the little wood sprite made everything she touched cheerier. What an amazing talent.

Reaching his destination, Alec knocked on the sitting-room door.

"Come," the duchess called from inside.

Alec pushed the door open and stepped into the homey room. It lacked the grandiose nature that characterized most of Castle Hythe. There were no expensive trinkets lying about. No pretentious golden accents. Just a warmly lit room with a settee, two comfortable-looking chairs, and, hanging above the hearth, a painting of the duke and duchess in their earlier days.

He smiled at the duchess who had half of London terrified and offered the orchid with outstretched hands. "Your surprise as promised, Your Grace."

Her old eyes, icy and shrewd most of the time, crinkled at the edges, and a smile broke out across her face. "Oh, Mr. MacQuarrie, wherever did you find a Dendrobium?"

Was that its name? Alec shook his head. "In your orangery, madam."

Her brow furrowed as she took the pot and looked it over, gently touching the bluish-purple petals. "But... that's not possible. Hythe gave one to me many years ago. He had it brought over all the way from Borneo, but it died."

"This is the very same flower, I assure you." Alec smiled at her. "Sorcha asked me to bring some special soil from her home, and as you can see, her attentions have rejuvenated your plant."

The duchess swiped at a tear, careful not to tip over her treasured flower pot. "I cannot thank you enough, Mr. MacQuarrie. This is the most thoughtful thing anyone has done for me in a very long time."

"It was all Sorcha, Your Grace. I only helped a little."

She clutched the pot even closer to her bosom. "That gel is special. There's something about her that makes me smile."

"Me too," Alec admitted.

An expression flashed in her eyes, but it was gone just as quickly. "Well, I suppose I should have Palmer place this somewhere special, and then we should head down to my ballroom." She rose from her spot and rang for her butler.

As a rule, Alec tended to avoid balls, had done so even before he'd become a vampyre. He'd never had a desire to be on the marriage mart. He'd always known he would marry Cait, so he had never had a reason to attend such functions. He had no reason to attend them now either, not in his current state. But he didn't have a choice this evening. Someone had to keep Sorcha out of trouble.

The little minx's mischievous prank that afternoon had left him fantasizing about tossing her over his knee. What was she thinking? She already had Bexley chasing her skirts. Now Loughton and Chilcombe were more than curious to learn the identity of the lady he'd had in his arms in the orangery. And if all of that wasn't bad enough, those bloody Lycans would be here this evening too.

After the duchess gave her butler strict orders to take her flower to the duke's bedside, she linked her arm with Alec's. "Thank you again, Mr. MacQuarrie."

"Your smile is thanks enough, Your Grace."

He led her through the corridors and down a cantilevered staircase to the main level of the castle. There they immediately encountered guests arriving for the ducal ball. Alec left the duchess with a pair of old matrons and entered the ballroom on his own.

The musicians had not yet started playing, and

guests were just beginning to find their way into the ballroom. Alec glanced around the room, noting white roses and ribbons draped across the ceiling. That must be Sorcha's handiwork. Innocence and beauty all rolled into one. He smiled at the thought.

The scent of wild mutts assaulted Alec's nose and his smile instantly vanished as four Lycans stepped into the ballroom. Caitrin hung on to the Marquess of Eynsford's arm as though she couldn't bear to separate herself from her husband. His wolfish half brothers trailed in their wake. Lord Radbourne caught Alec's eye and smiled wickedly.

Alec nearly shot him a crude gesture in return, but then he realized the wicked smile was not for him. It was directed over his shoulder. Alec turned his head to look behind him, and damned if he didn't see Sorcha standing there. The same thing that must have provoked Radbourne's wicked grin immediately entranced Alec.

Sorcha was a vision of loveliness. She walked toward him slowly, her gaze drawn down to her elbow where she tugged at the top of her white glove distractedly. Her gown matched her apple blossom scent, which reached him long before she did. She smelled so good that her scent nearly made his mouth water. The whisper of her garters, as one leg slid past the other, held his rapt attention. He wanted to find out if they were the same light green as her gown, so light it reminded him of the apple orchard on his estate in East Galloway.

Alec's gaze drifted up, leaving his thoughts about her garters behind when he saw the plunging neckline of her gown. He took a step toward her, fully prepared to wrap her in his own jacket to cover all that delectable skin. But before he could take a single step, a voice crowed close to his ear.

"Does that one have dirt under *her* fingernails, I wonder?" Lord Chilcombe bumped Alec's shoulder with his own. The man stumbled a little when Alec's body didn't give with the pressure of the gesture.

Alec forced himself to look away from Sorcha, just for the moment. "What are you babbling about, Chilcombe?" he asked, not even trying to remove the bite from his voice. He bloody well hated the Englishman. He couldn't deny it. He was a blight on society. He was about as useful as a teapot with no spout.

Chilcombe nodded toward Sorcha and said, "That's the one, isn't it? The chit who had you all mussed up when you left the orangery." He motioned toward Loughton and two more of his cronies, drawing them into their circle. "I believe I've finally discovered the identity of the lovely lady MacQuarrie dirtied and then abandoned this afternoon."

"Who is it, by God?" Loughton demanded. "Please do tell. I tire of examining ladies' fingernails."

"Indeed?" Chilcombe chuckled. "I thought it one of your favorite activities."

"I shall engage in my favorite activity once you divulge the lady's name." Loughton's eyebrow rose in amusement. "And then she can put her fingernails anywhere she'd like."

Let him try to touch Sorcha, and Alec would remove the man's hands from his arms.

"And just for the record, *the chit* was the one who

dirtied *MacQuarrie*," Viscount Dewsbury chimed in. "Not the other way around."

"My mistake," Chilcombe agreed. "You are most certainly correct, Dewsbury."

"Jealousy does not become you, gentlemen," Alec said, trying to maintain his jovial air. He failed miserably, he was certain. But he did try. Then he tried to appear unconcerned when he saw Radbourne making his way slowly across the ballroom toward Sorcha. There was no way he could leave the group of Englishmen and get to her first. If he did, he'd be painting her the very picture of a fallen woman. If he didn't, Radbourne would intercept her in barely a moment. Of course, he could strangle Radbourne as soon as no one was looking. And the blasted Lycan couldn't defile Sorcha with a ballroom full of witnesses.

Alec gritted his teeth. Just as soon as he could dispense with the irritating Sassenach peers, he'd make certain Radbourne and his unruly brothers kept their tails away from Sorcha.

"Is that Lady Eynsford?" Loughton murmured. "I don't suppose *she* was in the orangery this afternoon."

Chilcombe's dark eyes twinkled with merriment. "He always has had a fondness for the marchioness, hasn't he?"

"Fond enough to fondle her in the orangery?" Dewsbury smirked to himself.

"Are you saying I'm correct?" Loughton asked, his chest puffed out with pride.

Before Chilcombe could reply, the blasted Marquess of Eynsford himself was at Alec's shoulder. "Ah, MacQuarrie. I thought I noticed you."

More like the man heard his wife's name mentioned and thought to put a stop to it, especially as Alec's name was linked to hers. Much as Alec despised the wolfish marquess, the man's arrival would put an end to the unfortunate conversation. He grunted in greeting instead of actually having to speak to Eynsford.

"It's been an age," the marquess continued as though he and Alec were the best of friends. "Much too long."

Alec met Eynsford's eye and managed a grim smile. If he had his way, it would be countless ages before he saw the Lycan again, if ever. "Indeed. It has been forever since I've seen you or your lovely wife." Perhaps that would end the speculation that Cait had been with him in the orangery. He didn't want to see her reputation besmirched anymore than he wanted Sorcha's sullied.

"Well, Eynsford Park is very close. Perhaps you'll pay us a visit while you're in Kent."

Just as soon as hell froze over. "How generous of you." Alec's eyes strayed across the crowd to where Radbourne paraded Sorcha around the perimeter of the ballroom. He clenched his jaw at the sight. Damned Lycan. "Actually, Eynsford, there is something I'd like to discuss with you. How fortuitous that our paths should cross this evening." He looked over his shoulder at Chilcombe's group of debauched peers. "Do excuse us, will you?"

He didn't wait for a reply as he turned on his heel and started for the nearest corner. Eynsford was quick on his tail, and Alec found himself begrudgingly glad of the fact. It was better to get this over with sooner rather than later.

"What were those buffoons going on about?" the marquess demanded in *sotto voce*.

Alec squared his shoulders and leveled his most scathing gaze at his one-time rival. "Keep your mutts away from Sorcha."

Eynsford furrowed his brow. "Are you threatening me, MacQuarrie?"

"A threat is usually followed with an 'or else.' I demanded, not threatened. You really should know the difference. Keep your damn hounds away from her."

"Certainly has the timbre of a threat." The blasted marquess had the audacity to look amused. "What I am most curious about is why you think you have any right to dictate whom Sorcha can and cannot associate. Do you have some sort of arrangement with the lass I've not been informed of?"

A muscle twitched in Alec's jaw. "I have *always* cared about Sorcha's well-being."

"How noble of you."

Alec would have loved to pummel the smug look from Eynsford's face, but not in this setting. Not with all of these witnesses. "I won't see her suffer Caitrin's fate."

The damned man looked even more smug, though Alec wasn't certain how that was possible. "My wife has no complaints about her lot in life. If you don't believe me, feel free to ask her. In the meantime, I'll thank you to keep her name off scurrilous men's tongues. Chilcombe was lucky I didn't rip his head from his shoulders back there."

Alec actually wouldn't have minded the sight, though he doubted the duchess would have enjoyed her ball being disrupted by decapitated earls. "I have no control over Chilcombe or anyone else."

Eynsford shrugged. "And I have no control over Lord Radbourne or his brothers."

Alec noted the man didn't say *my* brothers; to do so would be to openly admit he had been born on the wrong side of the blanket. "I know that's not true. You're the pack alpha. So keep them away from her. Sorcha deserves better than a drooling Lycan."

"Does she?" Eynsford lowered his voice. "Do you suppose she deserves a vampyre instead?"

"I never said such a thing."

"But you've thought it, MacQuarrie. I can see it on your face. So let me make myself clear—you may have known Sorcha all her life, but that means very little to me. The lass is part of Cait's circle, which makes her part of *my* circle. And I will look out for her best interests."

"Then you'd better keep an eye on those brothers of yours," Alec growled as he noticed Cait closing in on them. He glanced in her direction, nodded a greeting, and stepped away. "Good evening, Lady Eynsford."

If that damned marquess wouldn't keep his pack in line, then Alec would have to do it for him.

Eleven

SORCHA GRINNED UP AT ARCHER HADLEY, VISCOUNT Radbourne, as he tucked her hand in the crook of his arm.

"You know," he began quietly as he directed her toward a less populated area of the ballroom, "I have thought about nothing but you since last night."

"You have?" she asked, not certain what else to say.

"Hmm." He dipped his head closer to hers. "It's a novel experience spending time with a lass who knows what I am. Rare indeed."

Havers! He still looked slightly discomfited by the fact that she knew about his Lycan heritage. "I meant what I said, Archer. I will never tell anyone yer secret," she said, trying to reassure him.

Archer smiled down at her, and his dark amber eyes glittered from the warm chandelier light above. "I trust you, lass. It's just nice not to have to pretend with you."

"Ta pretend ye're somethin' ye're no'." She agreed with a nod. Sorcha could most assuredly understand that. Only the families of her fellow coven sisters knew what she was. Well, and Alec. But, no one else. It was often difficult to walk the line of being who she truly was while keeping that part of her a secret from the rest of the world. "I understand completely."

He placed his hand over hers on his arm and squeezed. "Somehow I think you do."

"I am curious about the transformation." Her eyes glittered with excitement. "I'd love ta hear more about it, if ye'd like ta tell me."

A slight blush crept up Archer's neck and he glanced away from her as though he was embarrassed. "I've never told anyone about that. My brothers, of course, know all about it and our mother has never asked."

"Yer father probably told her," Sorcha suggested. After all, if *she* married a Lycan, she'd demand to know all there was about the creatures. Everything Cait and Elspeth had refused to tell her. That alone made the information worthy of knowing. If it was something mundane, there wouldn't be a need to keep secrets or blush to the color of ripe tomatoes whenever Sorcha asked for details, would there? Of course not. Perhaps Archer Hadley would tell her everything she wanted to know. "How does the change come on? Do ye feel it all day or—"

"Dear God," the viscount suddenly grumbled beneath his breath. "This is an experience I could have done without." A most stern expression crossed his face as he looked over her shoulder.

"I beg yer pardon," Sorcha began as she spotted Alec, a severe look upon his face, barreling in their direction.

"Every time I'm speaking with a pretty Scottish lass, some vampyre or another wants to steal her from me."

"Every time?" Sorcha couldn't help but giggle. That couldn't possibly be true. What a silly thing to say.

"Rhiannon and Blodswell," Archer explained. Then he waggled his brow suggestively. "What is it about the bloodsuckers that you lasses find so irresistible?"

"Perhaps it's the lack of drool," Alec drawled as he stopped at Sorcha's side and placed his hand on her shoulder.

Sorcha frowned up at him. "Alec! There was no need for that."

"Oh, there was a need," he assured her. Then he leveled his glare on Archer Hadley. "You can take your fleas and go bother someone else."

The Lycan arched one dark, golden brow. "Am I bothering you, Sorcha?"

"Of course not," she began, but Alec squeezed her shoulder in warning. When had Alec MacQuarrie become a brute?

"I have a few things I need to discuss with my countrywoman."

She was his *countrywoman*? Was that all?

"Sorcha?" Archer asked.

Well, she did need to speak with Alec, even if he only thought of her as his countrywoman. "I'll be fine, but do find me in time for our dance."

Archer nodded his head as gallantly as Sir Galahad, she was sure. "I wouldn't miss it for the world, lass." Then he started back toward his brothers and Cait, leaving Sorcha alone with Alec. Well, as alone as two people could be in a ballroom filled with revelers.

Sorcha poked Alec in the ribs. "I have never kent ye ta be so ill-mannered, Alec MacQuarrie."

His black eyes pierced her soul. "And I have never known you to be so careless. That little prank with the dirt you left all over my face and waistcoat this afternoon has caused quite the stir in the castle, in case you weren't aware."

She couldn't help the giggle that escaped her. He had looked perfectly ridiculous as he'd fled the orangery.

"I hardly find it amusing."

"Then ye must no' have looked in the mirror. Ye were positively the most disheveled sight I have ever seen."

Alec's eyes somehow darkened even more. How could black eyes appear darker? She wasn't sure, but they did. "And you've almost ruined yourself in the process. Hopefully, you don't find that so amusing."

"Ruined myself?" she echoed. What a perfectly ridiculous thing to say.

"Oh, aye. Chilcombe and his merry band of idiots have been scouring the castle in search of the chit who was my orangery assignation."

Lord Chilcombe! Was that why the earl had asked Maddie if she enjoyed spending her time in the orangery? And was that why Lord Loughton had tried to get a look at her fingernails? Sorcha groaned. She would never forgive herself if she ended up hurting Maddie, unintentionally or otherwise. "It was only a jest."

"One that could likely have you ruined, Sorcha Ferguson, should anyone find out about the situation."

That was the last thing Sorcha wanted. Her father would kill her. Or Alec. Well, her father couldn't really kill Alec, could he? But he'd give it his best try.

Then an idea popped into Sorcha's mind as her eyes found the punch bowl on the opposite side of the room. A little bit of dried eyebright leaves, ground into powder and added to the orgeat, ought to do the trick. "What if we made them forget they ever saw ye covered in dirt and escapin' the orangery, Alec?"

❧

Alec wasn't certain why, but the wicked little glint in Sorcha's eye was the most terrifying sight he'd ever seen. "I don't know what you're plotting, but put it out of your mind this instant."

She tipped her nose in the air haughtily. "But it's a very good plan, Alec. And they'll never suspect I've wiped their memories."

He was right. That look was the most terrifying sight he'd ever seen. "Is that what you did to that poor groom last night?"

Sorcha grinned at him. "That was valerian. Very different. I'm sure Johnny is just fine today."

"Just fine," Alec echoed. "I saw the poor lad, Sorch. Other than suffering from a broken heart, he'll live."

"He was a sweet lad. I dinna mean ta hurt him." Remorse flashed in her pretty brown eyes until she blinked it away. "But I'm talkin' about a bit of powered eyebright for Chilcombe and the others. It'll just make them forget whatever I say in the spell."

"That sounds like a truly bad idea, lass." It sounded like something that would backfire and get her into even more trouble. "Just behave yourself for a few days, and the situation will resolve itself."

She shook her head stubbornly. "I canna stand by

and do nothin', Alec. Maddie said Lord Chilcombe was askin' her about the orangery this afternoon. I dinna put two and two together then, but now I ken what he was askin'. And she could end up bein' blamed for my bit of fun. That's hardly fair. I willna do that ta her."

She would get herself into trouble. That's what she would do. "I'll take care of it," he finally sighed.

Her pretty little eyebrows scrunched together. "How?"

"Has anyone ever told you you're too curious for your own good?" He tried to scowl at her. But it was hard to chastise Sorcha. She was so damn adorable.

She laid her hand delicately on her chest and fluttered her lashes at him. "Who? Me?" A slow smile spread across her lips. His teeth began to ache, among other things. Why on earth was Sorcha suddenly calling to him the way she was? She was innocent. He was not. He hadn't been terribly innocent before his death. And he was even less so now. They couldn't be more different.

Sorcha broke into his self-recrimination. "Why do ye suddenly look so serious?" She lifted a hand and very briefly touched the side of his face.

Alec turned his head quickly and kissed the center of her palm, which made her giggle. Then he looked around the room to see if anyone had noticed his misstep. He shouldn't have done that. Yet she made him want to do things that would be so bad for her. He ran a frustrated hand through his hair.

"May I escort you in to dinner tonight, Sorcha?" he blurted out.

She looked as surprised as he was.

"Or has Radbourne already requested the honor?"

The corners of her mouth turned up in a grin. "Radbourne has no' asked. No' yet, anyway."

"Is that a yes?"

Her eyes narrowed as she appraised his face. Was she looking for sincerity? She might find that. He sincerely wanted to keep Radbourne from taking her in to dinner. But he doubted that was the kind of sincerity she would be looking for. She was looking for a pure heart. And, hell, he didn't even have a heart anymore.

"Perhaps." She said just that one word. Perhaps. Perhaps he'd just toss her over his shoulder and steal away with her. He could move so fast that only the very observant would see him. And even those people could be made to forget, just like he would do with Chilcombe and his cronies.

"Perhaps? Do not tempt me, Sorcha," he growled.

"Ooo, ye sound like a Lycan with all that growlin'." Her tinkling little laugh nearly made him crack a smile.

"Do not compare me to those beasts," Alec warned.

Sorcha laid one hand on his chest and patted him softly, her eyebrows mocking seriousness as she pursed her lips and crooned out, "Oh, that's right. Ye're a big, bad vampyre. Well above those Lycan beasts. Sometimes I forget. Thank ye for remindin' me of yer superiority." There went that tinkling laughter again. Alec fought not to grin. She was incorrigible.

"Do not take my condition so lightly, Sorch," he warned. "You may have bitten off more than you can chew, messing with me."

Her voice dropped to a silky purr as she leaned

closer to him. "I doona think I'll be the one who does the bitin'," she teased.

"Bloody hell," Alec muttered. His incisors descended right there on the outskirts of the ballroom.

"What's wrong?" The teasing left her voice as she searched his face. "Do ye have a headache?"

"Vampyres don't get headaches," he grumbled, fighting to hold his lips down over his teeth. He had to get out of the ballroom, away from the others. "I will retrieve you for dinner," he clipped out. But the very thought of dinner with her made him think about sinking his teeth into the delicate skin at the base of her throat.

"Are ye ill?" She continued to search her face.

"Nay, I'm just dead." Alec rubbed at his upper lip, hoping she wouldn't notice his fangs.

"That is no' humorous." Her pert little nose lifted higher in the air.

"No, it's not humorous at all. I'll retrieve you for dinner. So, please do not accept any invitations from Eynsford's relations." He'd hate to have to dispose of a body. But he could be led to commit homicide if one of the beasts put his hands on Sorcha. "Or anyone else for that matter," he amended. Bexley, Chilcombe, and Loughton weren't much better. "Understand?"

"Ye are no' handsome when ye act like a tyrant," she muttered. "No' a bit."

"Don't do anything magical with the punch while I'm gone. I'll see you in a bit," he said with a quick bow. He needed to make a quick trip to the butcher shop in the village to quench this suddenly insatiable thirst. But he also didn't want anyone to force him to

exchange pleasantries on his way out. He chose the
lesser of two evils and slipped into the garden and over
the garden wall.

He'd be back in a trice. He'd have just enough
time to drink his fill and then find Chilcombe and his
cohorts and help them forget what they'd seen outside
the orangery that afternoon. After all, there had to be
some good things about being a vampyre, didn't there?
It couldn't be all blood sucking and eternal damnation.

Twelve

SORCHA WATCHED ALEC FLEE THE BALLROOM AS THOUGH his life depended on a quick escape. What in the world was wrong with him? For a moment she'd hoped he was experiencing some of the pain Lords Kettering and Blodswell had suffered before they transformed back into human men. She'd hoped that perhaps the talk of his time with her in the orangery this afternoon and the event itself had sparked a bit of life in the man she had known all her life, but that had all been wishful thinking on her part. Foolish, foolish wishful thinking.

Alec apparently hadn't suffered any headaches, and she'd never seen him touch his chest as though to ease any suffering. But something had to be bothering him. How infuriating not to know what that was! She could ask Cait, not that she'd get an answer. The seer lived by a code as far as her powers were concerned. Of course, Cait *did* want Sorcha to help Alec see that he should be among the living. How could she get Cait to tell her…?

Maddie's voice interrupted Sorcha's thoughts. "Where is your Mr. MacQuarrie off to?"

Sorcha pasted on a cheerful smile as she turned and greeted her friend. After all, there was no sense in admitting that she had no idea what Alec was up to and that it was killing her. "He said he'll be back before dinner."

Maddie linked her arm with Sorcha's. "Stroll about the room with me, will you?"

Strolling was better than standing in the corner looking like a dolt, so Sorcha nodded in agreement.

They had only taken a few steps together before Maddie whispered, "You really do know Lord Radbourne. I saw you walking with him."

Ah, so despite her protestations, Maddie *did* want to meet the Hadley men. "Do ye want me ta introduce ye?"

Maddie's mouth dropped open in surprise. "Of course not! Grandmamma says he's the worst sort of fortune hunter."

Sorcha couldn't help the giggle that escaped her. "The worst sort? What is the best sort of fortune hunter like? Does he whisper sweet nothings to your guineas?"

Her friend's green eyes narrowed to little slits. "I hardly find that amusing, Sorch. I just wanted to warn you. Tell me you haven't set your cap for him."

Less than a sennight earlier, Sorcha couldn't have said any such thing. But now… well, now she didn't know what she wanted. That might not be entirely true. If she was being completely truthful with herself, she would admit that what she really wanted was for Alec MacQuarrie to feel something for her. Something real. Something that would make his heart beat once more, for *her*. But she knew that wasn't really possible. And she didn't want to be like him, pining away for something, for someone for the rest of her existence.

"I havena decided," she muttered quietly.

Maddie frowned in response. "Well, you should decide and quickly. He and his disreputable brothers are coming this way."

Sorcha turned her attention to the three very masculine, very Lycan gentlemen headed toward them. Weston Hadley reached them first and bowed in greeting. His hazel eyes twinkled, though he didn't smile. Maddie stiffened at Sorcha's side.

"I hope you didn't forget our dance, Miss Ferguson," the scarred Lycan said softly.

Maddie's grip on Sorcha's arm tightened as though warning her against such a foolish action. Sorcha smoothly extricated her arm from her friend's grasp and smiled at the gentleman. "I would be honored, Mr. Hadley."

"I asked her first," grumbled Grayson Hadley, coming up behind them.

Weston shot his twin a triumphant look. "Finally beat you, Gray." He offered his hand to Sorcha, and she happily allowed him to pull her closer.

"I wasna aware ye were competin'," Sorcha teased.

"Everything is a competition with these two," Radbourne said, his voice droll.

"But not you, my lord?" Maddie asked, surprising Sorcha with her impromptu question. Perhaps she truly did want to meet the trio after all.

The viscount smiled slowly at the heiress, which made a slow flush creep up Maddie's neck. "Why compete with them when I will win, regardless?" He very gently bumped Sorcha's shoulder with his arm. "Do introduce me, Miss Ferguson, so I can ask the lady to dance."

"And risk angerin' the duchess?" Her Grace would have an apoplectic fit if she knew Maddie was being pursued by the Hadley brothers.

Lord Radbourne chuckled. "Considering our past encounters, I believe you are fearless, lass. So do us the honors, will you?"

Sorcha ignored the warmth in her cheeks from his lordship's veiled comment. Though she wasn't certain if he thought her a risk taker for consorting with vampyres or for her attempt at folding a lifeless groom into a carriage all by herself. "Since when do ye wait for an introduction, Lord Radbourne?" she asked.

"True, true," he sighed. "Why should I stand on ceremony?"

He was going about this all wrong, and the duchess might very well have Sorcha's head; but what else could she do? "All right. Lady Madeline Hayburn, Viscount Radbourne and…" She tapped Weston's arm, which still held hers, "Mr. Weston Hadley and…" She nodded in Gray's direction, "Mr. Grayson Hadley."

"Pleasure to make your acquaintance." Radbourne grinned unrepentantly and reached for Maddie's hand, bowing regally over it. "May I claim this dance, Lady Madeline?" he asked, with a playful arch of his eyebrow.

Maddie couldn't very well say no, could she? Not if she planned to dance with anyone else for the rest of the night.

"Thank heavens for social propriety," Radbourne whispered to Sorcha as he led Maddie away. "She's too nice to even refuse me."

"Until her grandmother notices," Sorcha whispered back. "The duchess will have yer head."

But then Weston directed Sorcha onto the dance floor. "Your friend seems skittish as a kitten."

"Kitten?" Sorcha giggled. "An interestin' comment for a dog ta make."

A frown settled on Weston's face. "No matter what MacQuarrie might say, Miss Ferguson, my brothers and I are not dogs."

"I-I meant no offense," she muttered as the first chords of a waltz began.

Weston Hadley bowed before her and swept her into his arms for the dance. "Think nothing of it, lass."

But it was hard not to think about her comment when he looked so miserable. "Honestly, Mr. Hadley, I ken many of yer kind and I adore each and every one of them."

Finally he smiled, and she felt immeasurably better. "Truly, my dear, think nothing of it."

This time she believed him, and she smiled in return as he led her in a turn. She noticed his eyes settled on Lord Radbourne and Maddie just a few feet away. "She isna skittish," Sorcha said quietly, "just cautious."

❦

Alec rushed as quickly as he could to the butcher's shop in an effort to quench the insatiable thirst he felt for Sorcha. He was thoroughly amazed that he could even walk, as aroused as she made him, much less run, but he arrived within moments. Unfortunately, the butcher was still hard at work. But, lucky for him, that at least meant fresh takings, rather than the hours-old blood he'd had previously. He enchanted the butcher, partook of a few cups of the life-giving substance, and rushed back to the ball.

Yet when he arrived, he found that the mere smell of Sorcha's apple blossom scent had him thirsty again. Her scent reached him from all the way across the room, where she danced within one of the Hadley twins' arms. Damn the dog for putting his hands on her.

This single-minded attraction he felt for Sorcha was driving him mad. Not since he'd become a vampyre, and certainly not before, had he been this attracted to a woman. Not even Cait had appealed to him the way Sorcha now did.

Alec shrugged his shoulders back, forcing himself to think about what he'd just admitted to himself. He had an attraction for his lifelong friend. That much was certain. But he'd never felt such a depth of emotion for anyone but Cait. He not only wanted to be inside Sorcha, he wanted to know what was inside her as well.

"Why so serious, Alec?" a soft voice asked from his left. Alec looked down into the sky-blue eyes he'd always thought would be in his future.

"Lady Eynsford," Alec said with a stiff nod. "You're faring well, I hope." If he didn't look at her, perhaps she would go away. Not bloody likely, but it was worth a shot.

"Quite well," she agreed. "But I'm curious ta ken what has ye tied up in knots."

Blast her meddling soul. "Now you can read my mood as well as the future?" he asked, keeping his eyes on Sorcha and Hadley all the while. "Somehow I doubt that."

"Oh, ye hide it well. But no' well enough, no' from me," she countered. "Admit it. Ye're taken with her."

"With whom, Lady Eynsford?" Perhaps if he said her title enough times, she'd remember that she'd thrown him over for that damned Lycan and go away.

"With whom?" she taunted. "Ye ken quite well of whom I speak, Alec MacQuarrie. Ye havena been able ta take yer eyes off her since ye walked back inta the room. Ye're lookin' at her right this moment, in fact."

"If your husband's *relations* didn't seem bound and determined to hound her, I'd be able to enjoy my own pursuits." If he didn't look at her, she might believe him. If only he could believe it himself.

"Jealousy becomes ye, Alec." She giggled. The damn woman giggled. Blast her. "Ye need no' wish I was a man so ye could dispose of me," she whispered playfully.

"Get out of my head, Cait," he growled.

"I wasna in yer head, ye fool. I was makin' an educated guess." She inhaled deeply. "A correct one, obviously."

Alec jammed his hands into his pockets. It was either do that or let her see how much her observations affected him.

"It's all right if ye're infatuated with her," Cait said softly.

He ground his teeth together so hard that he was certain people could hear the sound in the next county. "I'm *not* infatuated," he grumbled.

"No. It's much more than that. Or it will be if ye let it."

He finally turned and looked down at her, hoping

he would get her attention. "Pardon me for being blunt, but whatever it is, it's none of your concern, Lady Eynsford."

She rocked her head from side to side, as though weighing whether it was or not. "Perhaps no'," she admitted as her blue eyes seemed to penetrate his soul. "But I want ye ta ken one thing."

Only one? "Which is?" he sighed.

"Ye're worthy of her, Alec."

He wouldn't argue that point, not with Cait; but there was no way that he'd force Sorcha to accept him as he was. He wouldn't condemn her to life with a parasite like him, not when she had a bright future ahead of her. Sorcha was all things good and kind and happy and alive. "Worthy of her, but not you," he remarked dryly.

"We werena meant ta be."

Alec spotted Eynsford walking in their direction, his eyes singularly focused on Cait as though he was ready to retrieve her. And for once, Alec would be happy to see her go.

"Truer words have never been spoken, Cait," he said quietly as he left her standing there at the edge of the room.

Alec circled the perimeter of the ballroom, keeping his eyes trained on Sorcha and the Hadley mutt all the while. Damn the Lycan for grinning at her and for being charmed by her, not that he could blame the man. But if the lout didn't put more space between them and hold her at a more respectable distance, Alec just might give him a second scar, this one across the center of his forehead. Or his groin. Alec wasn't certain which.

Sorcha spotted Alec, and her warm, brown eyes twinkled. She smiled at him, and Alec felt a bit of the tension in the back of his neck dissipate. He couldn't help but smile back. Just being in her presence made him feel better. Happiness was something he hadn't felt in a long time. And he wasn't certain he felt it now. But she made him feel good. That was close enough to discomfort him.

Thankfully, the excruciatingly long set finally came to an end, and Alec pushed through the crowd to intercept Sorcha before anyone else could claim her. "My dear Miss Ferguson." He bowed before her. "You do keep the most questionable company."

"I was just thinking the same," Weston Hadley growled.

"*Havers!*" Sorcha release her hold on Hadley's arm and brushed past Alec. "I'm no' sure if the lot of ye are children or grown men." She pushed her way toward the terrace doors and only stopped when that blasted Bexley stepped in her path.

"You do look so ravishing this evening, Miss Ferguson," the Englishman purred.

The earl was two seconds away from having Alec unceremoniously remove his head in front of an audience. "Evening, Bexley. Do excuse us." Alec captured Sorcha's arm and began to direct her toward her previous destination of the terrace.

"Not headed to the orangery, by chance, are you?" The man's voice floated over the din, smacking Alec squarely in his chest. Bexley knew. Somehow the little rodent knew about Alec's encounter with Sorcha that afternoon.

Alec released Sorcha's arm and turned back to face Bexley. If the man had any idea of the precarious situation in which he found himself, he didn't show it. A smug little smile tugged at his lips, and a quick glance in Sorcha's direction made Alec's vision turn a bit red at the edges. "I advise you to keep your own counsel, Bexley, or you will have to answer to me."

The earl tilted his head to one side as though considering the threat. Then he nodded and his grin deepened. "Until next time, my dear."

There wouldn't be a next time, not if Alec could help it. He returned his attention to Sorcha, placing his hand on the small of her back and directing her through the open terrace doors. If he wasn't already dead, she'd be the death of him. She wasn't a child any longer. She couldn't play as she once had. No more frolicking in orangeries. No more carelessly dancing through life. No more attracting the attention of every scoundrel within a five-mile radius.

"Why must ye do that?" She turned on him, her brow furrowed with irritation.

Was she actually annoyed with *him*? "You mean threaten blackguards like Bexley? Because *you* seem blissfully unaware of the havoc you create, Sorcha. This isn't Edinburgh. You're heavily ensconced in the cream of English society, and you can't continue in this manner."

Her perfect little nose scrunched up as though she smelled something distasteful. "That is no' what I was referrin' ta at all. And I do no' create havoc."

"Oh, aye, you do." Of which his jumbled emotions were testimony.

"Doona change the subject." She jabbed one pointy finger into his chest. "There's no reason for ye ta treat the Hadley men with such disdain. They havena done a thing ta ye. I'm no' sure I even recognize ye anymore, Alec."

That's what this is about? Those damned Lycans? Her precious wolf-men? The fellows she was bound and determined to catch no matter what? A bit of despair settled in the pit of his stomach, and Alec took a step away from her. "Perhaps you may have noticed, Sorch. I'm *not* the same as I once was."

"Nay, ye're no'. But ye were raised ta be a gentleman, Alec. That hasna changed. And for the life of me, I canna understand the incessant snipin' back and forth between vampyres and Lycans. Ye have so much in common. Ye should get along famously."

They had so much in common? Aside from their common lust over certain witches, Alec really couldn't concede her point and he snorted in response.

Sorcha folded her arms across her middle, raising the tempting mounds of her breasts higher. His eyes drifted downward until she began speaking. "Ye canna help what ye are, and neither can they. Ye live among humans but hide the truth of yerself, just like they do."

"The same could be said of witches, Sorcha. Yet you and I are like night and day." And it was true. Where he preferred quiet darkness and solitude, she was all that was sunny and cheerful. "I am death and you are life, lass."

Her face seemed to fall a bit, yet she took a step toward him. "It doesna have ta be that way, Alec."

She placed her hand on his chest, and the warmth from her fingers stirred something inside him. He almost felt alive again.

"I wish—" He shook his head. Wishes were better left unsaid. Particularly ones that couldn't come true.

Sorcha inhaled deeply but didn't remove her hand from the center of his chest. Those creamy swells of skin at her bodice rose and fell with her exhale, once again capturing his interest.

"Alec MacQuarrie, are ye starin' at my bosom?" She pulled her hand from his person and stepped back.

Of course he was starting at her breasts. They were probably absolutely beautiful, if one took the time to disrobe her properly. He coughed into his hand. "I was doing no such thing." A grin tugged at the corners of his mouth. Luckily, his teeth weren't descending. Not quite yet.

The skin at her throat suddenly pinkened, her freckles becoming even more pronounced. What he wouldn't give to taste them, each and every one.

"Ye *are* starin' at my bosom," she complained. But there was something in her gaze. Something he couldn't quite decipher.

Alec leaned closer to her and said softly, "If you don't want men to stare at them, perhaps you should cover them up."

She gasped. "Oh, aye, it's my fault. Should I have ta have cover up ta my ears too, just because men like ye canna control yer basic instincts?"

Oh, she had no idea how much he was in control. No idea at all.

Thirteen

SORCHA FELT QUITE CERTAIN SHE WOULD EXPLODE INTO flames at any minute. He was still glaring at her chest. He'd even licked his lips as he'd done so. She'd called his name, and it had barely grabbed his attention.

"I don't know why you women dress to show off your assets and then get upset when we look at them," Alec muttered beneath his breath but loudly enough that she could make out the words. That meant he wanted her to hear them.

"*We women* dress ta flatter ourselves. No' ta invite yer gaze." She tugged at her bodice. "And it's no' too low. I'm quite properly covered."

"I beg to differ." His curt reply was tempered by his roguish grin.

She narrowed her gaze at him in warning.

"We should go back inside before Eynsford or one of his pack starts a search for you," Alec said as he offered her his arm.

"Since ye have already ogled my bosoms, I'd like ta ask for a boon," she said quickly. It came out all in one breath. Then she wanted to hide her face in her hands.

But she did want him to kiss her again. She doubted she'd ever get tired of his kisses, not if she lived to be a million years old.

"Recompense for my lack of manners?" Alec looked affronted. But then he shrugged. "If you plan to ask me to help you win one of those mutts, the answer is no."

What a wonderful idea. Why hadn't she thought of it herself? He seemed to lose all rational behavior when Lycans were involved. She could certainly use that to her advantage, couldn't she? "I'd do no such thing," she lightly protested.

"Uh-huh," he challenged, nodding his head in agreement. "Of course you wouldn't." He inhaled deeply and then let the breath out. It was an action reminiscent of his old life, a habit that was hard to break. "What's this boon you'd like to collect in exchange for my ogling?"

What was the best way to go about this? Someone more adept at flirting would know just what to say. "Do ye find me pretty, Alec?"

"Good God, Sorcha," he moaned. "Fishing for compliments now, are you?"

"Never mind," she clipped out and moved to brush past him. She'd made a blasted fool out of herself with that misstep. But she'd never needed to flirt or use a man's jealous nature to her advantage before. Perhaps she could talk Cait into giving her lessons.

Alec grabbed her arm as she tried to escape back into the ballroom. "Sorch," he said, attempting to placate her. "Don't go." No, stay here and continue to make a fool of yourself, the amusement in his eyes seemed to say.

"Name one good reason why I *should* stay," she countered.

"Very well, I'll answer you," he ground out. Then he groaned, as though doing so was painful.

She straightened her shoulders and prepared for the worst. She had started this exchange, after all. She would have to take whatever he said in the spirit in which it was intended. And if it was truly awful, she'd run back to her room and cry her eyes out for the rest of the night.

"You'd like for me to be completely honest, correct?"

Havers! Must he drag this out? "No, I want ye ta lie ta me, Alec." She rolled her eyes dramatically.

He chuckled. It was a warm sound. Very much like the old Alec, before he'd been reborn. Before his low laughter could come to a stop, he moved quickly, his arm snaking around her waist and drawing her close to him. Sorcha pressed her palms against his chest in an effort to steady herself. He was so hard beneath her fingertips. This was exactly where she'd wanted to be all night. Perhaps she hadn't made such a terrible blunder after all. She should ask him on a regular basis if he thought she was pretty.

"Stop doing that," he warned quickly.

"Doin' what?" She tilted her head back to look into his face.

"Touching me," he clipped out.

"I believe it was *ye* who grabbed me. No' the other way around."

"True," he conceded with a good-natured shrug. "But that doesn't give you license to explore my person."

"I need a license ta touch ye? Somehow I doubt

that." Her fingertips flexed against him again. Then she moved to disentangle herself from his arms. He didn't budge. Didn't let her go.

"Don't do that," he said, his voice soft and hard at the same time.

"Now what am I doin' wrong?" she sighed.

"You're wiggling. Stop it. I want to talk to you." With his free hand, he tipped her chin up, forcing her to meet his dark gaze. "You are not pretty at all," he said slowly.

At once her heart ached and the sting of tears formed behind her lashes. She'd thought she could take whatever he had to say, but...

"You're bloody beautiful," he added before she could respond.

"I beg yer pardon?" He didn't make any sense at all. Hadn't he just said she wasn't pretty? He'd pulled her into his arms yet complained when she'd touched him. What a confusing man.

"You're so beautiful that you're nearly painful to the eyes, Sorch," he continued. "When you walk into a room, it lights up."

"Really?" She blinked back her unshed tears.

"Long ago, I thought the room lit up when you walked into it because of who you are." He let his fingertip drag across the expanse of her chest. "In here."

"In my breasts?" she queried. Then immediately wanted to bite the words back. What a ridiculous thing to say.

"There too," he chuckled. "But really, it was what was in your heart for me back then. That was what made you beautiful. Your open and giving heart."

"And now, my heart's not beautiful anymore?"

"I'm certain it is, but I'm so busy looking at the rest of you that I miss the heart completely."

His hold had gentled while they stood there, but Sorcha made no move to extricate herself from his grasp.

"And 'pretty' doesn't begin to describe you," he continued.

She couldn't help but smile. "So, I can safely assume that men find me ta be attractive?"

He snuffled, a harsh sound from his nose. "That's safe to say. I'm not the only one who has been trying to look down your dress."

"Ye were tryin' ta look down my dress?" She shook her head. "I thought ye were just glancin' at them."

"I was trying to look down your dress. Never doubt it. I might do it again later."

"Promises, promises," she murmured.

He laughed again. "Don't tempt me, minx," he warned.

Things were going better than she'd hoped, but he hadn't tried to kiss her yet. What to do about that? "So, ye think I'm pretty." She held up her hand when he went to contradict her. "Pretty enough," she corrected.

"Pretty enough for what?" he countered.

To care whether or not she set her cap for someone else? To drive him a bit mad at the idea? "Ta catch a Lycan. Is that no' what we were discussin'?"

"There's not a chance in hell that I'm going to let you hunt or catch a Lycan," he informed her. "Over my dead body."

She opened her mouth to once again comment about his dead body, but he was already speaking again.

"And I'd have to be dead again before I'd allow it. We don't die easily, just so you know."

"But Elspeth and Cait both have Lycans of their very own. And I've always wanted one."

A muscle twitched in his jaw, and she wanted more than anything to smooth it with her fingers. "Those men are not puppies you can bring home, let sleep in your bed, and train. They're much more than that."

"Are they?" she asked, her eyes moving from his jaw to his lips.

"Indeed. And I will *not* see you get hurt by one of them. I'd have to kill him. Then Eynsford would try to kill me. It'd be a bloody mess. Cait would be angry at me forever."

Of course, all of this had to do with Cait. As far as Alec was concerned, everything always went back to Cait. She'd been foolish to have thought otherwise. All she'd wanted was a kiss and she'd ended up with a broken heart instead. "Will ye ever be over her?"

She didn't expect an answer and berated herself for even asking. Alec didn't say a word. He just looked down at her, his black eyes fathomless.

"She loves her husband."

"I'm aware of that." His tone was brusque. But he didn't set her away from him.

"But ye're still pinin' for her."

"Right now, the only person on my mind is you," he admitted, though he avoided her gaze when he said it.

"Because I'm a nuisance. I understand. Ye probably hate havin' me underfoot."

His hand slid down over her hip. The other one

joined his exploration, smoothing her dress over her other side.

"I've had you in my arms for a few minutes. And you haven't even tried to get away."

"Why would I do that?"

"Because I'm dangerous."

She giggled at the very idea.

"Because you are much too good for the likes of me." For some reason, that comment felt like it had been wrenched from his soul, and Sorcha's smile disappeared. He couldn't really believe that, could he?

"Ye are good, Alec." She patted his chest lightly. "In here."

"The only place I'm good is…" He suddenly stopped. "Never mind."

"What were ye goin' ta say?"

"Nothing."

How could he say "nothing"? Not knowing would torture her. She shoved against his chest. "Ye shouldna start comments ye're no' goin' ta finish. It's ill-mannered."

"So is sinking my teeth into the skin of others to drink from their life force. Yet I do it to survive."

"The only place ye're good is…?" she prompted.

He leaned down close to her ear. "The only place I'm good, Sorcha, is…" He let his voice trail off as his breath tickled the shell of her ear. "In the bedchamber," he finally concluded.

The hair on Sorcha's arms stood up, and her belly dropped to her toes.

"I've shocked you." He laughed, his dark eyes twinkling with mirth. "It's about time." He let her hips go and stepped back from her.

Madness made Sorcha follow him and press her length along his. She reached her hand around his neck and tugged his head down so she could speak quietly in his ear. "Prove it," she whispered.

When her breath blew across the shell of his ear, Alec's teeth descended and she felt a hard bulge against her belly. Then she turned and quit the terrace as quickly as she could. She hadn't gotten her kiss, but she most definitely had gotten his attention.

∽

Alec's fingers shook, almost desperate to pull her back to him, but he managed to remain rooted to the spot and let her escape back into the ballroom. *Prove it!* Damn it to hell, he'd hear those softly muttered words in his sleep. He'd hear them every waking moment for the remainder of his unnatural life. He was more dangerous to her than those bloody Lycans.

"Whispering sweet nothings?" Bexley's voice from the shadows brought Alec back to the present.

He spun in his spot to find a self-satisfied grin on the earl's face. Faster than a blink, Alec pushed Bexley farther into the shadows. A look of horror flashed in the man's eyes.

"I-I," the Englishman stuttered.

Alec focused on the man's pupils. "You saw nothing."

Bexley stopped struggling, and his breathing returned to normal. "Nothing," he repeated quietly, in a voice that didn't even sound like his.

"You have no recollection of Miss Ferguson meeting me in the orangery this afternoon."

"No recollection."

"In fact, you hold Miss Ferguson in the highest regard and find her character to be exemplary."

"Exemplary."

"You will keep your distance from Miss Ferguson in the future."

"Yes, keep my distance."

Alec released his hold on Bexley's jacket and took several steps away from the man, moving back into the light from the ballroom. He leaned against the balustrade and stared out into the darkened Kent countryside.

"MacQuarrie?" Bexley sounded confused.

"Aye?" Alec glanced over his shoulder at the earl.

"Do you know why I'm outside?"

Alec frowned and shook his head. "No idea."

"Hmm," Bexley looked toward the ballroom. "Must've needed fresh air. A bit stuffy in there tonight."

"Indeed," Alec agreed.

"Suppose I needed a distraction."

Alec raised his brow in question.

Bexley shrugged as though the weight of the world rested on his shoulders. "Had a long conversation with my grandfather this morning. Dreadful business being an heir."

Alec didn't doubt the truth of that. Of the men he knew, the most troubled were those with titles. "Sorry to hear it."

"Me too." The earl leaned his elbows against the balustrade as well and sighed. "Hard to think of anything else. You haven't got a remedy for distraction, have you?"

Was that what he'd been doing? Focusing on Sorcha to distract himself from whatever he'd discussed with his grandfather? Well, he'd just have to find something else to occupy his mind. Alec shook his head. "You seemed to enjoy yourself in the village last night," he suggested.

A small smile appeared on Bexley's face. "Brilliant idea. Perhaps I'll make another trip this evening. You up for another jaunt into Folkestone?"

It wouldn't matter where Alec spent his evening; he'd never get Sorcha's tempting words out of his mind. "Perhaps," he replied noncommittally.

Inside the ballroom, the musicians stopped playing and the room fell silent.

"Grandmother must have called everyone for dinner." Bexley sighed.

And Alec was supposed to escort a very enchanting witch. How would he ever manage to sit beside Sorcha and behave himself?

Fourteen

QUITE PLEASED WITH HERSELF, SORCHA ENTERED THE ballroom and spotted Maddie near the main entrance, talking with her grandmother. Sorcha quickly made her way around the perimeter and linked her arm with Maddie's and grinned at the duchess. "Wonderful evenin'."

And it was. She might as well be floating in the clouds, and Alec hadn't even kissed her. But he would, and very soon, if she had correctly read his expression when she'd abandoned him to the lonely night air.

Her smile vanished when the duchess frowned at her.

"Miss Ferguson," Her Grace grumbled a curt greeting.

Sorcha gulped. The Duchess of Hythe hadn't called her "Miss Ferguson" since their first meeting at Rhiannon's wedding the previous spring. "Is somethin' amiss?"

"It's nothing," Maddie began, but the duchess halted Maddie from saying more by holding her bejeweled hand in the air.

"I don't quite understand Lady Blodswell's, Lady Eynsford's, or your devotion, for that matter, to Lord Radbourne and his brothers, but I do wish you wouldn't subject my granddaughter to men of their ilk."

Havers! Sorcha bit the inside of her cheek. She shouldn't have introduced Maddie to the trio after all, but they truly were wonderful men. "I—um," she started, though she wasn't certain what she would say.

"Lord Radbourne was quite the gentleman," Maddie added. "Honestly, Grandmamma, nothing untoward occurred."

"Yet." The duchess' scowl darkened. "But we'll discuss this later. This is hardly the place, and it is time for dinner." She waved her hand in the air to gesture the musicians to finish their set, and then she set about to inform the rest of her guests that it was time to make their way to the dining hall.

"Don't think on it, Sorcha." Maddie squeezed her hand, kind as always. "Grandmamma'll be fine in a while. And she adores you. She was gushing over the flower you restored for her just this evening."

Sorcha was hardly worried for herself, but she didn't want to make Maddie's life more difficult, and she shook her head. "I hope I dinna get ye inta trouble."

Maddie smiled. "So, I've had my first encounter with a rogue. I've lived to tell the tale, and I'm sure more degenerate fellows will await me in London next season."

That was probably true. The little imp inside Sorcha pressed her to ask, "And did ye like him?"

Maddie turned up her nose just a bit. "Grandmamma is right. Lord Radbourne is not the sort for me, but I'm certain he's fine for someone else."

Well, if Maddie hadn't decided to set her cap for the man, the duchess couldn't stay put out with Sorcha for too long, could she?

People began trickling into the corridor, and Alec and Lord Bexley entered into the ballroom from the terrace. Immediately, Sorcha sought Alec's eyes and tried not to blush as the memory of their last conversation replayed in her mind. Had she actually asked him to prove his virility in the bedchamber?

Within a moment, the Earl of Bexley stood before them with Alec close behind him.

"Maddie," Bexley offered her his arm, "Grandmother wanted me to escort you into dinner to make certain you don't fall prey to any lurking scoundrels."

Meaning the duchess wouldn't take the chance that one of the unruly Hadley men would focus their attention on Maddie. Sorcha shook the thought from her mind. None of it was her concern. The only person she wanted to think about was standing at her side. "Mr. MacQuarrie, how flatterin' ye havena forgotten me."

The look he shot her made it clear that he could never forget her nor the conversation they had shared on the terrace; his eyes nearly smoldered. Alec's heated expression caused Sorcha's belly to flip, and she quickly took his outstretched arm.

Maddie and Lord Bexley strode from the ballroom, and though Sorcha would have been happy to follow them, Alec apparently had other plans and remained rooted to the ground. Sorcha glanced up at him, wondering why they weren't following Maddie and her brother.

"You are a minx, Sorcha Ferguson." His voice rumbled over her like a caress and she shivered.

"I doona ken what ye mean, Alec MacQuarrie," she shot back at him.

He snorted. It was a most ungentlemanly sound, and she couldn't help but giggle.

"You know exactly what I mean. You shouldn't provoke me like that." His dark gaze bored into hers. "It's almost as though you've thrown down the gauntlet. And now I feel obligated to prove my prowess to you."

He did? Good heavens. How wonderful. "What's stoppin' ye?" she managed to croak out.

He began to tick items off on his fingers. "One, I've known you your whole life."

She interrupted him. "I'm no' a child any longer, Alec."

"I'm well aware of that," he grunted, his gaze again straying to the bodice of her gown. A flush crept up her face. But he continued anyway. "Two, you're an innocent."

She nodded. "I am. Ye say that as though it's a detriment."

"It is." He lifted another finger. "Three, I'm a gentleman."

"At times," she acquiesced.

"Beg your pardon?" he asked, his eyebrows scrunching together.

She waved her hand in the air breezily. "Ye're a

gentleman when ye need ta be. But when ye go off in search of a meal, there's no doubt in my mind that ye can be persuaded ta forget yer gentlemanly demeanor."

She knew immediately that she'd said the wrong thing when a muscle began to tick in his jaw.

"I chose my circumstances, Sorcha, but I wasn't fully aware at the time of what they'd be. Now it cannot be undone." That was the most she'd ever heard him say on the matter, and it didn't look as though he planned to say anymore.

"Did ye have more considerations? A four, five, and six, perhaps?"

"Four, I want you."

Sorcha's breath caught. "Ye do?"

"My teeth ache every time you're around," he admitted, but he didn't sound happy about the fact. Poor tortured Alec, she'd gladly let him take from her. All he had to do was ask.

"Ye want ta drink from me?" The very thought made her heart race.

A curt nod was his response.

"Five, my existence is a solitary one. For many reasons, some of which I cannot explain to you."

"Ye mean ta say, 'Five, I'm still in love with Cait,'" Sorcha supplied.

"No," Alec said with a brisk shake of his head. "She's not even on my mind."

Her heart nearly thudded to a stop. If he was over his infatuation with Cait, could they have something together? Something real? He did want her, after all. He'd said so. "What is on yer mind?"

"You consume my every waking moment." Then

he straightened his shoulders and began to lead her toward the dining hall.

She tugged at his arm. But it was like trying to stop a runaway horse. "Alec," she implored.

"What is it?" he asked, though he didn't even look down at her.

"I dinna mean ta say ye were less than a gentleman back there. That came out completely wrong."

He simply nodded, but his jaw tightened again.

When they reached the table, Alec pulled her chair back rather than wait for a footman, and she delicately sat down. He settled next to her.

"Can ye eat real food, Alec?" she whispered to him.

"No, I can't," he whispered back.

"Then what do ye plan ta do durin' dinner?"

"You'll see."

That was it? "You'll see." Apparently, their conversation had come to an end, not that she could stop thinking about it. Alec wanted her. She'd already suspected that. But he was too much of a gentleman to act on it. She shouldn't have questioned his station as a gentleman. Not at all. He still was all that and more.

Now he was obviously irked with her. And she had no idea how to bring back the playful Alec. She should have left well enough alone.

⁓

Had Alec not been required to escort Sorcha into the dining hall, he'd have made an escape. The urge to do so was still at the forefront of his mind. The little witch somehow managed to get too close for comfort, both with her questions and with her body. Damn, he wanted her. There was no need to deny it. Yet his doing so had made her question his very status as a gentleman. Bloody hell.

Gentlemen tumbled innocents every day. And they didn't have their positions in society revoked. Oh, they'd be referred to as rakes and whispered about by old matrons, but they were *still* gentlemen. But, by virtue of Alec's vampyre nature, his own status appeared to be in question. If he was less of a gentleman, he'd have already had her in his bed.

This gentleman facade would be his undoing.

"Ye need no' be so cross with me," the little witch said beneath her breath.

"I'm not cross with you," he clarified. He was in *lust* for her. But certainly not cross. He picked up his wine goblet and lifted it to his lips. But it was all for show. He didn't swallow or take a sip.

"Ye're very good at that," she remarked.

"Very good at pretending to be a gentleman? I do try," he replied dryly.

She frowned at his words. "Very good at feignin' yer ability ta eat and drink," she said, instead. Then she sighed heavily. "When was the last time ye fed?"

"Tonight," he clipped out.

She choked. "Tonight? Was that where ye ran off ta?"

"I didn't run off," he explained. "I was hungry, and I needed to feed."

"Who was she?" Sorcha's biting tone took Alec off guard, and he finally looked down at her.

"She?" he asked.

"The one ye took from. I assume ye choose a lady. Blaire said ye always choose ladies. So who was she?"

Blaire again? Who knew the warrior witch had the loosest lips? "The source of my meal would be none of your concern, Sorcha." She wouldn't let this one alone, he was certain.

And he was right. She leaned closer to him, so close that her shoulder brushed his. "I wish ye would just take from me," she whispered.

Alec tipped his head back and closed his eyes. The very idea of taking her had consumed all of his thoughts since he'd arrived at Castle Hythe. Taking from Sorcha as he gave her pleasure would be the quintessential moment. He knew it would be for him. And he'd make it so for her.

"Don't make offers you can't fulfill," he warned.

"I'm a Ferguson, and I would never make an offer I couldna make good on." She looked mildly affronted.

Good God! As proud a Scot as her father. Alec scrubbed a hand across his brow. "That wasn't what I meant, lass. Just let it be, will you?"

But she continued as though he hadn't spoken. "I'm tryin' ta help ye, Alec. It's just a bit of blood. Besides, Kettering did it with Blaire. And Blodswell did it with Rhiannon. It canna be all bad." She shrugged her delicate little shoulders.

Oh, but it *was* bad. A bad idea for Sorcha. Taking blood served a need for Alec. It fed him, and he traded passion in return. But he would never expect a lady he truly respected and admired to be his next meal. "Let it be, Sorcha," he warned. Already, his fangs were pricking at his upper lip, ready to make themselves known. That was the last thing he needed.

"I'm jealous," she said quickly.

Alec stared down at her. Sorcha's face was flushed, her freckles standing out in stark comparison across the bridge of her nose. "Jealous of?" he asked. He must sound like a half-wit. But he wasn't following her thought process at all.

"I doona want ye ta take from anyone else." She shrugged her shoulders again. "I doona like the very idea. I doona want ye ta have someone else in yer arms." She took a bite of her food and pretended they were having the same type of quiet conversation that all the other occupants of the table were having.

"Why not?" Alec prodded. What did she mean by that? If he had a heart, it would be stamping a beat within his chest.

She speared a carrot and ignored his gaze all together.

"Sorcha?" he tried again.

She laid her fork down. "I refuse ta spell it out for ye, Alec." Then she pointed toward his plate. "What do ye plan ta do with that? Claim a stomach ailment?"

He was much more interested in what she'd almost said, but she didn't seem likely to say any more. So Alec grinned slowly. "No. Watch this," he said. Faster than she could blink, he traded her plate for his. She looked up and down the table, but no one even noticed the switch. Alec couldn't help but smile. Sorcha wouldn't have noticed it either, if he hadn't bade her to watch.

"I had no idea ye could move so fast." She grimaced down into her plate. "But I'm no' certain I can eat this. I just finished mine."

She was tiny as a bird. No one would be surprised if she didn't eat as much as a morsel. "Shove it around on your plate, then," he groused. "Make a good show of it. Besides, with the gown you're wearing, I doubt anyone is watching your plate."

"My dress is just fine," she complained, but she did finally look at him as she said it.

"Just fine if you want to get yourself tumbled." He really should watch his tone, but it was blasted hard. Everything was hard. From the entire situation to his manhood. Thank God for draping table linens.

"If I dinna ken better, I'd say ye are also jealous."

Perhaps he was. That was definitely possible. After all, he didn't want other men gazing at her, certainly not the way Eynsford's blasted brothers did.

"Ye canna go and drink from a lass and then expect me ta be a paragon of virtue," she warned.

That did it. He tossed his napkin onto his plate. Alec wouldn't have her think him a scoundrel, not for one more second. For some ungodly reason, her opinion mattered to him. He leaned close enough to murmur in her ear. "I didn't take from anyone. I visited that little butcher shop you mentioned to me. And I had some blasted goat's blood. Maybe even mixed with something else just as bad." Vile stuff it was. But it quenched the thirst. Well enough, anyway. "That's all I've had since I arrived at Castle Hythe."

"No maids? No widows? No whores?"

What the devil? "Just what do you know about whores?"

Following his lead, Sorcha tossed her napkin to her plate as well. "I ken a great many things, Alec MacQuarrie." Then she pushed her chair back, nodded to the old codger who had somehow ended up on her left, and stalked from the dining hall.

Fifteen

SORCHA KNEW ALEC HAD FOLLOWED HER. SHE COULD sense him a few paces behind her, but she refused to turn around. She couldn't look at him. Not right now.

Oh, she knew all about the gentleman's club he frequented in London. Though "club" was a euphemism, according to Rhiannon and Lord Blodswell. The club was populated with whores waiting to give themselves up to vampyres, waiting to give themselves up to Alec in exchange for the pleasure he'd give them. That hadn't bothered her until now.

When she'd first learned of *Brysi*, she had been relieved that such a place existed. Relieved Alec had a sanctuary to escape to when he needed to do so. Relieved that he wasn't forced to scour the darkness in search of a meal. Of course, Rhiannon loathed the club and all its offerings and had shocked her husband with a slight jolt of lightning for having mentioned the club to Sorcha in the first place.

But now… Well, she had been honest at dinner. She *was* jealous. Jealous of each whore at *Brysi* who had found pleasure in Alec's arms. She knew she was being irrational. She had no right to be angry about the time he spent at his club. No right to be jealous of women who had shared their life's blood with him. But she was anyway. Irrationally jealous. Foot-stompingly jealous. Rip-a-lass'-hair-out jealous.

All things considered, it would be best if she escaped to the safety of her chambers and stayed there the rest of the night. Perhaps under the morning light, her good sense would be returned to her and she could have a rational conversation with Alec, instead of appearing to be a spoiled child who didn't like sharing her playthings.

"Sorcha!" Alec called after her.

But she shook her head, not trusting herself to utter a word to him. She made it as far as her chamber before his hand on her shoulder halted her.

"Why are you running from me?" He muttered so quietly in her ear that gooseflesh rippled across her skin.

"I doona wish for company, Alec," she bit out.

His fingers tightened on her shoulders and he stepped closer to her, drawing her back against his front. Sorcha closed her eyes, wishing she didn't revel in the feel of him as much as she did. When had life become so complicated? She'd come to Kent to capture a Lycan husband, and she now found herself standing in darkened corridors with a vampyre. The same vampyre she was unreasonably jealous over. The same vampyre who loved Cait, despite his protestations otherwise. The same vampyre who had throngs of whores waiting to be taken by him.

"You've been tempting me all evening, Sorch."

Only because the women in his club were too far away.

"You were supposed to save me a dance at least. Remember?"

Sorcha stepped out of his hold and grasped the cold door handle. "Next time, perhaps." Then she slipped through the door and shut it before she could do something foolish like toss her arms around him and beg to be kissed.

She flopped onto her bed and stared up at the ceiling. "Congratulations, Sorcha," she muttered. "Ye've made a fine mess out of everythin'."

&

Lying in his bed, Alec stared up at the ceiling, exhausted and more than a little irritable. He'd stayed up nearly half the night, wondering what he had done wrong the previous evening. One moment Sorcha might as well have offered herself to him on a platter, and the next she was fleeing to the safety of her bedchamber. He'd misstepped somewhere. That much was obvious.

Until recently, he'd thought he understood women. Then there had been the debacle with Cait. The insanity of Blaire and Rhiannon both giving themselves to vampyres. And now this, whatever this was, with Sorcha. Apparently, he didn't understand a damned thing. He doubted he ever had. He'd just been fooling himself for years.

That was certainly a lowering thought, especially since all he had to look forward to were more years than any mortal could dream of. Was the rest of his existence going to be one unpleasant surprise after another? Would nothing ever make sense?

A scratch sounded at his door, but before he could respond, the door opened and his valet, Forbes, strode over the threshold, looking as cheerful as the sunniest country morning. Alec scowled at the man. How dare Forbes get a restful night of sleep, while Alec had tossed and turned until after sunrise?

"Out," Alec ordered.

"About that, sir," the valet began, his voice nearly singsongy happy. Alec hated him at that moment. "Her Grace called for her lady's maid and gave her strict orders to find me and to make sure I had you ready for a private breakfast. I'm supposed to send you to her immediately."

The duchess might scare a great many people, but Alec wasn't one of them. "I said, 'out,'" he reminded his man.

But Forbes ignored him and opened the nearest wardrobe to remove Alec's dark grey jacket. "A bit morbid for the country, don't you think, sir?" He smoothed a hand across the front.

"No." After all, grey was quite fitting for his mood.

"Well, in any event." Forbes laid the jacket over the closest chair back. "Her Grace is annoyed that you never have breakfast in the breakfast room." He opened a drawer and retrieved a snowy cravat. "She must just be there at a different time than you, sir. For some reason, she thinks you take breakfast in your chambers." Forbes laughed as though that was the most ridiculous thing he'd ever heard. "Don't know where she'd get that idea. *I* would know if you ate breakfast in your room, now wouldn't I?"

"I'm not hungry this morning. Do send my regards."

Forbes shook his head. "Can't do that, sir. Hilda, the duchess' lady's maid, that is. Anyway, Hilda said if I didn't have you in the duchess' private sitting room looking your most handsome, I'd have to answer to her." The valet shivered dramatically. "Hilda fits her name, sir. There are some people I wouldn't mind answering to, but that woman isn't one of them. She's terrifying."

"You're terrified of a lady's maid called Hilda?" Alec leaned up on his elbows. Annoyed and tired as Alec was, Forbes had somehow managed to make him smile.

"I don't think Gentleman Jackson could take her, sir. In fact, I'd put my money on Hilda."

Alec sat up completely and scrubbed a hand down his face. "Please don't let anyone else hear that you'd wager good funds on a lady's maid called Hilda pummeling the life out of Gentleman Jackson. They'll think you've gone daft."

Forbes folded his arms across his chest. "Not if they saw her, Mr. MacQuarrie. Not if they saw her. Now come closer to the window so I can shave you properly. Hilda said you should look your most handsome."

Alec snorted. "You're to be the judge of whether or not I'm my most handsome?"

His valet scowled at him. "Well, sir, you're not the sort I usually fancy, but as I have taken good care of you for the last decade or so—I think I'm reasonably qualified to know if you're turned out looking your best or not."

Begrudgingly, Alec slid from the bed and moved to a chair close to the window. The sun glinted off his ancient signet ring, and Alec ran a finger over the engraved griffin on the side. Then he prepared himself to suffer Forbes' ministrations. Breakfast in the duchess' private sitting room. He'd endured worse in his life, but he still wasn't looking forward to placating Her Grace so early in the morning, especially as he had gone most of the night without sleep, and especially as Sorcha's image kept flashing in his mind.

Yet, thirty minutes later, he rubbed his cleanly shaven jaw as he traversed the corridors toward the duchess' suite of rooms and pondered why on earth the duchess would summon him to her sitting room so early in the morning. Or summon him to her sitting room at all. He'd already given her the blasted surprise, which he'd thought had pleased her a great deal. Certainly she'd not found disfavor with him over his dining habits? She didn't even know the worst of them.

The duchess' personal footman opened the door with a most ominous look on his face as Alec approached the sitting room. The man knew something was happening. Alec could nearly feel the reproach rolling off him in waves.

Alec stopped short before he reached the sitting room. He could hear loud sniffling and the snort of a person who was softly crying. "Pray tell me that noise is not what I think it is," he mumbled to the footman.

"I would if I could, sir," the man said, his expression still stoic despite the absurdity of the situation.

Whatever this was about, Alec wanted nothing to do with it. He turned from the door, but the footman stepped between him and the exit. Between him and safety. "I suggest you remove yourself from my path," Alec warned.

"I would happily take your suggestion, sir," the footman said as sweat broke out across his forehead. "But I fear for my safety much more with the duchess than I do against you."

Alec had to give the man credit for being astute. The duchess was a formidable woman, after all. But still, what the devil did crying chits have to do with him? He supposed there was no other way to find out, so Alec straightened his jacket and stepped closer to the door. The sniffling was definitely coming from inside the room. As well as the high-pitched whine of a distressed female. "How many are there?" he clipped out, his question aimed at the footman.

"Several," the man warned. "God be with you." Then he bowed and stepped from the threshold. Alec could just imagine him on the other side of the door, standing sentinel should Alec try to escape. A vampyre could take a footman down. But would that be in his best interests? Probably not.

Alec stepped into the sitting room. The duchess paced from side to side across the length of the room. If she didn't slow down, she'd wear a hole in the Aubusson rug beneath her feet. She did stop and glare at him when he coughed quietly into his hand to make his presence known.

"I have gone to great lengths to keep this meeting private," the duchess said, her face a cold mask that barely concealed her fury. Or Alec assumed it was fury. It could have been hatred. Or just as likely disgust.

"If you're in need of privacy, I'd be happy to leave," Alec remarked dryly.

The duchess was not amused. Not a bit. She

pointed to the pair on the settee, who Alec vaguely recognized as some Welsh baron's wife and her daughter. "You're obviously familiar with Lady Overton and Miss Overton."

Obviously familiar? What an odd statement. He'd seen them both at the house party. And had even danced once with the daughter at Rhiannon's wedding ball. But, if he remembered correctly, he'd returned the chit quite directly to her mother after she'd whispered some most inappropriate things to him during a waltz. He bowed lightly to the two ladies. "Good morning," he tried.

"What's good about it?" the baroness shot back at him. Then her eyes filled with tears again, and she began to snuffle into her handkerchief.

"There, there," the duchess soothed as she patted the woman's shoulder. "Mr. MacQuarrie, do take a seat." She motioned toward a high-backed chair not far from where he stood.

"I'd prefer to stand, thank you," Alec said. Running away quickly would be much easier if he was already standing.

"Sit," the duchess barked.

He was a vampyre, for God's sake. Not a Lycan who could be trained to sit, stay, and roll over. But he dropped into a chair anyway.

Her Grace took a deep breath. "We all know why we're here."

"We do?" Alec broke in. He had no idea why he was there.

"You do not play ignorant well, young man," the duchess warned.

Well, he should be thankful for that, shouldn't he? "Your Grace, if you might tell me why I'm here, I'm certain I'll fully understand in time. I must have forgotten." Forgotten that he'd hidden a body. Forgotten that he'd caused grievous harm to these women. Had he done something? Certainly not that he could remember.

"You've forgotten me already?" Miss Overton cried, which started a fresh round of tears.

Alec inhaled deeply. Though he no longer needed the breath, it did help to calm him. He lifted his hands, palms up, at the duchess. "Please take pity on me and tell me what the devil is going on," he pleaded.

The duchess didn't seem shocked by his language at all. She pursed her lips tightly together. Then she said very quickly, "You have the nerve to compromise this girl and then deny knowledge of who she is?"

Compromise Miss Overton? Alec's head spun so quickly that he was afraid it would spin right off his shoulders. "Beg your pardon?" he croaked.

Sixteen

SORCHA NIBBLED ON A PIECE OF TOAST IN HER CHAMBERS.
She didn't think she could take the activity of the breakfast room, not while she tried to come up with a plan
for her day. She'd made a muddle of things with Alec so
she'd need to apologize, though she had no idea what
she would say. "I'm sorry for bein' so jealous I couldna
see straight." Or "I do apologize for makin' such a cake
of myself." No, neither of those would do. She'd have
to keep thinking on it. How could she say she was sorry
without making herself look even more ridiculous?

Suddenly, her door flew open and her maid tumbled
into the room. "Miss, this just came for ye. It's urgent,
they said."

Sorcha knit her brows together as she took the
correspondence and opened the wax seal.

> *Sorcha,*
> *   You're needed immediately in Her Grace's*
> *sitting room. Alec requires your presence. Make*
> *haste. His future is at stake.*
> *   Cait*

His future was at stake? What an odd thing for Cait to say. She wasn't supposed to share the futures of others. It went against the very nature of her gift. She only did so in dire circumstances.

Sorcha tossed the missive onto the bed and dashed for the door. Luckily, she'd already pulled herself out of bed and dressed, but just barely. She certainly wasn't at her best. However, this obviously couldn't be avoided. Not if Alec's future was at stake.

She approached the closed door to the duchess' sitting room, but a slightly rotund footman stepped into her path. "Her Grace is otherwise occupied, miss. Would you like to leave a message?"

No, she would not like to leave a message. Nor would she. "Step out of my way," she ordered with an impatient flick of her wrist.

"I cannot do that, miss," the man said.

Oh, he could and he would. Sorcha glanced up and down the corridor, happy to find plants and flowers gracing the low tables along Castle Hythe's corridor. She willed the nearest plant to stretch its leaves and took great satisfaction as she watched the man's eyes widen in dismay while the vines closed around his wrists and ankles.

"Dear God," the man breathed as he tumbled to the floor. He tugged against the bindings, but they simply tightened with his every movement.

"Ye really should listen when a lady asks ye ta step aside," Sorcha scolded as she stepped past him and through the door. She would call the vines off in a moment, before anyone could see them. She dusted her hands together as she stepped into the duchess' sitting room.

"Sorcha," Alec gasped as he rose to his feet. "You should *not* be here." He pointed back toward the door with a stern look.

Sorcha walked closer to him and looked up into his worried face. "Cait sent a note that ye might need me," she said so low that only he could hear.

"Oh, you have no idea," he groaned. "But I still wish you weren't here."

But she was here, and Cait had to have had a very important reason for sending such a missive. There was no time like the present to find out what the problem was. "What's happenin'?" she asked.

Two women sat on the settee, their stunned faces streaked with tears, their eyes puffy with dreariness. Sorcha recognized them immediately. Miss Amy Overton had been less than friendly over the past sennight. Instead of exchanging pleasantries with any of the ladies at Castle Hythe, she always seemed to find the company of as many gentlemen as possible, as though it was a game. Friendly or not, Sorcha hated to see anyone reduced to tears. "Has someone died?" she asked.

"Not yet," Alec said quietly.

That was fairly ominous coming from a vampyre.

"You should go, Sorcha," the duchess ordered, tossing her regal head back like a queen.

Not even a royal decree from the Prince Regent himself could remove Sorcha from this sitting room. Not yet anyway. "I'll do no such thing," she declared. "I *will* find out what's goin' on." She squared her stance. "And I'll no' leave this room until I do."

"If Mr. MacQuarrie is in need of a friend right now and consents to you hearing his sordid little secret, who am I to complain?" The duchess flicked her wrist at Alec. "Tell her."

"I'd rather not," Alec remarked.

Sorcha was about to jump out of her skin. Patience had never been her strongest suit. "Tell me," she demanded.

"If you don't, I will," the duchess warned, "and you may not care for my choice of words, Mr. MacQuarrie."

Alec took another deep, cleansing breath. "It appears as though Miss Overton has been compromised. And the parties in this room have decided I'm to blame."

The jealousy that had gripped Sorcha the previous evening twisted at her heart once more. She suddenly couldn't draw in enough air.

Fury etched across Alec's face and he stepped away from her. "You should have left when I told you to," he growled.

She followed Alec toward the far wall, turned him to face her, and then stepped on tiptoe to speak so only he could hear. "Did ye do it?" The idea that he might be guilty of the crime bothered her far more than it should. She felt like she'd just been kicked in the chest by a horse. He said he'd only taken his meals at the butcher shop, but he hadn't said he hadn't bedded other lasses.

"I never touched the chit," he ground out. "I swear it. Everyone knows she's free with her favors."

Sorcha nodded slowly as a plan began forming in her mind. This was why Cait had sent for her—to save Alec. Sorcha only had one shot at this.

"Miss Overton, will ye permit me ta ask ye a few questions?" Sorcha tried to make her voice cheery and companionable. She must have succeeded, because the girl nodded slowly. Sorcha forged on. "Ye say Mr. MacQuarrie compromised ye here at Castle Hythe."

The girl nodded as Lady Overton began a fresh bout of crying. Good Lord, Sorcha had never seen so many tears.

"And when did this assignation occur?"

A few sniffles and the girl said between pouty lips, "Every night since we arrived. He comes to me after the household is in bed."

Alec groaned aloud, his fists clenched tightly at his sides.

"And why would ye allow a known defiler of women ta come inta yer room? Inta yer life? Inta... whatever else he came inta."

Alec threw his head back as though in defeat, the muscle in his jaw ticking.

"He promised to marry me," Miss Overton cried.

"Did he now?" No one in his right mind would marry the girl. That was probably why she'd chosen Alec. Once she'd gone down the list of peers at the castle who wouldn't have her, she'd settled for a wealthy gentleman instead.

Sorcha smiled despite herself. There was only one way to get Alec out of this mess. She wouldn't see him saddled with this brainless twit for the rest of the lady's life. Amy Overton would never be faithful, and he would be miserable.

"Did he come ta ye last night?"

The girl nodded quickly.

"What time?"

"After the ball," she sniffled, and then looked to her mother as though seeking confirmation. Lady Overton encouraged her with a nod.

Sorcha crossed her arms beneath her breasts and moved to stand beside Alec. "Ye're a liar," Sorcha said.

"How dare you!" The baroness jumped to her feet and probably would have attacked Sorcha's person, had the duchess not stepped between them.

"Why do you assume she's not telling the truth, Miss Ferguson?" Her Grace asked. Something flashed in her eyes. Pleasure? Enjoyment? But it was gone before Sorcha could identify it.

Sorcha shrugged and looked up Alec with the most flirty grin she could force onto her face. He looked positively green. "Because he was with me last night. All night. We left the ball early and went straight ta my room. And he was there until dawn. I would have kent it if he'd left."

Alec's body relaxed marginally. So, he wasn't put out by the suggestion. Perhaps?

"I-I meant the night before," the girl began.

"Did ye?" Sorcha broke in. "Hmm. He was with me until dawn that night as well." She shrugged. "In fact, he has been with me every night. All night. I quite find that I like wakin' up in his arms."

"Well!" the duchess said. She clucked her tongue for a moment. "This does change the situation a bit." She looked hard at Alec. "I can't believe, Mr. MacQuarrie, that you would take advantage of a dear, sweet creature like Miss Ferguson." Then she cast her eyes on Sorcha. "I suppose you can't be blamed for being taken in by such a rogue, handsome and charming as he is. And since you've disproven Miss Overton's claims, he's free to marry you instead, my dear."

Alec choked.

Sorcha bit back a grin. How fortuitous.

"I assume that you *were* planning an elopement, Mr. MacQuarrie?"

"No." Alec cleared his throat. "I intend to ask her father for her hand," he croaked out. "I'd planned to travel there next week."

Sorcha threaded her arm through his. "Under the circumstances, we might have ta do it a little sooner, darlin'," she cooed at him. "After all, I could be carryin' yer bairn." She patted her flat stomach and smiled brightly at those in the room. "And I couldna be more delighted."

Alec's face went from green to purple. He started to sputter, but nothing came out.

"Well, then, we'll have to ensure that this secret will remain among the occupants of this room," the duchess informed them all.

The tears from the two ladies on the settee had suddenly dried up, and they sat stone-faced, looking at the duchess. "Secrets such as this are hard to keep private," Lady Overton said, her nose raised slightly in the air.

"Yet they *will stay* private all the same," the duchess warned. "Or I'll be certain that the party who shares the news of the blessed nuptials will live to regret it."

Both women blanched. Alec snorted.

Then Alec bent and kissed Sorcha's cheek quickly with a glare that said, "We will discuss this." Oh, she could imagine they would.

❦

Alec was going to kill Sorcha, just as soon as he had her out from under the ever-watchful eye of the Duchess of Hythe. He captured Sorcha's elbow in his hand and tightened his grip. The little wood sprite didn't even have the sense to look remorseful about the string of lies that had just ruined her fate. "Come along, lass," he grumbled. "We have a lot to discuss."

"Oh, I imagine you do." The duchess' light eyes actually twinkled.

Damn it to hell, how could the duchess' eyes twinkle? Did she find the ruination of lovely young women amusing? He'd never thought of Her Grace as malevolent before. Alec frowned at the older woman, and then he directed his *fiancée* over the threshold.

As soon as they entered the corridor, Alec spotted the duchess' sentinel footman, wrapped up in vines and lying on the floor fast asleep. Good God! He tugged Sorcha closer to him and hissed, "What did you do to him?"

She shrugged. "He dinna want ta let me pass."

She should have listened to the footman. Instead, she'd destroyed any future she might have had. "Let the man go, Sorcha."

She heaved a sigh and then flicked her wrist toward the downed footman. Almost instantly, the plant released the servant and began to recede toward its pot. "Happy now?"

"Hardly. You can't go around revealing your powers and attacking poor footmen."

Sorcha giggled. "Oh, he willna remember a thing."

That was a terrifying statement. "Why not? Did you give him a potion too?" Alec frowned.

Sorcha giggled. "Nay, I just told the vines ta tighten right above his wrists. It helps ye get ta sleep if ye pinch right there. Did ye ken that? Elspeth showed me that a while back. Very helpful if one needs ta cure a bit of insomnia."

Insomnia? Good God! And he was supposed to marry this lass? The one who didn't think twice about drugging poor defenseless grooms or tying footmen up with vines and lulling them to sleep? Alec shook his head. He couldn't marry Sorcha. He refused to ruin her life, despite the fact that she was more than ready to throw it away on her own. He wouldn't be party to helping her with the actual throwing.

"Anyway, he'll wake up soon and think the whole thing was just a dream," Sorcha continued. "And he willna tell anyone about it because he willna want ta admit ta sleepin' at his post."

"Have it all figured out, have you?" Alec tugged her farther down the hallway, away from the now slightly snoring footman who was sprawled across the corridor.

"I wouldna say I have it *all* figured out. I'm just good at improvisin'."

"Good at getting yourself in heaps of trouble is more like it," Alec growled, scanning the corridor in hopes of finding a quiet salon or parlor in this wing. Shouldn't there be one nearby?

"I think ye were the one in trouble back there, Alec. I was simply helpin'. Ye're welcome, by the way."

You're welcome? She had to be joking! Alec stopped in his tracks and grasped both her arms in his hands, staring down into her innocent brown eyes, which were as guileless as those of a newborn fawn. "Helping? Do you have any idea what you've done, Sorcha?"

She nodded and smiled sheepishly. "Aye, I saved ye from having ta marry that connivin' lass. I promise ta be the best wife ye could have ever hoped for. I mean, I'm no' Cait, but—"

Damn it, they were back to Cait. Alec couldn't help but wince. Besides, that was hardly what he'd meant. Finally, he spotted a doorway just a few feet away. Thank God. He tugged her farther down the corridor and was relieved to find the small salon unoccupied.

"Don't move," he warned her, and then he shut the door behind them to keep anyone from happening upon them. Alec took a deep breath and then turned back to face the lady who had plagued his thoughts since his arrival in godforsaken Kent.

"Look, Sorch, I have no doubt you'd be the best wife any man could hope for, and somewhere out there is a man who'll thank his lucky stars every day of his life that he found you… But that man isn't me, lass. I can't marry you."

Her face fell at those last words. "But I thought…"

Alec would have given half his fortune for her to finish that statement, but she looked away from him as her lips pressed together in annoyance. Bloody wonderful! She'd tried to come to his rescue, and he'd ended up hurting her feelings, which was the last thing he wanted.

He tucked a stray lock of her dark hair behind her ear and let his finger linger on the corner of her jaw. "Sorcha, I'm not the sort of man *you* should marry. Tell me you see that."

"Would I have been better off if I'd kept ta my original plan and brought Lord Radbourne up ta scratch?"

Alec frowned, and it took every bit of strength he had not to shake some sense into her.

The damned Lycans again. "Keep your distance from those beasts, Sorcha."

Finally, she met his gaze, a question burning in the warm brown depths of her eyes. Then her finger poked his chest. Hard enough to make him wince. "I just saved yer wretched hide. And this is the thanks I get?" She stepped back from him. "Since it's clear ye doona want me, I doona ken what I'll do. I just told the Duchess of Hythe ye have been in my bed."

She'd set her sights back on that blasted Radbourne. He could feel it in his bones. "I never said I don't want you, Sorch. I said I can't marry you. I care too much for you to ruin your life that way."

Sorcha swiped at a tear that trailed down her cheek. "Lord Kettering dinna feel that way, and neither did Lord Blodswell."

Alec still couldn't believe the former vampyres had actually thought to foist themselves on women more deserving. "Selfish pricks, the both of them," he grumbled under his breath.

But Sorcha heard him and she gasped, most likely over his choice in language. "I canna believe ye said that."

"Sorcha, just help me find a way out of this mess."

Her stubborn chin jutted upward. "Ye're sayin' life with me will be a *mess*? Is that what ye really think?"

No, that wasn't what he really thought at all. Life with her would be an adventure he'd never forget, but for her—

"I thought we rubbed along well, Alec."

"We do—" he began.

"Then I doona see the problem. And with me ye wouldna have ta pretend ta be somethin' or someone ye're no'. Ye wouldna have ta enchant me, and ye wouldna have ta take sustenance from butcher shops or that awful club, and—"

"Beg your pardon?" Did she mean *Brysi*? How the devil did she know about his club? And was she once again offering her blood to him? Alec nearly groaned at the thought of sinking his eyeteeth into Sorcha Ferguson.

Sorcha continued as though he'd never said a word. "I ken what ye are, Alec, and I accept ye exactly that way. And ye ken what I am too. That's rare for us witches, and somethin' we only share with our spouses. There wouldna be any need for secrets. And—"

"All right, you win." He couldn't seem to shake the idea of taking from Sorcha whenever he wanted. His incisors started to descend. Damn it, why had she planted that thought in his head? He was turning out to be just as big a prick as both Kettering and Blodswell.

"Did ye say I won?" She gaped at him.

In a moment of weakness, he had. "Aye. You win," he said again.

What else could he do? She'd gone and ruined herself already with that Banbury tale she'd told the duchess. *Waking up in his arms every morning.* Good God, he couldn't believe she'd said that!

Besides, Alec reasoned, if he didn't take her in hand, she'd set her sights on one of those blasted Lycans again. None of them would take the care with Sorcha that Alec would. No matter what he thought about himself, he wouldn't see her tied to one of those drooling beasts. Not in this lifetime or the next. But the *real* reason that he'd acquiesced, the reason buried so deeply in his soul that he didn't even want to acknowledge it, was that he truly did want her.

He wanted her like nothing or no one he'd ever wanted before. He wanted to taste every inch of her and trail his fingers from one enchanting freckle to the next. He wanted the freedom to look down her *décolletage* anytime he wished without reprimand. He wanted to delve deep inside her, clutch her to him, and pierce her slender neck, and then do it all over again.

Sorcha threw her arms around Alec's neck and squeezed him tightly. "I'm happy we got that sorted out."

Sorted out. He'd be sorting this out for the next several years, he was certain. Alec was equally certain somewhere deep in his chest, where his heart had once beat, that Sorcha would regret the rashness of this decision. On the day that finally happened, he'd die a second death.

"Ye meant what ye said, dinna ye?"

He couldn't remember half the things he'd said in the past hour. "Which thing, lass?"

She rolled her eyes. "Did ye really mean ta ask Papa for his permission?"

Oh, that. Alec nodded. That was the least he could do, considering he was going to ruin her life. "Aye."

She leaned up on her tiptoes and kissed his cheek. "We'll start for home tomorrow, then?"

"Considering the fact that you thwarted Lady Overton's plan to trap me, we should probably leave this morning."

Seventeen

SORCHA BURST INTO HER CHAMBERS BUBBLING OVER with giddiness. However, her levity vanished when her eyes landed on Caitrin, who sat very primly on the edge of Sorcha's bed. "Cait."

The seer smiled softly and then rose from her spot. "So, I see ye arrived in time ta save him."

Cait had known exactly what would happen when she sent Sorcha to Her Grace's private sitting room. *Havers!* Was Cait sad about the fact? Perhaps a bit jealous? "Are ye all right with this?"

Cait nodded once. "Ta be honest, I wasna a few years ago, but I am now. Dash was my future. I just had never seen it. But I have kent for quite some time that Alec is yers."

Cait had *always* known? Sorcha took a staggering step backward. Was that why Cait had fought so hard against accepting one of his many offers?

"I would offer ye my congratulations, but yer journey is far from over, Sorch. Ye have more than a few obstacles standin' in yer way."

"What obstacles?" Sorcha asked, though she knew

her friend would never say.

Cait shrugged her answer. "Dash and I'll go with ye ta Edinburgh."

Sorcha shook her head. "That doesna seem wise, Cait. Dash and Alec together?"

Cait heaved a beleaguered sigh. "It isna up for debate, Sorch. Ye are no' yet married, and ye canna travel all that way with Alec alone. Ye do still have a reputation ta protect."

"But—" Sorcha began to protest.

"No buts," Cait interrupted. "Besides, our travelin' coach is already packed and ready ta go."

"I need ta pack my things," Sorcha mumbled. There was obviously no reason to argue. But as she glanced around the room, she noticed that her personal things were missing from the bedside table. She opened the wardrobe to find that all her dresses were gone. "Where is everythin'?" she asked of no one in particular.

"I had yer maid pack it all up," Cait answered with another shrug of her shoulders. "The coach is ready."

"Did ye have them pack Alec's things as well?" That seemed a bit forward.

"Even I wouldna do that," Cait sighed. She got that faraway look in her eye that meant she was seeing events that had not yet happened. "But as soon as ye go and inform him we're leavin', he'll be ready in no time."

"I'll have ta go find him," Sorcha grumbled. A small part of her hoped Alec would refuse to travel with Eynsford and Cait. They didn't need a chaperone. Cait certainly hadn't had more than a maid when she'd traveled to Scotland with Eynsford. And

Sorcha would revel in some time alone with her fiancé, truth be told.

"He's in his room," the seer chirped. "Or he will be in a moment." Cait avoided looking at Sorcha entirely. "Ye should run along. The sooner ye tell him, the sooner we can leave."

"What do ye see?" Sorcha bit out. Cait was keeping something from her; she could feel it.

"Ye ken I canna tell ye," her friend chirped again, still avoiding Sorcha's face entirely. But a grin tugged at the corners of Cait's mouth.

"Fine," Sorcha groused. It looked as though her fate had been decided for her. She would be traveling with a Lycan, a vampyre, and the witch who'd once stood between them.

*

Alec mumbled to himself all the way back to his room. He'd gotten himself into a hell of a mess this time. How dare those Overton women try to trap him? And Sorcha. Pretty little Sorcha had stepped up to his defense like he'd never expected anyone to do again. He wasn't worthy of such loyalty.

He'd take Sorcha as his wife, take her into his bed, and take her life force, and he wouldn't be able to give her a damn thing in return, aside from access to his wealth. He couldn't grow old with her. She'd continue to age, and he would always remain a young man. How in the devil would they avoid that? He couldn't give her children, either. In his mind's eye, he could see Sorcha with a child at her knee. She'd make a wonderful mother.

Yet she'd settled. She'd settled for him.

A knock at his door drew his attention. "Enter," he called out absently. He didn't even have to look up to know who it was. As soon as the door opened, Sorcha's apple blossom scent preceded her into the room. "You came to your senses, did you?" he asked as he leaned against the large wardrobe and folded his arms across his chest.

"Nay, I'm still an idiot, by yer standards," she replied, her voice droll. She closed the door behind her.

Alec couldn't help but smile at her. She had the sharpest tongue for such a sweet little lady. "I don't think you're an idiot, Sorch. I just think you took too much upon yourself when you decided to sacrifice yourself for me. And you should open that door. Someone could get the wrong idea."

Sorcha snorted. Such a dainty little sound. "I think it's a bit late ta worry about that," she reminded him.

"Only because you had to be a martyr," he shot back.

"So, wantin' ta save my friend from a fate worse than death makes me a martyr?"

"I already suffered a fate worse than death," he said quietly. "And lived to tell the tale. That would have been nothing." He stalked across the room toward her, with all of the pent-up emotions he hadn't been allowed to show rising to the surface. "And were you completely addled when you told the duchess I've spent every night with you? That you enjoy waking up with me in your bed?"

"So, I lied. What of it?" Her eyes flashed at him in anger.

"Aye, you lied. I feel certain I'd remember being in your bed." He'd never come out of it. He'd stay there forever and a day. And he'd keep her there with him.

"I should hope so," she snapped back.

So quickly that she startled and flinched, Alec reached out and grabbed her, drawing her flush against his body. "Since you're already ruined, Sorcha, I think we should take advantage of the moment."

"Beg yer pardon?" she choked.

Her hands landed flat against his chest, but she didn't pull away. Blast her for not pulling away. She was temptation personified. "More than one person thinks I've been in your bed." His hands slipped down her sides until he cupped her round little bottom. She still didn't retreat. "I can't stand for you to be thought a liar. So, I think we should remedy that."

He'd thought about very little, aside from taking her beneath him, since he'd arrived at Castle Hythe. And now she'd sealed her fate. Would he be the worst sort of cad if he took advantage of her?

Alec let his hands knead her bottom, not enough to scare her but enough to draw her closer to him, so close that he was certain she couldn't miss the bulge beneath his trousers.

"Ye'd like ta take me ta bed?" Sorcha asked.

"More than anything," he admitted. Then he cupped her bottom, picked her up with her feet merely a few inches off the floor, and very gently laid her in the center of his bed. She didn't protest. She didn't utter a sound, aside from a pleasant moan as she sank into the counterpane and he climbed up beside her. "Ye're a bit daft, you know that?" he whispered as he brushed her hair back from her face.

"Ye really ken how ta flatter a lady in yer bed, Alec," she protested mildly, shoving ineffectually at his chest.

"Look at me, Sorch," he prodded. His teeth had descended and they ached with the need to have her. He smiled at her when she finally looked at his face. "This is me. This is what I am. A vampyre."

She reached up to stroke the side of his face. "I ken what ye are," she whispered.

His lips touched the corner of her mouth. It took all of his concentration to be gentle. The pounding of her pulse filled his head like a soldier's drum might fill a battlefield. That excited him even more. "I want you," he growled as he cupped the side of her neck with his hand and pressed his lips to hers.

She tasted like jam and smelled like all the things he loved most in the world. She rose to meet him, her lips eager, her body loose and languid beneath him.

"You really should push me away," he warned when he finally lifted his lips.

"I wish people would stop tellin' me what ta do," she whispered to him, and tugged his head back down to hers.

When he slipped his tongue into her mouth, hers eagerly rose to greet it. He kissed her until his head swam with the need to take her. Then he lifted his head and looked down at her. "God, you're beautiful," he breathed.

"Ye say that like it surprises ye." She giggled.

"You surprise me every day. I didn't even know you were all grown up until recently."

"Until ye started lustin' for me." She giggled again, an animated sound that made him want to join her.

"You think this is amusing," he taunted. He didn't know when he'd fallen under her spell, but she was all he could think about. Right now, he wanted to be inside her. He wanted all of her. Every last inch.

"Quite," she affirmed. Her hands began to work the knot at his neckcloth, keeping at it until she was able to pull his cravat free and toss it to the floor.

"Just what do you think you're doing?" he asked. He liked it. He wouldn't stop her. But he'd like to know what was in her head.

"I want ta be closer ta ye," she admitted as she began to work the buttons of his waistcoat and helped him shrug out of it.

"Forbes is going to have your head," he warned. "He took great care dressing me today. For the meeting with Her Grace."

"Ye'll protect me." She sounded so sure of that. And she should. He would always protect her. From everything.

She tugged at his shirt until she'd freed it from his trousers and then pulled it over his head. "Now what?" he asked.

With a gentle little shove, she pushed him onto his back. "Now I can have my way with ye," she said as she climbed on top of him, her breasts pressed against the hair on his chest.

"Your turn," he warned as he began to tug at the laces at the back of her neck.

"Ye undress women much too well, Alec MacQuarrie," she teased as he opened the back of her gown and helped her pull it over her head.

"I'll never undress another woman again," he swore. When he looked down her body, he saw that she wore nothing more than a thin chemise and stockings. He groaned aloud. He could see the dusky pink of her nipples through her shift.

"I'll expect ye ta undress me on a regular basis," she teased.

"You don't count," he said as he reached up and pulled her lips back down to his. Then he rolled her to her back.

"Nice ta ken how much I doona matter." She rolled her eyes.

"Hush," he said gently as he took her mouth with great care. She arched against him, the fine muslin of her chemise tickling his chest. The broad points of her nipples brushed his bare skin. She trembled beneath him when he bent his head and rubbed his cheek against one of the little nubs. Her fingers threaded into his hair and tugged gently.

"Alec," she whispered.

But then he licked across her nipple, right through the fabric of her chemise, and she nearly came undone right there in his arms. Alec glanced up at her face to find her sparkling eyes dark with passion and hooded by heavy lashes. He reached for the hem of her chemise to draw it over her head.

But the pulse point that pounded at her inner thigh drew his attention with its frantic rhythm. He spread her legs and settled between them. Then he sat up on his knees so he could run his fingers over her inner thigh, searching for that pulse point. He wanted nothing more than to feel it pound beneath his fingers.

For surely her pulse was throbbing as hard as his manhood was. He could hear it in his head.

"What are ye doin'?" she asked.

He bit back a grin. Of course, she would ask. "Touching you."

"Why there?" A breathy little gasp left her throat when his fingers skimmed up her thigh toward her heat.

"Because it gives me pleasure," he replied as he let his fingers slide into the springy curls at the juncture of her thighs.

"Me too," she cried out, as he touched her center. She was wet, slippery with desire. He nearly spilled himself at his first stroke across her folds. Her hips arched toward him as he lowered himself on top of her again.

Sorcha tipped her head to the side as his lips touched the side of her neck. God, she tasted like nothing he'd ever had, and he hadn't even punctured her flesh yet. A cry rang out in the room as Alec stroked across the little nub that could drive her to completion. He'd take her over the top and then take her there again when he could be inside her.

"Please, Alec," she whimpered, her hips finding a rhythm against his gentle stroking.

Alec replaced his finger with his thumb and slid one digit inside her. She was like a warm silken glove that closed around him. She tugged at his hair and forced him to look into her eyes. He could drown there, never having seen such an utter look of surrender on anyone's face. Her eyes closed as her pants increased, those breathy little sounds nearly driving him mad. He wanted to work his way inside her and then hear them all over again. She only needed another moment, and then he would…

Her back arched when she finally toppled over that precipice. Her hands clutched the bedclothes as the force of completion racked her tiny frame. He continued his gentle stroking as she fluttered around him and caressed her until she was done.

Sorcha threw an arm over her eyes and groaned, "Oh, dear." The thump of her heart was still frantic, but it was beginning to slow.

"Was that a good 'oh, dear' or a bad 'oh, dear'?" He had to know.

She lifted her arm briefly and peered shyly from below it. "Very good," she whispered.

Alec adjusted his body so he could free himself from his trousers. "Are you certain you want this?" he asked. He searched her face as he looked for the answer.

She reached down and tugged his trousers over his hips. Apparently, she did. Alec situated himself between her thighs and probed at her center. The warm wash of her previous climb sucked at him. But just as he nearly pushed himself inside, a heavy knock sounded at the door.

"They'll go away," he groaned. But he held very still at the entrance to her warmth and listened for the door.

"Did ye lock the door?" she had the sense to ask. Thank God, because he had no sense at all in that moment.

"Did you?" he replied. Bloody hell. Neither of them had.

The knock sounded at the door again. Then a hard, extremely annoyed voice called out, "MacQuarrie?"

Eynsford! Blast and damn. Of course, the blasted Lycan would show up right when Alec was about to push his way into Sorcha's warm and willing body. She stiffened beneath him and shoved at his shoulder. "Oh, no," she cried.

"Miss Ferguson, are you in there?" Eynsford asked quietly through the crack in the door.

Alec put a hand over her mouth and shook his head. She didn't utter a sound.

"I know she's in there, MacQuarrie. I'm far from deaf, you know. I'll expect you to have her out here within the next five minutes."

Five minutes. Alec wouldn't even need five minutes. He'd like more than that, but…

"And I'm going to wait right here while you finish *talking*." Talking would be the operative word. There was little talking going on, and Eynsford could hear all of it with those blasted sensitive ears of his.

Alec bent and kissed Sorcha hard, a promise of things to come.

"Be out in a moment," Alec grumbled quietly.

"Oh, I know you will," Eynsford replied.

Alec rested his forehead against Sorcha's. "I hate that man," he whispered.

She winced slightly, which didn't bode well. "Then I should probably no' tell ye that he and Cait are travelin' with us ta Edinburgh."

What was left of Alec's ardor vanished instantly. There he lay between Sorcha's thighs, his manhood probing at her willing center, and his ardor vanished completely. He'd traveled the North Road with Cait and that blasted Lycan of hers the previous winter, and though their circumstances had changed drastically since that time, he had no desire to repeat the journey. "Are you trying to kill me?"

Sorcha giggled and very softly kissed his lips. "Ye are already dead, Alec."

Eighteen

THE MORNING SUNLIGHT CAST A GOLDEN HUE ACROSS the grounds of Castle Hythe. But all Alec could see was blackness before him. He towered over Caitrin and scowled, gesturing to his perfectly appointed coach. "I have my own carriage, Lady Eynsford, and I am more than capable of transporting my fiancée to her father's doorstep by myself."

With an arrogance that matched her husband's, Cait tipped her head back and smiled as though Alec was the country's largest dolt. "And yet ye'll be travelin' with Dash and me just the same." She gestured to her own coach, parked directly in front of his. "I've *seen* it, Alec."

And had she *seen* Alec strangling her pretty little neck too? "Don't think for one moment that you can use your powers to get your way in this, Caitrin. And I'm far past the days when you could manipulate me with a smile and a kind word."

Her smile broadened. "I am so glad ta hear it, Mr. MacQuarrie. However, as we are all part of the same circle, or will be soon enough, this little excursion will give us plenty of time for ye and Dash ta become friends along the way. We all need ta be in harmony."

"Friends?" Alec somehow managed not to snort. "Did your gift suddenly change into something that gives you the power to have way?" He tapped his chin with the tip of his index finger. Then he drawled sarcastically, "Oh, nay, I nearly forgot. You always get your way regardless. But not in this, Cait." He shook his head vehemently.

"We *all* need ta be in harmony," she said again, as though he hadn't heard her the first time. "If we're no'…" She shrugged. "Well, then our powers tend ta be a bit faulty. Someone could get hurt. I'd hate ta be around Rhi if lightnin' started explodin' every which way." She cringed. "And ye canna imagine the damage Sorcha can cause with plants. Ye'll have ta ask Benjamin about it some time."

Benjamin. Alec hadn't given his old friend another thought since his conversation with Sorcha on their return from Folkestone. They *all* needed to be in harmony? He wasn't certain he could ever be in harmony with either Benjamin or Eynsford. Perhaps he and Sorcha could escape to the continent instead of returning to Scotland. The Mediterranean had to be nice this time of year.

"Doona even think about it, MacQuarrie." Cait narrowed her clear blue eyes at him.

"You can't possibly know what I'm thinking."

"Oh, I ken ye and I ken how yer mind works. I also ken ye would never take Sorcha away from her father or her brother or from her coven."

He absolutely hated that she was right about that. Once again, he should have been less of a gentleman.

"Ah, look," Cait gestured toward the main castle door, "here's yer bride now."

Alec glanced over his shoulder to find Sorcha striding in their direction, her arm linked with that of the duchess' granddaughter. The sun glinted off Sorcha's brown locks, making her glow like an angel, and he couldn't help but smile. But at the forefront of his mind was the way Eynsford had thwarted his amorous attentions less than an hour earlier. "If we travel with you, Caitrin, I will not have that beast of a husband of yours interfering with my plans."

"And which plans would those be?" Cait crossed her arms and glared at him.

Of course, she knew his plan was to devour Sorcha at every opportunity. He'd had her in his bed, for God's sake. He'd seen her very nearly naked. Had watched her find completion at his hands. Alec adjusted the fit of his trousers. "Never mind," he mumbled.

"As long as ye're a gentleman, Alec, there'll be no need for Dash ta try ta interfere." Cait brushed past him toward the approaching ladies.

The duchess' granddaughter talked quietly with Sorcha. "Travel safe." Lady Madeline squeezed Sorcha's hand in farewell.

"I will. And promise ta keep an eye out for any lurkin' scoundrels."

Lady Madeline laughed. "I will miss you."

"I'll see ye in London for the season," Sorcha promised.

Alec supposed that was true. He couldn't remember a season he hadn't spent in London. How different the next one would be.

"I'll hold you to that." Lady Madeline folded her arms across her middle, as though to comfort herself.

Caitrin draped her arm around Sorcha's shoulders and led her down the gravel path toward Alec and the pair of traveling coaches. Sorcha's eyes sought Alec's. If he'd needed to breathe, she would have stolen his breath when she smiled at him.

Within a minute, the two witches stood before him. Youthful exuberance rolled off Sorcha in waves. "Have ye really agreed ta travel with Cait and Lord Eynsford?"

"Aye, he has," Cait answered before Alec could respond. "He pressed upon me how important it is ta him that he and Dash get along from now on, that our circle remains strong."

He was about to call the blond seer out for the liar she was, but Sorcha slid her arms around his waist and looked up at him, more than pleased. "Ye are so wonderful, Alec."

When she spoke, all he could think about was those wonderfully seductive noises she'd made in his chambers earlier. Would traveling with Cait and that blasted Lycan make her happy? He supposed, when one considered all she was giving up to marry him, that traveling with them was the least he could do. "Not wonderful," he corrected. "Conniving, lass. It is in my best interest to keep you happy, isn't it?"

"Forbes and Maggie can ride in Alec's conveyance along with my servants," Cait decided for them all. "Then the two of ye can share our coach."

"Perfect solution, angel." Eynsford appeared out of nowhere to drape an arm around his wife's shoulders. Where had the blackguard been? Had he overheard every blasted word Alec and Cait had shared? Most likely. After all, the man rarely let Cait out of his sight. The eavesdropping Lycan did not make it easy for Alec to even consider getting along with the man.

"I'd like ta get home as soon as possible," Sorcha said, releasing her hold on Alec.

His first thought was to toss her over his shoulder and whisk her away to Scotland on his own. They could be there in a matter of hours with his superior speed, but for some reason it seemed important to her that he try to make peace with Eynsford. Was that the harmony nonsense Cait mentioned?

"We'll go as fast as possible, lass." Eynsford winked at Sorcha.

If the Lycan thought he'd wink at Sorcha all the way to Edinburgh, he was greatly mistaken. Vampyres were stronger than Lycans, something Alec had been very happy to learn the previous spring, and he was not above proving the fact to Eynsford.

"Dash," Cait chimed in, as though she knew the direction of Alec's thoughts, "we should probably be on our way."

"You are right, of course, Caitie."

⌘

Sorcha snuggled against Alec and loved it when he pulled her closer on the coach bench. Ever since that morning when he'd kissed her, caressed her, and touched her in places she'd never dreamt existed, Sorcha had wanted to be at his side. Actually, she wanted to have him all to herself. There were things left unsaid, things left undone. Though she knew Cait was right about their traveling situation. Traveling alone with Alec would be highly inappropriate, no matter how much she might enjoy it.

She looked up at his strong jaw and remembered the wonderful things his lips had done earlier that day. He was hers. He was destined to be hers. Cait had seen it. The whole idea was still difficult to fathom, but Sorcha's heart leapt at the thought. No wonder Cait had been so adamant that Sorcha wouldn't marry a Lycan. She was *supposed* to marry Alec. And now that she knew the truth of that, it seemed so right, so fitting. And if there was more to experience in his arms—and she had a feeling there was—the rest of their lives was going to be more than wonderful, more than perfect.

Their lives.

Havers! If things remained as they were, Alec would live on and she would not. She shook her head. Since Alec was destined to be hers, he must transform the same way Lords Kettering and Blodswell had. She pressed her head closer to his chest and listened for the beat of his heart with all her might. But there was nothing, nothing she could hear anyway.

"Sorch?" Alec asked, "Are you all right?"

She sat up and nodded quickly. "Of course."

He frowned slightly but tugged her back against him.

Across the coach, Lord Eynsford snored slightly and Cait flipped through the most recent edition of *La Belle Assemblée*, but she had a greenish hue about her face. Sorcha leaned forward and touched her friend's knee. "Are ye feelin' all right, Cait?"

Cait dropped the periodical to her lap, looking positively miserable. She shook her head, and Alec promptly tapped on the carriage roof to signal the driver to stop. The jarring motion did nothing to help Cait's unfortunate color.

Before Alec could even help her down or Eynsford could fully wake, Cait tumbled out of the carriage and cast up her accounts mere inches from the coach.

"*Havers!*" Sorcha cried as she moved to follow her. Eynsford moved to accompany them, but Sorcha tossed him a smile, said, "I'll alert ye if we need ye," and closed the door promptly in his face. The sputtering noise Eynsford made was priceless.

Sorcha reached into her sleeve, pulled out a handkerchief, and passed it to Cait, who smiled weakly as she wiped her face. Sorcha couldn't help but giggle over the marquess' look of confoundment.

"I'm so glad ye find my situation so humorous," Cait groused.

"I was laughin' at yer husband, ye ninny." Sorcha gently rubbed Cait's back. "Are ye feelin' better?"

"A little," the older witch admitted.

"Ye were lookin' a might bit green back there. Was it somethin' ye ate?"

Her natural color slowly returning, Cait grinned and took Sorcha's arm and then pulled her away from the coach.

"Where are we goin'?" Sorcha asked as they got farther and farther away.

"I need ta tell someone," Cait hissed at her.

"Tell someone what?"

Cait raised a finger to her lips. "Whisper. Otherwise Dash will hear everythin' ye say."

"Alec too," Sorcha confided with a heavy sigh. "Though maybe he can hear whispers, as well. I'll have ta ask him."

"I had no idea vampyres could hear so well." Cait looked surprised.

"Vampyres are quite amazin' in their own right," Sorcha said with pride, as though she possessed the powers herself.

"I doona ken much about them."

"Me neither, but I plan ta learn." Heat crept up Sorcha's face as she realized Cait's husband had probably already told his wife what she'd been doing with Alec behind closed doors.

"Rumor has it that ye've already learned quite a bit." Cait smiled broadly.

"Yer husband is a menace," Sorcha mumbled.

"My husband has yer best interests at heart." Her friend giggled.

"Anythin' he can do ta thwart Alec seems ta give him pleasure."

Cait shook her head. "He'd actually prefer not ta be involved at all. I'm the one who sent him ta Alec's room."

Traitorous witch! "How could ye?" Sorcha gasped.

"Someone has ta protect ye. Ye're dead set on givin' yerself away." Cait shot her a telling glance. "I assume ye no longer have the need of anyone tellin' ye what happens in a marriage bed, now do ye?"

Sorcha took a deep breath. Truly, none of this was Cait's concern. Sorcha didn't hound *her* for intimate details. Well, she had asked for marriage-bed advice, which Cait had firmly refused to give her.

"Were ye no' casting up yer accounts just a moment ago? How did this become about me?" She pointed to her own chest. Then she turned to walk back toward the coach. "I'll send yer husband ta ye," she called over her shoulder.

"Doona go!" Cait cried. Then she whispered vehemently, "I have ta tell someone." Sorcha turned back toward her. "I have ta keep so many secrets about futures! I want ta blab ta the whole world about mine."

Sorcha took a few steps in her direction and whispered back, "What kind of a secret?"

Cait placed a hand on her belly and said, "I think I might be expectin'."

"Expectin' ta cast up yer accounts again? I'll go get yer husband for ye." Sorcha never had been one for sickness. She had a much too sympathetic stomach.

"No!" Cait cried. Sorcha saw the curtain move inside the coach as Lord Eynsford's head came into view. Nosy man. Cait glared at him and motioned for him to close it. He did so, but he didn't look very happy about it. Cait dropped her voice back to a whisper. "I think I'm expectin' a *bairn*."

Tears immediately pricked at the back of Sorcha's lashes. "A bairn?" she squeaked.

"Shh!" Cait fluttered her arms wildly, trying to get Sorcha to quiet.

"Oh, sorry!" Sorcha whispered as she folded Cait into her arms. "I canna believe it. I'm just so excited! I'm goin' ta be an aunt again." Then she narrowed her eyes at Cait. "Ye havena told yer husband?"

"No' yet. I want ta be certain." Cait laid her hand protectively over her belly again.

For a woman who saw everyone's future but her own, something like this must be driving Cait mad. Still… "With the way ye were castin' up yer accounts back there, I'd say it's fairly likely. Ye never get travel sick."

"I think so too," Cait said with a smile. "But I want ta wait a bit ta be certain. So, doona tell anyone. No' even Alec."

As though Alec would want ta know that the lass to whom he'd given his heart was carrying someone else's child. "I'll no' say a word." Then a brilliant idea flashed into Sorcha's mind. She narrowed her eyes at Cait. "If…" She let her voice trail off.

"If what?" Cait shot back, her blue eyes rounded in shock.

"If ye'll call off yer dog."

Cait looked more than mildly affronted. "Beg yer pardon?"

"Call Eynsford off. Doona send him chasin' after Alec and me. Let my future happen all on its own, without interference." She paused. "Please?"

"I canna believe ye called him a dog." Cait grunted.

"If the collar fits," Sorcha tossed back.

Nineteen

ALEC SAT ACROSS FROM THE MARQUESS OF EYNSFORD IN the carriage and struggled to hear what the pair of witches were talking about. He caught a word here and there, but not very many. And what he did hear didn't mean much.

"Your wife is a cunning woman," Alec tossed out into the silence of the coach.

"If cunning and conniving mean the same thing, then yes, she is," Eynsford replied. "Can you hear what they're saying?"

Alec shook his head. "Very little of it." He listened for another moment, but all he could hear was Cait's shocked gasp. "Sounds like they're arguing."

"Heaven help us if they are," the marquess grumbled.

"I have my own coach," Alec informed him. "I can take Sorcha and we can separate them." He'd like nothing better than that anyway. Harmony be damned. He wanted his little witch all to himself.

"Have you ever seen them really argue? Any of the witches? They're scandalous." Eynsford shivered dramatically.

"I've seen them do it my whole life," Alec reminded him. "That's why I volunteered to take Sorcha to my own coach. It's terrifying."

"Finally, something we agree upon," the marquess said drolly.

"That your wife and my fiancée are forces to be reckoned with? Aye, we're in agreement. But do me a favor and don't tell them that."

Eynsford inclined his head slightly.

"While we're speaking so openly, if you ever find yourself outside my door again and decide to intervene, I will do you bodily harm," Alec warned. "You know I'm capable, and you should know I won't hesitate next time."

"You can try." The marquess raised one amused eyebrow. "But my wife threatened to do me bodily harm, along with several other most severe punishments, if I didn't intervene. Unfortunately for you, her proclamations frighten me more than yours do."

From nowhere, a comment popped out of Alec's mouth. "You love her, don't you?" He wanted to bite it back immediately. But what was done was done.

Eynsford laid his head back on the squabs and regarded Alec for a moment. "With all my heart," he finally said.

There was nothing to say to that, so Alec simply nodded once. He was glad Cait had found happiness, even if it was with the overgrown dog sitting across from him. And Eynsford seemed the most smitten of men. Still, he'd rather not have to endure the man, if given a choice.

Devil take it! What was keeping the lasses so long? Argument or no argument, how could they possibly think to abandon Eynsford and himself to each other's company? Alec tossed open the coach door and quickly exited, only to find Sorcha headed in his direction.

She wore an impish smile that made all of Alec's annoyance drain right from him. She was so full of life; she almost made him remember what it felt like to be human. He wanted to wrap her in his arms and revel in the energy that coursed through her. It still wasn't too late to toss her over his shoulder and make a run for it, was it? Probably. But he wouldn't rule that out for the future.

"Everything all right?" he asked, as he closed the distance between them.

Sorcha nodded and gestured toward Cait a few paces behind. "A little travel sick is all."

Behind them, Alec heard the coach groan as Eynsford alighted from the conveyance and then rushed past to take Cait's arm. "I've never known you to get travel sick, angel." The marquess caressed his wife's cheek. "Is there anything I can do?"

Alec towed Sorcha closer to the carriage and lowered his voice. "And the argument?"

Sorcha shrugged. "That's how we always talk ta each other. Ye should ken that, Alec."

Oh, he knew it. "Worse than sisters," he agreed.

Sorcha's brown eyes twinkled with joy. "That's how ye ken we love each other. We only get worked up because we care."

"And is that why you argue with me too?" He couldn't help but ask, though he bit his cheek as he waited to hear her answer.

She nodded emphatically. "Of course. I've cared about ye my whole life, Alec."

Her admission warmed him from the inside out, and he softly pressed his lips to hers. "The feeling's mutual, Sorch."

Somewhere behind them, Eynsford grumbled, "If I have to watch that the whole way to Edinburgh, I'll be travel sick myself."

"Hush," his wife complained. "I think young love is adorable."

Alec almost took a step back. Young love? He couldn't love Sorcha. He adored her; he cherished her; and he wanted her beside him always. But he couldn't love her. He didn't have a heart anymore.

Sorcha blushed a bit, but thankfully, she didn't seem to notice Alec's distress as she stepped from his arms toward their traveling companions. "After watchin' ye moon over Cait, I think ye're the last person who gets ta complain, my lord. Now, where is my green travelin' valise?"

"Should be with MacQuarrie's coach," Eynsford replied.

Sorcha glanced up and down the road. "Are they in front or behind us?"

"Why does it matter?" the marquess asked.

"Because," Sorcha turned to stare at the man as though he was an imbecile, "I have my herbs in there. A bit of ginger will help settle Cait's stomach."

"Ginger would be just the thing," Cait agreed.

"Renshaw!" Eynsford barked, stalking to the coach with newfound purpose.

"Yes, sir?" The coachman spun in his box to answer his employer.

"Has MacQuarrie's coach passed us?"

"Not yet, sir."

"Very good." Eynsford turned back to the small group. "Then why don't we wait for them here? We'll snatch your little valise up and keep it with us from now on. How does that sound?"

Sorcha agreed with a nod. "Perfect, my lord. Thank ye."

"No thanks necessary. Just help her, lass."

"I may no' be as good as Elspeth at this sort of thing, but I'm better than Blaire or Rhiannon. So if ye canna have El, ye're very fortunate ta have me along for this journey."

Cait snorted. "I'd rather have ye instead. El doesna go anywhere without that annoyin' lapdog of hers anymore."

Eynsford coughed in surprise. "Caitie!" He gestured to his person, as though reminding her she'd married a man of the same breed as Ben Westfield.

"I would never say such a thing about ye, my love. But Benjamin canna help but get on my very last nerve with all the hoverin' and dotin' and—"

"He's much better," Sorcha began, "ever since Rose was born. Now he dotes on the little bairn like…" Then her face nearly turned scarlet and she turned away from the group.

What was that about? Why should talk of Ben and his daughter cause such a reaction in Sorcha? Alec glanced from Cait to Eynsford, wondering if his fiancée's response made any sense to either of them. And that's when it hit him.

Cait was expecting. He could see it in her bluer than blue eyes.

The travel sickness. Sorcha's instant embarrassment

at the mention of a bairn. A slip of the tongue, obviously. Still Eynsford didn't seem to have figured it out. His concern for Cait might as well have been etched across his brow for all the notice he paid to Sorcha's words.

So Cait was to be a mother. Would she birth a little witch or a litter of Lycans? He discovered it didn't really bother him either way. If he'd stumbled upon this news a month earlier, it would have sent him into a downward spiral of self-pity and anger he was sure; now he was simply happy for her. After all, this life was apparently what she wanted.

Alec followed Sorcha toward a line of trees so they would be closer to Alec's coach when it approached. He tapped her shoulder, and she nearly leapt out of her skin.

"Oh!" She spun around and then smiled when she saw it was him. "I thought ye were Cait."

Alec laughed. "I've never been mistaken for her before."

Sorcha's adorable nose scrunched up. "Nay, I'm just certain she's furious with me."

Alec grasped her hand and pulled her into his arms. "Eynsford is dense, lass. He didn't realize what you said."

Her mouth fell open, and instant regret flashed in her eyes. "Ye mean—"

"It was just a matter of time, wasn't it?"

"I-I suppose." She looked so concerned, so worried for him.

Alec adored her all the more for it, and he pressed a kiss to her forehead. "There's no reason to worry about me, Sorch. I've told you time and again that

I'm over Caitrin. It's true. You don't need to try to protect me."

Her hands slid around his waist, and she pressed her head to his chest. "Ye canna tell a soul or she'll boil me in a cauldron of oil."

Cait's temper was legendary, but Alec doubted cauldrons of oil would be necessary in this case. "Why doesn't she want him to know? I'm sure he'd be over the moon."

"She wants ta ken for certain," Sorcha said against his chest. "She canna see her own future, ye ken."

"Is that what your argument was about?" Alec tipped Sorcha's chin up so she had to look at him. "You thought she should tell him?"

Sheepishly, Sorcha shook her head. "I was tryin' ta blackmail her. I told her I'd keep her secret if she'd call off the marquess, if she'd let us just be and let us make our own decisions."

Alec nearly roared with laughter. "My conniving little witch!" Here he thought she'd taken the high moral road, wanting to keep everything open and honest, but she was actually blackmailing Cait! Or trying to. He wiped a tear of mirth from his eye. Sorcha was priceless. "Oh, lass, you do make life interesting."

She frowned at him. "I canna believe ye're laughin' at me, Alec MacQuarrie!"

"Not at you, Sorch," he amended, bringing his levity back under control, "at the situation. You—" The sound of an approaching carriage caught Alec's attention, and he looked over Sorcha's shoulder. "There's my coach now!"

Twenty

SORCHA SPOTTED THE BLACK HORSE INN FROM HER window and breathed a sigh of relief. Cait hadn't fared particularly well, even with the ginger. As soon as Sorcha had a room to herself, she could concoct something a little stronger. So much for getting to Edinburgh quickly. They'd be lucky to make it there by Michaelmas at this rate.

"Almost there, Caitie," Eynsford soothed, caressing his wife's arm.

"I am sorry," Cait mumbled as the coach rumbled to a stop.

"It's no' yer fault." Sorcha smiled at her friend. "As soon as I can steep ye a special pot of tea, ye'll feel better than ever."

Eynsford snorted. "Not me. I made a vow to myself never to drink tea a witch offers me, at least not while traveling."

Even in her fragile state, Cait elbowed him in the stomach. "I canna believe ye can joke at a time like this."

"Sorry, angel. Just breaking up the tension."

Eynsford opened the coach door, climbed out, and then scooped Cait up in his arms.

Neither Sorcha nor Alec had made a move to depart the conveyance, at least not yet. Alec chuckled to himself. "The man really is dense. How could he not see what is going on with her?"

Sorcha shrugged. "More worried than suspicious, I suppose."

"Well, I suppose we should get you to your room so you can steep this magical tea." He alighted from the carriage and offered her his arm.

A grin tugged at the corners of her mouth. "Ye're accompanyin' me ta my room?" She stepped forward, laid a hand flat on his chest, and then batted her eyes at him in what she hoped was a coquettish move.

He leaned down a little to say quietly in her ear, "I don't see any hovering Lycans lurking about to stop me, do you?"

"Eynsford is hoverin' around Cait right now." Sorcha glanced furtively around the courtyard. "How long do ye think we have?"

"It won't take me very long," she thought she heard him mumble.

"What did ye say?"

"I said we can have as long as it takes to make the tea, I'd assume," he clarified.

She narrowed her eyes at him. That wasn't what he'd said. But she'd leave it be.

When they entered the inn, they found that the marquess had already secured their rooms for them. Hers was directly beside Eynsford's and Cait's. And Alec's was on the other side of the establishment.

"Interfering mutt," Alec muttered.

Sorcha couldn't keep from giggling. Alec reached into his pocket and passed the innkeeper a coin. "My wife would like some tea, but she prefers to steep her own. Could you please send whatever we require to my chamber?"

"Your wife, eh?" The innkeeper nodded dramatically and winked at them. Alec appeared none too pleased, however, and something in his expression must have worried the stodgy old man.

"Beg your pardon, sir. I'll take care of it immediately for you and your wife. It'll be my pleasure."

◦◦◦

No, it would be Alec's pleasure, as soon as he had Sorcha alone in his chambers. But the innkeeper need not know that. He ushered her up the stairs as quickly as he could get away with. The delicate sway of her hips as she climbed the steps in front of him nearly had his mouth watering. He wanted her unlike anything he'd ever wanted before. Like a drowning man craves a breath. Like a starving man craves a meal.

The thought of a meal had his teeth descending before he and Sorcha even stepped into the room.

Sorcha chattered on about something. He wasn't certain what, but he must have nodded at appropriate times because she kept talking. She didn't stop until they had finally walked over the threshold of his bedchamber and he had closed the door behind them.

"Are ye all right?" she asked, her face clouded with worry.

"I am now," he grunted as he grabbed her arm,

tugged her to him, and dropped his mouth to hers. She didn't pull back. She didn't shy away. In fact, she rewarded his ungentlemanly behavior by stretching up on her tiptoes and pressing her lips tighter against his. "Sorch," he groaned against her lips.

He'd have to slow down or risk scaring his little innocent. He threaded his fingers into the hair at her temples and very gently stroked her. She purred as she pressed herself against his hand.

After a moment, she opened her eyes. And they grew round as saucers. "Why did ye no' tell me?" Her eyebrows snapped together in consternation.

He had no idea what he'd done. "Tell you what?"

"That ye're hungry," she informed him as her gaze returned to his mouth. Of course, she saw his descended incisors.

"I always seem to be hungry for you," he admitted. "Do I have to tell you all the time?" He tugged her hips closer to him. "Can't I just show you?" His lips dropped to the side of her neck. She warmed beneath his lips, her pulse thumping beneath the delicate skin of her throat. The thump, thump, thump of her heart nearly overwhelmed him, and his teeth ached in cadence with the rhythm of her life force.

Sorcha gave a gentle shove against his chest. He ignored it.

"Alec," she protested as she slapped him a little harder. He raised his head and looked at her. She wasn't unaffected by his kisses. But she obviously had something else on her mind. She turned her back to him and pulled her hair over her shoulder. "Help me out of this dress, will ye?"

Alec didn't need to be asked twice. He had her unlaced before she could even inhale and then shoved her traveling gown down over her hips just as quickly. When she stood before him in only her shift, he stepped back to look at her. "God, you're beautiful," he breathed.

"Where do ye want me?" she asked, her voice terse and clipped.

He'd annoyed her? Of course he had. He was acting like an untried lad. He couldn't keep his hands off her. Alec turned away from her and swiped a hand down his face. Maybe if he didn't look at her, some of the ache to take her would ease. "We should get you to your own chamber," he said quietly without even looking at her.

"Over yer dead body," she taunted. He glanced over his shoulder to find her index finger pointed at him. "Alec MacQuarrie, ye *will* take me. And ye *will* take me now."

"I will?" This was bloody confusing.

"I'll no' let ye be hungry. No' when I can fill that need for ye." She stepped forward and stroked a hand across his back. "And I *want* ta fill that need for ye."

She thought he was hungry for her blood? Dear God, he was. But that was nothing compared to his desire to become one with her. "Sorcha, I'm not worried about dining," he said as he turned and faced her.

"Ye have ta eat." She pointed toward his mouth. "Yer teeth are tellin' me ye're hungry."

Alec fought his grin. "My teeth do that at the strangest times. Not just when I'm hungry for *food*."

"Ye're sayin' ye're no' hungry?" She was beginning

to look a little irked, standing there in her chemise and stockings. She crossed her arms beneath her delightful breasts.

He *was* hungry, truth be told. But it was a distant second in the race to get inside her body. He shrugged. "It can wait." He advanced toward her again.

She held up a hand to stop him. "Nay," she barked.

"Nay?" He probably sounded like an addled parrot. But his teeth ached as much as his manhood did. His mind was not his own.

"Nay," she said again as she walked slowly toward him and laid a hand on the center of his chest. Then she shoved him. He allowed her to push him back a step.

"Sorcha, I'm sorry," he started. For God's sake, he was going to marry this lass. He was going to be with her forever. Or at least as long as her forever lasted. And he was treating her like a common tavern wench.

She shoved him again. This time, the backs of his knees hit the edge of a high-backed chair. "Sit," she commanded.

"I'm not trained to sit and stay, Sorch," he remarked playfully.

"Sit, please?" she tried. Her pretty little lashes swept against her cheeks like dark fans as she smiled at him.

Alec was completely under her spell, and he sat like the most well-trained dog. He reached for her hips as she stepped closer to him. But then her hands landed on his shoulders and she moved to straddle his lap. "What are you doing?" he croaked.

"Makin' it so that ye canna get away," Sorcha said quietly as she slid closer to his body. Instinctually, he reached and grabbed her bottom, drawing her flush against him. She gasped at the rough movement.

"Sorry," he mumbled, but he couldn't make his fingers let go of her bottom.

"I ken ye *could* force me from yer lap any moment, Alec," she whispered, her lips a mere breath from his. "But I am also well aware that ye willna do so."

There was nothing more than his trousers between his manhood and her softness. Sorcha wiggled her bottom in his lap, trying to get even closer. "Easy, lass," he warned.

"Sorry," she said with a giggle. "This is fairly scandalous, is it no'?" she questioned. Her heart was still thumping like mad.

"Perfectly scandalous," he grunted. She was almost naked in his lap. Bloody hell, he wanted her.

Sorcha lifted her delicate little wrist close to his face and turned it toward him. "Do ye want me here?" she asked. Her adorable little nose scrunched up. He took her wrist in his hand and brought it to his nose. The apple blossom scent of her, combined with the knowledge that those delicate blue veins pounded just below the surface, nearly had him disgracing himself in his pants.

"Something tells me you'll find fault with it if I take you there," he said. He had no idea why she would. But she obviously had some preconceived notions.

"It's no' where Blodswell took Rhiannon." At his dumbfounded expression, she clarified, "I saw the marks when I helped dress her hair for the weddin'."

Alec shoved Sorcha's hair from her shoulder and tugged her chemise until it hung off her shoulder. Those freckles winked at him and tasted just as wonderful as he'd thought they would, like springtime and Scotland all rolled into one. He pressed his lips where her shoulder met her neck. "Did he take her here?" he whispered.

"Yes," she whispered back. "Right there," she cried out as he very gently nipped her sensitive flesh.

"There are other places where I could take you," he informed her quietly, but he continued his assault on that sensitive flesh. The scent of warm apple blossoms was driving him mad.

"Like where?" she breathed.

His hand reached for her knee and slid forward until he nearly found her heat. "Like here," he said, stroking his fingers across the pulse that pounded in her inner thigh.

"Ye'd have ta put yer head down there?" She looked appalled at the suggestion.

"You'll love it," he chuckled. Then he raised his hand to stroke her center.

"Alec! We canna do that. No' right now," she chided him. "Ye're havin' dinner," she reminded him.

"Aye, I am. I can't wait," he mumbled against her shoulder. But he didn't remove his hand; in fact, he used his finger to bring some of her desire forward, to slicken the little nub he knew would send her over the precipice.

"Alec," she cried as she buried her face in his neck, turning her head so that her neck was fully exposed. Her hips began to move on him, and the friction between his trousers and his manhood was nearly painful. He reached between them, freed himself from his confines, and then pulled her forward so she could ride the ridge of him. The slickness of her desire washed over him, and he almost exploded.

Alec concentrated on gentling her, rather than stoking his own desire. He was past the point where he could stop. She would be his in mere moments, and that seemed to be what she wanted.

"You're certain you want to wear my mark?" he ground out, his lips heavy against her neck, his teeth poised and ready.

She rocked her hips against his hand, let out a healthy little mewling sound, and tugged the back of his head. Alec abraded her flesh with his teeth, allowing them to scrape over her delicate flesh as he stroked her higher and higher. When she cried out, he pierced the tender skin of her throat.

Sorcha's passion was unlike anything he'd ever tasted. She rode the waves of completion, giving her pleasure to him as she took his in return. Her hands slipped around his body as she hugged him even more closely to herself. If he could draw her into himself, he would. He supped on her delicate life force, taking her into his body, into his life, into his very being, and she came willingly.

And then he did the same. He couldn't even control it. When she found completion, he found his along with her, spilling his seed between them. He groaned aloud and drank her in, taking in every last whimper and every last cry. Finally, when she collapsed against him with her head on his shoulder, he forced himself to withdraw his teeth and lick across the wounds he'd made to close them.

"You're mine now," he grunted as he ran his hands up and down her back. He'd never felt like this before. Never wanted to hold and cuddle a lass after sharing her pleasure. But this was Sorcha. *His* Sorcha.

"I'm yers," she whispered back. "But what about ye? Ye dinna get ta…" She let her voice trail off as an embarrassed flush crept up her neck.

"I did," he admitted. When he slid her bottom forward, she must have felt the sticky wetness between them because she giggled. "And if you tell a single one of your coven sisters that I couldn't even wait to be inside you to do that, I'll not be very happy."

"Quite shameful, is it no'?" she asked.

"Quite shameful that I wasn't inside you when I did that?" All right, his pride was aching a little. He might as well be sixteen all over again.

"No, quite shameful that I enjoyed it so much. I never imagined…"

"Neither did I, lass," he admitted.

A heavy knock sounded on the door.

Twenty-One

SORCHA GASPED AND THEN LEAPT OFF ALEC'S LAP AS the knock sounded again, a bit more insistent this time. She glanced down at herself and realized she couldn't possibly open the door. Not so scantily clad anyway.

Alec frowned as he rose from the chair and buttoned his trousers. "Damn Lycan," he grumbled under his breath.

It was Eynsford? Sorcha almost squeaked in distress. They couldn't let the marquess find them like this. "Alec!" she hissed as he started for the door.

With a look of chagrin, he shrugged. "It'll be all right, lass." Then he opened the door just a crack. "Don't you have a wife to look after?"

Though Sorcha couldn't see Lord Eynsford from where she stood in the corner of the chamber, she could hear him grumble, "You certainly don't waste any time, do you?"

"It *is* of the essence."

The marquess growled a warning. "I intercepted a tavern maid with a tea tray. Not certain why she was instructed to deliver her wares here, so I redirected her to *Mrs*. MacQuarrie's room instead."

Oh! Cait's tea! "I'll be right there," Sorcha called as she retrieved her gown from a nearby chair. "I'll need all my herbs and seeds."

"And a bath," Alec added. "As you've taken on the role of footman, Eynsford, would you be so good as to order *Mrs.* MacQuarrie a bath as well?"

Actually, a bath was in order. Sorcha slid her gown back over her head. "Please, my lord, if ye doona mind. That would be lovely."

"I only live to serve, lass." Eynsford's sarcasm could be detected even through the door. Then he snorted. "You smell like you could use a bath yourself, MacQuarrie."

"Do feel free to order me one then. Just see to Sorcha's first, will you?"

"Just as soon as she sees to Cait's tea."

Sorcha slid her feet back into her slippers and started for the door, though Alec still stood there, blocking her from Eynsford's view. She placed her hand at his back, and he glanced over his shoulder at her.

"I'm ready."

"She'll be there shortly." Alec closed the door and then turned and raked his gaze across her once more. "The gown is about to fall right off you, Sorch. Let me get the buttons."

"Why did he say ye smell like ye need a bath?" She inhaled deeply. "Ye smell fine ta me." She lifted her hair from her shoulders so Alec had better access to her fastenings.

"That muzzle of his is much too sensitive. He can't help being a beast," Alec teased. A moment later, he kissed her cheek and took a step backward.

"If you need help undoing them for your bath, do send for me."

Sorcha rolled her eyes. "Ye are incorrigible."

"One of my better traits," he agreed, though he looked a little more serious than she would have expected.

"Are ye all right? Are ye still hungry? I can—"

Finally a smile tugged on his lips. "I will survive for the time being, lass. Go bewitch that tea for Cait or we'll never get rid of her overgrown mutt."

Sorcha lifted up on her tiptoes to press a kiss to his chin. "Be nice ta him. We do all need ta get along."

"Harmony?" he asked with one raised brow.

"Precisely," she agreed with a nod. "Mama and Fiona Macleod had a fallin'-out and things were miserable for everyone else because of it for a very long time. We've been fairly fortunate with our generation, and I doona want ta be the one ta mess it all up."

"I will try to be nice to him, but only for you."

Only for her. What a sweet thing to say. Sorcha's heart pounded in her chest. What a wonderful man she was destined to marry. Cait must have been exaggerating when she said they had obstacles to overcome. Sorcha couldn't ever imagine not being in harmony with Alec. He was perfect. Or he would be once his heart started beating again.

She smiled at him once more and then exited into the tiny hallway to find the marquess still waiting for her. *Havers!* She had thought he'd returned to Cait as he hadn't made a sound. "Are ye goin' ta escort me ta my chamber?"

Eynsford winked at her, and she could still see the warmhearted man she had met all those months ago, the one desperately in love with Cait from the moment he'd laid eyes on her. "It would be my honor, Mrs. MacQuarrie."

She took the marquess' proffered arm and allowed him to direct her toward her chamber. "I suppose it will take some time to get used to that name," she said conversationally.

"I wish you luck with it, lass." He stopped in front of a room, took a key from his pocket, and quickly unlocked the door. "Cait's sleeping. How long will your cure take?"

There was no *cure* for carrying a bairn, other than birth, but Sorcha could help make the journey more comfortable for her friend. "About ten minutes, my lord. But she'll need ta drink all of it and more in the mornin'."

The look of concern he'd worn all day once again settled on his face. "Do you know what's wrong with her?"

Sorcha shrugged. Why wasn't Cait awake to answer his questions? Sorcha was certain to make a blunder of it somehow. "Just a bit of travel sickness."

"I've traveled the length of Britain with her more than once. I've never seen her like this."

Blast Cait for not telling him the truth. Sorcha didn't want to see the marquess suffer unnecessarily. Just as soon as Cait awoke, Sorcha would demand that her friend tell Eynsford the truth, or what she suspected the truth was. "Just allow me ta get the tea ready, my lord, and we'll go from there, all right?"

He nodded and then said in a low voice, "You were always my favorite of the bunch, you know."

Sorcha's mouth dropped open. "I beg yer pardon?"

Sheepishly, he smiled. "You were the only one to accept me in the beginning. You were the first to lend your support. You never shocked me with a bolt of lightning or anything like that. You are the embodiment of sweetness, Sorcha."

She'd had no idea he'd felt that way. "Thank ye, my lord."

"And from what I understand, you were the same way with Westfield and Kettering and my undeserving brothers. Unblinking acceptance."

Sorcha wouldn't really put it that way. And why did he think his brothers were so undeserving?

"Just be careful, lass," the marquess continued as his eyes lingered on her neck. "I know your fate is on a certain course right now, but I'd hate to see you lose the sweetness that is your nature. Not *every* entity is worthy of your acceptance."

Meaning Alec. He didn't have to say it; Eynsford's meaning was clear. But she'd known Alec her whole life, and she'd trust him with her heart, her body, and her future. She didn't want to have that particular conversation with the marquess, though, and certainly not in the hallway of The Black Horse Inn. So, she simply nodded her head instead.

Sorcha stepped inside her chambers to find a tray with a couple cups and a steaming teapot placed on a table near her bed. Luckily, all of her valises and portmanteaus that contained herbs, flowers, and seeds were awaiting her as well.

She quickly went to work and removed the lid of the teapot. In short order, she added a healthy dose of chamomile and another pinch of ginger for good measure. Then she retrieved a tiny flaxseed and placed it in the palm of her hand and made a fist. Sorcha imagined Cait smiling, healthy, and happy with just the right coloring to her face.

Sorcha opened her fist, touched the seed with the tip of her index finger, and couldn't help but smile as it turned to dust in her hand. Then she added the powder to the teapot and breathed in the soft aroma of chamomile. Cait would feel better in no time.

Just as Sorcha was about to toss the door open to inform Eynsford that the tea was ready, she found her maid, Maggie, in the hallway wearing the most confused expression. "Oh, there ye are, miss. The innkeeper is havin' a tub brought up for Mrs. MacQuarrie. I think he thinks that's ye, Miss Ferguson."

Sorcha bit her bottom lip. She supposed someone should tell her poor maid what was going on. Or some of it anyway. "Maggie, I am Mrs. MacQuarrie." How odd it felt to say those words aloud. At her servant's rounded eyes, Sorcha hastened to explain, "I mean I will be just as soon as we get home and talk ta Papa."

"Oh! That is wonderful news." Her maid grinned, but then her face fell. "But the innkeeper said…"

How was she to explain this so Maggie would understand but not think badly of her at the same time? "The innkeeper must have misunderstood, but tryin' ta explain it now will just make it more confusin'. A tub is on the way up, ye say?"

"Aye, miss."

"Wonderful." Sorcha smiled at her maid. "I am covered in travel dust. I need ta peek in on Lady Eynsford and then I'll be right back for my bath. Will ye help me with the tray?" She pointed to the table beside the bed.

Maggie bobbed a courtesy and then bustled across the room to retrieve the tea tray. Sorcha stepped into the hallway and knocked on Cait's and Eynsford's door.

"She's still sleeping," the marquess said softly as he opened the door.

"Well, she'll need ta be awake ta drink my special brew." Sorcha gestured to her maid a few steps behind.

Eynsford quickly ushered them both over the threshold. "Thank you, lass."

"This should work wonders," Sorcha promised as her maid deposited the tray on a table near the room's lone window. "Thank ye, Maggie. I'll return ta my chamber in just a moment."

As soon as her maid departed, Sorcha turned her attention to the marquess. "Ye should leave us for a bit too, my lord. I'll wake her and make certain she starts right in on the tea."

A series of expressions flashed across the poor man's face. He appeared completely lost, not knowing what to do about Cait. "But—"

Sorcha had some things to say to her friend that she didn't particularly want the marquess to overhear. "Why doona ye go for a quick walk and stretch yer legs? Ye've been all folded inta that coach for quite some time. Yer legs must be as sore as mine are."

He frowned. "Places like this bother her. All these strange people. If I'm not here to keep the images at bay, every future of every person in this inn will start to invade her thoughts. It's almost painful for her. My touch clears her mind."

Which, of course, Sorcha knew. Yet if Cait was right about her condition, then a piece of Eynsford was already with Cait and the troublesome images would keep their distance from the seer. However, Sorcha couldn't say as much to the marquess, not since she'd given her word that very day. "I need ta have Cait's full attention for the tea ta take effect, my lord. Just for a few minutes."

He looked nearly pained himself as he agreed with a nod and silently slid from the room.

Sorcha smoothed Cait's blond locks from her face. "Caitrin, ye need ta wake up," she began soothingly.

Cait groaned and her blue eyes fluttered open. "Sorch?"

"Hmm." Sorcha moved from Cait's bedside to pour a cup of her special tea. "I want ye a drink this."

Cait pushed up on her elbows and then sat up straight. "I feel awful."

Sorcha pressed the cup into Cait's hands. "Ye're no' the only one. Yer poor husband is nearly beside himself with worry. Ye have ta tell him, Cait."

But her friend shook her head stubbornly, as only Cait could. "No' until I ken for certain."

But she did know for certain; she just hadn't realized it. "Caitrin, ye are in The Black Horse Inn. Are ye plagued with any unwanted futures?"

Cait blinked at her as though she had just realized she wasn't bothered by the awful images. "Nay," she whispered. "My thoughts are my own."

"It's because ye are expectin' a bairn, Cait. Ye're expectin' *Eynsford*'s child. He doesn't need ta touch ye ta keep the futures from floodin' ye because he's already with ye."

The happiest smile Sorcha had ever seen graced Cait's face. "Aye, that makes sense."

Sorcha sat on the bed beside her friend and squeezed Cait's hand. "Please tell yer husband. The man is positively miserable."

Cait agreed with a nod, but then she shook her head at the last moment. "But, Alec... We have a long trip ahead of us, Sorch. I doona want ta make it more difficult."

"Alec already kens."

Cait almost dropped her tea. "Ye told him? Ye promised ye could keep yer trap shut." She smacked Sorcha's arm and somehow managed not to slosh any tea from the cup.

"I dinna tell him. He's a smart man." Sorcha rubbed her ill-used appendage. "And doona hit me, Cait."

Cait lifted the tea to her lips and inhaled. "Flax?" She turned up her nose like a finicky child.

Havers! Sorcha heaved an impatient sigh. "Drink the blasted tea, Cait. It'll help ye feel better."

"Flax?" Cait complained.

"It was *one* tiny seed." Sorcha tapped the bottom of the cup, silently encouraging Cait to drink. "If ye doona mind, I'd like ta cure yer travel sickness so we can get ta Edinburgh."

"Someone's in a hurry ta marry," Cait said with a soft, sarcastic whistle and a wink. Then her gaze dropped to Sorcha's neck. She sat forward on her knees to get a better look. "Sorcha, what is that?" she cried as she reached toward Sorcha's bite wound.

Sorcha covered it with the palm of her hand. If the marquess hadn't been so persistent, she'd have had time to cover it. "It's nothin'," she quipped, and stood up to bustle about the room.

"That is *no'* nothin', Sorch," Cait cried as she reached out, grabbed Sorcha's hand, and then tumbled her back onto the bed. "Let me see that thing," she ordered.

"It's really none of yer concern, Cait," Sorcha said as she felt the heat of embarrassment and anger creep up her face.

"He bit ye, did he?" Cait sat back against the headboard with a knowing grin.

"If ye must ken," Sorcha returned hotly, "he did."

"And how was it?" Cait nearly vibrated with something Sorcha didn't understand.

Sorcha took a deep breath. "Cait, I ken ye willna understand about this since ye have normal relations with Eynsford. But please try no' ta judge."

"Judge?" Cait cried, looking much too pleased with herself. Then she tugged at the collar of her own gown and showed Sorcha the mark at the base of her neck. "I am the last person ta judge ye, Sorch." She giggled.

"Ye had a vampyre bite ye as well?" Certainly Alec hadn't…

"*Havers*, no! Dash did it." She looked supremely pleased by that fact. "It's his mark. I like it." She shrugged. "I have wanted ta tell ye all about it for so long." Cait looked like she could dance across the room at any moment. "Now that ye've had relations with Alec, we can talk about everythin'."

Sorcha gasped and jumped to her feet. "I havena

had relations with Alec." She thought about it a moment. "Well, no' all the relations. No' that I'm aware of." Then she held up a hand to stop Cait's pending questions. "I'm fairly certain there's more ta it than what I've experienced." Then beneath her breath she muttered, "At least I hope there is. It's perfectly scandalous, is it no'?" She winced at the last.

"Dash bit me before he married me too."

"Tell me more," Sorcha prompted.

"He bit me the night he met me. After only a few moments. Then he was irrevocably tied ta me."

"Poor man," Sorcha teased. "He dinna even see ye comin'."

"I dinna see him comin' either," Cait lamented. "Is it no' wonderful?" She sobered. "What was it like?" She gestured toward Sorcha's neck.

"Amazin'," Sorcha sighed.

"Mine is just a mark. A way of solidifyin' our bond. Yers is more than that." She quieted. "Did he drink yer blood?"

Sorcha groaned. "Doona judge, Cait. Please?"

"Was it as wonderful as Rhiannon claims? Could ye feel what's inside him? Could ye feel his love for ye?" Cait reminded her of a child waiting for a birthday gift, all anxious exuberance and wanting.

"It was wonderful." But she hadn't felt his love for her. She'd felt his passion. And his grief. And his pain. And it had all overwhelmed her at once. His pleasure had taken the forefront. But she hadn't felt any love. Now that she thought about it, she hadn't felt that at all. She'd always assumed love would wash over her like a tidal wave. Like a loud song sung at the opera.

Like Rhiannon's wind when she was angry. Like… nothing she'd felt in Alec.

"Why so sad all of a sudden?" Cait asked, obviously growing alarmed at Sorcha's introspection.

"I couldna feel his love for me because he doesna love me." Sorcha probably shouldn't have said that aloud, and certainly not to the one woman Alec *had* always loved, but it was too late to take her words back once they had left her mouth.

Cait's face fell and she reached for Sorcha's hand. "I'm sure—"

"Stop, Caitrin." Sorcha scrambled from her spot. "I, um, have a bath waitin' for me."

"But, Sorch—"

"Just drink yer tea, Cait." Sorcha fled the room as quickly as she could before Cait could see the tears that had begun to pool in her eyes.

Twenty-Two

ALEC SAW A FLURRY OF SKIRTS RUSH FROM EYNSFORD'S room and into Sorcha's. Then the door slammed closed with a thud. What the devil? If that Lycan had hurt Sorcha, he wouldn't live to see the next full moon. Alec stomped down the corridor, but before he could even knock, soft sniffling from inside halted him.

"Sorcha," he called through the door. "What's wrong, lass?"

The sniffling stopped with an abrupt gasp. A second later, she said with feigned cheerfulness, "Nothin'."

But *nothing* wouldn't have made her bolt into her room as though the devil was chasing her. And *nothing* wouldn't make her cry like this. "Sorch, tell me what happened."

Not a sound came from within the chamber.

Damn it to hell! What the devil had happened? She'd been perfectly fine when she'd left his arms. Obviously something had transpired since their interlude. Sorcha was so sweet and sympathetic to a fault. Alec racked his brain, searching for an answer. "Did something happen with the tea? Is Cait all right?"

"Please just go away, Alec," Sorcha begged, her voice sounding constricted and anguished.

The hell he would. Alec wouldn't move from this spot for all the blood in London. "Sorcha, open the door."

Another sniffle, and Alec's chest hurt. He rubbed at it absently. He didn't really need her to open the door, not with his strength. He could reduce the door to a pile of splinters with one well-aimed hit. Alec lifted his arm…

"Sounds to me," came Eynsford's arrogant voice from the staircase, "as though the lass would like some time to herself, MacQuarrie. Can you not take a hint?"

Damn Eynsford! Alec looked over his shoulder as the Lycan ascended the final step. "Mind your own affairs."

The golden-haired Lycan stalked toward Alec, his dark amber eyes filled with fury. "I told you once before that I'll look out for Sorcha's best interests."

"No need any longer." Alec glared at his onetime rival. "As she's my fiancée, her interests are mine, Eynsford. Now do be a good dog and go lie down out of my way."

The Lycan snorted like an indignant wolf. "I don't care," he said so low that no one other than the two of them could possibly hear his words, "that she wears your mark like a brand. And I don't care how many of them she sports. Until your ring is on her finger, Miss Ferguson is under my protection. And in the meantime, should she come to her senses where you're concerned, I'll do everything in my power to help her extricate herself from your hold."

Wasn't it enough that the Englishman had already stolen one lass from Alec? Certainly, he didn't think he could take Sorcha from him too. She was sunshine and happiness and everything the remains of Alec's soul needed. At the very thought of losing her, his vision turned red at the edges.

"Perhaps I should remind you of what my kind is capable of. Sorcha is *mine* for now and for always. If you make one move to spirit her away from me, your wife will find herself wearing widow's weeds in the blink of an eye. Black is not Cait's color. She'd be very put out with you."

"Threats again, MacQuarrie? Don't you tire of making them?"

Where Eynsford was concerned? Hardly. "Leave my fiancée alone, unless you want to find out whether or not the threats are empty."

"Dash!" Cait's voice filtered into the hallway. "Is that ye?"

Eynsford's eyes flashed to his own doorway. "Yes, lass, I'll be right there." Then he turned back to Alec. "We are supposed to be making an attempt at getting along."

Alec hadn't yet ripped the Lycan's head from his shoulders. As far as he was concerned, he *was* making an attempt to get along with his old nemesis. "I believe your wife awaits you. Considering her coloring in the carriage all day, I'd hasten to her side, were I you."

Eynsford shot Alec a fierce look before he turned the handle to his own door and escaped inside the chamber, presumably to the bedside of his wife.

Alec turned his attention back to Sorcha's door and knocked softly. "Sorcha, let me in."

It seemed like forever before she said, "I doona feel quite like company right now, Alec. Please leave me ta myself."

Well, he wasn't going to force himself on her. Alec leaned his head against her door, missing the sparkle that was normally in her voice. How had things gone from bliss to... *this* in so short a time? Somehow Sorcha Ferguson had the ability to tie him up in knots like no else ever had. He'd spent the previous evening tossing and turning because of the lass, and he wasn't anxious to repeat the ordeal. "You know where to find me."

A sniff was her only reply.

Sorcha sent her regards for dinner. She still didn't feel quite like socializing with anyone, at least not until she could sort through her own thoughts. Alec was destined to be hers. Cait had apparently always known that. So why didn't he love her? Shouldn't he love her? After all, she loved him. She wasn't quite certain when that had happened or when she had realized it—but it was most definitely true.

She wouldn't feel so despondent otherwise. In fact, she probably wouldn't have concocted that outrageous Banbury tale about Alec spending every night in her room back in Castle Hythe if she didn't love him. There was no *probably* about it. She most definitely wouldn't have done something so foolish if she didn't love him. She hadn't given any thought to the one-sidedness of their situation until now.

She supposed it wasn't Alec's fault that he didn't love her. One didn't get to choose whom one loved. You either loved someone or you didn't. Wishing the situation was different wouldn't change the fact. Crying her eyes out over the matter wouldn't change the fact. Pounding her fist over and over into the lumpy inn bed wouldn't change the fact.

Things simply were what they were.

So what if all of her coven sisters had found men who loved them more than life? Two of them, in fact, loved their wives so much that they had physically changed from immortal vampyres to mortal men as a testament of that love. Most marriages weren't love matches. Her friends were abnormally fortunate in that regard. All four of them. Sorcha tried not to grimace at the thought. She didn't wish unhappiness on any of her coven sisters; she just wanted a little for herself. That wasn't so bad, was it? Even if the odds weren't in her favor.

Look at their mothers, for example. Of the previous generation of *Còig* witches, only three of the five could point to happy, love-filled marriages. Fortunately or unfortunately, depending upon how one looked at it, Sorcha's parents had been among the lucky ones. It had been fortunate for them. But perhaps it had been unfortunate for Sorcha because she'd always assumed she'd be loved and cherished as much as her mother had been.

Alec *did* care for her. She knew that. She'd always known that. She could feel it when he held her and kissed her and pleasured her. But it wasn't the same. It wasn't what she truly wanted. Though she'd made her bed as far as that was concerned. She'd made outlandish statements to the Duchess of Hythe that would ruin her if she didn't marry Alec, and she *had* let him pierce her flesh with his teeth. He'd marked her, and she was his.

No, she was most definitely past the point where she could change her mind about all of this. And she *did* love him. And he *was* destined to be hers. Could her love for him be enough for the both of them?

∽

For the second night in a row, Alec slept fitfully, if one could even call tossing and turning and pounding his pillow all night "sleep." He'd even paced the hallway for at least an hour, but that was different. That was so he could be closer to Sorcha, as he hadn't laid eyes on her since the brief flurry of her skirts when she'd dashed from Caitlin's room into her own.

Did Sorcha's crying have something to do with Cait? Had Cait seen what had transpired between Alec and Sorcha and blistered the little wood sprite's ears over it? Caitrin always was a little high in the instep. Certainly she didn't think to lecture *his* bride, not after the way she'd conducted herself with Eynsford on that blasted journey last winter.

That couldn't be what she was upset about, could it? Or did it have something to do with Cait and the bairn she carried? Could that be it? Was Sorcha already regretting the fact that she'd be marrying a man who couldn't give her children? That she'd be wasting her life on a dead man and giving up all she'd ever held dear? Everything she'd ever dreamed about for her future? That must be it.

It wasn't too late to set her free, was it? He could free her from her promise to marry him and tell the Duchess of Hythe that the lass needed a husband who loved her much more than she needed to prevent a scandal. That was it. He'd go to her and tell her she didn't have to live up to her end of this fool's bargain.

Alec dressed quickly, putting on his trousers, pulling a shirt over his head, and then stuffing his feet into his boots. It was the middle of the night. Very few people would be about. He slipped out the door, skulked quietly down the corridor, and quickly found himself outside Sorcha's chamber door.

He stood at her door and listened to her soft breathing through the crack in the doorframe. She was sound asleep. So, she'd obviously found some peace, or at least enough to let her rest. Should he bother her? He'd just look in on her. If her cheeks were wet with tears or her face blotchy from crying, he'd never forgive himself for making her suffer through the night. But, if she rested peacefully, he'd wait until the morning to free her from her promise to marry him.

With a hard turn of his wrist and a jerk to the door, he opened the door with a nearly silent click. He slipped inside and crossed to the side of the bed where he could look down at Sorcha's sleeping face. She looked like a little angel. She'd looked like a siren that afternoon when she'd ridden his lap in the throes of passion. And now she looked like a fresh-faced lady. The collar of her frilly white nightrail nearly covered the mark he'd left on her neck, the only evidence of their encounter aside from the one that was indelibly burned into his memory.

The look on Sorcha's face when she'd offered herself up to him had very nearly been his undoing. She'd quite naturally assumed that the prominence of his teeth meant he was hungry. And he had been. But he was hungry in more ways than one. Even looking down into her sleeping face made him want her. But he also saw more when he looked at Sorcha.

He saw long evenings by the fire with her cuddled in his arms. He saw long walks in the woods. He saw himself devouring her on every surface within the orangery he'd have to build for her after they were married. He could make her happy. He'd buy her anything she could ever want. And he'd even tolerate her coven sisters and their husbands, within reason.

Sorcha stirred and rubbed the side of her face into the pillow. Then her eyes suddenly blinked open. She smiled softly at him. "Alec?" she mumbled, her voice husky with sleep. "What are ye doin' here?"

He sat down on the side of the bed. "I just came to check on you. I was worried when you didn't come down for dinner. You made me suffer through a meal with Eynsford." He brushed a lock of hair from her forehead with gentle fingers.

"Where was Cait?" She reached up to rub the sleep from her eyes and rolled to her back.

"She was there," he said with a shrug.

"She's feelin' better?"

"Much better, apparently," he informed her. "Eynsford was grinning from ear to ear. It was purely sickening to watch the two of them."

"She told him?"

"She must have. I certainly didn't."

"They must be very happy," Sorcha said with a pleased sigh.

"He didn't stop touching her all night," Alec pretended to grouse. "It nearly spoiled the lamb for me."

"It still bothers ye ta see them together," Sorcha said quietly. She scooted away from him in the bed, moving as far to the other side as she could. Then she rolled to her side to face him and tucked a hand beneath her cheek.

"It doesn't bother me at all to see them together," he said. And it didn't. He wasn't sure when it had happened, but he no longer felt the same about Cait as he once had. "Why would you say that?" Alec reached down to tug his boots from his feet and then slid beneath the counterpane to join Sorcha. She didn't move. She barely blinked. But she didn't roll into his arms, either. He stayed to his side of the bed, tucked the pillow beneath his head, and just looked at her.

She regarded him quietly. Waiting. Waiting for what, he wasn't certain. But he could lie there in the quiet with her all night and not complain.

When she didn't respond, he continued, "Things between Cait and me were complicated for much too long. Eynsford is the one she was destined to be with. And she obviously knew that long before I did. I'm all right with it. I'm not brokenhearted over her anymore."

That was a contradiction if there ever had been one. He didn't have a heart to break. So, of course, he couldn't be brokenhearted. He couldn't fall in love, either.

He reached out and took her hand in his, the one that lay flat on the bedclothes. He covered it with his own and just looked at her. Finally, he broke the silence. "Why were you crying, lass?" he asked and then he watched her face closely.

"It's nothin'," Sorcha replied, and she tried to tug her hand from his.

"Don't," he warned. He held on to her fingertips until she gentled again and let him thread his fingers through hers. "I only came in here to be sure you were all right. I should probably go."

"Eynsford is probably already aware ye're here. It's too late ta sneak out now."

"I do not sneak," he said, mildly offended by the suggestion. He took a deep breath to fortify himself, although he didn't need one to live. "I came here for another reason too," he confessed.

Her eyebrows lifted marginally.

"I want to free you from your promise."

Her eyes narrowed. "Which promise would that be?"

"The one where you offered yourself up like a sacrificial lamb to save me from the certain agony of being married to that Overton chit." He watched her expression closely. "If you want to back out, Sorch, I'll tell the duchess you had a change of heart and that nothing happened between us that is outside the bounds of propriety."

"But it did," she whispered. And tears shimmered on her lashes again, building up like a dam that was about to overflow. He let her pull her hand back and watched as she laid her palm over the bite mark on her neck. She held her hand closely there against her pulse. "Somethin' outside the bounds of propriety did happen."

"Nothing that irrevocable," he reminded her. "You're still an innocent."

Her eyes narrowed. "I sincerely doubt that anyone would consider me an innocent at this point. I certainly doona think so."

"You could do better than me," he said quietly. Then he watched her face.

"Aye, I could." That was all she said. And she didn't smile. She didn't flinch. She didn't show remorse. She just yawned widely.

"Then why do you want to settle for someone of my ilk? You could have children. And a husband who doesn't need to feed on the life source of others. Particularly yours."

"If ye think ye can stop offerin' me pleasure that way, now that I've tasted it," she whispered, "ye better think again."

He couldn't keep from smiling at her.

"And yer heart could wake." She scooted closer to him in bed and laid a hand over his chest. "Just like Kettering's and Blodswell's did."

"That's not going to happen for me, Sorcha. Don't go into a marriage with me assuming that will be the outcome. Marry me because you want to spend your days by my side and your nights in my bed. Marry me because you want to spend your time with me."

"What if I fall in love with ye?" she whispered quietly.

He reached out for her hip and tugged her closer to him. "Then I will be the most honored of men."

"But ye willna be able ta love me back, is what

ye're sayin'?" She spoke from where her head rested beneath his chin, so he couldn't see her face.

"I'll be a good husband to you. And that's all I can offer." He waited, afraid to move. Afraid she would toss him from the room. Afraid she would cry again. Afraid she wouldn't care enough to have any emotion at all.

"I'll take it," she whispered as she spun in his arms and pressed her bottom into the spoon his body made when he wrapped around her. She settled peacefully within moments, and he lay awake for not long after, listening to her breathe. This was how it would be for the rest of their life together. Sorcha in his arms. Sorcha in his life. Sorcha in his bed. But he couldn't love her, though he wished he could. It was a shame to make the wood sprite settle, but he was just selfish enough to do so. And if Seamus Ferguson wouldn't accept his offer, Alec wasn't sure what he would do.

Twenty-Three

A SLEEPING SORCHA BURROWED CLOSER TO ALEC ON the bench, and he tightened his hold on the wood sprite. Over the last week, he had grown accustomed to having the lass at his side, and he smiled down at her. So peaceful, so trusting, so wonderful: he didn't deserve her.

Across the coach, Eynsford shifted in his seat and Alec briefly glanced at the Lycan. After more than a sennight of traveling with Sorcha, Caitrin, and Eynsford, Alec wasn't certain he liked the Lycan any better than he had before their journey began, but he could at least tolerate the man's company now. Most of the time, anyway.

The marquess still kept a close eye on Sorcha and made Alec's attempts at getting the lass alone more than difficult, but he also took the gentlest care with Caitrin. At one time, Eynsford's doting would have been one more reason to hate the man, but Alec instead found himself quietly envious. Not of Cait's affections, but of the Lycan's mortality. Eynsford *could* be the husband Cait needed. Eynsford *could* give Cait the children she deserved. Eynsford *could* grow old with his wife.

Alec knew he was a scoundrel for going ahead with the plan to make Sorcha his wife, but as the journey had turned into days upon days, he couldn't imagine letting her go. Of course, if Mr. Ferguson tossed Alec out of Ferguson house on his vampyre arse, he wouldn't have a thing to say about it. And there was every chance Sorcha's father would laugh Alec's offer right out the door. Seamus Ferguson had more wealth than most Scots. He didn't need Alec's fortune or connections to ensure his daughter's future. And he might not be keen on inviting a vampyre into his family.

Every time Alec mentioned as much to Sorcha, she'd giggle and remind him that her father had always been fond of him. But that had been Alec the mortal. Alec the vampyre was an entirely different person. Of course, he didn't have to reveal his true nature to the man who hopefully was his future father-in-law, but Alec couldn't start his life with Sorcha by deceiving her sire. It wouldn't bode well for their future, and they needed every bit of good fortune they could get their hands on.

Across the carriage on the opposite bench, Caitrin groaned slightly as she opened her eyes. At once, her husband offered her a flask of Sorcha's special tea. "We'll stop after we cross the border, lass. You can stretch your legs and get a breath of fresh air."

Cait only nodded in response. Then she once again closed her pretty blue eyes and fell back asleep against her husband's shoulder.

Alec somehow found himself smiling at his old nemesis. "You certainly aren't what I expected at our first meeting."

Warmth twinkled in the Lycan's golden eyes. "Our first meeting? You mean when I was covered in mud and dripping enough rainwater in that little inn that I had to pay extra for the mopping?"

That seemed like a lifetime ago. Alec had gone north to a friend's hunting box. He and a couple of the fellows had headed off to a local taproom to quench their thirst in both spirits and wenches. They were there when a gust of wind blew Cait inside the warm tavern. Eynsford wasn't five minutes behind her, all arrogant Englishman, using Cait's Christian name and barking orders as though he was already her husband. "You looked like a drowned rat, an enraged one."

Eynsford grinned. "Oh, I was furious that evening." He gestured with his head toward his now-sleeping wife. "She'd put a sleeping potion in a pot of tea and served it to me with the sweetest smile. I slept for two days, woke up with the worst headache of my life, and then nearly killed my driver with exhaustion to catch up to her."

"She was trying to escape you?" Alec had never known that bit of the story. Why hadn't Cait said something at the time? Probably because Alec had behaved like a most spectacular arse that evening. He almost cringed at the memory. He'd actually told Cait that if she wouldn't marry him, he didn't want her in his life at all. She'd nearly burst into tears at his pronouncement.

"She was trying to escape a future she couldn't see," Eynsford explained, breaking into Alec's reverie. "Caitie is a stubborn lass when she sets her mind on something."

Alec snorted. "Cait is a stubborn lass without even needing to set her mind on something. It's just who she is."

"Indeed," her husband agreed, good-naturedly. "But it was fear that had her running from me back then. Fear of the unknown, which I imagine for a clairvoyant must be fairly terrifying."

Fear of the unknown. Alec could relate to that feeling. He'd been living with it ever since his life had been taken from him beside a freezing loch in the Highlands and he was transformed into the parasite he'd since become. And now that fear was even stronger. He had no idea what the future held for him and Sorcha, and that was more terrifying than he could have ever imagined. If only he could be assured that they were making the right decision.

"Luckily," Eynsford continued, "she took that leap of faith, and I will be grateful for the rest of my life."

"A leap of faith," Alec muttered softly, but the Lycan, with his exceptional hearing, caught the words.

"I might have been a little boorish earlier, MacQuarrie. I hope you'll let me apologize."

"Boorish?" Alec echoed.

Chagrin settled on Eynsford's face. "I can be a bit overzealous as far as Cait's coven sisters go. Until recently, I never had a family of my own. These lasses welcomed me into their circle. Well, mostly anyway. And I can't help but try and protect them. It's my nature."

Alec had thought he knew everything there was to know about the *Còig*. He'd known all of its members his whole life. Was there something he didn't know? As he was about to marry one of them, he probably should find out if there was more. "What do you mean 'mostly'?"

Eynsford frowned and then glanced back at his wife as though to make sure Cait was still sleeping. "There's been a slight rift between Caitie and Elspeth Westfield."

Westfield. Just the name was like a dagger in Alec's no-longer-beating heart.

"It's nothing they can't overcome," the Lycan hastened to explain. "At least I hope it's not."

At one time, Cait and Elspeth had been the closest of all the witches, nearly inseparable. Alec couldn't imagine a rift coming between the two. "What happened?"

Eynsford sighed. "I did," he admitted. "Suffice it to say there is no love lost between me and the brothers Westfield. Each lass is loyal to her husband, which means the two of them are not as close as they once were."

Alec wasn't as close as he had once been to Benjamin Westfield, either. "What about this harmony thing Cait keeps going on about?"

"You'd have to ask her. I know their powers are stronger and more predictable when the five of them are getting along with each other than when they're not."

This generation of witches did seem stronger than the previous one, now that Alec thought about it. "Sorcha's and Cait's mothers were not fond of each other."

"That's certainly a euphemism." Eynsford nodded as though he was well aware of the fact. "From what I've been told, Fiona Macleod made a habit of over-stepping her bounds and manipulating the others with faux visions. When Bonnie Ferguson learned the truth about Fiona's deception, the two had a falling-out."

Fiona Macleod had manipulated the others with untrue visions? What a horrible thing to do to one's coven sisters. Alec had never heard that, and he gaped at the Lycan.

Eynsford took pity on him and explained, "Mrs. Macleod was an enterprising lass. She managed to keep Elspeth away from her father *and* was responsible for Lord Kettering's imprisonment. Apparently, she wanted to keep the coven pure of such mangy creatures as Lycans and vampyres."

But Bonnie Ferguson apparently had felt differently, just like her cheerful and inviting daughter. Alec glanced down at the sleeping witch curled up beside him. Hopefully, Seamus Ferguson was more in line with his late wife's way of thinking. He couldn't lose Sorcha.

In an attempt to lighten the mood, Alec caught Eynsford's eye once more. "I wouldn't really call vampyres *mangy*. Lycans, on the other hand…" He let his voice trail off and shrugged. Then he chuckled at Eynsford's feigned scowl. At least Alec assumed it was feigned; there was no fury in the man's eyes.

Once the four of them reached Edinburgh, Alec didn't imagine he'd ever seek Eynsford out of his own accord. But should they end up in the same parlor or ballroom, the two of them might be able to behave as gentlemen. Maybe.

～∞～

The motion Sorcha had become so accustomed to came to a stop, and she fluttered open her eyes. Beside her, Alec smiled the roguish smile she had quickly come to love. "Where are we?" she asked and rubbed the sleep from her eyes.

"We are in Scotland, lass." He tucked a curl behind her ear.

"Home?" she asked, unable to keep the smile from her voice. They'd made excellent time. She had thought they were still a few days away. But all the days on the road did tend to blend together after a while.

Alec shook his head. "Not home precisely, not yet anyway. We are finally off those Sassenach roads as we've just crossed the border into Gretna. And Eynsford promised Cait we'd stop for the night."

Gretna! What were the odds that Sorcha could talk Alec into an anvil wedding? It would certainly keep the Marquess of Eynsford's snout out of their affairs for the rest of the journey. And she could finally have Alec all to herself.

"Alec," she tugged his jacket and brought his face closer to hers, "we could have a blacksmith marry us here. Today. Right now."

He kissed the tip of her nose. "And have your father drive a stake in my heart once we reach Edinburgh? I'd rather not face his wrath, if you don't mind."

Sorcha giggled. Papa did not have a wrath to be feared. He was the most kind and generous man in all of Scotland. "He willna mind. I promise. Besides, ye dinna hear Mr. Crawford at Blaire's weddin'. He was adamant about no' performin' any more irregular ceremonies. And I doona want ta wait another three weeks for the banns."

This time Alec gently touched his lips to hers. "Crawford can be dealt with. And though you may not think your father would mind, I have to disagree with you, Sorch. You're his only daughter and the light of his life. He will want to be present at your wedding, and I cannot take that away from him."

Alec was right. She knew he was. Papa would be hurt if she married without him there to walk her down the aisle. But... Wait! Alec *couldn't* wait for her at the altar. Alec *couldn't* step foot inside the church. Why hadn't she thought of that before now?

"What is it, lass?" Alec tugged her from the darkened coach into the waning daylight as though to see her better. "Your heart is pounding. Is something wrong?"

Everything was wrong, and he looked so concerned, so handsome. She didn't know what to say. "Ye canna marry me in the church," just tumbled out of her mouth before she could stop it.

Realization seemed to strike him too, at that moment, and Alec shook his head. "Nay. But we'll figure a way, Sorcha. It just won't be a Gretna wedding."

Well, what other way was there? "But, Alec!" she complained. "How will we—"

He placed a finger against her lips to silence her. "There are other ways, lass."

"But—" She tried to talk around his finger.

"We *will* talk to your father before we're married. We *will* have his blessing. After that, if we have to come back to Gretna or declare ourselves publicly, we will do so." He pulled her into his embrace and Sorcha sighed, loving the feel of his arms around her. "I'm just as anxious to have you all to myself, Sorcha. Don't doubt that."

She nodded against his jacket and wished that she could hear even the faintest beat of his heart. Foolish, she knew. How many times did he have to tell her he wasn't going to change? But she couldn't let that bother her, not right now anyway. Alec was hers, after all. And she was only going to get married once. She should enjoy it.

Then his earlier words hit her and a giggle escaped her throat. "Did ye say we could declare ourselves publicly?" Why hadn't she thought of that herself? Because it was positively ridiculous. Such things weren't done anymore.

Alec pulled back from her and seemed to search her face, for what she wasn't sure. "Would that bother you?"

Sorcha grinned and shook her head, imagining their friends' faces. "Nay. It just seems so unorthodox. Mr. Crawford would have an apoplectic fit."

Alec's dark gaze bore into hers. If she wasn't mistaken, she'd think the blackness of his eyes had lightened just a bit. "Sorch, you're a witch and I'm a vampyre. Unorthodox goes without saying."

She supposed he was right. And the idea of marrying Alec by simply stating that they were married in front of everyone they held dear—no church, no clergyman, just the two of them and their friends—warmed her heart just a bit. All things considered, it was a bit more romantic than marching down the aisle, more intimate in a way. "We could declare ourselves here," she prodded, gesturing to the coaching inn. "Right now. Ta Cait, Eynsford, and whoever else is inside there."

He laughed and tucked her hand into the crook of his arm as he directed her toward the open doorway. "Aye, and we *could* have a blacksmith marry us here too. But we'll wait for your father, just the same."

"All right, all right." Sorcha rolled her eyes playfully. "Stubborn vampyre."

"Enchanting witch," he countered.

The Marquess of Eynsford stepped from the inn, and his amber gaze shifted from Sorcha to Alec and back. "Do tell me I'm not going to have to sit guard outside your room again, Miss Ferguson. *Please* tell me as we are close enough to Edinburgh that the pair of you can be trusted for an evening or two more."

Alec grumbled something unintelligible under his breath. Whatever he'd said, Sorcha was certain Eynsford had caught it because the marquess' brow furrowed and a scowl settled on his face.

"Perfect," Eynsford growled. "Keeping a lass' virtue intact is more difficult than sending a camel through the eye of a needle."

"Not really the way that quote goes," Alec drawled.

"Close enough."

Twenty-Four

ALEC WAS NEVER HAPPIER THAN WHEN HE SAW THE skyline of Edinburgh come into view. He had started to believe their journey would never end, that he would never hold Sorcha's attention all by himself again. That he'd never get to draw her close to him. That he'd never get rid of Eynsford.

Despite the peace between them the past few days, the wolf had never stopped sniffing into Alec's matters both day and night. He'd waylaid Alec outside Sorcha's quarters two evenings in a row. So, when Eynsford asked for a special concession, Alec couldn't quite believe his ears.

"Say again," he prodded, peering at the Lycan across the dimly lit coach.

Eynsford shrugged. "I said, would it be terribly remiss of me to ask that the carriage take us to Macleod's house first and then continue on to the Fergusons'?"

"I would like ta tell Papa about the bairn," Cait added quietly, her face expressionless and her blue eyes darkened by the waning light inside the carriage. "And I am so tired."

Alec pretended to be affronted as he turned his gaze on the Lycan. "You mean to say that you'll trust me with your precious baggage, Eynsford?" he gasped with mock outrage. Then he grinned down at Sorcha and leaned to kiss her forehead.

But she elbowed him in the side instead. "I am no' baggage," she giggled.

"I trust that you can return the lass to her father," Eynsford said with a nod. "And once you deliver her to Mr. Ferguson, she'll no longer be my responsibility."

"Ye'll need ta take her *straight* home," Cait scolded, but now her eyes were twinkling with something.

"I'll take her straight home." Straight to his house. Straight to his bed. He'd just *take* her. Alec had spent days with her pressed against his side in a carriage. He had felt her breast against his arm for the past few hours. And she seemed to be oblivious to it all. "Don't worry. I'll take care of her." He fought the grin those words provoked. Oh, aye, he would most certainly take care of her. Over and over again.

"Excellent," the marquess said with a grateful sigh. "I'll owe you a good turn, MacQuarrie."

He wouldn't owe him a damn thing. Because Alec was about to have the one thing he wanted most in the world—Sorcha. "I'll hold you to that," Alec replied absently, already somewhat lost in thoughts of how long he'd have with his witch before he had to return her to her father or have Seamus Ferguson come looking for her. He tugged at his jacket and adjusted his trousers in a sad attempt to hide his reaction to the thought of finally taking her, of having her all to himself.

Alec hadn't eaten in days. He could reasonably control his thirst for a week or better, and the amount of blood he needed was somewhat dependent on how active he was. As he'd been locked in a carriage for quite some time, he was all right with not having dined. But he couldn't go forever. He wanted Sorcha with a single-minded determination. He wanted to taste her, to drink her in. All of her. In every way.

Eynsford scowled at him. "You're certain you're capable of returning her to her father?"

"Oh, aye…" Of course, he was. He'd just need a few moments alone with her. Or more than a few. As many as he could take.

"Why does something tell me I'm making a bad decision?" the Lycan muttered.

Cait broke in, "Ye can trust Alec ta take care of her." Her lips lifted in a silent smile aimed at Sorcha, who flushed delicately and hid her face in his arm.

Thank goodness the sun was setting, or Eynsford would have certainly seen. And he would be none too happy to know his wife and her coven sister were pulling the wool over his eyes. The two of them were conspirators. Hell, Cait *knew* what was going to happen, and she was still more than happy to give her aid.

Cait laid her head on her husband's shoulder and said quietly, "He willna let any harm come ta her. I trust him."

"If *you're* certain," the marquess finally gave in.

The coach rumbled to a stop outside the elegant Macleod townhouse, and Eynsford alighted quickly and then held his hand out to Cait. But before Cait could escape into the waxing darkness, she leaned in, hugged Sorcha tightly, and said, "Ye willna need me ta educate ye about anythin' at all." She giggled as Sorcha let her go and shooed her from the carriage.

Sorcha lay back heavily against the squabs and closed her eyes, and then she groaned aloud.

"What is it, lass?" Alec asked. He wished he could read her mind. But she was such a mystery to him.

She turned her head slowly toward him and looked up and down the length of him. "Alone, at last," she purred.

"It's about damn time," he grumbled as he reached for her. She giggled as he picked her up and deposited her directly into his lap, her back against the carriage wall, her legs draped across his. He cupped the side of her neck and drew her head down. "Sorch," he groaned in protest, his mouth a mere breath from hers.

Sorcha fisted her delicate little hands in his shirt and tugged with all her might. "If ye change yer mind about marryin' me, I'll have ta do ye bodily harm, Alec MacQuarrie."

"Never," he grunted and punctuated his words with a quick kiss. Never would he surrender her. Not now. Not ever. He was a cad for not taking her immediately to her father. But he needed time with her. Time to be alone. He'd take her to her father shortly. Right after he'd thoroughly devoured the man's daughter. Oh, blast and damn, that would never do.

❧

Sorcha began to work at the fastenings on the front of her traveling gown, as desperate to be with Alec as he seemed to be with her. Her hands trembled as she worked until Alec finally brushed hers away with an impatient swipe. "Let me," he ordered. He didn't stop kissing her as his fingers worked. And within seconds, he had her bared down to her chemise, her gown shoved low around her hips. "We don't have long," he lamented.

"We doona need long," she whispered back against his lips. She felt rather than saw his smile.

"I mean we don't have long before the coach stops, Sorch," he chuckled. "I plan to take my time when we get to my house."

"Ye do?"

"I do," he affirmed. "Assuming Eynsford's man can be bought." With a roguish grin, he pounded on the coach roof and then called loudly out the window, "Renshaw, take us to my home and you'll be hand-somely rewarded." Alec turned his attention back to Sorcha and whispered across her lips, "There, I plan to taste every inch of you."

She flinched as he tugged her chemise from her shoulder and let it fall, and then did the same with the other side. She clutched at the material as though she needed it. She was naked beneath it. Didn't he know that? He couldn't just disrobe her completely in the carriage. Alec very gently tugged her hands from where she clutched the fabric and raised them to his lips, kissing the knuckles of each one in turn. Then he let his gaze devour her.

His teeth were fully distended, as was his manhood, which she could clearly feel beneath her bottom. She squirmed in his lap but instantly froze when she saw the darkness of his hand in the moonlight as he cupped the fair flesh of her breast and raised it toward his waiting mouth. "Alec," she breathed.

His gaze rose to meet hers, but his mouth did not. Instead, it covered that aching little bud that strained toward him while he looked into her eyes. A gentle tug from his lips and tongue had her reaching for the back of his head to draw him closer, to never let him go.

"*Havers!*" she whispered harshly. Even when he'd drunk her blood, he hadn't touched her this way. He'd touched her most intimate of places, but he hadn't embarked on this gentle, mind-blowing seduction. He hadn't attacked her with his lips and tongue and demanded her very soul in return.

With one last tug, he raised his head and kissed her lips softly, and then he dipped his head back toward her waiting breast. In the moonlight, his hair was black as night, his eyes as dark as nothingness, his lips as light as a feather, his tongue as tender as a baby's breath.

"I love ye, Alec," she couldn't keep from saying. He raised his head and looked at her, as though she'd surprised him. Then he began to right her clothing. "What is it? What did I say?"

He chuckled. "You said you love me. You can't take it back. I heard it with my own two ears, Sorch." He worked quickly at the fastenings of her gown.

"Then why are ye dressin' me?" *Havers*, she'd made a mess of things, which was the very last thing she wanted.

"My wanton little witch," he grumbled playfully. "We're home." He shrugged. "Well, we're at my home.

And, with your permission, I'd like to take you inside and finish what we started."

"Will ye do what ye just did, again?" she asked quietly, hoping her desperation didn't show in her voice. But the blood pumped through her veins so loudly that even she could hear it. Her belly had been in a constant plummet directly to her toes.

"I'll do it again and again and again and as many times as it takes." He laughed like the old Alec. "Or as many times as you'll let me."

The carriage rolled to a stop, and Sorcha could see Alec's large home outside the window. He gave her a small push to move her from his lap and followed her out the door when Lord Eynsford's driver dismounted to open it. "Thank you, Renshaw." Alec nodded to the coachman. "You're a good man."

"Of course, sir."

Alec offered his arm to Sorcha, which she readily accepted. She leaned heavily into his side as they started up the stone walkway toward the front door. "Do I look presentable?" she whispered.

"You looked dressed," he groused. "I quite prefer you the other way, if you must know the truth." He drew her toward the front door, his steps hurried and anxious. He wanted her. She could tell, and that made her heart pound even faster.

"Will yer servants talk?" she hissed at him.

"They're not expecting me," he assured her. "So, I'll just sneak you upstairs and no one will be the wiser." He kissed her quickly. "I feel like I'm sixteen years old again," he admitted and smiled like the old Alec she'd always known.

He slid a key from his pocket and quietly opened the front door. Then he slipped inside, pulling her in along with him. But before he could even take a step, a loud, very obnoxious cough sounded from the corridor. When it happened again, Sorcha couldn't help but think someone was choking in the hallway.

Alec groaned loudly. "You may come out, Gibson," he called.

His stoic butler peered around the corner and then bowed. "Mr. MacQuarrie, Miss Ferguson, so glad ye're home."

"Are ye all right, Gibson? I can make ye a tonic for that cough," Sorcha offered.

The butler very gently cleared his throat as though testing it. "I believe I'll be just fine, miss, but thank ye."

"You may excuse us, Gibson," Alec said crisply. That was a bit rude but obviously necessary since the man was lingering.

"I would if I could, sir," the butler said, his face pained. "But ye have a guest. A few of them, in fact. And I doona ken what ta do with them."

"Who might that be?" Alec asked as he pulled his gloves from his fingers and shook out of his coat.

"I doona rightly ken, sir. The man says he's Mr. Browning. And, uh, he brought his... sisters?" The last part came out as a question.

Charles Browning? Alec leaned back to peer down the corridor and listened closely. He could hear the dulcet tones of an *acquaintance* of his from London. He listened harder. He could also hear Tillie, a whore from *Brysi*, the club for vampyres where Alec had previously found sustenance.

"Who is it?" Sorcha whispered. "Do I ken Mr. Browning?"

"No," he clipped out. And she never would. Not if he could help it. "Let's go," he barked, as he dragged her back toward the front door with a tug of his fingers. "Inform my guests that I'll return shortly," he growled at Gibson.

The butler blanched at Alec's tone.

Damn it, what were the chances that a vampyre and a whore they'd both shared for a time would show up at his respectable home in Edinburgh on the *very* night he arrived home with his intended? Only in his very unlucky world. First Eynsford and now Browning. At this rate, he'd be married to Sorcha for a decade before he had her all to himself.

"You are right, dear!" Charles Browning's deep voice filtered down the corridor. "MacQuarrie *is* here, and he's got a morsel of his own."

Twenty-Five

SORCHA SLID FROM UNDER ALEC'S ARM TO SEE A TALL, auburn-haired man depart a parlor and stride in their direction. His black-as-night eyes told Sorcha more clearly than words that he was a vampyre. Alec's hand grasped her shoulder and pulled her closer to him. "Is this a friend of yers?"

At least she assumed he was a friend. The unfamiliar vampyre smiled rakishly and didn't appear a dangerous sort. "MacQuarrie, I had hoped you'd be here."

"Browning." There was a tightness to Alec's voice and Sorcha cocked her head to one side to better see her intended's face. "I can't even imagine what brings you to Edinburgh."

The English vampyre chuckled. "Oh, I'm sure you can. Tillie and I imposed on your staff until your arrival."

"For how many days?" Alec grumbled.

"Just a few. Do join us in your parlor so we can speak more openly."

Alec shook his head. "I would love to, but I must return Miss Ferguson to her father's care."

But Sorcha had no intention of returning to her father's side. Not while strange vampyres made themselves at home in MacQuarrie House. Not until she figured out why Alec was suddenly so on edge. "Alec, would ye mind if I had a spot of tea first? I find I'm quite parched from the journey."

"I'm certain your father has plenty of tea and biscuits awaiting you, lass," Alec said through gritted teeth.

"No' if Wallace is at home." Her brother had been accused more than once of eating the Fergusons out of house and home. It wasn't just a saying, but a fact as far as Wallace Ferguson was concerned.

Alec's irritated gaze sent Sorcha a warning, but it was no use. The interloping vampyre bowed low before her. "It doesn't appear that our friend is going to introduce us. Charles Browning at your service."

Alec huffed in annoyance. "Sorcha Ferguson, Charles Browning. Now really, Charles, I need to see the lass home."

Mr. Browning smirked. "Not so quickly, Alec. The chit said she was parched. And I, for one, would like to become better acquainted with your... friend."

"Fiancée," Alec corrected with a grumble.

The English vampyre chuckled. "So I heard, just wanted to see if the rumors were true." He reached a hand out to Sorcha. "Come along, Miss Ferguson. I promise not to bite."

Sorcha blinked at Mr. Browning. "How could ye possibly have heard our good news, sir?"

"Not in the corridor," Alec complained. He brushed Browning's arm aside and directed Sorcha toward the parlor his friend had exited minutes earlier.

Then he tossed over his shoulder at Gibson, "Tea, please. I'm certain the ladies could use refreshment."

Sorcha stepped into the parlor, and her eyes landed on a very pretty girl sitting on a black settee. The girl pushed her long brown hair over one bare shoulder, and Sorcha nearly gasped at the number of bite marks along the girl's neck and bare skin. *Havers!* She looked like a pincushion. The marks were tiny, but Sorcha knew what to look for, after all. She covered her own neck with the palm of her hand for a moment. Then she realized what she was doing and jerked it down.

Behind her, Alec cleared his throat. "Um, Sorch, this is…"

"Miss Harris," Mr. Browning put in smoothly, sliding into the parlor and crossing the room. He squeezed the girl's shoulder and gestured for Alec and Sorcha to take a seat. "I feel as though I've usurped your hosting duties, Alec."

"What does that tell you, Charles?" Alec muttered as he led Sorcha to a high-backed chair and then took its twin beside her. "That perhaps you shouldn't take over someone else's home and enchant their servants to do your bidding?"

Mr. Browning laughed again and dropped into the spot beside Miss Harris. "Your accommodations are better than staying at some musty inn. Besides, I couldn't take the chance you'd keep your lovely bride from me."

Alec frowned. "And Till… Miss Harris?"

The Englishman shrugged. "We all need our sustenance. Besides, Tillie has only ever seen London and not the good parts. She *wanted* to come with me."

Miss Harris nodded enthusiastically. "Scotland is so pretty. Very green."

A sinking feeling washed across Sorcha as she focused once again on Miss Harris' plethora of marks. How well did Alec know this girl? "Ye dinna answer me, Mr. Brownin'. How did ye hear that Alec and I are ta be married?"

Browning's dark eyes twinkled and he winked at her. "Heard a couple fellows at a hazard table talking about it a few days ago." Then he looked at Alec. "Radbourne has the worst possible luck. One would think that as a man with pockets to let, he'd stay away from games of chance."

"Damn Lycan," Alec growled. "What the devil was he thinking?"

The Englishman leaned forward as though they were conspirators and tapped his ear. "No one but me could hear them. The fellows seemed to think Miss Ferguson was too good for you. After hearing that, I knew I *had* to meet the chit." He smiled at Sorcha again.

Alec tensed beside her. "Miss Ferguson is not a chit, and I'd appreciate it if you'd take a more respectful tone with my intended, Charles."

Mr. Browning sat back in dazed amazement. "Never thought I'd see the day Alec MacQuarrie would be laid low by such a little slip of a thing." The man's gaze darted down the side of Sorcha's neck. "The offerings must be tempting, indeed."

"That is not up for discussion," Alec barked.

"My apologies," Mr. Browning shot back, but Sorcha could tell he wasn't sorry in the least. His black eyes twinkled in amusement.

Alec raked a hand through his hair. "Where are you off to next?" he asked.

The vampyre regarded him with a blank expression. "Off to? Do you mean to say that I'm not welcome at MacQuarrie House?" He placed a hand on his chest and feigned a look of surprise.

"I run a respectable household," Alec informed him. "Miss Ferguson is one of the only people who even knows what I am. I'll not have you ruin my life here with your whoring and ungentlemanly ways." He sighed heavily. "No offense, Tillie," he said more softly to the English girl.

"None taken," she chirped back, sitting a little higher in her chair.

Had he just called her by her given name? Sorcha bristled. "Just how is it that ye all ken each other?" she asked.

"Oh, from *Brysi*," Miss Harris said with a light wave of her hand.

Brysi!

Mr. Browning opened his mouth to speak, but Alec cut him off. "It's a gentleman's club for those of our kind, lass," he explained.

Oh, she knew exactly what it was. She just couldn't believe one of the club's whores was sitting a few feet from her. "And what does Miss Harris do there?" Sorcha retorted.

Alec avoided her gaze.

"Alec?" she prompted, wondering if he would be honest about the situation.

A voice from behind Sorcha's back made the hair on her arms stand up. "She's a lady's maid. Mine, in fact."

Sorcha jumped to her feet and spun around, while Alec mumbled something to the other vampyre under his breath and came to his feet as well. In the doorway stood a breathtaking woman, her light hair loose about her shoulders, her green eyes flashing. Her gown was cut scandalously low and showed a bit too much of her ankle as well. But she was beautiful by anyone's standards. In fact, she looked a little like Cait, except for her eyes and pointy chin.

"I'm a lot of things, miss," Miss Harris said hotly. "But a lady's maid ain't one of 'em."

"Yet for this trip, that's the ruse we all agreed upon," the blonde snapped.

"No. We agreed we'd be sisters."

"As though I'd be *your* sister."

Mr. Browning looked mildly amused by the whole situation. "Now, now, no need to fight over me, my dears," he said with a chuckle. "Or MacQuarrie."

"Why did you bring *her*?" Alec shot at Mr. Browning.

"Why, for you, of course." He dropped an arm around Miss Harris' shoulders and whispered something to her that made her blush furiously. Then he raised his head, looked directly at Sorcha, and said, "Tillie's for me, but I thought Alec could use a bite to eat. I know how squeamish he is about enchanting the innocent." His gaze dropped to Sorcha's neck again. "Though that appears to have changed."

Sorcha threaded her arm through Alec's and leaned into his side. "Introduce me ta the lady, Alec," she said softly.

No one had ever mistaken Delia Sewell for a lady, at least not that Alec was aware of. Then again, the first time he'd laid eyes on the Cyprian she'd been lounging on a divan at *Brysi*, wearing rouge on her cheeks and not much else. God, he'd rather keep all of that from Sorcha.

In the chair beside him, Sorcha huffed out an impatient breath of air. He had to say something soon. Damn Charles to hell for bringing this *mess* to his doorstep. Frustrated, Alec flopped his hand between the two women. "Miss Ferguson, meet Miss Sewell."

"It's very nice ta meet ye," Sorcha said, her voice quiet and sure. She smiled in greeting, which caused Delia to look down her nose at Sorcha. How dare the Cyprian take a superior attitude with his intended? Sorcha was worth ten of Delia. And even more than that.

"Likewise," Delia replied with a dismissive nod.

"How was yer journey ta Edinburgh?" Sorcha asked.

Delia stepped farther into the room and perched herself on the arm of Alec's chair as though she belonged there. "As eventful as any other." She looked at Alec from beneath hooded lashes. "Do you remember the time *we* went to the country for the weekend, just the two of us?"

Alec managed a grunt, but that was all. Had the woman lost her blasted mind? A muscle along his jaw began to twitch, and he could just imagine that his face was a brilliant purple.

"We had the most splendid trip." Delia shot Sorcha another superior glance. Damn her.

"I really don't think—" Alec began.

But Delia spoke over him, "It rained and we spent most of the time in bed, when we weren't snuggling together in the coach." Her deep throaty laugh nearly took over the room. Alec remembered that trip well. He'd paid her handsomely to go along with him, to be his paramour for a short time, just for the convenience of having her life force at hand. Obviously, she'd thought more of the occasion than he had.

Sorcha visibly stiffened in her seat, which made Alec rise from his spot. "We'll need to be on our way," he tossed out to the room at large. "I promised to have Miss Ferguson back to her father posthaste." He looked down into Sorcha's eyes as she gazed up at him. "Are you ready, love?" Storms brewed behind her lashes. Thank God, Rhiannon wasn't nearby or a true storm would be brewing indoors.

Sorcha rose from her seat, squared her shoulders, and said, "I can see myself home just fine, Alec." Then she started for the door.

He caught her arm and pulled her back to him, and then he whispered, "I'll accompany you. I had planned to have a talk with your father tonight, anyway."

"Regrettably, Alec," she shot back, her voice cracking only once, "I find myself in need of some time alone. Renshaw can see me back ta my home." She glanced around Alec's town house. "This certainly isn't it."

She started again for the door, and he found himself chasing after her like a puppy at her heels. "Sorch, wait," he tried.

"It was nice ta meet ye all," Sorcha said properly to the group. Then she turned on her heel and quit the room, her nose held high in the air, her shoulders proudly back.

It wasn't until she was outside the front door that she allowed the facade to crumble. Sorcha caressed a strand of ivy that trailed up the house front. She whispered to the plant as she stroked it lovingly.

"Sorch!" Alec's hand on her shoulder made her jump.

"Oh, Alec." She frowned at him. Then she shook her head quickly and started down the steps toward the coach. "Ye should have told me."

"Told you what?" he asked as he reached for her fingertips.

She stopped and turned back to face him. "That ye have a *mistress*, Alec," she whispered. Her hand came up to stroke the day-old beard stubble on his face. "As much as I love ye, I refuse ta share ye." She inhaled deeply and graced him with a watery smile. "She's beautiful, by the way. Such a resemblance ta Caitrin. Miss Sewell will suit ye well until ye find a wife of yer own."

"I've already found a wife of my own," he ground out. How dare she assume his feelings had changed? How dare she let Delia's presence change anything? How dare she throw Caitrin's name at him again? "It's *you*, Sorch."

"Then what is she ta ye?" She watched his face closely.

"She's a whore," he bit out. "Nothing more. Nothing less."

"Ye've bitten her?" She looked so sad as she said the words.

He nodded. He wouldn't lie to her. But what did she expect? He *had* to drink blood to survive. And he'd not apologize for that.

"Ye've shared her bed?" She stroked his face again, her voice silky soft.

"Sorcha, this is not a fitting conversation for a gentleman and his bride-to-be." He knew he sounded like an arse before the words even came out of his mouth. But he couldn't help it. Discussing a mistress with a fiancée just wasn't done, and she was making him more than uncomfortable.

"I ken ye have shared her bed. I can see it in the way she looks at ye."

"You see an opportunistic woman who lets any number of vampyres into her bed in exchange for pleasure and a few coins."

Sorcha looked thoughtful for a moment. "I'm goin' home, Alec," she finally said. He made a move to follow her. But she held up a hand. "The way I see it is this—she offers ye the same thing I did, my body and my blood, in exchange for a bit of pleasure and some coin." She looked at his house and then down at his fine clothing. "So, what makes us different?"

There were so many answers to that question that he couldn't even pick one. "You are mine," he ground out.

"Yet ye said yerself ye can never, ever love me, so I doona ken what's so different about us after all." Then she fled into Eynsford's still waiting carriage and departed. She was gone before Alec could even gather enough thought to chase after her.

❧

Sorcha settled back against the squabs and fought the heavy need to cry. She'd been fortunate to find a man to love. And unfortunate that he was a man who couldn't love her back. He'd bitten that woman. That whore. That piece of perfection. And the woman who was head over heels in love with him.

Sure, he'd bitten Sorcha too. And he'd given her pleasure. But he'd never given her his heart. In fact, he's given her his staunch resolve that it wasn't his to give. She'd thought she was all right with that. And she probably would have been, had Miss Sewell not sauntered into Alec's parlor, reminding Sorcha that one woman's blood was as good as another's. She was nothing special to Alec, and she never would be. And she didn't think she could live with that after all.

Alec hadn't asked her father for her hand yet. There was still time to undo what hadn't yet been done. Sorcha knocked on the roof of the carriage and called out to Renshaw to take her to the Westfields' instead of driving her home. Perhaps Elspeth could heal a broken heart before it shattered into a million pieces.

Twenty-Six

As soon as Sorcha spotted Westfield Manor through the coach window, she took a calming breath. More than anything in the world, she wanted Elspeth to wrap her in comforting warmth. She wanted the healer to ease all her pain. She wanted to feel happy. Or to feel nothing at all. *Nothing* was preferable to the dull ache that slowly constricted her heart.

The carriage rumbled up the stony drive and Sorcha closed her eyes, feeling every bump until the conveyance finally came to a stop. The coachman opened the door and offered Sorcha his hand. Worry lined the man's face, and she tried her best to assure him with a smile. "Thank ye for everythin', Renshaw. Ye should probably head back ta Mr. Macleod's. I think I'll be here a while and then I'll return in Lord Benjamin's carriage."

"Is everything all right, Miss Ferguson?"

Oh, she wished he hadn't asked that. Tears stung the backs of her eyelids. "Aye. Just please doona mention any of this ta Lord Eynsford." Cait would know anyway, and that was awful enough.

Reluctantly, the coachman nodded. Then Sorcha scurried past him up the stone steps to the large oak door. Before she could even knock, the Westfields' young butler opened the door. "Miss Ferguson! I had no idea ye were back home." He held the door wide. "Come in, come in, lass."

She crossed the threshold and tried to smile at the exuberant butler. "Please tell me Lady Elspeth is in, Burns." It would be just her luck to show up here and have Elspeth aiding a midwife on the other side of town.

He winked at her and shut the front door. "Her ladyship is in the nursery, Miss Ferguson."

The nursery. Thank heavens she was home. "I ken the way, Burns. I'll surprise her, if ye doona mind."

Burns nodded; warmth and cheer nearly radiated from him. "I think she would like that, lass."

Sorcha climbed two sets of stairs and wound her way down one corridor and then one more before finally reaching the massive nursery. One would think Lord Benjamin planned on raising an entire pack of Lycans from the sheer size of the room. Thus far, he had only filled it with a fiery-haired witch-to-be, a tiny one at that. From the doorway, Sorcha heard little Rose Westfield's childish giggle, and the sound nearly brought her to tears, though she wasn't certain why.

She must have made some sort of anguished sound because an instant later, Elspeth stood just inside the nursery, concern etched across her brow. "Sorcha!" she wailed, her red locks bouncing about her shoulders. "*Havers!* I thought ye were in Kent."

Kent, where all her plans for a Lycan-filled future had gone awry. Sorcha couldn't hold back the tears any longer, not when she was standing so close to the one witch who had always seemed like more than a coven sister. Sobs so deep that Sorcha didn't know where they came from threatened to cleave her in two. Elspeth caught her and held her close.

"Oh, Sorcha! What is it, love?" the healer crooned. "Surely it canna be this bad."

But it was every bit as bad as that and worse. Sorcha couldn't even speak. She wanted to, but words just wouldn't come. All she could do was sob.

Then the baby started to cry too. A second later, quick footsteps pounded up the staircase. "Ellie!" Lord Benjamin called from somewhere below. "What the devil?"

"It's Sorcha," Elspeth called back, smoothing a hand down Sorcha's back. "I think Rose is cryin' sympathetically. Come and take her, will ye?"

Havers! Sorcha didn't want Lord Benjamin to see her like this. She tried to stop her own crying, which only made her hiccup loudly. It was one thing for Elspeth to see her like this. Elspeth was like the older sister she'd never had. The healer was the kindest, most caring soul Sorcha knew. Elspeth could heal her broken heart. But Lord Benjamin was a *man*. A Lycan man at that. And Alec MacQuarrie's oldest friend, or ex-oldest friend. Either way it didn't matter. She just didn't want to see him. Not right now.

Before she could even semi-compose herself, Lord Benjamin Westfield stood behind her. "Good God, Sorch!" he breathed. "Are you hurt?"

Oh, she was hurt more than she ever had thought possible. But she didn't want to tell *him* that. He sounded so concerned, which only made her humiliation that much worse. And she hated it when he handed her a handkerchief. She must look a sight.

"Stay with Rose and let me see ta Sorcha," Elspeth suggested, and she began to tow Sorcha down the corridor.

Sorcha let her friend lead her into a softly lit private parlor and dutifully sat on a comfy chintz settee. Elspeth settled in beside her and grasped Sorcha's hands. "Take a deep breath, love."

Sorcha nodded and did as her friend asked. Her jagged breathing started to smooth out, and she began to feel like the most foolish idiot in all of Scotland.

"Can ye talk now?" Elspeth leaned close, looking into Sorcha's eyes.

She thought she could talk, so she nodded. "I-I need ye ta heal me, El."

The worry didn't vanish from Elspeth's face, and she just squeezed Sorcha's hands tighter. "I doona feel any sickness in ye."

Sorcha closed her eyes so she wouldn't have to see her friend's face. "My heart is broken, El. I need ye ta fix it. I just want ta be myself again. I want ta start over."

Elspeth sighed heavily. "Oh, Sorch. That's no' somethin' I can do. Matters of the heart are beyond my powers."

Sorcha's eyes flew back open. Elspeth *had* to help her. She just had to. "But—"

"Who broke yer heart? Was it one of Eynsford's scurrilous brothers? Which one was it? What did he do?"

Sorcha choked on a sob. How she wished she'd stuck to her original plan. "Nay." She shook her head. "Lord Radbourne or one of the others would have been better. One of *them* could have at least fallen in love with me. *Why* did I lose sight of my goal?"

Because she'd stupidly, foolishly, shamefully fallen for a man who could never be hers. Not in the way she needed him to be.

"What happened?" Elspeth's calm voice floated over Sorcha like a warm blanket.

"It doesna matter. I just need ta be healed. I want ta be whole again. There must be somethin' ye can do. Please, El."

Elspeth smoothed a tear from Sorcha's cheek. "If there was somethin' I could do, Sorch, I would have done it for myself when Ben broke my heart."

"Blasted men," Sorcha grumbled. "Always breakin' hearts. They ought ta be drawn and quartered, the lot of them."

Elspeth's eyes grew wide, and she shot out of her seat. "*Havers!*" she cried, rushing toward a potted iris in the corner of the room. At least it used to be a potted iris. Now it was a cloud of black smoke. "I've never seen ye make a plant burn up like that before." Elspeth fanned the smoldering plant, as though to air out the room. "Ye better tell me what this is about or there willna be a flower, shrub, or tree that is safe in yer presence."

It was hardly the poor iris' fault that men were such feckless creatures, but Sorcha was afraid to try and even help the poor plant for fear of making it worse. "What did ye do, El? How did ye get over the heartache Ben put ye through?"

The healing witch looked toward the doorway as though she expected her once-feckless husband to appear. "I had ta forgive him."

"Forgive him?" The last person she wanted to think about forgiving right now was Alec MacQuarrie. He could rot with his friend Mr. Browning and the two English whores for all Sorcha cared.

"I had ta make peace with the situation," Elspeth explained.

From the doorway, Lord Benjamin cleared his throat and Sorcha turned a scathing glare on the man she normally adored. He bounced little Rose in his arms, though concern still clouded his eyes. "Rose was worried about her godmother."

"Ben," Elspeth chided, "we are talkin'."

He pointed to his left ear with a look of sarcasm on his face. "And I can't help overhearing, so I might as well join you." Then he glanced again at Sorcha. "Am I to take from the tears and damaged iris that your Lycan hunt didn't go as planned?"

"Ben!" Elspeth hissed. "Ye are no' helpin'."

Lord Benjamin shrugged, stepped into the room, and then dropped into a chair across from Sorcha. "Tell me your problems, lass. I may have a different way of looking at them."

Meaning he was a *man*. Her eyes dropped to her lap and she said nothing.

"Come now," he said softly. "I know you had your heart set on one of Eynsford's brothers. But you wouldn't want to be a relation of *his*."

Elspeth returned to the settee and resumed her spot beside Sorcha. "Ben, ye're no' helpin'," she said again.

"Besides Cait has told her more times than I can count that a Lycan is no' in Sorcha's future."

"Cait can go hang," Sorcha grumbled, which earned her twin gasps-from both Elspeth and her Lycan husband. But Sorcha wouldn't take it back. She didn't want to hear another word about Cait or her visions. No, there were no Lycans in Sorcha's future, according to Cait. The only man she could look forward to was a vampyre who could never love her. It wasn't fair! "If I want a Lycan, I doona think I should let Cait's vision stand in my way. Besides…"

"Yes?" Lord Benjamin sat forward in his seat, shifting Rose from one arm to the other.

"I ken what Cait has seen for me, and I doona want any part of it."

"She told ye?" Elspeth gasped. Everyone knew it was unspeakable for Cait to share the futures she saw. It went against the very principles of her gift.

Sorcha turned back to her coven sister. "Do *ye* ken what she saw for me?" It would be beyond the pale if Cait had told others, but never her. Elspeth simply blinked at her, which really didn't answer Sorcha's question in the least. "Well, it doesna matter. I willna marry a vampyre who canna love me. Ye healed a wolf who was broken, El. There's got ta be a way ta mend my heart. Tell me ye'll try."

"Vampyre?" Benjamin echoed. "Caitrin says your future is with a vampyre?"

"It doesna matter what Cait says. I'll make my own future. Just as soon as Elspeth heals me."

"For yer heart ta be broken, ye must have fallen for this creature. Perhaps ye should listen ta Cait."

"Perhaps ye should just—"

"Alec," Benjamin muttered.

Sorcha sucked in a breath and stared at the Lycan. How had he figured that out so quickly?

He shook his head as though he hardly believed the story. "It is him, isn't it?"

Tears sprung to her eyes again. "I doona want ta talk about him."

❦

Alec paced back and forth at the foot of his bed, trying to decide how on earth he'd gotten into this mess. One minute, he'd had Sorcha in his arms and very nearly had her in his bed, and the next, she was gone, leaving him with a rakish vampyre and two whores, one of whom appeared to be suffering from that vague human affliction called love, or perhaps it was simply jealousy. He scrubbed his forehead in frustration.

When Sorcha left, she'd taken everything that was bright in his life with her. His passion. His happiness. His future. She'd walked right out the door and taken it all with her. Now he had to get it back. He just had to. The utter look of devastation on her face would have broken his heart, if he still had one. In his case, it just worried him. It worried him to no end that he'd messed up his only chance with her. He worried that he'd somehow hurt her. And that was just intolerable. He'd kill anyone who dared to wipe the smile from his witch's face. Here he'd gone and done it himself.

A scratch sounded at his door. "Go away," he groused at the noise.

"Mr. MacQuarrie," Gibson called out hesitantly. "I'm sorry ta bother ye, but ye have a visitor."

Alec opened the door with such force that the old man tumbled into the room. "Haven't you let enough people into this house for one day?" he snapped.

The butler adjusted his jacket and squared his shoulders. "I admitted the others a few days ago," he amended. "Mr. Browning assured me that he and his sisters were great friends of yers from London. And that ye'd be highly irritated if I didn't see ta yer wishes and allow them ta stay until yer return."

Alec shot Gibson a look of incredulity. "You know good and well that those women are not his sisters," he scolded. "You let a couple of whores into my house."

"I dinna ken that at the time, sir. But I do ken it now. That's why they have been removed ta the Thorne and Rose for the duration of their stay. I assured them ye'd be most happy ta pay for their lodgings." The butler looked supremely satisfied with himself.

"I thought it would be more difficult than that," Alec muttered, scratching at the day's growth of beard stubble that itched his cheek. Then he narrowed his eyes at his butler. "I'd have sacked you if you hadn't figured out how to do that."

"I can be crafty when necessary, sir," Gibson said, still smiling a satisfied grin. "But ye have another guest in the parlor, sir. Lord Benjamin has come ta visit."

"You can tell Lord Benjamin to go straight to the devil," Alec said. That overgrown dog was the last person he wanted to see. Now or ever.

Alec sniffed at the air. He could already smell the

Lycan's stench inside his home. Bloody perfect. All he needed to make the evening a complete disaster was a meeting with Ben Westfield.

A voice roared from belowstairs. "If Gibson tells me to go straight to the devil, I'll put him in a cupboard until the morning, and then I'll come and find you myself!"

Gibson's jaw dropped open. There had never been any love lost between his butler and Ben Westfield.

"He would do no such thing," Alec assured the old man, though he wasn't so certain himself.

"Yes, I would!" Ben called from belowstairs again. "Try me and see, MacQuarrie."

"How did he hear that, sir?" Gibson asked, lowering his voice in surprise.

Damn Ben's Lycan hearing. He could hear a pin drop in the house next door. Of course, he could hear Alec's and Gibson's mutterings.

"Sound carries in this house," Alec replied.

"No' that well," the butler contradicted.

"It won't be the only thing being carried if you don't get your arse down those stairs and come talk to me!" Ben bellowed, his voice growing louder and louder. The damn neighbors would hear him at this rate.

Alec glanced at his astounded butler. "Lord Benjamin was dropped on his head as a bairn. It obviously affected his hearing. And his common sense."

"My common sense is fine!" the irate Lycan belowstairs bellowed again. "It's my house that's in a state of upheaval. An enchanting lady who normally has a green thumb is destroying every plant and flower

I possess. And I am fairly certain she would be most pleased with me if I buried your lying arse somewhere on Arthur's Seat!"

Sorcha was at Westfield's? Alec shot out the door and down the stairs so fast that the old butler could only stand and stare. Alec's oldest and dearest friend leaned casually in the doorway of the parlor and glared at him with a look of bemusement. "Finally got your attention, did I?"

"Sorcha's at your home?" Alec managed to choke out.

"So nice to see you too," Ben drawled as he crossed his arms over his chest.

"I wish I could say the same."

Ben started down the corridor toward Alec's study.

"Where are you going?" he called to his friend's retreating back. Then Alec followed. Damn, who was the dog here? Him or Westfield?

"I assume you still have whisky, even though you can no longer imbibe," Ben mumbled as he shuffled through Alec's sideboard. He grinned broadly as he found the decanter he wanted and poured himself a tumbler full of the amber liquid. Then he dropped into a wide chair across from Alec's desk.

"Do make yourself at home, why don't you?" Alec groused as he dropped into his own chair behind the desk.

"I believe I will, since my own is in a state of upheaval. And it's all your fault." Ben took a slow swallow from his glass. Then he leaned forward and speared Alec with a glance. "I quite like sleeping with my wife."

"I don't need to know about your bedroom

proclivities, Westfield," Alec said as he tried to look affronted by the mere suggestion.

"I like sleeping with my wife for a lot of reasons, though the likelihood of that happening this evening diminishes each moment Ellie tries to soothe Sorcha, and all because *you* had the stupidity to bring your mistress into the sight of your intended. Now tell me, what kind of a fool does that?"

"You're a fine one to talk about being foolish." If they were to tally up each of their mistakes, Ben's list would stretch from here to Aberdeen.

Ben shrugged. "We can discuss my sins if you'd like, though I hardly see the point as doing so won't help you with Sorcha."

"I don't need your help with Sorcha." He didn't need anything from his old friend, other than to have the man turn tail and depart his home.

"Oh, I beg to differ. You need all the help you can get."

"My situation is none of your concern." Alec tried to sound arrogant and unconcerned himself, but he'd failed miserably, he was afraid.

"But it is," Ben countered. "Ellie and Sorcha are connected, and therefore my wife's state of mind is very much my concern."

That damn harmony thing again. Alec nearly groaned.

"Now who installs their mistress in their home?" Ben pressed. "Does this woman mean something to you?"

For the love of God! "She's not my mistress. She's a whore. Nothing more, nothing less."

Ben drew in a deep breath and leaned back in the chair. "Don't ever let Ellie catch you saying that."

Whatever the devil that meant. "Just leave, Ben."

His onetime friend sighed. "I know you detest my kind, Alec." He held up a hand when Alec would have interrupted. "But I can't change what I am any more than you can."

"You could have told me," Alec muttered.

"No, I couldn't. There are covenants that prevent that." He shrugged his shoulders. "And Simon would have had my head if I'd even tried." He looked so directly at Alec that he wanted to look away, but he refused to do so. "I did want to tell you more than once throughout the years. It just wasn't possible."

"But now I know." Alec wasn't certain whether that was a good thing or a bad thing.

"Just as I know what you are," Ben retorted.

"At least you *like* what you are," Alec said quietly.

But Ben heard him anyway. "Not always. There was a time when I detested what I was. It made me feel out of control. I even hurt Ellie because of it. Thank God, she forgave me. I couldn't live without her."

Alec made a gagging sound that brought a smile to the Lycan's face.

"You are not immune to love, my friend," Ben informed him.

"I have no aspirations of love," Alec scoffed. But something within him ached, like a piece of him was being torn in two. He rubbed at his chest absently.

"Something wrong?" Ben asked, his face etched with concern.

"No." Alec waved the Lycan's questions aside. "Where is Sorcha now?"

"She was at the Manor when I left, begging Ellie

to heal her broken heart." Ben took another sip of his whisky. What Alec wouldn't give to taste that again, to feel numb from it. "She has cried until there are no tears left. I can't tell you how painful it is to hear her profess how much she loves you, even being willing to settle for someone who can't love her back. But she's not willing to settle for someone who can't be faithful to her. She's a smart lass, that one."

Alec hurt again. He hadn't hurt since he'd been turned. What the devil? "Will Elspeth help her?" All things considered, Sorcha would be better off if she didn't love him. Of course, he'd be utterly destroyed if she stopped, but it would be in her best interest.

"She doesn't have that kind of power." Ben took a deep breath. "But you do."

"I don't know what to do." The pain of separation between him and his old friend began to ease somewhat, and Alec felt calmer than he had in quite some time. The only person who made him feel better than this was Sorcha. His Sorcha.

"You know, there's an old saying that we Lycans live by."

"And I assume you'll burden me with it?" Alec quipped.

"It speaks of the fact that a Lycan cannot love another until he learns to love himself. I know you hate what you are now." When Alec would have interrupted, Ben held up a hand. "I know you do. I can see it all over your face. But you can't change it. You can either continue with this futile self-loathing, or you let that lass love you and give her the best life she could have ever dreamed of."

"She deserves better than a life with me. But I'm

just selfish enough to keep her from having it." He hated that about himself. But the thought of sleeping in a cold and empty bed for the rest of his life made him feel hollow inside.

"As things stood when I left home, she wouldn't have you if the Regent ordered her to do so right now. So, I'd suggest you dust off your courting clothes and get to work on persuading the lass, not to mention her father, that you're the right one for her."

"What if I'm not?"

"Then you'll have to work on that." Ben shrugged. "Besides, there's obviously something about you Sorcha fell in love with, MacQuarrie. You just have to remind her of what that was."

Remind her of the passion she felt in his arms? That wasn't likely to happen, not if the scathing glare she'd cast him as she'd escaped his doorstep was any indication. "Men like me don't court women," Alec muttered, though the man he had once been would have done so.

"They do if they want to win them, you dolt." Ben launched himself to his feet and laid his empty tumbler on Alec's desk.

"You needn't call me names," Alec murmured.

"The next time that lass comes to my house in tears, I'll do worse than call you names."

"As though you could take me," Alec taunted.

"I'd have a damn good time trying," Ben admitted. "Then I'd tell Wallace Ferguson that you bit his sister and sit back and see what happens."

"She *told* you that?" Alec couldn't believe she'd divulged that information.

"She had your scent all over her when she got to my house." Ben shrugged. "The rest was easy to figure out."

"I keep forgetting about that blasted nose of yours," Alec said.

"And I keep forgetting you're an idiot. Then you remind me all over again." Ben shrugged. Then he sobered and stared directly at Alec. "Make it right, old friend."

Alec nodded absently. If only he knew how to go about doing that.

Twenty-Seven

ALEC STRODE UP THE STEPS OF BEN WESTFIELD'S NEWLY constructed home. Caitrin had called it a monstrosity, and she was not far off. Just outside of Edinburgh proper, Westfield Manor was a sprawling neoclassical home with decorative arches and ornate columns, exuding the feel of an English country estate. In fact, the manor rivaled that of Ben's oldest brother's home in Hampshire, both in size and grandness. How very Westfield it was.

Before Alec reached the final step, a man who was too young to be a proper butler opened the door, a cheerful smile upon his youthful face. "Good evenin', sir."

"Good evening. I—" Alec began.

"Ye must be Mr. MacQuarrie." The fellow gestured Alec over the threshold. "His lordship said I should be expectin' ye."

"Did he, indeed?" Alec hadn't decided on this fool's errand until at least an hour after his old friend had departed. He handed his beaver hat to the butler when the man held out his hand for it.

"Aye. I assume ye are here ta see Miss Ferguson."

He *was* there to see Miss Ferguson. He just wished he had some idea what to say to the lass. The ride from MacQuarrie House to Ben's country manor hadn't yielded any answers to that problem. "Is she still here?"

"Miss Ferguson?" The man smiled again, and Alec had the sudden urge to send the young butler crashing through the closest door. Clearly the man was besotted with Sorcha, just by the way he said her name. Damn Ben for hiring a mere lad for this position. A butler should be stoic, old, and not so bloody cheerful. "I believe she is in the nursery, sir." Then the man leaned in conspiratorially. "Lord Benjamin said I shouldna announce ye, or ye'd scare the lass off. Follow me."

Scare the lass off? Hardly. Sorcha wasn't afraid of him. She could blister his ears better than anyone else. Still, she might refuse to see him, which was another thing all together. And if she wouldn't see him, what then? He still had no idea what he'd say when he did see her; he just needed to lay his eyes on her again.

Alec nodded to the exuberant butler. "Lead on." Then he followed the young man up a flight of stairs. "Have you worked for the Westfields long?"

The butler glanced back over his shoulder at Alec. "Ever since I arrived from Glasgow. Her ladyship said she liked my outlook on life."

That explained the man's employment. Tender-hearted Elspeth had spent most of her life in a tiny cottage. She wouldn't know the first thing about hiring proper servants. The enormous house and the comical staff would be wildly amusing any other day. But Alec could only think about seeing Sorcha again.

After a second staircase and what seemed like a labyrinth of corridors, Alec found himself just outside a spacious nursery. Soft, melodic humming filtered into the hallway, and Alec silently nodded for the butler to leave him. Once alone, he leaned his shoulder against the doorjamb and watched Sorcha fuss over a little red-haired bairn.

God, she was beautiful. So ethereal, so sweet, so wholly deserving of more than he could give her. He should turn on his heel and quietly leave her to live her life with some lad who could share everything with her—heart, body, and soul. He really, truly should.

The bairn spotted him across the room and reached her pudgy hand in his direction. Sorcha followed the child's action and gasped when her eyes landed on Alec. He couldn't leave now. Not now that she'd spotted him. He'd look like a damn fool. "Sorcha," he mumbled, for lack of anything better to say.

"What are ye doin' here?" How was it possible for brown eyes to turn cold? And so quickly? Alec nearly shivered.

He took a fortifying breath and stepped into the nursery. "I, um, heard that all plant life at Westfield Manor was in danger and in need of rescue. So I thought I'd see if there was something I could do."

Sorcha returned her gaze to the bairn in her arms. "Yer papa is a meddlesome gossip, Rose. Shall we bind him up in ivy and then toss him inta Dunsapie Loch for good measure?"

Little Rose Westfield giggled, though it wasn't possible she understood a word Sorcha said.

"Oh, I think so," Sorcha cooed to the child.

"Turning the little one against her father?" Alec asked as he took a few steps closer to her. "Ben will be devastated."

"Then I suppose *Ben* should mind his own affairs. I made it very clear I dinna wish ta see ye."

"Sorch," Alec lowered his voice. "Allow me to explain. I deserve that much consideration, don't I?"

Finally her eyes rose to meet his once again. "I canna imagine what ye need ta explain, Alec. I might be young, but I grasped the manner of your relationship with Miss Sewell."

"I don't think you did."

She rolled her eyes heavenward. "Doona patronize me, Mr. MacQuarrie. I doona appreciate it."

What he wouldn't do to grasp her to him and kiss the hurt from her lovely face. "What will you do, Sorch?" He smiled hoping to see her do the same in return. "Bind me up in ivy and drop me into Dunsapie Loch right alongside Benjamin?"

"Nay." She cocked her head to one side as though she was thinking. "There's a crumblin' castle near Strathcarron in the Highlands. It's the perfect place ta keep a vampyre. I just need ta get the keys from Aiden Lindsay."

The castle where the previous generation of *Còig* witches had left Lord Kettering to rot for two decades. The castle where Alec had lost his human life. "I've visited there before and would rather not see the place again, if you don't mind. How about Birks End instead?"

She stared at him quizzically. "Birks End?"

"My home in East Galloway." He closed the gap between them and ran his finger along her jaw. "We can escape to Birks End and you can bind me up in all the ivy you want, just as long as you're there with me."

Her heart pounded so loudly that he could hear it in his ears. Blood coursed through her veins, and the memory of tasting her essence rushed into his mind.

"Ye should take Miss Sewell with ye," she whispered. But he could tell she was softening toward him because her eyes had warmed a bit and a touch of pink stained her cheeks. Thank God she wasn't immune to him, even if her words said otherwise.

Little Rose Westfield squirmed in Sorcha's arms, and she grabbed Alec's neckcloth with her fist. He looked down at the smiling bairn. Well, at least he had charmed one of the witches in the room, even if Rose was only a few months old. "She really does look like Elspeth, doesn't she?"

Sorcha tried to pry the child's fingers from Alec's cravat. "She's the prettiest little witch ever," she crooned.

"She *is* adorable, but I wouldn't say she was the prettiest witch ever." Alec flashed Sorcha a smile when her eyes rose to meet his. No, the prettiest witch ever had to be Sorcha. It wasn't just her angelic looks; it was her inner beauty that shone through in everything she did—whether it was gushing over Ben's bairn or throwing herself on her own sword to save him from the Duchess of Hythe. No one, witch or otherwise, was lovelier than Sorcha Ferguson.

Skittishly, she backed away from Alec, with Rose in her arms. "Ye better no' let Benjamin hear ye say that. He'll challenge ye ta duel in Holyrood Park."

Alec chuckled. "*He's* hardly a challenge. But, you... I'm enchanted by the challenge of you, Sorch."

She shook her head. "Doona say such things, Alec."

"But it's true." He stepped closer to her, this time being careful to avoid Rose Westfield's clutching fingers.

"But that woman—"

"Means nothing to me," Alec professed. "She never did, Sorch."

"She looks like Cait."

Dear God! "Because they're both blond? I swear to you, lass, the woman never meant anything to me, other than as a meal. I do *have* to eat. Surely, you can't fault me for that."

She turned away from him and crossed the floor toward a large window. There was nothing but blackness outside, but she stared out as though she could see across the ocean on a clear day. "I canna be Caitrin," she finally muttered after the longest time. "I can only be me."

Only Sorcha was more than everything he wanted. Alec was at her back in the blink of an eye, his hand on her waist. He inhaled the apple blossom scent of her and buried his face in her pretty, brown hair. "I don't want Cait." He kissed her shoulder, clutching her back to his front. "I want *you*, Sorcha."

She gasped when his lips touched her skin, but she didn't pull away from him and Alec silently rejoiced.

Rose Westfield chose that moment to cry.

Alec raised his head to look down into the bairn's scrunched-up face. She was positively enchanting in her own right, all pink flesh and pudgy little rolls. She even smelled like blueberries, if that was possible. *Was* that possible? Or was his nose playing tricks on him? A small part of him wanted to admit he would miss having children. He'd always assumed he'd be a father some day. He'd have a little boy who looked like him. Or a little girl he could dote on who looked like Sorcha. He groaned.

"Ye sound like ye have the weight of the world on yer shoulders, Alec," Sorcha said quietly as she leaned her head back against his chest.

"When I have you in my arms, all is right with the world, Sorch." He squeezed her gently. "Your father is going to worry if I don't deposit you into his loving care very soon," Alec reminded her. He didn't want to give her up, but they couldn't stay in Westfield's nursery all night.

The Lycan's voice rang out from the corridor. "Everything all right in here?" Ben asked, his voice full of playful suspicion. As always, he was as subtle as a rock. "I was beginning to think you'd have him tied up in vines and be dangling his sorry hide out the window by now."

"So sorry to disappoint you," Alec replied.

"I did think about it," Sorcha interjected. "But the window seemed so very ordinary. I'd prefer a tree. Or the side of a cliff."

"Or the top of Arthur's Seat." Ben winked at her.

"Exactly." Sorcha sighed with feigned content-ment. Little witch.

Ben sobered and leaned closer to Sorcha to whisper dramatically, "Your father sent a coach to collect you, lass. It appears as though he knows you've returned and that you haven't come to greet him."

"Oh, dear," Sorcha cried as she passed the bairn over to Ben. "If he's gone so far as ta send a carriage, I had better hurry." She started from the room. But then she turned back and looked over her shoulder. "Are ye comin', Alec?"

Of course, he was. Wild dragons couldn't pull her from his side, not now that he had her back.

❧

It seemed like forever since Sorcha had been home. A month or so with Blaire and Lord Kettering in Derbyshire. A couple weeks with Rhiannon and Lord Blodswell in London. A month with Maddie and the Duchess of Hythe in Kent. Then more than a fortnight on the North Road with Alec, Cait, and Eynsford. But now that she was home, it didn't quite feel right. Everything sounded the same, and the slight hum of activity was comforting. Home looked the same with its brightly colored walls and gleaming gold accents. It even smelled the same, like sandalwood shaving lotion and like the cinnamon biscuits Papa and Wallace devoured on a regular basis. Yet it wasn't the same at all, not that Sorcha could name what exactly was different.

Before she could say as much to Alec, her father's voice boomed from the opposite end of the corridor. "Did ye forget yer way home, lass?" An instant later, she found herself wrapped in his arms and the air nearly squeezed from her lungs.

"Let go, Papa," she giggled.

But he didn't. He only held her tighter. "I missed ye so much. I thought it was some kind of mistake when Eynsford sent a note this evenin', makin' sure ye made it home all right."

Behind them, Alec ground his teeth together, which only made Sorcha laugh harder. "Please, Papa! I need ta breathe."

Slowly he released her. He beamed down at her as he took a step back. Pride and love shone in his gaze, and Sorcha couldn't help but smile back at him. Whatever was different about home, it certainly wasn't Papa. The size of a small ogre, he still had a full head of dark hair and hazel eyes that twinkled with happiness. "Ye are a sight for sore eyes, but I thought ye were goin' ta stay with that duchess a while longer."

That had been the plan, but Sorcha shook her head. "Papa, I have somethin' ta tell ye."

But his gaze had found Alec before she could say more. "Alec MacQuarrie! *Havers*, it's been ages! I thought ye left us for good last year."

"Well, sir, I—"

"Come in, come in. Have ye had dinner, lad?"

"I—um…" Alec struggled.

"Ye must join us." Sorcha's father gestured down the corridor. "I'm sure Wallace will love ta see ye."

"Thank you, sir, but—"

"No buts. I want ta hear what ye've been up ta, lad." Then he began to lead Sorcha toward the dining hall. "Come along, MacQuarrie."

Sorcha glanced back over her shoulder at the vampyre she loved. He trailed behind them, a look of pure amusement on his face. At least he wasn't put out with Papa's heavy-handed ways. There would be time for them to share their news after dinner, when her father wasn't so excitable and was actually able to listen instead of gushing.

"*Crivens!*" Wallace Ferguson leapt to his feet, knocking his chair over in the process. "Sorcha! I thought Eynsford was daft, sayin' ye were home." Her giant half brother rushed forward and drew her into an embrace just as tightly as their father had.

"Watch your strength, Ferguson," Alec said. "You don't want to break the lass in two."

Wallace released his hold on Sorcha and gaped at Alec. "Good God! Alec MacQuarrie! I thought ye were dead."

Twenty-Eight

SORCHA WATCHED CLOSELY AS ALEC FROWNED AT THE food on his plate. There was little she could do to help him. Ever since Wallace had made the unfortunate statement about Alec's mortality, or lack thereof, her vampyre hadn't quite seemed himself. She wished she knew why her brother would say such a thing. Who had he been talking to?

Alec made a good show of shoving his salmon from side to side to make it seem like he was eating. But she knew he wasn't. He reminded her of a wee lad who would tuck brussels sprouts in his pockets to keep from having to eat them, only to have servants find a handkerchief of them in an odd place. What else was he to do? She'd ended up seated between her brother and father at the table. Alec couldn't switch their plates from that distance. Although her family had been solely focused on her ever since they assumed their places.

Already she'd been asked to describe every aspect of Blaire's home in Derbyshire. She'd had to detail her weeks in London and the entertainments she'd enjoyed with Rhiannon and Lord Blodswell. And she'd had to tell them all about the Duchess of Hythe and her new friend, Lady Madeline. Her jaw had begun to ache from all the talking.

"Sorcha, how was it traveling with Eynsford and Cait all the way from Kent? That's an awfully long way. Were they terribly poor company for an unmarried lass?" her father asked as he speared a carrot from his plate.

"Ta be honest, Cait was a tiny bit ill. Aside from that, though, the trip was just fine." She raised a sly glance at Alec. "But Alec traveled with us, Papa. He may have a different opinion."

"How about it, MacQuarrie?" Her father finally turned his attention on Alec. "Were they sickenin' with all that love babble? The pair of them nearly turns my stomach with their flagrant adoration for one another."

"Must we discuss this at the table, Papa?" Sorcha interjected. Not only was it a touchy subject for Alec, but it was also impolite to discuss such things at a family meal. Alec shoved a potato across his plate. Poor man. He must be terribly uncomfortable.

"No' hungry, MacQuarrie?" Wallace asked. "Cook will be inconsolable if ye send back yer whole plate. Prides herself as the best in four counties." He patted his stomach as though that was all the proof anyone needed to confirm such claims.

"Oh, no. It's wonderful. But I only recently ate." Alec's gaze dropped to the neck of Sorcha's gown and a warm rush washed up her cheeks, she was sure. He *hadn't* recently eaten. But he would probably like to. And soon. She'd like it quite a bit herself.

"Are ye all right, Sorch?" Wallace asked, his eyebrows arching together with concern. "Ye doona look well."

Sorcha fanned her face. "It's a bit warm in here, is all."

"And we've been makin' ye talk nearly nonstop." Her father frowned. "So, let me tell ye what ye've missed…" As he began to drone on about all the things that had happened in her absence, Sorcha tried to figure out a way to help Alec with the food on his plate. Then she had a brilliant idea.

A nice potted plant sat in the middle of the dining room table, its vines and leaves trailing delicately over the sides of its container. Sorcha reached over and gently rubbed the plant, which woke beneath her fingers. She giggled as it rubbed itself on the back of her hand like a cat that'd missed her.

"Stop playin' with the plant, Sorch," her father grumbled. "And eat yer dinner."

"Yes, Papa," she conceded with a small smile.

But with a quick mention in her mind, she told the plant exactly what she wanted it to do and then laughed inwardly at the reaction she expected from Alec. She watched out of the corner of her eye as a sneaky little vine slid across the table and tickled the underside of his palm. He jumped in his seat and then immediately looked up from his plate. His eyes met hers, a warning in their dark depths. He was so adorable when he was discomfited. She wanted to wiggle in her chair with excitement.

The tiny little vine sneaked across the table and under the edge of his plate, then reached over the edge and snatched a small potato with its greedy little grasp.

Then it retreated into its container with its prize. One potato down, only three more to go.

Alec mouthed at her to stop her antics, adding a violent slash of his hand when her father wasn't looking. But she was having way too much fun.

After the little vine had absconded with all of his potatoes, it moved on to his salmon. The fish proved to be much more difficult to grasp, however, so the vine had to enlist the help of a few leaves onto which Alec could rake the salmon from his plate. Then all of the bits disappeared.

Sorcha was positively delighted when dessert arrived. Raspberry creams had always been one of her favorites. But the cream would prove to be much trickier to remove from the dish. She gave it a lot of thought and smiled when she finally figured out what to do.

Soon the cream was delivered and Wallace, as she'd hoped, devoured two servings of the dessert before Sorcha could even put a spoon to her own sweet treat. Of course, Alec hadn't touched a bite of his. A switch would be simple, especially as it looked like Wallace might steal the one in front of Alec right out from under his nose. So Sorcha encouraged a pretty little flower to slide over to Alec's dish, drop itself directly into the gooey mess, and swish around so that its leaves were coated.

All the while, Alec looked positively mortified, but her father and Wallace were discussing the latest shipping investment and were much too engrossed to even realize she wasn't paying attention to them, much less that she was tormenting Alec with her powers.

Alec shot her a storm-filled glance when the little

flower, laden with heavy, creamy dessert moved up his waistcoat and bumped the end of his nose, leaving a blob of its gooey pink mess behind. Alec swiped at it with his napkin and grumbled beneath his breath. She asked the flower to do it again, only this time he moved his head to avoid the plant and it caught his cheek.

Sorcha covered her mouth as a giggle finally escaped her.

"Sorcha," her father boomed from beside her.

"Yes, Papa?" she asked, forcing her gaze away from Alec's disaster of a dinner.

"Why is it that Mr. MacQuarrie has been made aware of yer powers? Ye've plagued him with them the whole night. Is there somethin' I'm missin'?"

Alec coughed delicately into his hand before he spoke. His voice only quavered a little when he said, "It's because I'd like to marry her, sir."

❦

All eyes were on Alec, and he swallowed uncomfortably. "I—uh—probably should have asked to speak to you privately, Mr. Ferguson."

Seamus Ferguson glanced quickly at his daughter and then turned his attention back to Alec. "Is that what all yer inarticulate stammerin' was about when ye arrived? I've never kent ye ta sound so sheepish, MacQuarrie."

Sorcha gasped. "Papa!"

Her father frowned, which was something of a rarity for the man who was generally the epitome of jovialness. "Wipe yer cheek, lad. Then meet me in my study."

Sorcha pushed out of her seat only to be rewarded by a stern glance from her father.

"Sit," Seamus commanded.

Sorcha sat, but she pouted at the same time. "Papa, ye should at least hear me out."

"It's all right, Sorch." Alec swiped the bit of raspberry cream from his cheek and rose from his seat. "Your father's right."

Seamus Ferguson didn't even look back over his shoulder to make sure Alec was following him from the dining hall. Not that it mattered. Alec was right behind him. This was the moment Alec had thought about ever since the stream of fabrications had fallen from Sorcha's lips in her attempt to save him from the Duchess of Hythe's wrath. Well, he'd had other thoughts along the way, more carnally motivated ones, certainly. But this, asking for her father's blessing, had stayed with him through the journey.

If her father had any sense, he'd refuse Alec's offer. And if there was one thing Seamus Ferguson had, it was sense. Actually, he had a number of things. A mind for business. An ability to size a man up. A devotion to his daughter. And on top of all of that, Alec had to tell the man the complete truth.

As soon as Alec stepped into Seamus Ferguson's study, the old gentleman shut the door to keep anyone else from overhearing their conversation. "Whisky?" he asked, keeping his now shrewd hazel eyes leveled on Alec.

"No need for liquid courage, Mr. Ferguson."

A ghost of a smile lit the man's face, but it was gone an instant later. "Sit down, lad."

Alec complied, not wanting to do anything that would irritate Sorcha's father. Not when he needed his approval.

"Finally got over yer infatuation with Caitrin Macleod, did ye?"

"Eynsford, you mean," Alec corrected. Then he nodded his head. He wasn't certain when his everlasting devotion to Cait had come to an end, but somewhere along the way it had. "I wish Lady Eynsford every bit of happiness."

"Good." Seamus Ferguson settled on the corner of his desk to look down his aristocratic nose at Alec. "Because I willna have my daughter playin' second fiddle ta anyone."

Alec shook his head. "There's no comparing them, sir. Sorcha is…" What was the best word to use? What was the best thing to say to her father?

"Aye…? Sorcha is what?"

"Sorcha is the reason I look forward to the day. Who else would beckon flowers to smear cream on my face in the middle of dinner? Who else would bind footmen in ivy just to get her way?" Her father looked a little discomfited by that, so Alec rushed on. "I have no idea from one day to the next what she'll do. And I want to know. I want to be there just so I can share some of her contentment. I want… her."

Seamus Ferguson heaved a sigh and folded his arms across his chest. Then a broad smile spread across his face. "And does my daughter return yer affections?"

She loved Alec, which was more than he was capable of. But he nodded anyway, hoping her father wouldn't ask that specific question. "I believe she does, Mr. Ferguson."

"And ye clearly ken about her powers." He sighed. "I was supposed ta explain all of that ta her intended husband."

Alec smiled at the man. "I've known for some time, if that makes you feel any better. I know about the whole coven." And they knew about him.

"Well, then, I guess there's nothin' left ta do except talk ta Mr. Crawford in the mornin' about callin' the banns."

Relief swamped Alec. Seamus Ferguson had just given his permission. Yet, dread settled in his belly at the same moment. He couldn't set foot in the church. "I was hoping we wouldn't have to wait the three weeks, sir."

Sorcha's father laughed as he rose from the corner of his desk. "Aye, well, someday when ye have a daughter of yer own, ye willna be in a hurry ta see her married off and ye'll understand."

No. That would never happen, either. "I can't wait, Mr. Ferguson."

Confusion clouded the old gentleman's eyes. "Why canna ye wait the three weeks, Mr. MacQuarrie?" He folded his arms across his wide chest. "Are ye in that much of a hurry?"

Well, he *could* wait the three weeks. It was the whole church thing that was impossible. And Sorcha's father deserved the whole truth, or as much of it as Alec thought he could take. "Because of what I am, sir. Attending services is out of the question for me. I had hoped we could declare ourselves. Though Sorcha seemed keen on an anvil wedding. Truly, I'd be fine with either option."

"Because of what ye are, attendin' services is out of the question for ye?" A frown settled on Seamus Ferguson's face. "Just what exactly are ye, MacQuarrie?"

Alec took a deep breath he didn't really need. Then he looked straight in Sorcha's father's eyes. "I'm not your *average* man. And—"

"Well, I should certainly hope my daughter wouldna settle for an *average* man." Mr. Ferguson rummaged in his desk drawer, more than a little distracted.

"That's not exactly what I meant."

"Ye can support my daughter, can ye no'?"

"Of course, I can. But—"

"But, nothin', MacQuarrie. Do ye want ta marry my daughter or no'?"

"My wants are not in question." *I want her in every way possible.*

Seamus Ferguson's gaze finally rose to meet Alec's. "Forgive an old man for his stubbornness, but I'm fairly certain I doona want ta hear about yer *other* wants with regard for my daughter."

A smile tugged at Alec's lips. Mr. Ferguson went back to his desk drawer and finally pulled the drawer from the desk and upended it on the scarred and well-loved mahogany surface. He shuffled through scraps of paper, bits of memorabilia, and broken writing instruments until he finally located what he was looking for. He held up two small keys on a golden ring, one made of tarnished metal and the other gleaming copper. "Found them." He grinned.

Alec wasn't certain what to say to that, so he simply watched as Seamus Ferguson suddenly bounded to his feet and said, "Come along, lad. The day is wastin'."

Then he disappeared into the corridor, much more quickly than Alec would have expected from a man of his advanced age. Alec followed him down every twist and turn in the vast home until he finally stopped at the end of a corridor. He rapped his knuckles very lightly on the wall and continued down it until the knock began to sound hollow. Then he pressed hard and the wall moved.

Alec rubbed at his eyes, not quite believing what he was seeing. Had the wall actually moved?

"Doona stand there gawkin'," Seamus Ferguson commanded. Then he lit a small taper from the lamp on the wall and slipped inside the concealed space. He held the door open wide for Alec. Once they were inside the secret room, Sorcha's father lifted the candle high, illuminating another wooden door with a star carved into the middle. "For the five of them," he said, his voice distracted. "Though Sorcha's mother used this room more than most."

"It's a hidden room." Alec blurted out the obvious, still astounded by the fact that he'd slipped inside a wall and now stood at the threshold of a small room carved with a five-pointed star.

Mr. Ferguson chuckled. "Try ta keep up with me, lad. I ken it's a lot ta take in at once. But, ye'll get the idea of it soon enough."

"I am trying," Alec muttered.

Sorcha's father fitted the key into the lock and turned it slowly, as though he was afraid he'd break the portal's entrance. The click of the lock when he turned the key rang about the room like a harbinger of things to come. Be they good or bad, Alec was uncertain, but he was quite interested in what stood behind the second door.

"This was my late wife's secret room," the old man explained as he shoved the door open. Then he stepped into the dark alcove and lit lamps that lined the walls, casting the room in shadows, but at least Alec could see the contents. Large apothecary drawers lined one wall, each one marked in a bold but very feminine scrawl. Alec couldn't even dream of pronouncing most of the labels. Another wall was lined with shelves that held treasures of every kind.

Alec spun around slowly, absorbing sights he'd never seen before.

Mr. Ferguson held up a heavy piece of glass that shot out shards of light in every direction. "This is what happens when lightnin' hits sand. It forms a most brilliant piece of glass. Kind of wild and uninhibited, would ye no' say?" He raised his eyebrows in amusement.

"Did Rhiannon do that?" Alec asked.

The old man shook his head. "Her mother. It was a special talent of hers. I would imagine Rhiannon could do it too, if she was of a mind."

Alec let the tips of his fingers trail over another item on the shelf, the cool surface of the stone taking all of his attention. "An enchanted mortar and pestle. For makin' potions." Seamus Ferguson shrugged. "I never understood how it became enchanted. But they made many a mess usin' that thing, the five of them." He chuckled again. "Elspeth's mother had a similar room beneath the floor of her old cottage, but it was tiny compared ta this one. This one consists of ages and ages of tradition."

"Sorcha knows about this?"

"Aye, she learned of it last year when that first vampyre came inta their lives, no' that she is aware of all it contains."

What had the man just said? Alec's head spun around quickly to face the old man.

But Seamus Ferguson just smiled and shook his head slowly. "Ye thought I had no idea of what ye are? Who my daughter would be marryin'?"

He looked so thoughtful that Alec wasn't certain he was supposed to answer. So, he didn't.

"Ye were doin' a fine imitation of a suitor who was ready ta spill his life story ta an expectant father-in-law. But ye were about ta start flounderin', lad, so I thought I'd help ye." He chuckled aloud.

Though what the man found so amusing had Alec completely floored. "You know what I am." It wasn't a question. Just a statement of fact. The man did know what he was. He could see it on his face.

"Aye. It's all right here." Seamus Ferguson moved to the corner of the room and wiped the dust from the top of a locked wooden box. Then he took the copper key and fit it in the lock. He removed several ledgers, the top one of which he flipped open on a long table that stood in the middle of the room. "Oh, I probably should no' have read the books, but my Bonnie was gone and I missed her. Made me feel closer ta her."

What exactly was the man getting at? "Are you saying there's mention of *me* in those books? Of what I've become?"

Mr. Ferguson sighed. "They're no' filled with prose

about ye, MacQuarrie, but there is some mention of ye, aye."

Alec reached for the ledgers, but Seamus Ferguson placed a protective hand on the pile. "They're no' for yer eyes."

"*You've* seen them," he accused. If something about him was written inside those books, no one was going to keep him from seeing it, either.

"Aye." Ferguson agreed with a nod of his head. "But I've already lived what has been foretold about me. Ye, lad, have a ways ta go."

Alec frowned at his future father-in-law. "If you're not going to let me see the books, why even bother showing them to me?"

"Because I think ye should ken that it has been prophesied that ye'd take my Sorcha ta be yer wife."

Alec's mouth fell open. All of those long-ago conversations with Caitrin echoed in his ears. Each time she'd refused his proposal. Each time she told him he'd find happiness with someone else. Each time she told him that his path lay along a different one than hers. Cait had known all along. What else had she known? "And it says I'd be a vampyre?"

Seamus Ferguson nodded. "Which was confusin' ta me, I can assure ye, since I'd kent ye since ye were a wee lad, and I've watched ye grow inta the honorable man ye've become. But then Wallace overheard Kettering and Blaire discussin' yer untimely death, and it all made sense." He smiled sadly. "Sorry ye had ta go through all of that."

What was Alec to say to all of this? He was *supposed* to become a vampyre? Hardly a future he would want for himself. It might have been nice to have a bit of warning or for Cait to *not* have sent him ta Briarcraig Castle in the first place.

"I see yer mind tryin' ta make sense of things."

"Why would Cait let me endure this fate?"

"It's no' her fault." Seamus Ferguson frowned. "And, well, things havena actually taken place the way they were foreseen, lad."

"Beg your pardon?" Hadn't Ferguson just said he'd read everything in the old ledgers?

"It was foretold many, many years ago that this generation of witches would marry men not of their own kind, but Fiona Macleod wasna happy about the prophecy and did everythin' she could ta keep it from happenin'."

Which was something Eynsford had alluded to. "Is that possible?" Cait always made it seem that the future was etched in stone.

"Oh, aye. The future will eventually right itself, or so it seems, if the wrong path is taken. For example, Elspeth *should* have been raised with both her parents, followin' the drum and Major Forster across the continent from one campaign ta the next. She *should* have met Benjamin through their fathers years ago. But Fiona made certain Forster was disposed of. She couldna have seen what would eventually bring Westfield ta Elspeth's door because she changed the immediate future, just no' the eventual outcome."

"And me?" Alec muttered, not sure what to make of Ferguson's tale.

"Well, I'm no' certain how ye were supposed ta become a vampyre, originally that is. Most of the writin' is about the witches, of course. Poor Kettering should have never been locked in that castle. But Fiona thought it would keep him away from Blaire's destiny. And ye got messed up in all of that. But, like I say, the future has a way of rightin' itself. And yer future has always been with my Sorcha. Vampyre and all."

Alec scrubbed a hand across his face. He still couldn't quite believe that he was supposed to be a vampyre. This life had been his destiny. And, apparently, Sorcha's. "And you're all right with that. You're all right with handing your daughter over to a man like me?"

Finally, Seamus Ferguson flashed him a toothy grin. "Well, of course. Like I said, I've kent ye since ye were a wee one, MacQuarrie. I ken the sort of man ye are. And if I was ta try and let old prejudices keep ye from Sorcha, I'd be no better than Fiona, now would I? My Bonnie wouldna be very happy about that, I can assure ye."

"So if Mrs. Macleod was still alive, you're saying she'd try to keep me from Sorcha?" After what she'd done to Elspeth and Kettering, Alec didn't even want to think about what the crafty witch would have come up with for him. The idea almost made him shiver.

Seamus tapped the old books with his fingers. "The *Còig* is an ancient entity. It served its purpose in past centuries, but the times are changin'. The world is changin'. Ye ken those locomotives they've been fiddlin' with the last few years? Trevithick and the like?"

Alec nodded absently. He knew a little about the contraptions. Their usage seemed a little far-fetched, but his interest had always been more history related.

Though he figured he'd see plenty of history happen
in his never-ending lifetime.

"Soon there'll be a public railway takin' people
from one end of Britain ta the other." Seamus touched
his nose. "A smart man would invest in such ventures.
It's no coincidence the family of the seers has always
done relatively well financially speakin', if ye ken what
I mean."

Seamus Ferguson always did have his mind on
business matters, yet Alec wasn't certain how they'd
ended up talking about locomotives and investments.
"I suppose so."

Sorcha's father nodded as though he'd made a valid
point. "Well, poor Fiona couldna see that. Human
advancements were one thing, but changes within the
coven were somethin' else. She couldna let go of the
past traditions long enough ta embrace the future. She
wanted ta ensure that the strength and purity of the
coven would always remain intact."

Meaning that marriage to Lycans and vampyres
would destroy the fabric of the coven. Ferguson didn't
have to say the words aloud; Alec could see the truth
of that in the old man's eyes. "Does Sorcha know all
of this?" She certainly hadn't let on if she had.

Her father shook his head. "Bonnie wanted ta make
certain this generation of witches would meet their
destinies without interference from any other seers.
Luckily, Caitrin is a bit more forward thinkin' than her
mother. But Bonnie couldna ensure that was the case.
So she took these books from Fiona and hid them away
from everyone, except for Wallace, it seems. The lad
was just as enamored with Bonnie as I was and sat at

her feet, silently watchin' everythin'. After she passed away, God rest her soul, Wallace showed me the books. And I kent she'd want me ta keep them safe."

"These books were Fiona's?"

"Oh, of course." Seamus continued. "Traditionally, the prophecies were always kept with the seer. But Bonnie felt Fiona had misled the coven, and so she absconded with them." He smiled wistfully. "She was pretty and soft as flower petals, but my Bonnie had a spine of steel and an innate sense of right and wrong. She dinna believe Fiona could be trusted with the relics any longer. After ye marry Sorcha, I'll return them ta Cait. The lass has proven herself worthy in my estimation, and I think Bonnie would agree."

Alec didn't necessarily care who kept the books; only their contents mattered. "It's a little hard to come to terms with the fact that my life is on a path over which I have no say. That one way or the other, the future will right itself, as you said. That I was supposed to be this way."

"I ken it's difficult." Seamus Ferguson turned his back on Alec to reach up onto a high shelf in the room and retrieve a long wooden object. Alec watched closely until he realized what it was.

"Don't make me disarm you, Mr. Ferguson," Alec warned as his teeth descended.

"Ye mean take this little thing from me?" the old man teased as he tossed a wooden stake from one hand to another. "Sorcha made this little instrument. Well, so ta speak anyway."

She had? Alec was certain he looked like a dolt with his mouth hanging open. The lass he was to marry had fashioned a wooden stake? That seemed like something a vampyre should be made aware of.

"It was for that vampyre, the one who showed up last winter tryin' ta finish Kettering off," Ferguson explained. "Needless ta say, a slight battle ensured. In the midst of the brawl, Sorcha asked a nearby elm ta create this weapon for her."

Alec hadn't been present for that battle, but Rhiannon had told him enough about it that he felt as though he'd seen it with his own eyes. He hated that Sorcha had had to witness such a horrible event. After her close call with that malevolent vampyre, the same one who was partially responsible for Alec's own death, it was still hard to believe Sorcha could accept him as he was.

"As I ken what yer kind is capable of, MacQuarrie, it seems hard ta believe that a little piece of wood can fell ye."

Except that the stake in Ferguson's hand couldn't really be described as little. "I'd rather not put it to the test, sir," Alec replied, trying to maintain a casual air.

Mr. Ferguson tossed the stake to him, and Alec caught it in the air. "That was all that was left after the fellow burst inta flames."

Just the thought of such an occurrence made Alec queasy. "Are you warning me, sir?" He tucked the stake high on a shelf behind him.

"If ye hurt my daughter, MacQuarrie, I'll no' have ta worry about buryin' yer carcass. The *Còig* will do it for me."

"They like me," Alec muttered and was glad for the truth of it.

"Keep it that way. And put yer teeth away, damn it," the old man growled. "They make me a little nervous."

"Thank God for small favors."

"Speakin' of God, ye'll marry my daughter properly in a ceremony. No declarations. No anvil wedding. Her mother would be furious if I allowed such a thing. It willna be in a church, but it'll be legal and binding and holy. Do ye understand?"

"I'm still surprised you'll let me marry her at all, considering my circumstances."

"I'd be a fool ta stand in the way of destiny. Besides, ye are an honorable gentleman. Ye always have been. And that is why ye will marry my Sorcha." His eyes bored directly into Alec. "And make her yer Sorcha." He coughed as though trying to dislodge a lump in his throat.

"Aye, sir," was all Alec could get out, because instead of a lump of emotion in his throat, he had a pain nagging in the center of his chest.

Then Seamus pulled an envelope from his jacket pocket. "Special license with yer name on it. And Sorcha's."

A special license? Alec reached for the letter, and Mr. Ferguson handed it to him without the slightest delay. "How?" was all he managed.

His soon-to-be father-in-law shrugged. "It was in with the letter Eynsford sent this evenin', tellin' me Sorcha had returned. Apparently that English duchess who seemed so enamored of my lass had this drawn up a month or so ago, from the date."

Alec gaped at the license in his hand. Fate, or whatever it was that went about "righting" the future, sure had some interesting friends. The Duchess of Hythe had been in on this little charade with Cait from the beginning. Good God! Who *else* had been conscriped to place him on his destined path? Miss Overton and her mother? Radbourne and his brothers? Bexley? The list made his head hurt. But he was a vampyre, and vampyres' heads never hurt.

Twenty-Nine

SORCHA PACED BACK AND FORTH ACROSS THE DINING hall. Certainly, if her father planned to deny Alec's suit, he'd guide him back this direction before he kicked him out of the house. Then she could rush into the corridor and throw herself upon her father's love for her. She'd swear never to see Papa again if he didn't permit the marriage to take place. That was it. That would work. He'd never accept her total absence from his life. He loved her too much.

Alec was a fool for even thinking about telling her father what he really was. And she knew he was thinking about it. She could see it in his dark eyes when he'd followed Papa from the dining hall. His foolish honor would ruin everything. After all, what father in his right mind would give his only daughter to a vampyre? Sorcha knew what Alec was. Why couldn't her father leave it at that? She was the one who was marrying Alec. And she accepted him exactly as he was, pointy fangs and never-ending life and all.

"Ye look green," Wallace remarked as he shoveled another bite of raspberry cream into his mouth.

"I do no' look green," she insisted, and hoped she was right. Showing her nervousness wouldn't help her cause with Papa.

"Suit yerself." Her brother shrugged and took a sip of wine.

Sorcha frowned at her much older brother, as she finally stopped her pacing a dropped into a spot across from him at the table, still keeping her eyes on the main doorway.

"Do ye ken why everyone has come home?" Wallace asked.

Why must he speak so cryptically? Who was everyone? Alec and herself? "I'm no' in the mood for idle chitchat, Wallace."

"Nay." He placed his goblet back on the table and smirked. "Ye're preoccupied. Yer mind is lingerin' outside Father's study, wonderin' if he'll decapitate MacQuarrie."

Papa wouldn't try something so foolish, would he? She leapt to her feet.

"Sit down!" her brother commanded. "Neither of them will appreciate it, Sorch, if ye involve yerself in somethin' that's no' yer concern."

She didn't sit. She punched her hands to her hips instead and glared at her ogre-sized brother. "Who I marry, Wallace Ferguson, is most definitely my concern."

He chuckled. Blasted brother.

Out of the corner of her eye, she looked to her beloved potted plant once more for help. The stem leaned toward Wallace and poked him in the eye.

Wallace laughed again as he rubbed at the pain. She

hadn't told the plant to hit him hard enough to do damage but had told it merely to annoy him, much like he was doing to her. "Oh, I have missed ye, lass. What will I do when ye move inta MacQuarrie House and leave me all alone?"

Sorcha sank back into her seat. "Ye think Papa will give his blessin'?"

Her brother shook his head as though he couldn't believe she'd even ask such a question. "Has he ever refused ye anythin' ye wanted, Sorch?"

Not that she could think of, but she'd hate for him to start now, of all times. At that moment, the sound of male laughter filtered into the corridor and she leapt back to her feet.

"All that pent-up energy," Wallace began, "is goin' ta give ye a stomachache."

She glanced briefly at her brother, who was just now finishing the last of his raspberry cream. "Somethin' ye should ken a lot about, Wallace." Then she turned her attention back to the dining hall door and held her breath until her father and Alec walked back into the room.

"Ye look a little green, Sorch," her father said, concern marring his brow.

"Told her the same thing," Wallace said from the table. "She chose no' ta pay me any attention."

Normally, Sorcha would have bantered with her brother. She would have told him that only a fool would pay him any attention. But all she could do was seek Alec's black-as-night gaze, hoping to find some sort of reassurance there. Unfortunately, what she saw reflecting back at her was an expression she couldn't quite read. In fact, she didn't think she'd ever seen him wear such a look before.

"Go on," her father urged, pushing Alec in her direction. "Tell her the good news, or she'll faint dead away. Look at her color."

Alec finally smiled at her as he crossed the distance between them. He grasped her hand in his and brushed her knuckles with his lips. "Sorcha Ferguson, your father has given me his blessing to marry you."

Relief filled Sorcha's lungs. Then she squealed with delight and threw her arms around Alec's neck. He held her tightly for a minute before he stepped back and placed her from him. "He'd like for us to say our vows in the morning, lass. Is that acceptable to you?"

In the morning? She was surprised her father had agreed so readily. "Where shall we make our declarations?" She nodded eagerly.

Behind them, her father loudly cleared his throat.

Alec shook his head. "No declarations, Sorch. It seems the Duchess of Hythe was kind enough to secure a special license for us."

The Duchess of Hythe? Sorcha couldn't help but frown. How could the duchess have possibly secured a license in so short a time? She'd barely ruined herself verbally before she and Alec, Eynsford, and Cait... It was Cait. She knew it in her heart. For once, that meddlesome witch had done something grand.

She wasn't quite certain what to think about her friend's interference, and she shook her head. "She kent all along."

Alec's dark eyes twinkled. "It appears as though she did. Someone must have been whispering in Her

Grace's ear for the license to have been procured more than a sennight before my arrival."

A giggle escaped Sorcha's throat. "That's why ye were invited. Maddie couldna figure it out. Ye were no' the same as the others."

Which was an understatement. Alec's brow rose in question, and then he shook his head. "Don't tell me. I'm sure I don't want to know what you meant by that."

Sorcha's father stepped forward and clapped a hand to Alec's back. "All right, lad, ye better be off if ye're ta be here bright and early in the mornin'. And I have ta go pay a visit ta our good vicar."

"Ye're throwin' Alec out?" Sorcha protested.

"Ye've got the rest of yer life ta spend with the man, Sorch. One last night for yer old Papa is no' too much ta ask, is it?"

Tears started to well up in her eyes, and she shook her head. Tomorrow, she'd leave her father's home for good. One last night was not too much to ask at all. "I'll just see him out then."

Her father winked at her as Sorcha linked her arm with Alec's and ushered him toward the main entrance.

As soon as they were alone in the corridor, she glanced up at him. "What did he say?"

"He said aye."

She smacked his arm. "That's no' what I meant at all, and ye ken it. Did ye tell him? I mean, did ye tell him everythin'?"

Alec shook his head. "He told me. He knew it all. What I am, that you were predestined to be my wife, everything."

So there was nothing to hide from her father. She breathed a sigh of relief. How wonderful not to have to keep any secrets from Papa. She smiled up at Alec and noted that he looked a little pale. *Havers!* It had been too long since he'd fed. "Alec, ye doona look well. I think ye need a bit of blood."

He stopped dead in his tracks. "I can't, Sorch. Not right now."

What a ridiculous thing to say. It wasn't even a secret that he was a vampyre. Her father knew and seemed all right with the circumstances. "Why ever no'?"

A pained look spread across his face, and he pulled her into his arms. "Because, lass, I want ye more than anything. And I don't think I'll be able to stop with just a bit of blood."

She didn't want him to stop with just a bit of blood. She could tug him up the steps to her room, and there'd be no reason for him to stop this time. "Then take all of me."

He groaned. "I've managed this long, Sorch. I can manage one more night."

"But—"

"You mean more to me than just a bit of blood, Sorcha. Let me show you the respect you deserve by having you after we've said our vows. Let me do that right, will you?"

He looked so sincere, so much like the Alec she'd always known. Her heart pounded in her chest, threatening to overflow with affection. She nodded.

Very softly, Alec touched his lips to hers, and tingles raced across her skin. She would never tire of Alec's kisses. Not if she lived a million years, right along with him.

He stepped away from her and bowed slightly. "Until the morrow, Miss Ferguson."

"Tomorrow, I'll be Mrs. MacQuarrie," she said with a giggle.

"Indeed, you will," Alec called over his shoulder as he walked toward the front entrance.

"Oh, Alec," she called to him.

He looked back, distraction on his face.

"Never mind," she said with a shake of her head. She really should tell him about the spell she'd whispered to his ivy, but there was no need. Not now.

"Get some rest, Sorch," he teased. "I plan to keep you very busy tomorrow."

"Oh, the weddin' will be just fine." She brushed his comment aside.

"I meant *after* the wedding, love," he said. Then he disappeared inside the carriage and it pulled away. Sorcha's belly dropped all the way to her toes.

❧

Exhausted, Alec climbed the stairs of his home and pushed open his bedchamber door. Clearly, Forbes had arrived in one piece at MacQuarrie House. Alec's black robe lay across a striped Hepplewhite chair and…

Alec's head jerked to his four-poster. Lying across his counterpane, wearing nothing more than a smile, was Delia Sewell. She lay on her side, with her head resting in the palm of her hand.

"What are you doing here, Delia?" Alec snapped as he picked up his robe and tossed it in her general direction. She let it fall beside her but didn't bother to cover her nakedness.

"I thought you might need me," she purred.

"I don't," Alec tossed back. "You can see yourself out the same way you saw yourself in." He turned his back on her. "How *did* you find your way inside?" he asked. He'd serve any member of his staff up on a platter if he found out one or more of them had helped her gain entrance to his home, much less his bedchamber.

She cooed from behind him. "Alec dear, you know you want me."

But he didn't. She didn't appeal to him at all. Not even the smallest bit. He turned back around to face her, to tell her just that. As he turned to face her, she parted her thighs and laid a hand on the pulse he knew beat beneath that wizened, well-used skin. "Actually, Delia," he began with a sigh, "I do *not* want you."

Her lips formed an unattractive pout. "But you and I, we have been together so long."

He remembered it quite differently. It had been a month at the most. They'd shared some moments. He'd drunk her blood and paid her well for it. "You knew what our arrangement was back then. You still do." He picked up his robe again and draped it over her body like a coverlet. She batted at the length of it, but at least she tucked it beneath her armpits. "A bit of coin, a bit of pleasure. There was never any relationship between us."

Her face fell. "You woke in my bed, day after day," she insisted.

"You traveled with me so I wouldn't have to charm anyone into being my meal. And you were well compensated." He narrowed his eyes at her.

"Any business relationship we had is over. I'm getting married tomorrow."

"To that little mousy Scot?" she gasped as she jumped to her feet and glared at him.

"To Miss Ferguson," he reminded her.

"Your Miss Ferguson doesn't have the skills that I have."

He knew exactly what skills he was referring to. "Thank God for small favors," he said with a light chuckle.

Her face reddened in anger. "How dare you?" she gasped. "I served you well."

"And I paid you well," he quipped. "Gather your things and dress. I'm certain you can find another of my kind who can offer you what you desire."

"I desire *you*," she snapped.

"Then I am sorry for you," he returned. "The only woman in my life from now on will be my wife."

"But—"

Alec jumped when his bedroom window gave a loud squeak as it was pulled open from the outside. What the devil? He was on the upper level. There was no way that window could be opened by anyone.

Finally, Delia clutched the robe around herself. "What's going on?" she asked.

Alec wished he knew. "No idea," he mumbled as he stalked to the window. He looked out the open portal, but all he could see was some ivy and the rose bushes on the trellis outside his window. They appeared to be a little greener than they should be that time of the year. Perhaps Sorcha had given them a stroke? But what had opened the window? He reached to close it. But a thorny little vine shoved at his arm. "Ouch!" he cried as a thorn scraped the back of his hand. Then the vine tickled the underside of his palm. "Oh, good God," he mumbled.

Alec watched helplessly as a large clump of vines crept over the window sill and spread across the room. Two of them went for Delia's slippers, which lay on the floor beside his bed. The vines grasped them in their greedy little clutches and pulled them back to the window where they tossed them into the dark night.

"Umm, Delia," Alec said helplessly. "You might want to dress."

She hopped on top of the bed when some of the vines trailed in her direction. "What's going on, Alec?" she cried. "What are they?"

Alec chuckled. That little witch. She'd put a spell on his plants. Alec tossed Delia her shift just as the vines tugged her stockings from the back of a high-backed chair where she'd draped them. "Again, I would suggest that you dress," Alec urged. "The quicker the better."

She dropped the robe and tugged the shift over her head. The vines retreated out the window, tugging her stockings along with them. Alec leaned over his sill to peer down to the lower level, where her stockings and slippers now lay in the garden.

Alec reached for her dress when the vines grabbed it, but they were too strong. While one of them tugged the dress out the window, another wrapped around his hand to keep him from grabbing for it. Now all of her clothing, aside from her shift, lay on the garden walkway below.

Delia danced around on his bed, her feet sinking into the soft surface as she screamed, "Those are my clothes!"

"Indeed, they are," he chuckled. "I did warn you."

Her gaze shot to him. "You didn't say anything about thieving plants!" She narrowed her gaze. "How the devil is that happening?"

Alec shrugged and leaned casually against the edge of his four-poster bed. He whistled softly. "I can just imagine what they're coming for next." His Sorcha wouldn't leave the job half done. She'd pitch Delia from the window as well. "Or, who."

A particularly tricky little vine crept up the side of the bed and sneaked around Delia's wrist like a shackle. Then it tugged. She nearly toppled headfirst from the bed, but she found her footing after a moment and ran toward the window as the vine pulled her. She stuck her head out and looked down at her belongings.

"Have a good night, Delia," Alec called to her as the vines bodily picked her up and—rather gently, truth be told—carried her from the window and deposited her on the garden floor.

Her screams would certainly wake the neighbors. But he was enjoying the performance so much that he didn't particularly care. He could make them forget tomorrow. Just as she could be made to forget. He walked to the window and looked out once more. Delia was frantically putting her clothes on as the vines stood sentinel. When she was done, they gave her a shove, much like a man would shove another man he really wanted to get rid of. Delia wasted no time. She didn't even look back up at Alec. She ran. She left one of her slippers behind and didn't seem to care. But the vines must have noticed it at the same moment Alec did because one of them picked up the discarded footwear and tossed it at her, hitting her square in the backside. Delia stopped and picked up the shoe.

It was a damn good thing she did, or the slipper would have kicked her arse all the way back to the Thorne and Rose.

Alec hadn't laughed so hard since he'd become a vampyre. "Oh, Sorch," he said to himself, "I believe I'm in for a challenge. One I will enjoy almost as much as I enjoy you."

Tomorrow he would marry a witch with extraordinary powers. Powers that could toss a lass out a window and throw shoes at her head. Powers that could tie people up. Powers that were quite possibly endless.

Tomorrow he would marry. He would marry Sorcha, and he would make her happy. Because heaven forbid what she would do to him if he didn't.

Thirty

SORCHA HAD STAYED UP HALF THE NIGHT TALKING with her father and promising him that she truly loved Alec. Her father had never mentioned Alec's condition, and she hadn't, either. She knew he was well aware of the truth, but her love for Alec was more important than Alec's life after death.

Dressed in her soft yellow gown, she entered her late mother's favorite salon. She didn't even have time to glance at the daffodils and lilies she'd spoken with the night before. She knew they were draped across the room overhead, but she was so stunned by the other occupants of the room that she noticed nothing else.

On one settee sat Elspeth and Lord Benjamin, who held their tiny red-haired witch in his arms. Not far away, Caitrin sat with Lord Eynsford on her mother's prized, white brocade divan. In one of the high-backed chairs, a very expectant Blaire struggled to her feet when she spotted Sorcha. But she wasn't quick enough to intercept her, as Rhiannon appeared out of nowhere and threw her arms around Sorcha's neck.

"Oh, Sorch!" Rhi gushed. "I am so happy for ye."

Sorcha clutched the weather-controlling witch to her tightly. "Rhi! What are ye doin' here? Ye're no' gonna cry, are ye? I doona ken if the flowers will survive a downpour."

Rhi pulled back and swiped a tear of joy from her face. "I'll be careful of yer flowers, ye goose."

Sorcha glanced around the room and now noticed Lords Kettering and Blodswell hovering nearby as well. "Where did ye all come from?" Rhi and Blaire in particular should be at their new homes in England.

"Do ye think we would miss yer weddin', Sorcha?" Blaire asked, stepping forward to squeeze Sorcha's hand. "Ye were the only one, ye ken, who was at each of ours."

That was true, but, "How?" Was this what Wallace had meant when he'd said everyone had come home?

But she knew the answer to that, and her eyes found Cait, still seated on the divan beside her husband. "Ye are the slyest witch ever born, Caitrin."

The blonde grinned. "We all have our talents, Sorcha Ferguson."

Sorcha sighed and shook her head. "We will have a long talk, ye and I."

Cait tipped her head sideways as though she was seeing the future event in her mind. "Aye, we will."

Where was Alec? And Papa? And Wallace? And Mr. Crawford, for heaven's sake?

"Relax, lass," Lord Blodswell said quietly as he came to stand beside his wife. "Alec is in with your father and the vicar, signing some papers."

"How did ye ken what I was worried about?" she asked.

He grinned back at her. "After six centuries, one learns to read expressions fairly well."

How she adored Lord Blodswell's calm demeanor. "Thank ye again, my lord, for savin' him." For turning him into the creature he was now. If he'd died beside that icy loch, she never would have found her one true love. The situation wasn't ideal, but it was so much better than if she'd never had him to begin with.

"Oh, I think you're the one who has saved him, lass."

But she hadn't. Not in the way Rhiannon had saved Blodswell. Not in the way Blaire had saved Kettering. Alec hadn't become human. He hadn't become human because he didn't love her. Sorcha grasped Lord Blodswell's arm and dragged him into the far corner. "I havena saved him," she whispered. "Ye must ken that."

With a genuine smile, Blodswell tipped her chin up so she had to look into his soft green eyes. "We're all saved in different ways, Miss Ferguson. The man I saved, the man I tutored to live this life, was angry and bitter. He had no care for anyone or anything other than his own damaged heart. Never doubt that you saved him, my dear."

"But…" He was still a vampyre. Still incapable of returning her love. But Sorcha couldn't bring herself to say the words aloud.

"Love him, lass. Love him with all your heart."

"I already do," she admitted.

Blodswell winked at her. "I know. I can see that too."

From the doorway, Sorcha's father cleared his throat, signaling his arrival. "Well, I see everyone is here. It appears, lass," he looked directly at Sorcha, "that your weddin' party is larger than I anticipated. There are even more in the ballroom. Shall we join them in there as I doona believe they'll all fit in here?"

Sorcha crossed the room to her father and took his proffered arm. "I canna believe all of my coven sisters are here! I never even dreamed of hopin' for such a thing."

Her father began to direct her toward their ballroom, and he sighed. "They all love ye, lass. And who can blame them? As soon as Cait ordered everyone home and explained why, they came in droves."

Upon entering the ballroom, Sorcha scanned the throng of people. Cait and Rhiannon's fathers stood together, talking to Rhi's silly sister, Ginny, and her new husband. Lord Radbourne and his twin brothers nodded their welcome in her direction. Blaire's two brothers each had linked arms with her new sister-in-law. All of MacQuarrie House seemed to be present, as did every neighbor and friend Sorcha or Alec had ever possessed. "*Havers!*" she muttered under her breath.

"Indeed," her father agreed. "If ye were less loved, we could have performed the ceremony in yer mother's salon."

Then Sorcha spotted Alec at the far end of the ballroom beside a large window, talking with the bald-pated vicar, Mr. Crawford. Alec looked across the room at her, his dark, penetrating eyes so focused that Sorcha almost missed a step. Her heart pounded so hard that she thought for certain it would leap right from her chest.

"Careful, love," her father whispered as he led her through the guests and to Alec's side.

Once she reached him, she realized he had the silliest collection of apple blossoms tucked into his lapel. She couldn't help but laugh. "What are ye doin' with those?"

Alec shrugged. "Found them in a magical orangery and couldn't help but take a few."

Sorcha's father placed her hand on Alec's arm and then nodded for Mr. Crawford to begin the ceremony. "We are ready."

The vicar looked from Alec to Sorcha and back and repeated the old Scottish blessing, *"Slainte mhor agus a h-uile beannachd duibh."* Then he nodded at Alec. "Repeat after me, sir. 'Before God and these witnesses, I, Alec Lachlan Colin MacQuarrie, take ye, Sorcha Ivy Ferguson, ta be my wife, ta have and ta hold 'til death do us part.'"

Alec squeezed Sorcha's hand. "Before God and these witnesses, I, Alec Lachlan Colin MacQuarrie, take you, Sorcha Ivy Ferguson, to be my wife, to have and to hold 'til... death do us part."

Sorcha swallowed, wishing he hadn't paused on that last bit. But death would part them, wouldn't it?

"And now ye, Miss Ferguson. Repeat after me—'Before God and these witnesses, I, Sorcha Ivy Ferguson, take ye, Alec Lachlan Colin MacQuarrie, ta be my husband, ta have and ta hold 'til death do us part.'"

Sorcha stared up into Alec's dark eyes. "Before God

and these witnesses, I, Sorcha Ivy Ferguson, take ye, Alec Lachlan Colin MacQuarrie, ta be my husband, ta have and ta hold forever."

One of Alec's dark eyebrows rose in mild amusement. "You always surprise me, lass."

Mr. Crawford coughed delicately.

Alec turned his gaze on the vicar. "You may continue, Crawford."

"But she didn't say it exactly."

"She said what she meant," Alec replied, all pompous Scotsman. "Now continue, Crawford."

The vicar stood a little taller, although a frown now marred his brow. "Do ye have a ring, Mr. MacQuarrie?"

Alec nodded and then reached into his pocket. He retrieved a beautiful ruby ring, the color of a nice claret. Then he slid the ring onto Sorcha's left hand.

Heavy mist hung in the air. Sorcha glanced over at Rhiannon, who wiped a tear from her eye. "I'm sorry," she mouthed back at Sorcha. Then she shrugged and leaned into her husband's arms. The mist began to clear as he whispered in her ear.

"With this ring, I thee wed," Alec said quietly, drawing her back into the ceremony.

Mr. Crawford's voice rang out. "Ye may kiss yer bride."

Alec attempted to gather her gently into his arms. But she'd have none of that. She launched herself at him and threw her arms around his neck, nearly knocking him over in the process. But he just chuckled and grabbed her, lifting her to meet his waiting lips. Suddenly Alec yelped and dropped her to her feet.

All the eyes of the coven sisters and their husbands shot to Rhiannon. She shrugged. "My emotions are gettin' the better of me," she said.

Lord Eynsford laughed aloud as his brothers looked on, completely unaware that Alec had just been zapped by a witch with a lightning bolt for being too amorous with his end-of-ceremony kiss.

&

Love him with all your heart. Lord Blodswell's advice had echoed in Sorcha's ears all morning. And an idea had taken root. Truly, the idea made all the sense in the world. Though she would miss her old life, at least she thought she would, spending the rest of eternity with Alec was worth every sacrifice.

"I'd really rather not have a convergence of your circle in my parlor just now. We've already been surrounded by half of Edinburgh for most of the day," Alec complained as his coach stopped before his home, or their home, really.

Sorcha couldn't help but grin at him. "It willna be for long, Alec. Besides, Cait said it was important." And Sorcha had a feeling she knew why. Cait must have seen the future and realized Sorcha wouldn't be counted amongst the *Còig's* numbers much longer. It wouldn't do to leave the others exposed. One last coming together was the least she could do for her lifetime friends.

"It's already too long, and we haven't gotten inside yet."

"Be a good host, will ye?" she admonished.

"So I should greet them with a smile and then tell them to turn around and leave my wife to me?" His brow rose suggestively. "We have some unfinished business to attend to, lass, and I am more than anxious to finally attend to it."

Warmth crept up Sorcha's cheeks. She was more than anxious to attend to their business as well. But her final act as a *Còig* witch needed to be handled first. She owed that much to the others who had been such an important part of her life up until now.

The driver opened the door, and Alec bounded from the carriage. Then he offered his hand to Sorcha. "Mrs. MacQuarrie." He smiled and scooped her up in arms as he started toward their front door.

Sorcha giggled. "I can walk, Alec."

"Tradition, lass, tradition," he replied as he bounded up the steps.

Before the door opened, a strand of ivy reached toward her and caressed Sorcha's hand. Alec's eyes grew wide at the contact. "Welcoming you home?" Awe laced his voice.

Sorcha bit back a laugh. Not a welcome per se, more like a quick recounting of a most delightful tale. "Something like that," she murmured as the front door opened and Gibson nodded at the pair.

"Welcome home, sir, madam."

Sorcha had never been called madam before. It made her feel a bit older than her years, though that would be a common occurrence from here on out, wouldn't it?

Alec gently returned her to her feet and turned his eye on their butler. "We have guests right behind us, Gibson. Pray direct everyone to the green parlor."

"Of course, sir."

"And refreshments, Gibson," Sorcha added.

The butler nodded and then started for the kitchens as Alec led Sorcha to the large front parlor where sunshine poured into the cheerful room. "Such a lovely day," she commented.

Alec pulled her into his embrace. "I never really noticed before that every plant leans toward you like the sun. You should tell your little friends that your husband is the jealous sort."

Sorcha laughed. "And ye should tell all of yer friends that yer wife is the jealous sort."

Something flashed in his eyes, and Sorcha had the feeling it had to do with a certain whore being chased off his property the night before. "I have no friends anymore other than you, lass."

"Well, then," she reached up on her tiptoes to kiss his jaw, "ye are rather lucky ta have me."

"Lucky indeed," he agreed.

"I'll say," boomed Benjamin Westfield's voice from the corridor. "No need to direct us, Gibson, I know just where to find Mr. and Mrs. MacQuarrie."

Alec rolled his eyes. "Gibson hates him."

Sorcha smiled up at her husband. "He's yer friend, ye ken. Ben has always been yer friend."

He tweaked her nose. "Aye." He sighed. "I suppose there's no getting rid of the dog, is there?"

Benjamin chose that moment to direct everyone into the green parlor. "Man's best friend, you know." He winked at the pair.

Almost instantly, the other four witches surrounded Sorcha, making it clear they required her presence. "Ye doona mind do ye, Alec?" Rhiannon asked sweetly.

A mild look of annoyance settled on his face. "After the blast you gave me this morning, Lady Blodswell, don't think you can just charm me with the bat of your pretty eyes."

Rhiannon giggled. "Ye deserved it and ye ken it, MacQuarrie."

"We willna take up too much of her time," Elspeth promised.

"You better not, or I'll be forced to whisk her away the same way Ben did you, El."

Her only response to that was a smile.

Once the five witches had sequestered themselves in one of the parlor's corners, Sorcha's eyes began to water. She knew she was making the right decision, but she would miss her friends, her coven sisters, dearly.

"Doona ye dare cry," Blaire admonished. "He'll throw us out."

Sorcha tried her hardest to smile, but then her eyes landed on Blaire's wedding ring. Once upon a time it had belonged to Lord Kettering and had allowed the man to walk amongst the living in the daylight. The ring was an exact duplicate of Alec's, well almost. Lord Kettering had had his resized to fit Blaire after their wedding.

Blaire followed Sorcha's line of sight and squeezed her hand. "Ye are like bottled sunshine, Sorch. We willna allow ye ta spend the rest of yer days hidin' from the light. It wouldna be right."

Rhiannon reached into her reticule, retrieved something, and then opened her hand, revealing Lord Blodswell's identical ring. "Matthew doesna have need of it anymore. We want ye ta have it."

Sorcha couldn't stop the tears from trailing down her face at that, and her heart threatened to burst. "I was so afraid ye wouldna understand."

Elspeth dabbed at Sorcha's cheek with a handkerchief. "Did ye think we would abandon ye, sweetheart?"

She hadn't been sure what their reaction would be and Sorcha shrugged.

Elspeth swiped at a tear of her own. "Ye were the most loyal and true ta all of us. We will always be here for ye, for as long as our family lasts."

Up until now Cait had been very quiet, which was most certainly a rarity for their seer. Sorcha looked straight at the blonde witch. "Ye willna try ta stop me?"

Cait shook her head. "I had the most interestin' conversation with yer father today. He has an unusual theory on prophesies and the future rightin' itself. I'm no' my mother, and I willna stand in the way of yer future or yer happiness. Just follow yer heart, Sorch. That's all I ask."

Sorcha nodded. "I am."

"I ken," Cait replied. "And I ken ye are goin' ta be very happy with Alec. Love him with all yer heart."

Almost exactly the same thing Lord Blodswell had said earlier that day.

Across the room, the men laughed at something, and Sorcha turned her attention to the vampyre she would spend forever with.

Thirty-One

AFTER SEVERAL HOURS OF ENTERTAINING THE *CÒIG* AND their husbands, Alec had endured all he intended to. Why wouldn't they leave? It seemed like he had waited for Sorcha forever, and he didn't plan to wait one more second. He had warned Elspeth that he wasn't above whisking his wife away, and that was exactly what he planned to do.

"I know that look." Ben chuckled.

"Aye, you should," Alec agreed. "I've seen you wear it often enough."

"Doesn't he, though," Eynsford put in.

"You're one to talk." Alec snorted. Then he looked at the quartet of men surrounding him. "The lot of you can stay or go. I really don't care any longer. But I'm done entertaining you."

He paid no attention to the twin expressions of amusement that adorned Blodswell's and Kettering's faces as he left their circle and strode across the floor to retrieve his wife. Alec nodded at Sorcha's coven sisters as he placed his hand on his witch's shoulder. "Do excuse us, ladies."

Then he bent at the knee and scooped Sorcha up in his arms. She gasped but didn't look unhappy.

"Feel free to visit any time," Alec tossed over his shoulder as he strode from the parlor and started up the main steps.

"Alec!" Sorcha giggled.

He carried his bride across the threshold to his chambers, with her clutching him as closely as she could. "I know. I'm a terrible host in my own home," he groused.

She playfully smacked at his chest and scolded, "I canna believe ye left them all belowstairs and whisked me away."

"The interlopers stayed too long."

Her warm brown eyes twinkled. "They're our friends and they're perfectly delightful. Ye could have been a little more gentlemanly."

"What will be delightful is when I have you naked in my bed," Alec growled, giving her a good look at his distended teeth. He wanted to disrobe her slowly. But after suffering through the ceremony, then the after-wedding assembly, and then the well wishes from her coven, he was too damn anxious to be inside her to even care about taking his time with her clothing.

He dropped her to her feet, allowing her to slide slowly down his body until her feet hit the floor. He cupped the back of her head and pulled her in for a kiss. "Welcome home," he whispered, just before his lips touched hers. She tasted like wedding cake. And smelled like apple blossoms. Apple blossoms and sin.

Her heart beat rapidly within her chest. He could hear it. "Nervous?" he asked when he finally lifted his head.

She ducked her head shyly. "Maybe just a little."

"Don't be. I know what I'm doing."

"Thank heavens one of us does." She bit her bottom lip, making the plump flesh pout a bit. "But I doona like that ye have been with other women."

"There's not much I can do to change that," he admitted, as he thought about her complaint. Then he drew her into his arms and she automatically laid her head on his chest. "But since the moment I saw you at Castle Hythe, I've wanted no one else." He tipped her chin up with his finger. "You're the one I want. For the rest of my life."

She raised a fingernail to nibble on it. "Speakin' of the rest of our lives. There's somethin' I want ye ta do for me, for us."

He spun her around and began to work the buttons of her yellow gown. "Can you tell me about it later? I've been waiting and waiting. And now the only thing I want is to make love to my wife."

"Ye do?" she asked quietly. As though she couldn't tell from the frantic way he was disrobing her. When he had her down to her chemise, he began to remove his clothes as well, shucking them piece by piece and tossing them across the floor. It was only when he was down to his smallclothes that he stopped.

"I do," he whispered. God, he wanted to touch her. He wanted to surge inside her. He wanted Sorcha.

"Did ye change yer bedclothes since last night?" she suddenly blurted out.

Alec raised his head and looked into her eyes. "Beg your pardon?"

"Well, Miss Sewell was here last night, so I was hopin' ye would have changed the bedclothes since she left." She looked as mischievous as he'd ever seen her.

"Ask your vines. If not, perhaps you can call them in here to do it for me."

She giggled until he shucked off his unmentionables. Then he tugged her chemise over her head, leaving her as naked as he was, aside from her stockings and garters. He bent in front of her to roll them down and off her feet.

"Alec!" she cried, as she shoved at his head.

Not that he could be blamed for his inability to keep his eyes off her. Alec took her hips in his hands and spun her around. "There, now your modesty is intact," he said with a chuckle. The view of her backside was just as nice.

Her face was scarlet when she looked at him over her shoulder. "That's no' much better," she mumbled.

"It's just fine for me," he teased as he pulled the last stocking over her toes and ran his hands up the backs of her thighs. Then he leaned forward and nibbled the flesh on her hip very gently. His teeth were fully distended and had been since the moment they'd walked upstairs.

Alec appraised her body as he stood up. She was absolute perfection. He could look at her all day. He might do that very thing after he finally got to have her. Just keep her in bed for the rest of the day, naked, so he could explore her whole body. Maybe he could even count her freckles. Alec turned her back to face him and dropped his lips to her shoulder. He wanted to taste every part of her.

He cupped her bottom and raised her against him, letting her feel how much he wanted her.

"That was a very naughty thing you did last night. I have never seen Miss Sewell so put out. How did you know she would come here?"

"I dinna ken for sure," she said with a shrug. "But I had an inklin' so I just whispered a little somethin' on my way out yesterday. Yer ivy told me the whole tale when we arrived this mornin'." She giggled. "Did her slipper really hit her in backside?"

"You are a force to be reckoned with, my devious little witch. And you look so sweet on the outside."

"I am sweet," she whispered, and Alec nearly shivered as she pressed her lips to his shoulder and trailed a tiny path up the side of his neck.

She was sweet and then some. "Stop that," he warned. "Or I'll disgrace myself like I did the last time we were together."

"One of my coven sisters says that's fairly normal."

He jerked her back gently to look at her face. "You told them about that?" He might have to toss her over his knee for the infraction.

"Well, one of them brought it up when she was talkin' about her experience with her own vampyre," she said sheepishly. Then she raised her hands as though surrendering. "I promise I dinna tell them about ye. But it was interestin' ta hear it happens ta more men than just ye."

"One of the former vampyres, eh?" he asked absently as he tugged the pins from her hair, letting the dark locks cascade over her shoulders. "Which one? I'd like to give him a hard time about it."

Sorcha's mouth dropped open in surprise. "Ye would no' do such a thing."

He might. It would all depend on whether it was Kettering or the oh-so-noble Blodswell. "Which one?" he asked again.

"I'll never tell," Sorcha teased. Then she squealed as Alec once again picked her up in his arms and carried her to the bed. He very gently placed her in the middle and wasted no time crawling up to seat himself between her thighs. "Now?" she asked, a little hesitance in her voice.

He gazed down into the depths of her eyes, in awe of what he saw staring back at him. She trusted him to take care of her. And he would, for the rest of his days. Or the rest of hers at least. "Not yet," he whispered as he dipped his head and took the tip of her breast into his mouth. Sorcha arched her back, her hands sliding into his hair as she tugged him closer to him.

"Alec," she cried. "My heart is beatin' so hard."

"I know," he said as he switched to her other breast. "I can hear it." Then his head dipped again. She even tasted like apples. It had been so long since he'd eaten that ripe fruit that he was momentarily put off by it.

"Somethin' wrong?" she questioned as she sat up on her elbows.

"You taste like apples," he admitted.

She laughed. "I get ta maneuver the trees," she said with a shrug. "It's a benefit. For now, at least."

"For now?"

"Ye said ye wanted to talk about that later," she reminded him.

Not that he needed a ton of encouragement to return his complete focus to her delightful apple essence. "I wonder if you taste like that everywhere?" He kissed his way down her belly. It fluttered beneath his lips as she began to squirm.

"No' there, Alec," she cried, attempting to close her legs.

"There," he affirmed, just before his fingers parted her folds and his tongue found her entrance. "Lie back and enjoy it."

Her mouth fell open and her head fell back as he licked across her center. "Alec," she cried, his mouth moving across her most sensitive skin as she begged and pleaded for release. Alec replaced his mouth with his thumb and strummed across that little bundle of nerves he knew would drive her crazy as he turned his head and licked her inner thigh. Her pulse beat beyond that delicate skin. "Allow me to take from you?" he asked.

"Aye!" she cried out as he got her closer and closer to release. Just as she toppled over the barrier and into bliss, Alec bit into the silky flesh, finding her pulse point as he drank her in. Her pleasure hit him first. His manhood throbbed for release, but he continued to milk the vein in her thigh as he strummed across that delicate little nub. Her pleasure nearly swamped him as she cried his name over and over, and she took his joy at pleasuring her in response.

When her hips slowed and her body unclenched,

Alec licked across the wounds he'd made to close them and heard her sigh from above him. He climbed up her body until he could kiss her tenderly. Her lips were soft and pliant beneath his, and her heart still beat a mad rhythm. "Will ye take me now?" she asked quietly.

He continued to kiss her as he probed at her center, his manhood hard and ready, nearly screaming for release. Wetness surrounded him as he slid into her chamber slowly, allowing her time to stretch around him.

Sorcha held tightly to his forearms, her tiny little fingernails digging into his skin like pleasurable talons of delight. "Are you all right?" he stopped to ask.

Her legs rose to tug him farther into her and locked behind his back. "Please," she whispered against his lips.

"Slow down just a moment," he warned as her feet tugged him farther inside her. She flinched beneath him. He'd suspected it was coming. But he'd never taken an innocent before. "Sorch?"

"Make it better," she said quietly as her legs wrapped more tightly around him. He slid his full length inside her and stopped when he was fully seated within her sheath.

"Tell me I didn't harm you," he prompted, staying still within her.

"I'll harm ye if ye keep tryin' ta treat me like I'll break," she replied. Her gasp when he began to move hit him like an anvil over the head. The breathy little moans she made nearly tore him in two. He pulled back and then sank inside her, and she willingly accepted every inch of him.

"Sorch," he murmured into her hair as he tried to

hold off. He wanted to bring her over the pinnacle with him, so he reached between them and strummed her back up to those heights he'd had her at a moment before. And she burst at the same time he did, screaming his name loudly as he finished inside her. She quivered around his flesh, wringing every drop of pleasure from his body as she settled in his arms. When they were done, he rolled to his side and drew her to lie on his chest. "You're sure you're all right?" he asked as he placed a kiss in her hair.

"Better than all right," she said, her voice sleepy and sated. "I love ye, Alec," she whispered. He heard her quite well. And the place where his heart had once been ached as she lay draped across him, her slender, naked body arousing him anew. "My coven sisters gave me no clues it would be like that." She inhaled deeply and then said, "I will miss them so much when they're gone."

"I'll take you to see them any time you wish."

Her fingers trailed in small circles through the light hair on his chest. She raised her head and looked directly at him. "That's no' what I meant."

He must have had a blank look on his face, because she rushed to continue. "I mean when they're old and dead and gone." She looked at everything but him. "I'll miss bein' a witch, but I love you more than I love the *Còig*."

"Sorch, I don't understand." And he didn't. Why would she stop being a witch? No one had said a thing to him about that. All the other witches were still witches.

She raised herself up on her elbows to look into his

face. She was so beautiful, with her trusting brown eyes and passion-bruised lips. "I have decided I want ye ta turn me. So we can be together forever."

Forever. Was that what she had meant in the wedding ceremony? Had she lost her mind? "Turn you?" Alec sat up and glared at her. He must sound like an idiot. "I'm not going to turn you. Not into what I am." Where the devil had she gotten that idea?

"But it's the only way we can be together forever, do ye no' see?" Her eyebrows scrunched together. "Ye want ta be with me for always?"

He wanted nothing more than to be with her until the end of time, but he wouldn't curse her the same way he had been. Seeing Sorcha turned to a parasite like him would certainly kill him as quickly as a well-placed wooden stake.

"I'll miss bein' a witch," she continued, seemingly oblivious to his tortured thoughts. "But the others assure me I should follow my heart."

She was willing to give up her life? To give up her powers? To give up her mortality? To give it all up for him? Sorcha loved him enough to do all of that? To change her life so completely? To love him over everyone and everything she'd ever known?

A searing pain hit Alec's chest, swamping him even more than her pleasure had. He fell back to the bed as the excruciating ache within his chest nearly cut him to ribbons.

"Alec, are ye all right?" Sorcha cried as she hopped up on her knees to hover over him.

Her voice sounded farther and farther away as the pain grew worse.

Then all he knew was darkness.

❦

Havers! Sorcha took Alec by the shoulders and shook with all her might. "Alec!" she called loudly. "Alec, what's wrong?"

A moment earlier, they'd been joined together and it had honestly been the most amazing moment of her life. He might not love her, but he did care for her, and it showed in his tender touch, in the way he looked into her eyes as he took her beneath him, in the way he saw to her pleasure first.

But now he was lying lifeless, and Sorcha thought she might expire right alongside him. "Ye're finally mine, Alec MacQuarrie. Doona do this ta me."

A knock sounded at the door as it opened just a crack. "Are you all right, lass?" Lord Blodswell's voice crept around the door.

"Please help me!" Sorcha cried as she scurried to the foot of the bed, retrieved the counterpane, and covered Alec with it.

"Are you decent, Mrs. MacQuarrie?" Lord Kettering's disembodied voice asked from the corridor.

She glanced down at her own nakedness. She was quite indecent, now that he mentioned it. She snatched her chemise from the floor and threw it over her head. "Aye." Modesty be damned, there was no time to wait for her to be properly attired. Something was wrong with her husband.

Blodswell and Kettering tumbled into the room, one right after the other. She could have sworn she saw a concerned Lycan or two hovering behind them. But Lord Blodswell kicked the door shut and she heard a loud curse from beyond the closed portal.

"Meddling Lycans," Kettering mumbled, as he brushed a lock of hair from his face. Another loud yelp sounded from the corridor. "However, it sounds as though your wife has them well under control."

Blodswell chuckled. "Lightning does have its uses, outside of storm building."

How could they laugh? "I doona ken what ye think is so amusing. Where is Elspeth?" Sorcha demanded. "Ye have ta get Elspeth ta heal him!" Hot tears tracked down her face, and she dashed them away with her fingertips.

"None of this is amusing, lass," Blodswell informed her, the grin leaving his face as soon as he realized how upset she truly was.

"Well, the fact that your wife just shocked the trousers off Eynsford *was* particularly satisfying," Kettering said with a wide smile.

"James," Blodswell chastised and gestured with his head toward Sorcha.

"Not to worry, lass." Kettering stepped toward her. "Lady Eynsford must have known this was going to happen. Otherwise, she wouldn't have insisted we all stay here."

Blodswell pointed to Alec who lay prone in the bed. "What happened?"

"What *did* ye do to him, lass?" Kettering asked, a grin tugging at the corners of his mouth. Blodswell punched him in the arm, which knocked the grin from his face but not the teasing tone from his voice.

Heat crept up Sorcha's face. Alec was naked, and

she was wearing nothing more than her chemise. What on earth did they think she'd done to him? *Havers!* She hadn't hurt him, had she? She hadn't really done this to him?

"It's all right," one of them soothed from across the room. "You didn't harm him." She was too embarrassed to look up and see which one had spoken.

"Is he dead? He willna wake." They must have heard the quiver in her voice because they both finally approached the bed and looked at her sympathetically.

"He was dead prior to today, lass," Blodswell reminded her. Then he reached out and put a crooked finger under Alec's nose. He held it there for a moment and then looked back at Kettering. "Just as we suspected."

"Indeed?" Kettering's blue eyes widened in surprise. *Havers!* This was awful. "Oh, Alec," Sorcha moaned and crawled back onto the bed and lay her face against her husband's chest. But then she felt it. His chest rose and fell. She sat up on her hands and knees and looked at him. "Alec?" she asked. Then she addressed the interlopers. "Is he breathin'?" She put her own finger under his nose and felt his hot breath against her skin and gasped.

"Something like that," Kettering muttered.

Alec groaned from beside her on the bed. "When I remember how to breathe and talk at the same time, the two of you will be thrashed," he said quietly, gasping the words out.

"Alec?" Sorcha cried. "Alec, please tell me I dinna harm ye."

His hand reached out to squeeze hers. "Sorch, if you

didn't, I'll give you ample opportunity to try it again later," he said. He finally opened his eyes and looked at his onetime mentors who stood staring at him, both of them obviously holding back hysterical laughter.

Kettering even coughed into his closed fist. "Wonder if I looked just as pathetic when my heart started to beat."

Alec narrowed his eyes at the pair. "The two of you look awfully satisfied with yourselves."

"This from the man who said he'd never be human again," Blodswell reminded him. "Nice to have you back in the land of the living, MacQuarrie."

Everything was happening so quickly. "Wait," Sorcha begged. "Ye're human?" She'd given up that hope so long ago. Was it truly possible?

Alec's once-again brown eyes twinkled at her, and she knew it was true.

"It would appear so, love," Alec said with a smile as he brought her hand to his mouth and placed a lingering kiss in her knuckles. Then he held his other hand out to her. "Take off the ring and let's see."

Sorcha didn't waste a moment tugging the signet ring from his finger.

The sun shone brightly through the window, and a beam of light skittered across his face when she moved to look more closely at him. "Aye, human," he grunted. He didn't go up in flames. He didn't burn. He just lay there with the sun on his face.

But it didn't make any sense. "I doona understand." She must sound like a ninny. Her gaze shifted to the two former vampyres and then back to Alec. "Ye doona love me," she reminded him quietly.

"That's obviously not the case," Kettering teased.

Alec's glare speared the intruders. "I think you both have worn out your welcome."

Kettering and Blodswell looked at one another with mock surprise on their faces. "I don't remember being invited into his bedchamber, much less being welcomed."

"Go find your wives and gloat," Alec ordered. "And take those Lycans with you," he added. But his eyes were on Sorcha as he reached up and brushed a lock of hair from her face. He wrapped his hand around the back of her neck and pulled her gently down until his lips could meet hers. Then he addressed his former mentors, who still hadn't moved. "You might want to leave now, because my wife is going to be naked in about three seconds," he said aloud.

Sorcha gasped and batted at his grasping hands as they moved to the straps of her chemise. Her heart skittered a frantic beat within her chest as he took control and started to tug the soft fabric from her body.

"I believe that's our cue to exit, my friend," Blodswell said to Kettering.

"But just so you know, Alec, neither of us fainted like a lass when we received our humanity. You, on the other hand..." They both chuckled.

"Out!" Alec ordered. They were out the door in a flash, closing it solidly behind them. "They'll never let me live that down," he said quietly to Sorcha. "I swooned. Good God, what's the world coming to?"

Sorcha could hear an argument going on outside the door, but Alec was taking all of her attention as he tossed her chemise across the room and flipped the counterpane over them both. He drew her body flush against his, her breasts pushed against his naked chest.

"Are ye really alive?" she whispered, still not quite believing it.

"It would appear so," he replied as he ran his hand down her side and tugged one leg over his hip. He was hot and hard and pressed at her insistently. But he didn't seem to want anything more than to be close to her.

"But how can that be?" she asked, sorry to hear the quiver in her own voice. Tears were pricking at the backs of her eyelids, and she had no control at all.

"I never thought I'd be able to fall in love," he tried to explain.

"So, all it took was tumblin' ye in the bedchamber ta make ye fall in love with me?" She shoved at his chest. If she'd known that, she would have seduced him at Castle Hythe.

"I've been tumbled, as you so indelicately put it, many times in the past, love," he said quietly.

"Doona remind me," she sulked.

"And that leads me to believe that it wasn't the fact that I bedded you that changed me."

Then what was it? "I dinna do anythin' else." She hadn't done anything out of the ordinary, aside from marrying and making love to her husband.

"I was living in a fog until you, Sorch," he said quietly. "I was existing from day to day but not living. Not for a moment of it. Then you walked back into my life. And it changed. I became more than I was. It's all because of you." He touched his lips to hers.

"You were willing to give up your coven for me. They're more than family to you. And you would have given them up, along with your powers, for an eternity with *me*."

"I still would," she said quietly. He looked so intent. So, thoughtful. It was different looking into his eyes now that they weren't black as night.

"That's when it hit me. And it hit me hard."

Sorcha tried to swallow past the lump in her throat. But it was nearly impossible.

"I love you, Sorcha," he said quietly. Then he rolled her beneath him and looked deep into her eyes. "I couldn't live without you. I need you, like the air that I need to breathe."

A tear trickled a hot path down the side of her face into her hair. He leaned over and kissed it away.

"I want you," he said softly as he rocked his hips and pressed at her center. "For now and always."

"I'm yers," she cried as he slid inside her.

"And I'm yours. Though why you'd have me is beyond my comprehension."

She giggled beneath him, which made her grip him more tightly. She lowered her voice to a small murmur and said close to his ear, "It's because ye're really good in the bedchamber." Then her mouth fell open and a cry she didn't even recognize fell from her lips.

"Thank heaven for small favors," he replied, before his lips dipped toward her breast, and then neither of them had enough air in their lungs to keep talking.

Epilogue

"Tell me how your heart startin' beatin' again, Papa." Ivy MacQuarrie climbed up into Alec's lap at his study desk. He was so engrossed in the Stockton and Darlington Railway papers before him that he hadn't even heard the door open.

He ruffled the top of the little imp's head. "I'm certain you could tell me the story since you've heard it so many times, lass."

"But it's better when you tell it," she insisted the way only a five-year-old can.

Alec lifted his daughter's hand to his mouth and placed a kiss on her palm. "After you've finished playing with your friends, I'll tell you the tale again, Ivy. Now run along."

She tipped her head back to see him better, and her brown curls bobbed over her shoulders. "But Lia keeps tellin' me what ta do, and I doona want ta play anymore."

That was hardly surprising. Alec chuckled. Lady Aurelia Thorpe was just as haughty as her mother had been all those years before. Perhaps more so. The future seer was spoiled rotten by her father. "I am sorry, my little sprite. Let's go see how much longer your mother and the others are going to be, shall we?"

Ivy nodded and hopped back to the floor. Alec pushed from his seat and took his daughter's hand.

"Mama's probably tired anyway."

Sorcha had been awfully tired as of late. She hadn't been getting enough sleep and was doting on her plants more than usual. He'd have to find out what that was about, but for now he turned his attention back to his daughter and her five-year-old problems. "Have you ever thought of teaming up with Lucien, Ivy? Aurelia never tells *him* what to do." At least he'd never seen the little witch dictate orders to her twin brother.

Alec led Ivy toward the orangery where Sorcha and the other witches were convened.

His beautiful daughter looked up at him and wrinkled her nose like she smelled something bad. "He's a *boy*," she replied, as though Alec had suggested she throw in her lot with the French.

"That he is," Alec agreed. "Don't know what I was thinking."

They entered the orangery, and immediately the five witches rose to their feet. Only Sorcha was able to meet Alec's gaze. What was that about? "Hope we're not disturbing you," he said, stepping closer to the coven.

"I need ta be on my way anyway." Cait rushed past him. "Are Lia and Lucien still in the nursery?"

Alec looked down at his daughter and she nodded. "Apparently so. Do send our regards to Eynsford."

"Ye can tell him yerself," Cait tossed over her shoulder. "Since ye'll be our guests at The Park next week."

Now Alec knew why none of the others had met his eyes. He glanced at his wife. "Are we headed to Kent, love?"

Sorcha nodded her head. "We have a bit of *Còig* business ta attend ta."

So everyone was going, were they? Alec shrugged. Truth be told, he'd found a camaraderie with Eynsford, Kettering, Blodswell, and his old friend Westfield somewhere along the way, and he couldn't imagine his life without all of the witches and their husbands. "Then, I suppose we'll have a grand time."

Elspeth, Blaire, and Rhiannon slid past him, muttering their farewells, and Alec and Ivy walked farther into the orangery to where Sorcha still stood rooted to the floor. Her brown eyes sought out Alec's and she smiled. "Cait gave me a glimpse of the future."

Alec frowned. "That's against the rules."

Ivy dropped his hand and wrapped her arms around Sorcha's legs. "What did she say, Mama?"

Sorcha winked at their daughter. "She said it's high time we got ye a governess, lass."

Ivy's mouth dropped open. "But, Nurse—" she started to protest.

"Nurse will have her hands full."

Alec's mouth went dry. "Her hands will be full?" The meaning of those words touched his soul. "Are you saying you're expecting, Sorcha?"

"Expectin' what?" Ivy demanded, and at the same time Sorcha nodded her head.

Alec pulled her into his embrace and buried his face in her apple blossom-scented hair. "Oh, love, are you feeling all right? Is that why you've been so tired?"

Sorcha pulled back to looked at him, her radiant smile making him fall in love with her all over again. "A boy."

"A boy?" Ivy echoed. "A boy what?"

Sorcha looked down at their precocious daughter. "I'm goin' ta have a bairn, Ivy. Ye're goin' ta be a big sister."

Ivy's nose scrunched up again. "A boy?"

Alec laughed as he scooped up the tiny lass in his arms. "Of course, a boy. We already have such a delightful girl."

Ivy giggled as he tickled her. "Papa!"

"Let's retire to the nursery, lass, and I'll tell you that story again."

Ivy nodded. "Mama, too."

Sorcha wrapped her arm around Alec's waist and pressed a kiss to Ivy's forehead. "What story are we ta hear, lass?"

"The one where ye made Papa's heart beat again."

"My favorite of them all." Then Sorcha rose on her toes and kissed Alec's chin.

About the Author

Lydia Dare is a pseudonym for the writing team of Tammy Falkner and Jodie Pearson. Both are active members of the Heart of Carolina Romance Writers and Romance Writers of America. Their writing process involves passing a manuscript back and forth, each one writing 1,500 words after editing the other's previous installment. Jodie specializes in writing the history and Tammy in writing the paranormal. They live near Raleigh, North Carolina.

If you're captivated by Lydia Dare's

Regency vampyres, wait until you meet her

roguish, aristocratic werewolf heroes!

From

A CERTAIN
WOLFISH
CHARM

Available now from
Sourcebooks Casablanca

LILY COULDN'T REMEMBER EVER BEING SO ENRAGED. How dare the blackguard refuse to see her? How dare he hide out in his study? She pounded louder on the door. "I am not leaving until you see me."

Nothing.

Not a sound came from the study. He *was* in there, wasn't he? She knew he was. She'd seen him vanish into the room with her very own eyes. Unless he'd climbed out a window, he could hear every word. Despite last month's mention in the society papers, where he was touted for slipping out Lady T.'s window while the butler helped the inebriated Lord T. to bed, she simply couldn't imagine him folding his big body in two and going out the window just to get away from her.

Lily crossed her arms over her chest. Really, who could imagine the powerful Duke of Blackmoor would be afraid to see *her*?

Over the years, ignoring her had apparently been easy for him, but that was when she was in Essex. Out of sight and all that. It took real effort to ignore her when she was pounding on his door. "I am a most stubborn woman," she warned him. "I'll wait right here as long as it takes, Your Grace."

Still nothing.

Lily jiggled the handle. Locked.

She heaved a sigh and leaned her head against the large oak door. She knew he could hear her, and she was at a loss. Perhaps talking to him would be easier without his penetrating gray eyes focused on her. What did she have to lose?

"I'm worried," she said softly. "Something is not right with Oliver and… Well, I know you don't care for the boy, but his father made you his guardian. So that means I'm stuck with you."

The door was suddenly yanked open, and Lily stumbled forward, right into the muscled arms of the Duke of Blackmoor. She sucked in a surprised breath. Men never held her in their arms. Yet his closed around her as he steadied her. She couldn't really call it *holding her*, since she'd fallen into him like a great oak tree whose roots had suddenly given way.

Lily froze. The heat of his body, coupled with the manly scent of him, was enough to knock her off her feet once more. She steadied herself by placing her hands on his chest. The muscles rippled beneath her fingers. She raised her eyes to his untied cravat and then to the open neck of his shirt, where an improper amount of skin was exposed. She'd never seen such an amazing sight. The light dusting of hair across his chest mesmerized her.

Lily realized that she was standing on her own two feet, yet his arms were still around her. With her great height, she looked most men in the eye. But she had to tip her head back to look up at Blackmoor. His warm, mint-scented breath blew across her face. Lily closed her eyes and inhaled.

Suddenly, the duke pushed her away from him, a scowl marring his ruggedly handsome face. "Miss Rutledge, shouldn't you be in Essex?"

Shaking off his effect, Lily squared her shoulders. "Do you even read the letters I send you?"

"How much?" he growled.

"How much?" Lily echoed, blinking at him.

"How much money will it take to make you leave?"

Money! Why did it always come to money with this man? Oliver's estates brought in plenty, which Blackmoor would know if he paid the slightest bit of attention to his ward's accounts. She didn't care if she never saw one farthing of Blackmoor's fortune, for heaven's sake. Lily leveled him with her haughtiest glare. "There is more to being a guardian than proper funds, Your Grace."

"And that's why Lord Maberley has *you*, Miss Rutledge." Then he stepped away from her, stalking down the corridor toward his gray-haired butler. "Is the coach ready, Billings?"

Lily chased him. He couldn't dismiss her so easily. How dare he try to escape her? "There is only so much I can do, Your Grace. We're entering a realm in his development I know nothing about. Oliver isn't the same boy he was before and…"

The duke turned back to face her. His nostrils flared. His gray eyes darkened to black orbs. A muscle twitched in his jaw. He looked more like a dangerous beast than a refined nobleman.

Lily swallowed her next words, gaping at the imposing duke as a shiver of fear trickled down her spine.

"If you are incapable of caring for his lordship any longer, Miss Rutledge, I will find a replacement. In the meantime, I suggest you return to your nephew."

Replacement? Someone who would care even less about Oliver than Blackmoor did? No one would take Oliver away from her. Not even this great hulking, surly duke. Lily found her voice. "How dare you threaten me? I am concerned about Oliver's well-being, and you won't put me off. *You* are his guardian, for better or worse, and you have duties where he's concerned."

Blackmoor's eyes darkened even more, which Lily hadn't known was possible. She gulped nervously, panicking slightly when she realized his gaze focused on the movement in her throat. The duke had never seemed frightening until now. Of course, she hadn't laid eyes on him in years. Upon reflection, perhaps it was good he hadn't been to Maberley Hall in the last six years.

"No one," his voice rumbled over her, "orders me about, Miss Rutledge, and it would be good for you to remember that." Blackmoor turned his piercing gray eyes on his butler and spoke through clenched teeth. "I assume the coach is prepared, Billings."

The butler simply nodded.

"You can't run away from me, Your Grace," Lily sputtered.

"*I'm* not running away at all." He scooped her up in his arms. "But you, my troublesome Miss Rutledge, are returning to your nephew."

Lily's mouth fell open. "How dare you…"

"You ask that quite a bit. I *do* dare, Miss Rutledge. That is all you need to know."

She squirmed in his arms, though it was no use. They were like steel bands wrapped around her. "Put me down."

"In due time," he growled.

Before Lily could respond, they were on the front stoop and then he was depositing her inside the Maberley coach. "Your Grace!" she managed before he shut the door on her.

She reached for the handle, but the coach started off with a jerk, throwing her back against the squabs.

TALL, DARK AND WOLFISH

BY LYDIA DARE

REGENCY ENGLAND HAS GONE TO THE WOLVES!

He's lost unless she can heal him

Lord Benjamin Westfield is a powerful werewolf—until one full moon when he doesn't change. His life now shattered, he rushes to Scotland in search of the healer who can restore his inner beast: young, beautiful witch Elspeth Campbell, who will help anyone who calls upon her healing arts. But when Lord Benjamin shows up, everything she thought she knew is put to the test...

Praise for *A Certain Wolfish Charm:*

"Tough, resourceful, charming women battle roguish, secretive, aristocratic men under the watchful eye of society in Dare's delightful Victorian paranormal romance debut."

—*PUBLISHERS WEEKLY* (STARRED REVIEW)

978-1-4022-3695-2 • $6.99 U.S. / £3.99 UK

THE WOLF
NEXT
DOOR

BY LYDIA DARE

REGENCY ENGLAND HAS
GONE TO THE WOLVES!

Can she forgive the unforgivable?

Ever since her planned elopement with Lord William Westfield turned to disaster, Prisca Hawthorne has done everything she can to push him away. If only her heart didn't break every time he leaves her. Lord William throws himself into drinking, gambling, and debauchery and pretends not to care about Prisca at all. But when he returns to find a rival werewolf vying for her hand, he'll stop at nothing to claim the woman who should have been his all along, and the moon-crossed lovers are forced into a battle of wills that could be fatal.

"With its sexy hero, engaging heroine, and sizzling sexual tension, you won't want to put it down even when the moon is full."

—SABRINA JEFFRIES, *NEW YORK TIMES* BESTSELLING
AUTHOR OF *WED HIM BEFORE YOU BED HIM*

978-1-4022-3696-9 • $6.99 U.S. / £3.99 UK

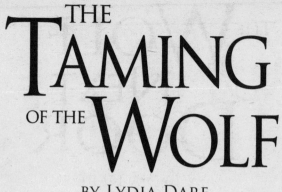

THE TAMING OF THE WOLF

BY LYDIA DARE

REGENCY ENGLAND HAS GONE TO THE WOLVES!

Lord Dashiel Thorpe has fought the wolf within him his entire life. But when the moonlight proves too powerful, Dash is helpless, and a chance encounter with Caitrin Macleod binds the two together irrevocably. Though Caitrin is a witch with remarkable abilities, she is overwhelmed and runs back to the safety of her native Scotland. But Dashiel is determined to follow her—she's the only woman who can free him from a fate worse than death. Caitrin will ultimately have to decide whether she's running from danger, or true love…

Praise for Lydia Dare

"**The authors flawlessly blend the historical and paranormal genres, providing a hint of the Lycan lifestyle with a touching romance… lots of feral fun.**" —ROMANCE NOVEL NEWS

978-1-4022-4437-7 • $6.99 U.S. / £4.99 UK

It Happened ONE BITE

By Lydia Dare

❧

HE'S LOST, TRAPPED,
DOOMED FOR ALL ETERNITY...

Rich, titled, and undead, gentleman vampyre James Maitland, Lord Kettering, fears himself doomed to a cold and lonely existence—trapped for decades in an abandoned castle. Then, beautiful Scottish witch Blaire Lindsay arrives, and things begin to heat up considerably...

UNLESS HE CAN PERSUADE HER
TO SET HIM FREE...

Feisty Blaire Lindsay laughs off the local gossip surrounding her mother's ancestral home—stories of haunting cannot scare off this battle-born witch. But when she discovers the handsome prisoner in the bowels of the castle, Blaire has no idea that she has unleashed anything more than a man who sets her heart on fire...

978-1-4022-4510-7 • $7.99 U.S./£4.99 UK

Uncertain Magic

BY LAURA KINSALE

New York Times bestselling author

A MAN DAMNED BY SUSPICION AND INNUENDO

Dreadful rumors swirl around the impoverished Irish lord known as "The Devil Earl." But Faelan Savigar hides a dark secret, for even he doesn't know what dark deeds he may be capable of. Roderica Delamore, cursed by the gift of "sight," fears no man will ever want a wife who can read his every thought and emotion, until she encounters Faelan. Roddy becomes determined to save Faelan from his terrifying and mysterious ailment, but will their love end up saving him… or destroying her?

978-1-4022-3702-7 • $9.99 U.S./$11.99 CAN